THE SOOTHSAYER

THE SOOTHSAYER

For Kel

you started me on this journey, and I owe you everything.

Special Thanks To:

Todd Johnson & Shannon Gray

for your early support.

Kimberly Laurel

whose copy editing skills were invaluable.

Meg Ashley

who gave me the writing bug and guidance I needed.

THE LANDS OF
ATLANTEA
SAMUEL'S
SHACK
GILEAD
N
S
E
W

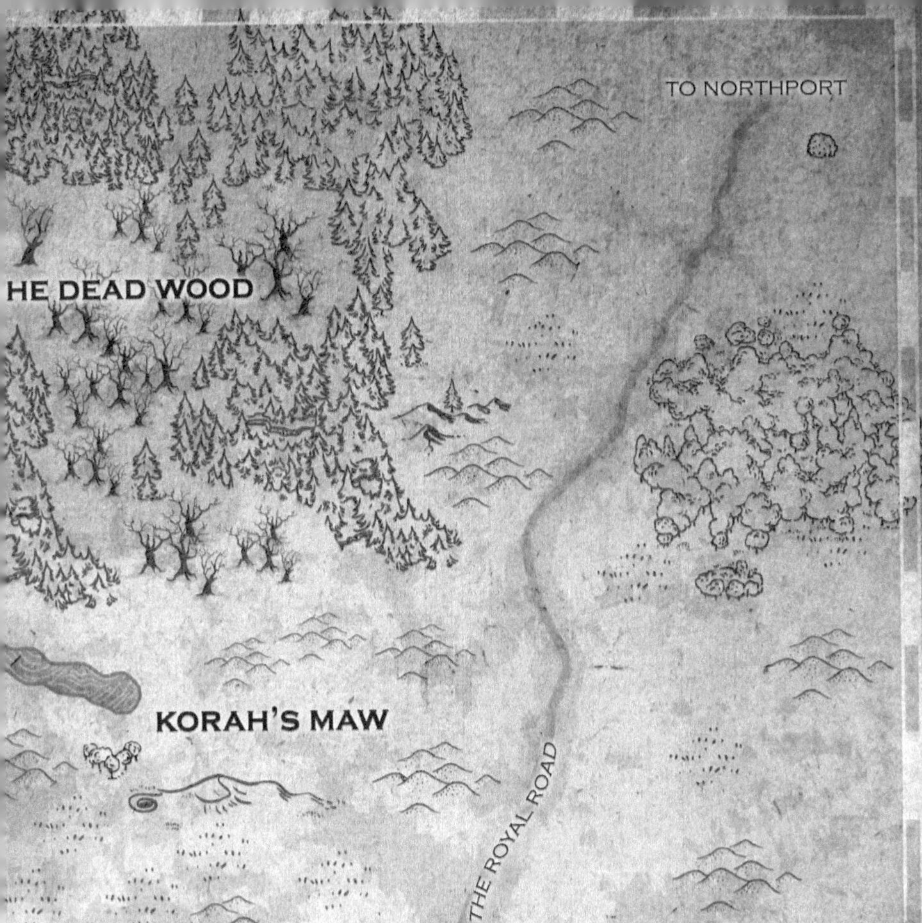

TO NORTHPORT
HE DEAD WOOD
KORAH'S MAW
THE ROYAL ROAD
EASTERN
MOORS
TO SANHEDRIN MTS

THE SOOTHSAYER

A NOVEL BY

GLEN GABEL

THE CITY OF
GILEAD
CASTLE COURTYARD
AMBASSADOR'S SQUARE
WESTERN GATE
LION'S MAW

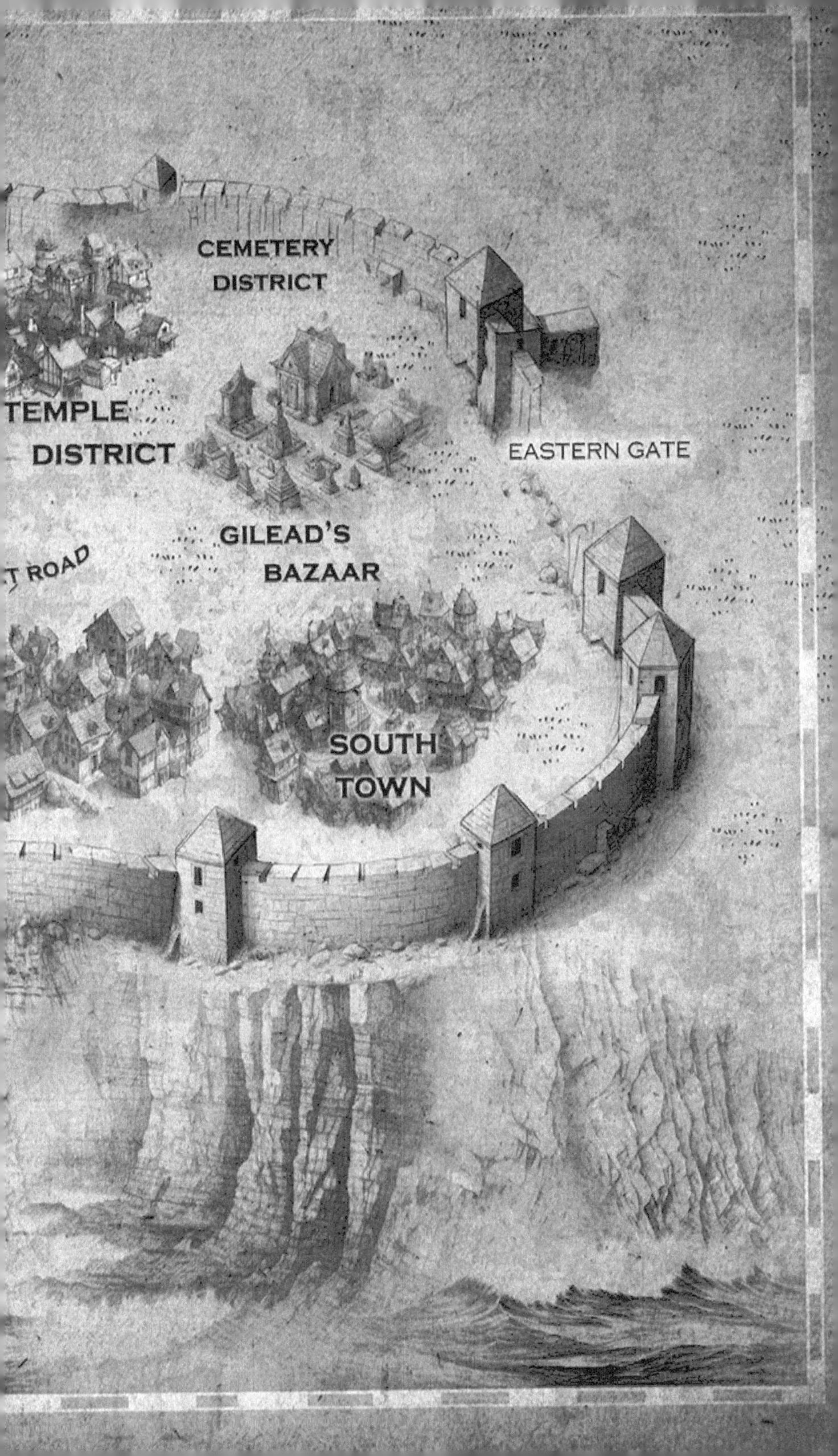

CEMETERY
DISTRICT
TEMPLE
DISTRICT
EASTERN GATE
GILEAD'S
BAZAAR
T ROAD
SOUTH
TOWN

PROLOGUE

As dawn crept into the fog-laden harbor, Colin Deveroux raced through the mist, clutching a puzzle box he no longer wanted. He ran past empty parking lots and darkened windows of stores and restaurants to a ramshackle shop that stood apart from the others. Colin's thin frame ached and the stitch in his side screamed until he stopped a few feet from the shop's door to catch his breath. Twenty-four hours ago, life had been simpler—if not any happier. Twenty-four hours ago, he still had his name, and monsters only existed in dreams.

CHAPTER I

The Dying of the Light

A day earlier, Colin lay on the sun-baked blacktop of the school's basketball court. Though his hands and arms had taken the brunt of the fall, his body ached. The asphalt's slow burn into his thigh barely registered in his brain. His head was swimming. His brown locks covered the smattering of freckles across his forehead and obscured the figure who loomed over him. The copper taste of blood trickled into his mouth.

This can't be happening. God, please get me out of this.

"R-Red, s-s-stop!" Colin stuttered.

Red Arnold cracked his knuckles as he looked down at Colin. A lean and muscular junior with a shaved head, Red was known throughout San Clemente High School for sporting a black flight jacket and steel-toed Doc Martens, smoking, and handing out beatings to anyone he felt deserved them. Colin had often heard the wails of Red's other prey coming from the out-door quad near the track as Red screamed into the faces of his victims, "I'm kicking ass and taking names!"

"S-s-stop!" Colin tried to cover his midsection as he folded his knees to his chest.

"D-d-d-duh," Red mimicked. "You sound like a retard. You going to crap your pants next?" Red delivered a swift kick to Colin's ribs. "Get up, punk!"

Pain stabbed Colin's torso, but he knew the next kick might be more aptly placed to his face or groin. He only had so many hands.

"Punk." Red spat and walked away.

Colin heard footsteps and looked up to see Jennifer Straten running toward him.

"Are you okay?" she asked.

He couldn't keep her gaze. Unlike the league of perpetually tanned girls that stared into their cell phones at lunch, Jennifer was fair-skinned, quiet, and reflective. She'd just moved from England late in the school year. Her long golden locks accented a warm smile and the brightest blue eyes Colin had ever seen. While other students teased her for how she spoke, Colin liked her accent. She was shy and wore little to no makeup, but Colin thought she didn't need to. The first time they'd met, he had bumped into her in passing between classes, and now when they had lunch together, she'd tell him about her home or read passages from her Gothic books—mostly Edgar Allan Poe. She was weird, and he liked it. She didn't make him talk. She understood.

One lunch, Jennifer hadn't come to their usual spot. She'd wandered by the track instead. From a distance, Colin had followed her, and as he approached, he saw Red had hemmed her in against a fence.

"I really like your skin, it's soft," Red said as he grabbed her hand. "Someone like you might need a friend over here in the States."

Colin felt helpless watching the exchange, but he forced his feet closer. He couldn't walk away from her, not like this.

Red put his hand on Jennifer's arm. "Is it true what they say about English chicks? They like spotted dick?"

"I don't know, I need to go," Jennifer said.

"J-J-Jenn, I th-think the office is l-looking f-for you," Colin called out.

Red spun around and glared at Colin. Jennifer saw her chance and pushed past Red, grabbing Colin's arm as she walked away.

Red's cold stare that day had told Colin all he needed to know. He was next on the list.

"Colin?" Jennifer's voice bought his mind back to the present.

Colin stood up and limped past her, his legs aching from the beating. "I-I h-have to go," he mumbled, too ashamed to keep her gaze.

SNIDE REMARKS AND SNICKERS DOGGED Colin throughout the school day until he was finally free to leave. He rode his rusted black Huffy bicycle past countless apartments and condos, following Avenida Pico as it snaked toward the Pacific Coast Highway. Dana Point Harbor was four miles away, but the sidewalks along the Sunset Highway faced the Pacific. As he rode north next to the shoreline, he looked past the breaking wash to the sea, and the rolling surf soothed him. The sun was setting across the water, reflecting reds, oranges, and yellows as if the sea were on fire. Gulls floated across the watery flames like ships crashing into each other, echoing their cannon calls for miles.

If only I could live in this place, this one moment, forever. The thought crossed his mind as he pedaled, but he knew it was temporary. His English teacher had forced his class to memorize a poem the year before. He'd chosen "Nothing Gold Can Stay," by

Robert Frost. The images of light it evoked made him think of his childhood, his father, and how all good things had to end. He wished that weren't true.

As Colin rode into the harbor's large parking lot, he saw the last rays of the sun dip past the many shops and boats, then below the horizon. When he'd been a child, his father, John, had regaled him with stories of pirates, bounty, and especially, Captain Richard Henry Dana. Dana had brought a brig, *The Pilgrim*, into the protected cove and laid anchor to trade with Spanish merchants. Colin's mother, Lane, would roll her eyes as John stretched facts and spun stories to say that Dana was, in fact, a pirate who battled savages and hid stolen treasure in the many caves up and down the rocky cliffs of the coastline. Colin remembered how one night, years before, the family had even toured a replica of *The Pilgrim*—now a permanent tourist fixture anchored in the harbor.

Deep down, he had known his dad was making up the stories, but he had loved them anyway, and he knew that his mother secretly had as well.

But nothing gold stays. Colin learned that the night his mother had suddenly pulled him into her arms, crying, after receiving a phone call. This truth was only reinforced as he watched his father slowly slip away in a hospital bed—a victim of a senseless hit-and-run. Despite pleading and praying, his father never opened his eyes again. Colin hadn't honestly believed it was over until he stood over his father's grave, clutching a 2x3 photo of them camping.

Colin pulled his bike up to a bike rack outside the Jolly Roger Restaurant. The bay-front eatery, once considered fine dining, had fallen into disrepair over the last few years. What had been an hour-wait waterfront treat now towered over an empty square of tourist shops with darkened windows. He didn't mind. The smell of salt air and the cry of the gulls were an escape when the world closed in around him. No matter how wretched the waves of life tossed, he knew the harbor was his hideaway. A bit of debris to cling to, reminding him of how things used to be.

LANE DEVEROUX CHECKED THE WALL clock behind the family eating at one of her tables. Her break was about to start, and she needed it. The Jolly Roger's typical Friday night rush extended when a score of families arrived, all starving and ready for immediate service.

"Excuse me, waitress?" A man was standing in his booth to get her attention. "Would it be possible to take a quick one for us?" He waved his phone at Lane.

She was already five minutes into her break and desperate for a breather, but she nodded and took his phone, a manicured smile on her face. Good service meant good tips. And she needed the money.

"Okay on three guys—Go Dodsons!" The man beamed at his wife and two teenage daughters.

"Dad, seriously?" One of the girls sighed while the other rolled her eyes.

"Humor him, girls," their mother said, gently smiling. "You'll share these photos with your kids one day."

That one hurt. Lane's smile broke for a second before she quickly took the picture and handed the phone back to the man. The scene played over in her head as she strode to the kitchen to hang her apron and clock out. How often had her family passed on a photo they could've taken? How many memories were lost in time?

She unhooked her late husband's oversized brown cardigan from the waitstaff's coat rack and wrapped herself in it. It was a comfort in the chilly night air and dwarfed her thin frame. It still held his scent of aged bourbon and sandalwood. She caught a glimpse of her reflection in some glass as she went to the restaurant's back door. Worry lines had found a permanent home on her once-youthful face. Lane adjusted her brunette hair back into a bun, and saw the bags settling under her eyes.

Too many sleepless nights. And it won't get any easier; she thought to herself as she made her way to the sidewalk railing that overlooked the docks and boats below. After John had passed, she'd prioritized spending more time with Colin to keep their little family tightly knit, but bills came due, and then . . .

She wouldn't let herself go there. Without thinking, she pulled a pack of Virginia Slims from her coat pocket and lit one, taking a long drag to stifle the tears welling inside her. Once upon a time, she had held hope for them. A month after the funeral, she'd surprised Colin by taking the day off from work to kidnap him from school.

"Mom, you m-m-missed it," Colin had mumbled as they blew past the offramp to San Clemente High School.

"Don't I know it," she'd said with a devious smile. "I think it's time we have a day for us. A ditch day on life. What do you say?"

Colin's eyes brightened. "Are you s-serious? You sound like Dad."

"Your father was not the only fun one in the family, mister. In fact, I had to introduce him to roller coasters, because he'd never been on one."

"D-Dad?" her son smiled. "How'd he r-react? W-what coaster?"

"Well he almost puked, if you must know, and I thought I'd take you there to see for yourself."

Her son's downcast demeanor had lifted that day as they rode every ride she secretly dreaded—but it was worth it.

"We're still a family, hon," she had told him, "and I'm always here when you need me."

But even that promise was about to be broken. Her ongoing cough had led to tests and X-rays and blood panels. Even before the oncologist had sat her down for the talk, she'd known something wasn't right. She'd spent the last week letting it sink in, but at some point, she'd finally have to tell her son the truth. The kid had been blindsided too many times already. He'd be here soon, and she prayed the words would come.

As Colin approached her, Lane put out her cigarette and hugged him. "Baby, what did they do to you?"

"It's f-fine," he mumbled.

"You don't have your jacket either? The fog's supposed to be rolling in tonight." She looked him over and put her hand to his bruised head, wiping a smudge away with a sleeve that hung past her wrist. "What do you want me to do?"

"Stop w-w-with those." He glanced at the cigarette she held in her other hand.

She sighed. "I know. You're right, hon, more now than ever."

Colin's eyes searched hers. "W-what is it?"

"Walk with me, baby. We need to talk about something." She turned back towards the sea walk overlooking the murky waters of the harbor. Colin followed her around the side of the restaurant. Lane leaned against the railing, took a smooth stone lying on it, and rolled it in her hand. She stared at the quartz lines that swirled in concentric circles across its dark surface—avoiding her son's gaze.

"I told you I had a doctor's appointment last week?"

"Y-yeah?"

"I didn't tell you all of it. They think they spotted something in my lungs. Some kind of cancer." She handed Colin the stone as she searched his face for understanding.

"Are you s-serious, Mom? Why didn't y-you say anything?"

Lane saw her son's face flush red and his throat tighten. This wasn't going to be easy to swallow.

"Babe, I just found out a few days ago, and I didn't know how to say it, and then if I did . . ." She brought a fresh cigarette to her lips, then paused and tossed it aside.

"Th-they can cut it out r-right?"

"Honey, it's pretty far along." Her voice faltered. "I'm not sure that's possible."

"I was s-supposed to just find out when you d-died?" he screamed at her.

"Colin I am so, so sorry." Tears welled in her eyes. "Your father and I—"

"No! D-don't bring Dad into this." His face flushed. "He gave up, and you're just l-like him. J-just lay down and d-die? How could you, Mom? How could you? I h-hate you!"

Colin turned and ran from her into the night.

Lane clenched the railing to stop herself from following him. She had no more promises to give.

CHAPTER 2

TRINKETS AND TROUBLES

Colin ran down the sea walk until his lungs ached. Eventually, he stopped and slumped against the railing as tears rolled down his face. Clouds shrouded the moon, and fog crept around the darkened shops and patios lining the marina. A foghorn echoed in the distance.

Just once, couldn't things be right for us? If Dad were here, Mom would've never started smoking. We wouldn't be stuck here. It'd all be different.

"I'd b-be different," he whispered. He hurled the stone in his hand back towards the curtain of mist that now hid the shops from view. The rock skipped and jumped until it disappeared into the gloom.

The sound of breaking glass echoed out.

"Oh, gr-great," Colin sighed. The fog moved in to surround him as he strode toward the storefronts. All of them were closed. When the tourists arrived in a month, they'd be open till nine and bustling, but during the off-season, the marina was a ghost town. Passing a long line of Spanish adobe shops and terracotta overhangs, he came upon a quaint New England-style shop set a little apart from the others, one he had never noticed before. *Potter's Curios* was printed on a hanging sign in the shape of a fish. The nine-pane display window badly needed cleaning, and he saw the damage his stone had done on the bottom right. That pane was shattered.

He approached and glanced around the sidewalk, but the stone was nowhere to be seen.

I'm probably on about five security cameras right now.

A vision of having to pay an ungodly fine and picking up trash along the highway flashed in his mind. He peered closer through the fractured glass.

Across an old velvet-topped table were seashell-covered music boxes, *Precious Moments* figurines, and carved wooden beer steins with pirate faces.

No wonder this place is closed. How cheeseball can you get? Colin shook his head.

A store light from within blinked on. He stumbled back.

"Is somebody there?" a rough voice called out.

Colin turned and ran. He didn't need this kind of trouble tonight. The fog became thicker as he hurried past bushes and benches and bumped into a parked van before stumbling across the old dirt trail that led to the tide pools. Again, the distant foghorn called, but this time it was answered by a second horn, lower in pitch and less powerful.

He looked around. He had covered more ground in a few minutes than he had expected, but it was impossible to tell which direction to turn. The world was blanketed in gray. He listened for any sound of the shopkeeper giving chase but heard none. Again, the first horn echoed in the night; again, a softer response.

Why would they need a second foghorn? he wondered as he moved towards the sound. *It'll just confuse the ships.* The crash of the waves on the rocks was louder now, and he saw the cracked old concrete steps that led down to the sand and the waterline ahead of him.

Okay, I'm definitely going the wrong way. He turned back. Not fifty feet behind him in the mist was a gnarled figure of a man in a patched cardigan and brown pants that hung from his bony frame. His shaggy beard matched his thick head of white hair. He held an old square glass lantern lit by a meager candle.

"I see you there! You, son, you need to come with me!" The man's gruff call was unmistakable. It was the shopkeeper.

"G-g-got to be kidding." Colin shook his head and ran back toward the steps, taking them downward two at a time. He knew exactly how many would take him to the sand; he had counted them hundreds of times, climbing up and down them as a child. The beachhead was thin here, and the waterline always came close to the concrete stairway, with barnacled boulders standing sentinel beside them. The rock jetty was no more than six feet high. He'd be on the sand with five more steps. But the steps weren't there.

What the hell?

He fell headfirst into the fog and then the icy foam of sea-water. It was as if the waves had devoured any remnant of the beach and now waited at the edge of sight, ready to pounce on any prey that dared to cross the man-made concrete thresh-old. A black wave broke over Colin's head and sucked him back into darkness. His fingers clawed the bottom stair for a grip. Nothing. The waves tossed and smashed him against the nearby rocks. A thousand crusted barnacles ripped into his back like icy knives. Colin screamed as the saltwater flooded his wounds. Another wave sucked him under again. He grabbed hold of the rocks and refused to let go. His face broke the water's surface, his lungs ached for breath. The waves pulled back past him, but he held on tight. As the water receded, he climbed over the rock on his hands and knees and coughed up seawater—*some kind of freak wave.*

As if in answer to his thoughts, he heard the shopkeeper call out, "No, my boy, it's the coming of the lawless ones, with all power, false signs, and wonders. Take my hand."

Colin looked up. The shopkeeper stood at the edge of the broken steps, still holding his lantern. The candlelight flickered across his wrinkled face.

Colin's knees were weak, and he sensed something great and terrible in the old man's eyes. The shopkeeper looked past Colin to the dark wash behind. In a louder voice, he called out at the sea.

"Back with you! You don't belong here! Get back into the night!"

Colin turned to see three shadowy forms move in the shoals less than twenty feet from him, just beyond the breaking waves. They glided through the darkness and drifted across the water, larger than a man, black as night, with eyes that glowed a murky yellow. A cold shiver raced down his neck as they stared at him, and somehow, he knew that only the old man's authority kept them at bay.

"Come with me, boy. Take my hand," the shopkeeper said again as he lowered himself to one knee and reached out his hand. Colin backed towards him across the rock, his eyes still locked on the creatures. A long slow *hiss* echoed above the crash of the waves before their bodies melted back into the water.

"Focus on me, boy." The shopkeeper's voice had softened.

"You might need some help," Colin said while picturing the fiasco of pulling the geezer down on top of him, but he reached up anyway.

In one motion, the shopkeeper pulled Colin up onto the steps as if he weighed nothing.

"How?" Colin started.

"Now is not the time, my light's growing dim," the old man replied.

"Who?" Colin whispered as he looked at the aged face.

"I'm Mr. Potter. Now follow me back to my shop. There are dark things in the wind, and we have much to discuss." Mr. Potter turned and led the way as if the mist were nonexistent.

Colin, dumbstruck, followed the light through the gloom.

AFRAID OF WHAT HE MIGHT see again in the shadows, Colin looked away from the nine-pane window. He was sitting on a wicker chair that hadn't seen a dusting in ten years. It groaned slightly as he shifted his weight and leaned back.

I'm resting on a museum piece; he thought and looked around the cluttered little shop. The tchotchkes lining the display window now seemed a ruse to dissuade anyone from looking farther in. All around him were artifacts of varying age: a chipped goblet here, a medieval tapestry there, a suit of armor that looked to have seen battle, a Roman-style gladius. Gazing at the blade from his chair, Colin realized it was much older than him, perhaps even older than his grandfather.

Mr. Potter rustled and rumbled in the back room, kicking and pushing past old boxes and crates until he returned with a blanket and a steaming mug. "Here you go, dry off." He handed Colin the blanket. "You wanted a drink?"

"Coke, please," Colin responded.

"Earl Grey, it's better for you." He handed Colin the mug.

The warm cup of tea didn't burn his hand as he'd expected, but its heat crept up his arm and stilled his shivering. The slight taste of citrus was a welcome surprise from the dark tea, and as he drank it, his head cleared. Mr. Potter seemed frailer now, smaller in stature than he had appeared in the darkness.

That all-encompassing darkness, the terrible wave, and the creatures Colin had seen somehow seemed less real now, as if he had awakened from a bad dream and its last images were sliding away.

"Those things, were those real?" Colin asked.

Mr. Potter nodded. "I'm afraid so."

"What are they?"

"They were scavengers, not meant to be seen, trying to trespass on my property," Mr. Potter said and pulled out a pair of wire bifocals that he placed haphazardly on his nose. "Now then, let me get a look at you." He gazed intently at Colin.

The old man's stare was piercing, as if he were looking past Colin's eyes to the deepest reaches of his thoughts. Mr. Potter's eyes betrayed a sense of purpose that made Colin uneasy.

What the hell am I doing here?

Colin imagined Mr. Potter snatching kids. Maybe he kept them locked up in a basement, then killed them and mounted their heads in the back.

But Mr. Potter's eyes brightened. "No, my boy, you've nothing to worry from me, as long as you pay your debt."

Did he just read my thoughts? Colin wondered. "Wait, you said 'your property.' Did you mean the tide pools? The steps? The harbor?"

"Uh-huh, that's right." Mr. Potter leaned back and smiled.

"I've never seen you before."

"Oh, I'm always around. I'm not always here, but I'm always present." Mr. Potter folded his hands as if he had been expecting this line of questioning. "What's your name?"

"Colin. Just Colin." Colin gulped down the last of the tea, hoping the man wouldn't ask beyond that. He felt vulnerable like some part of him had been laid bare.

Mr. Potter tilted his head, studying the boy's face. "No, no that won't do at all. You're much more than just a Colin. Perhaps you'll find it."

He's senile, completely bonkers. The excuse flashed in Colin's thoughts, but he knew there was more to it. He shook his head, "Look, Mr. Potter, I don't know what you want, but . . ."

Mr. Potter frowned and stood up. "Perhaps not. Now, you owe me a debt. You broke my window, and I can't allow you to leave until something is given."

"I, uh . . ." Colin searched his pockets and pulled out his wallet. He retrieved a wet, crumpled five-dollar bill. "This is all I've got on me."

"Afraid it's not enough." Mr. Potter turned his back without even looking at the money.

"I can have my mom stop by after her shift and pay it off," Colin offered.

"Then she'd be paying your debt. No. Each man must answer for his own actions in this life."

Colin stood up, tossing the blanket aside and setting his mug down. "Then I've got nothing for you. I have to go. I'm sorry."

Mr. Potter spun around, his voice commanding. "Sit down!"

Colin immediately sat, and the chair groaned in protest.

"'Sorry' is a sorry excuse. What I want, 'Just Colin' . . . is your name." Mr. Potter's eyes gleamed. "I'll hold it for you, until you find a better one."

"Uh, okay? It's Colin Deveroux. Take it, whatever." Colin looked around. His mind echoed the line from *Forrest Gump*: *"Stupid is as stupid does"—except this old codger is crazy.* Colin slowly stood again. "So . . . can I go now? Mr. Potter?" He eyed the doorway and wondered what would happen if he ran for it.

Mr. Potter's face softened as he glanced about the store. "You've paid your debt, but no one leaves my shop without something in hand. A souvenir if you like." Mr. Potter looked about casually. "I seem to be out of those little calendars, so go find something to take with you."

"Really, it's okay, Mr. Potter. I've been enough trouble." Colin said.

"No, I insist. Peruse." The old man nodded at the wares surrounding them.

Colin sighed as he ran his hands across the different dusty shelves. At first, he resigned himself to finding some random bit of tourist junk he could toss the minute he stepped outside, but as his gaze shifted from item to item, he imagined himself using each of them. A vintage photo of the Sutro Baths he could possibly sell on eBay. *Too much effort.* His eyes shifted to the gladius he had spied earlier.

"Belonged to many a soldier, but I'm afraid it's seen too many battles to serve you," Mr. Potter called out.

Colin's eyes roamed to a glass bauble with a rattlesnake's head preserved within, fangs out, ready to strike. The eyes of the serpent seemed to watch him, and Colin shivered when he realized they were the same color as the eyes of the creatures he had witnessed in the shadows of the shoals.

"That would be too heavy for you to carry, I think," Mr. Potter said as he watched the boy.

Colin's finger next came to a small wooden box with a strange symbol carved onto the top. He didn't recognize it, though it resembled a skewed letter *A*.

"Now that's an interesting choice," Mr. Potter said.

Colin took it from the shelf and ran his finger around its six-inch diameter. There were no hinges, clasps, or locks. "How do you open it?"

"It's a puzzle box, said to have been owned by Captain Dana himself as he sailed on *The Pilgrim*. Opening it is up to you."

"Cool." Colin studied it. It looked made of ashen driftwood, yet it felt heavier as if something was inside.

"Then we're in agreement. The debt is paid." Mr. Potter smiled and opened the front door of the shop.

"Thanks, I appreciate it," Colin said as he moved past Mr. Potter and out the doorway onto the still-foggy sea walk.

"Turn left, boy, and be wary of the mist. And boy—"

Colin turned to look at the old man.

"Remember, you'll have everything you need, once you open the box. Never doubt that."

Colin looked down at the puzzle box in his hand. "What are you talking about?" He glanced up.

Mr. Potter was gone. The store was closed and dark, as if the whole exchange had been a dream.

"Hello? Mr. Potter?" Colin called out and tried the handle. It was firmly locked. "How the hell?" He stared at the window display. The glass pane he had smashed was intact, with not a scratch on it. He took a step back, amazed. He turned left and began moving through the fog back toward the Jolly Roger, re-playing the entire conversation with Mr. Potter in his mind. Then it struck him, he hadn't stuttered once.

CHAPTER 3

The Shadows' Embrace

As Colin approached the Jolly Roger, he immediately noticed the restaurant's windows were dimmed. The large wooden door opened, and a stream of patrons walked out. A busboy followed carrying a Closed sign and hung it just below the wooden placard displaying the famous ship that made up the restaurant's logo.

"Are you closing early?" Colin asked the employee.

"Nope, we're done for the night. Sorry, we're open again at eleven tomorrow." He turned back towards the door.

"Wait, is Lane Deveroux here?" Colin tapped the young man's arm.

The busboy pulled back from him. "The waitress? She went home hours ago. Excuse me." He walked quickly to the door, opened it, and slammed it shut as he went through. Colin heard a latch snapping into place.

Hours? How'd that happen?

His mind raced. To him, the whole affair—the water, the things that lurked in the waves, the shop, meeting the old man—had only perhaps been an hour at most. The wounds on his back still burned. *It couldn't have been that long. He drugged me. That old coot must have put something in the tea.* But that explanation seemed flimsy, at best. He couldn't recall losing consciousness, and he certainly didn't remember hallucinating. The yellow-eyed creatures returned to his mind. Before he'd ever met the old man, he'd seen *them.* Mr. Potter couldn't have made those things appear from thin air. Colin rubbed his temples. Perhaps some part of his brain had finally snapped? None of it made sense. Even now, he could be dreaming. He looked down at the puzzle box, still in his hand.

But this feels real.

He slipped the artifact into his cargo pants pocket and unlocked his bicycle from the rack. He glanced at a nearby clock mounted to an abandoned kiosk—it confirmed it was nearly midnight. A feeling of dread crept over him as he pedaled from the marina back to the Pacific Coast Highway.

Mom's going to freak out, he thought as he made his way along the shoulder of the road. It was at least a forty-five-minute ride to get to their one-bedroom condo on Pelayo Avenue, bordering north San Clemente. As he pedaled, it occurred to him that she'd probably called the police.

They'll be looking for me now, or maybe she collapsed, or maybe something happened to her—thoughts began to swirl in his mind.

Night after night, he heard her gasping in her sleep from his makeshift bed on the couch. He had always dismissed it as a bad cold she couldn't quite shake, yet deep down, he knew it was something much more. Her news tonight had confirmed it.

And you left her there in tears, you jackass.

He pictured her unconscious on the floor, barely breathing, and he pedaled faster. His legs were aching when he finally reached his street, and as soon as he came to the apartment complex, he dumped his bike by the trash cans and raced to his front door.

He unlocked the door and immediately felt something was amiss as he entered their living room. The lamps were in place; the couch, TV, and books—all were undisturbed. And yet something . . .

"Mom?"

Nothing. Colin turned the corner to the small hallway and his mother's bedroom. He opened the door. A distinct chill hung in the air. His breath was visible in the cold. The darkness seemed tangible, conscious—as if it were watching him. He could barely make out his mother's form, lying deathly still on her bed. He approached and knelt.

"Mom, I'm home," he whispered.

She didn't move. Colin took her hand. It felt like ice.

"Mom!" He pulled on her arm. "Mom, wake up!"

A slight hiss emanated from the corner of the room where the shadows were darkest. Colin looked and saw a pair of eyes. The yellow vertical slits of their pupils were all too familiar.

He froze.

Slowly reaching back, he pulled the chain of his mother's bedside lamp, and the meager light flicked on. Whatever this thing was, he had to see it.

The corner was empty, but the presence was still there.

The *hiss* sounded again.

He looked around. "G-get o-out of here!" he cried, throwing his arms across his mother's body.

This has to be some sort of sick dream.

His mind raced. He put his ear to her mouth and felt the slightest stirring of her breath.

"Mom! Mom, are you okay?" He shook her, and her chest rose a little. In the flickering lamplight, he saw two small punctures in her neck—black holes, perfectly aligned, like a snake's bite.

"Where are you?" he screamed as his eyes darted around the room, his anger overcoming his fear—but there was no response. Colin turned back to his mother. Shallow breaths labored from her lips, and he ran toward the phone.

THE AMBULANCE RIDE TO SAN Clemente Memorial Hospital was a blur of sirens and tight turns. The EMT in the back of the ambulance had pushed an IV into Lane's arm and was monitoring her vitals with a stethoscope. He looked across the cramped cabin to Colin and frowned.

"How long has she been unconscious?" he asked.

Colin stared down at his mother, his mouth agape. "I d-don't know."

The ambulance stopped outside the emergency room doors, and Colin hopped out to let them wheel his mother inside. Then she was rolled down the hall, out of sight, and the waiting began. The nurse at the desk eyed him before handing him a clipboard with two forms attached. "Are you eighteen?"

Colin shook his head.

"If you could fill out the top form then, we'll have to wait on the rest. Someone will speak with you soon."

Sitting in the ER waiting room, staring at all the forms, he could barely lift a pen to paper. The clock on the wall kept time at a snail's pace. For every tick of a minute, he felt an eternity pass. Finally, a nurse approached him.

"We can have you fill these out later. Is your dad coming?"

He shook his head.

"What's your name, sweetheart?"

He opened his mouth, but the words didn't come.

"It's okay. You're upset. I'm gonna have the doctor come out and talk with you." The nurse turned away.

Colin let his gaze fall across the waiting room walls and dwell on a kiosk of medical pamphlets. In neat rows, the pamphlet covers displayed images of women and children smiling together as they conversed with doctors, men listening intently to positive diagnoses, and families laughing as they ran across sunny meadows.

It's all crap, Colin thought.

Here and now, he was living a nightmare so surreal he could barely process it. There were no clear-cut answers, no reasoning that would come close to touching what he'd witnessed, and sinking below the mire of the bizarre he'd seen was his mother—now dying. He clutched the arms of his chair as if his body were waiting for a sudden drop. He'd be totally alone. How could anyone understand it, let alone explain it? How could God let this all happen?

The few times Colin had been to church as a child, he'd heard stories of God breaking through the heavens to save his people, pillars of fire and smoke, prophets that could wash away an army with the flick of a hand, and a savior who could lead humanity to an eternal paradise. But if God allowed for those miracles, where was Colin's miracle now? Maybe the man upstairs had given up on them; perhaps it was all a pipe dream brought on by some desperate wish to find meaning in all the madness. Colin's mind veered to Mr. Potter. *Madness. The old man, the damned old man! Could that stupid deal have been real?*

Colin realized the puzzle box Mr. Potter had given him still bulged in his pocket. He pulled it out. The ashen wood box was still closed.

He said it had everything I needed. Is this what he meant? Colin again looked for some seam. Nothing. He pried at it with his hands until his fingers cramped. Nothing.

The doctor approached—a woman who'd seen too many late shifts. She sat across from Colin in another chair.

"Are you her son?" she asked.

He nodded.

"What's your name, hon?"

Colin gagged as he tried to speak it, and his voice fell silent.

"No, it's all right." She took his hand. "I'm sorry to have to say this . . ."

"Sh-sh-she's dead!" He stuttered, his eyes filling with tears.

The doctor shook her head and put her hand on his knee. "No! No. But she's very sick. She has a severe stage four cancer. It's spreading, spreading faster than I've ever seen, and it's caused her to have an embolism—an obstruction in her heart," the doctor continued gently.

"B-bite on her neck," Colin said.

The doctor paused. "No, no spider bite would cause that." She searched his eyes. "We will do everything we can. I promise."

He shook his head no. She didn't understand. She hadn't seen it. How could he explain what he felt to be true? What he knew to be true? Hers was a world of empirical data, not monsters in the shadows and deals with the devil.

"I'll have an orderly drive you home," she said as she took the forms in hand.

THE SUN HAD RISEN ONLY an hour before, and the marina was still cloaked in fog. Colin stepped out of the car, nodding at the orderly to assure him this spot was as good as any. The car pulled away, and Colin went down the sea walk, heading back to where the madness had begun.

Mr. Potter can have the stupid box. This deal is bullshit. Colin started to run. He'd make the old man explain what was happening. The world was falling apart around him, and it had all started when they had met.

He raced to the curio shop, pausing a few feet from the door to catch his breath. The lights were out. A Closed sign hung from behind the display.

"Mr. Potter!" he yelled as he banged on the door and pulled on the handle. "Th-this is n-not . . . you can't—" he tried, but the words were trapped in his throat. Colin kicked the door hard, but it held. He threw the puzzle box at the door, and it bounced off, landing flat on the sidewalk. He turned to face the railing and the water beyond, burying his head in his hands. The old foghorn again echoed across the bay.

I can't stand up to anyone; I can't save my mother, can't even talk. The brutal truths echoed in his mind. *God, if you're there, give me something to hold onto.*

The box clicked.

Colin slowly turned. Taking shaky steps, he picked it up. Something had triggered it. He traced his thumb along the lopsided *A* on the top, and with another click, the box opened.

CHAPTER 4

Baptism by Fire

The lid lifted only slightly. Colin saw that its hinges were wooden, exquisitely hand carved, and sitting inside the lip of the container. He pried the lid open further. In the middle of the box, on top of an old, stained, and folded piece of paper, was his stone—the one he'd thrown through the window. The same concentric quartz circles across its surface confirmed it.

How the hell? How could he have known I'd pick this? How could this even be in here?

Perhaps Mr. Potter was a magician, but he was better than any Las Vegas celebrity act. Colin took the stone. This was no illusion; something very real and unreal had happened.

He pulled the paper from the box. It wasn't the cheap-lined stuff from his school notebooks or even the reams of white paper his mother sometimes used in their printer. It was thicker, almost consistent with fabric, and tattered along the edges. He unfolded it.

Strange symbols were written across it. They looked familiar, almost like Latin or Greek, and yet the accent marks and occasional curves suggested a language that was alien to this world and this time. The ink was old and faded to the point of being almost transparent in some areas.

He turned the paper around and instantly recognized what he saw: hand-drawn latitude and longitude lines over a rocky coastline. A sharp outcropping was the most dominant feature. A different ink had been used here, written by a different hand. It was still old but was not fading from the page.

It's a map. A real map. Colin looked around. The fog had cleared a little. He stared at the sharp cliffs of the marina, the sun peeking just above their rocky points before hiding again in the clouds.

Colin's eyes raced back to the map. There, scribbled in the margins, smeared by several ink blots, were the words "435 paces northwest off the point." Slightly below that was written the phrase, "There lies the balm of Gilead, to soothe the serpent's sting, the cave . . ." And below that appeared the rough initials "R.H.D."

No, no way. This couldn't be his . . .

Richard Henry Dana. Mr. Potter had mentioned the box belonged to him.

Maybe he was right. It must've belonged to Dana. But why would he hide this balm thing? Why would he need to? Unless there was something more to it. Did those creatures come for him too?

The foghorn called out, and then he heard it. That strange second horn call, the same as from the night before. He moved instinctively forward toward the tide pools. He paused.

What the hell am I doing? I don't have time for this.

But some part of him seemed to understand what his conscious mind did not. *Balm. Balm of Gilead. Healing. Is there a balm in Gilead? Tell me. I implore . . . quoth the raven . . .* Poe's words crept up from his subconscious. It was no coincidence that his world was spinning out of control and that here was a lifeline. If there was even a chance he could find this balm and save his mother with it, he had to try.

He walked away from the shops, back to the broken steps, and down to the sand. The water's edge had receded again. The sun was slowly burning through patches of fog here, and he saw no sign of the terrors he had witnessed the night before. He paused on the steps, peering into the few shadows melting into the waves.

Gone. They're gone.

He jumped down onto the sand and, leaving the sidewalk and railing behind, made his way along the edge of the cliffs, past the beach area. He followed a narrow footpath that curved between the high cliff walls on his right and the treacherous reefs to his left, still exposed from the ebb and flow of the tide.

What's a pace? Five feet? Four yards? He wished he'd looked up the term before trying this venture. Finally, he settled on a foot and a half, and with each step, he counted.

The trail was easy enough at first. Tourists often made their way along this shore to collect shells. But the farther he walked, the narrower the path became until it disappeared altogether. The strange foghorn sounded again. It was louder now and, unlike the marina's horn, seemed somehow deeper, earthier.

The water line came closer as Colin continued to count the distance, and as he made his way over larger and larger rocks, he could feel the spray of the waves reach toward him. He gingerly folded the map fragment back into the box and stuffed it into his jeans pocket. *Good enough for now*, he thought, as he continued his journey.

As the tide continued to creep in, Colin's worry began to

grow. *I'm going to be stranded if this comes in any farther. Maybe Dana's cave was covered in a landslide? Maybe it never existed.*

Then, as he rounded a sharp corner, he found it. Before him, set deep in the rock, was a narrow opening roughly six feet high but only a few feet wide, something only one thin person could fit through at a time. The wash of the waves poured into the gap. Colin peered into the cavity. The water was deep, and the passage within twisted out of sight.

He spotted a light across the dark stone walls as if someone inside had lit a torch.

Colin's voice echoed into the passage: "Hello? S-someone there?" The light blinked out. He looked down at the water, pulling out again.

Now or never.

He jumped into the icy foam. His eyes widened. The current was so cold that he wondered if California's sun had ever warmed these waters. He waded into the cleft between the rocks. The water rose around him as the tide pushed another wave in.

Shouldn't the tide be out? he wondered as his feet struggled to find purchase on the sandy surface below. *It must be at least six feet in here.*

Colin grasped at the slippery walls but to no avail, so he began swimming outright down the passage until his hands touched sloping pebbles and rocks. He crawled out of the water and saw the passage had led him to a vast empty cavern.

The ground was covered in sand, shells, and stones. The smell of salt and the faint scent of decaying fish filled his nostrils. Colin stood and walked forward. The wash of pebbles played against the stone walls like a muted hum of rain. To the left of the passage, the mouth of the cave opened wide to the ocean. He realized he would never have been able to see the big opening by walking along the waterline. Piles of rocks and boulders barred any line of sight. He watched the waves as they broke on the rocks at the cave mouth and pierced the remnants of the fog bank that hung just above the water, like an unwanted guest loitering at the door.

Colin pulled the wet map from the box in his wet jeans and opened the parchment. He had tried his best to keep it dry as he swam, but keeping his head above the water had been hard enough.

Thankfully the seawater hadn't ruined the ancient letters. Colin kicked the stones near his feet as he studied Dana's script. There was no mention of where this treasure might be found, and of course, he hadn't brought any shovel.

He heard a rolling mass and turned to the mouth of the cave. With a great wind, the strange foghorn's call echoed throughout the cavern. He dropped the parchment to cover his ears. A rogue wave broke through the mouth and slammed Colin against the back wall. Water ripped and spun him around. In an instant, he was pulled out into the open ocean.

Colin's head broke the surface, his mouth full of water. He spat out the acrid wash. His eyes burned, the sting of the saltwater blurring his vision. He twisted his body, flung his arms forward, and kicked against the powerful undertow, but he made no progress. A rhythmic gurgling echoed over the breakers surrounding him. His sight cleared to see a vortex forming ahead of him. Water rushed into the dark hole from all sides. He paddled desperately to escape, but the draw of the hole was too great. It was a mouth intent on a meal. He clutched for a handhold and found nothing.

His screams met only water and foam as he was swallowed into darkness.

"PULL HIM, BALAAM! TIME IS not our friend here!"

Colin heard her voice first. It was hushed and accented like Jennifer's.

A muffled, strange-sounding voice responded, "Pull the bilge rat yourself then."

He instinctively reached into his pocket. The map and box were gone. However, his fingers brushed the soaked 2x3 photo of his father and him camping. He breathed easier. It was an anchor to reality. Colin felt something large and hard against the nape of his neck, pulling on his shirt. He opened his eyes. The saltwater stung and blurred his vision again. But as his eyes began to slowly clear, he saw a young woman standing over him.

"Balaam, look—by the waterline. That parchment washed in behind him." The girl stepped out of view and returned, clutching his map.

Jennifer?

The resemblance was uncanny, yet this twin in front of him had fiery red hair and wore what Colin could only guess was some strange reject of a gown from a Renaissance fair, a mix of purple and brown, torn and shabby. The other figure was darker and bulkier somehow—or perhaps closer to the ground—but hard to make out with his still hazy vision.

"What's your name, boy?" the red-haired young woman whispered.

Colin gasped, but again, no words came.

"The water has dashed his brains," the other snorted.

"Wh-who are you? W-where . . ." Colin finally stuttered.

The girl knelt next to him. "Quiet your voice! My name is above your station until I know your intent. The kingdom of Gilead has enough enemies."

"W-what? Gil-Gilead?" Colin rubbed his eyes.

"Has the water deafened you as well?" the other voice replied.

Colin turned to find the muzzle of a donkey inches from his face. The jackass stared at him for a second before turning to the girl. "I think we should throw him back in."

Colin's mouth dropped, and his vision narrowed. This was beyond him. The world began to spin.

"Something I said?" the donkey's voice echoed in Colin's ears before consciousness shrank to a tiny point, then disappeared.

CHAPTER 5

AN UNWELCOME DUTY

&gan, chief warrant officer of Gilead's guard, shifted uneasily in his saddle. His tousled dirty-blonde locks hid the worry lines that had cemented themselves across his young face. Before taking his position of authority, he'd looked like of any fair-complexioned aristocrat, but his time on duty had left him unshaven, rough, and ragged. His green eyes searched the shadowy horizon. They had grown accustomed to the darkness that permeated the landscape and marred the hilltops like a stain. The intermittent moonlight cast deep shadows across the walls and towers of the city as if to mourn the sun's death. Only the bags under his eyes betrayed his many sleepless nights while protecting the city.

He still remembered the day that morning had never come and the panic that had slowly spread across the faces of his men as they tried to calm the people's fears. Hours had turned to days and then days to weeks of eternal darkness. Now the sun's face was a distant memory, barely mentioned in greeting. Though tall,

Egan sat bent over in his saddle and, when walking, had the gait of a man three times his age, the responsibilities of his position lying heavy on his back.

Two of his men had returned with nothing to report, but the third was still away. Fog rolled across the grassy moors of Gilead's highlands, spreading before him. The night mist still seemed unnatural to Egan, though all the queen's sages said it was merely a cycle of the winter equinox. Still, men could be wrong. Enemies could hide in the gloom or in any bush or cave. His gut told him something more was out there. He'd learned to trust his instincts over others' words. It's what had helped him rise so far, so fast.

He wished his father were here to see him now. At a young age, Egan had seen the esteem his father held. As a previous chief warrant officer of the city, his father had led a battalion in parades, and wherever he walked, people would bow in respect. When Egan came of age, he entered the Calling of the Squires and fought well with a stick, bow, and lance, but when his name was called in victory, the people flocked to his father's side, casting a shadow over his win. Egan had risen to warden in only a few years and then to first officer soon after that. Time passed, but his father's shadow never shrank. Now, he was the newly appointed chief warrant officer, the same station his father had held, a knight protector of the kingdom. At the age of twenty-five, he was the youngest ever to do so. Still, he noticed his men speak of the senior with nostalgia and shake their heads as the "lesser chief" walked past.

"Rely on your sword arm," his father had instructed him the day before the Calling. "You need nothing else."

Egan remembered how they'd sat on the shore and stared across the sea. His father leaned on his notched cedar staff as Egan skipped stones perfectly across the waves with his leather sling. His father appeared to choose his words carefully.

"You carry the family name, but you must earn the respect it brings. Remember gods fall, people fail you, but your blade will never betray you."

"What if I fail to hold the blade? What if I falter?" Egan asked.

"When you were a newborn, we lived east of the moors, in a little sod house by the Altain River. One night, a pack of wild sabers surrounded our house. Normally, those fierce panthers hunt alone, but they'd smelled the birth, smelled you, and they altered their tactics. I didn't have a bow or arrow or steel of any kind to protect your mother and you. Nothing but this." His father gripped the staff firmly. "I stood at the door and saw a dozen eyes staring back. I hollered my voice raw to keep them at bay. Beat my club across the walls to scare the pack. Some still came at me though, one by one, then two or three at a time, all night long. They came until their carcasses littered the doorway and the rest realized I wouldn't move. I would've done it with my hands if I'd had to."

Egan looked down at his own small hands.

"Look at me, boy." His father gazed into his eyes. "Protect the kingdom—that is your charge. To your dying breath. Do that, and I'll always have a son."

His third messenger broke through the fog, bringing Egan's mind back to the present. He reined in his horse and motioned to his men. "Come, we'll meet him."

Being young for his station, he had had to fight at first for his men's respect, but they had slowly given it to him as they saw his hand was fair in all dealings. Unlike many guards who could be found in bawdry houses on most nights, Egan patrolled the city with his men and saw to their needs as best he could. The opportunists who had joined due to rumors of lavish quarters and extra coins from merchant shakedowns quickly transferred to the queen's retinue, leaving a few remaining loyal soldiers in Egan's squad that he knew he could count on.

The messenger caught his breath as Egan and the riders approached him on the hilltop. "Chief, I spotted a cottage roughly a league south of here on the cliffs . . . hidden away in a grove of olive trees. There's a chance the old man lives there."

Egan sighed. "Well then, I guess we should investigate." He moved past the messenger and led his troop across the sloping grasslands. His official orders were to track down a zealot soothsayer, but his duty was to protect the kingdom. Not even the king's missing daughter took precedence over capturing the prophet now. Priorities had changed, whether he agreed with them or not. As he led his men to the bluffs and into the grove, he instinctively reached for his old sling, rolled tightly around his belt like a charm of protection. He wondered if the enemies he had sensed had already breached the kingdom's boundaries.

THE BLACK GALLEON SWAYED AS it pulled behind the Amorite fleet. A pair of green reptilian eyes gazed out from the captain's quarters toward the distant shore. The echo of the conch was unmistakable, and even from such a distance, Dagon could hear its call. The sorcerer put a black bone whistle to his lips and gently blew a note. In the distance, he heard the conch echo the refrain with a low earthy tone. There could be no mistaking it. The horn was near. Events had played out just as his master, the Dark Lord, had foretold. Dagon turned to leave his cabin but paused. Someone had come through from the other place. His scavengers had found the doorway again only two nights past, and he had allowed their excursions if only to sate their ravenous appetites. But someone had followed them back.

A boy, the dark whispers told him. Dagon licked his lips as a faint memory tickled his brain. *The other place . . .*

He shook his head. It didn't matter. All would come to bow before the Black Throne. He left his cabin and called to his men.

CHAPTER 6

The First Gift

olin awoke again on the shore. The surf echoed in his ears, and his hands grasped the coarse sand of terra firma under him.

I'm alive.

His fingers found something smooth at his side. He opened his eyes and saw it was the stone from the box. Without thinking, he pocketed it and turned to see the girl who had pulled him from the water. Her body was illuminated in the dim moonlight, and as he looked around, he saw they were between a dune and a copse of olive trees. The girl held a glowing conch shell, and its soft blue light danced across her face as it sounded a single low note of its own accord that echoed across the shore.

"What in the Maker's name?" she said before quickly covering it with a leather rag and stowing it in a nearby pack. Moving by him, she peered past the branches of one tree to a nearby path and then turned back to face him.

"Don't speak. The queen's men approach."

"Wh-wh-what's going on?" Colin shook his head. He glanced over to the donkey. It ate on some grass nearby. Colin rubbed his eyes.

Dreams within dreams.

"Hush!" the girl whispered, then walked out onto the path.

Colin sat up and leaned forward, spying from behind the tree before him. A young man in his twenties rode a white horse up to her. The man wore what looked to be a padded vest and a tunic richly embroidered in red and purple. Three knights in worn chain armor rode behind him.

The young officer reined in his horse when he saw the girl in the shadows. "I'm Egan, chief warrant officer of Gilead. Forgive me if I startled you," he said, his eyes instantly meeting hers.

"Egan, I remember you. Have your eyes grown so dim since our last lesson? You lead these men now?" The girl looked past him to his men and fidgeted with her dress.

Egan glanced back at the soldiers behind him and shifted in his saddle. "Of course, I remember you. You're the court scullery maid." He winked subtly at her. "We're patrolling for a sooth-sayer . . . an old man; he leans on a staff. Have you come across one in your, ah, travels?"

"Has Gilead no viler enemy than an old man? I'd think there'd be a greater need for the chief warrant officer elsewhere." The girl said with a smile and nodded across the shore to the dark sea beyond.

Colin followed her gaze. He could barely make out ships of some kind in the distance, lit by torchlights onboard.

How far up the coast am I? Colin wondered. *Or am I just drunk and delusional, passed out on the beach? Maybe I washed up behind the jetty.*

Egan dismounted and motioned to his men. "Head back to the city and report to Salain at the docks. There's nothing here."

"Sir, we still need to search the cottage," one of the soldiers replied.

"I said we're done here!" Egan snapped.

The soldier saluted him. "Understood." The three knights turned around and headed back towards the moors.

Egan turned back to the girl. "We can speak more freely now, Princess. The recruits are loyal to the crown but have no understanding of who wears it."

"It's been some time since I last saw you. Are you well?" the girl asked.

"Well enough, though the queen seems to favor me as an errand boy and not much else at this point. The city guard has been stripped down from five thousand honest men to a mere five hundred, most of whom care little for the job."

"I miss our training. The swordplay was the only highlight of my days before I left. Though I fear I've not improved or had a chance to," the girl said.

"What skill you have may serve you well, Princess. I can keep your whereabouts hidden for a time, but sooner or later, the queen will find out. She has eyes throughout the kingdom."

Colin peered out from the shadows of the trees. *I've stumbled into a Dungeons & Dragons convention, great. No, no good. I need out of here, now.* He stood and moved around the olive trees. "H-hey I need to—"

Egan lunged forward, grabbed him by the collar, and threw him against the ground. "Hold! Where did you come from?"

"G-get off me!" Colin yelled and threw a wild punch at the man's face.

Egan dodged the blow and slammed his fist into the side of Colin's head.

"Egan, stop! He's not a threat!" the girl cried. "I fished him out of the water. He's some fool who fell off a ship."

Still holding Colin down, Egan pointed toward the ships in the distance. "If it's a ship, then chances are he's from the Amorite fleet. I'll not report you to Queen Mariselle, but I can't let a spy roam freely!"

"Look at him," the girl sighed. "Does he look like a spy?"

Colin stared up at Egan's disgusted face. He wanted to tear it off.

"No," Egan said. "He's a scrub, at best."

"Yes, so leave us." The girl touched Egan's arm. "Take your watch to our shores. My friend awaits us."

Egan's face softened. "Is he well? Does he have need of anything?"

The girl shook her head. "No. Only to see our fair kingdom restored."

Egan nodded and stood, releasing Colin at last. "Then I'll say farewell, Princess. Should you have a need, please find me." He hoisted himself up onto his horse. "Safe journeys."

"And to you." The girl smiled at him.

Egan turned his steed and rode off. The girl looked down at Colin.

Colin lay still, holding his pounding head as his eyes swam. He moaned.

The donkey approached the girl and said, "I hope this one's worth the trouble."

The girl turned to the donkey. "He'll need better care than I can give here. Would you?"

The donkey sighed and brushed his muzzle into Colin's face. With a huff, he breathed, "Rest."

Light and shadow shifted into a solitary point in Colin's eyes, and he felt his legs buckle while his consciousness ebbed away.

COLIN AWOKE ON A STRAW mat covered with a hide. He'd lost time. He hadn't been asleep but had no memory of how he'd come here. Above his head, a small earthen oil lamp hung, its flame flickering in a slight breeze that danced across his aching cheek.

Water, I was drowning, rocks, and fighting a . . .

Colin sat up. An ancient man sat at the foot of his bed. Wrinkles ran their course in every direction on his face and up to his bald scalp. Only a smattering of long gray hair grew to the sides. His milky white eyes suggested a complete lack of vision, yet he stared at Colin directly. The figure leaned on a wooden staff as he sat, his head slightly nodding.

Colin slowly lifted his hand and waved it in front of the centenarian. The old man remained still and silent. Colin looked around. The room appeared made of a stucco-like substance, some kind of stone that was off-white in color, with a thatched roof several feet overhead. A kiln sat in the opposite corner, and several hooks and small nets hung from the rafters, holding various fruits, gourds, and dried plants.

Great, I've gone from Shrek *to* Little House on the Prairie, Colin thought as he leaned back against the wall and sighed.

"Ah, you're awake I see," the man suddenly said. "Well, not as I see, no, but certainly you've awakened." The old man stood with a slight groan. "Alexandra and Balaam were right in bringing you to me. I daresay it's the safest place you could've rested."

"W-who are you?" Colin's voice scratched out, his throat still raw from the salt water.

"I am Samuel, seer and soothsayer to King Braeden, though he hasn't called on me in quite some time. Who might you be?"

Colin. The thought was clear as day, but Colin gasped at his name, as if the words had died in his throat. He tried again.

Colin. Damnit.

He gagged, but the words wouldn't come. Only the many bruises across his body called out as he moved his legs. Colin winced.

"Ah? Speak up, boy. My hearing is going the way of my sight these days."

Mr. Potter. He wasn't kidding. I can't seem to say it. The bastard. Colin pictured his name in his mind, but his throat was silent when it strained to speak the syllables. He shook his head. "I-I've lost my n-name, I guess. It's a long story."

"A boy with no name? Well, well." Samuel turned his head slightly as if Colin's reply had somehow jogged his memory. "To be unnamed can be a blessing, or a curse."

"T-then call me what you like."

"I wouldn't dare," Samuel replied. "Every soul must find their own; it defines them. To give someone their true name can elevate or destroy them."

"Fine," Colin said. "How did I get here? Where am I?"

"That would be the work of Balaam. He has a peculiar talent I've never quite understood. He can make people forget things for a short time by breathing on them—though I rather think the stink of his breath leads one to shock more than anything else."

A soft knocking came from the door.

"Come," Samuel called.

The door opened, and the girl from the beach entered, followed by the donkey.

"I stowed the conch in Balaam's pack. I think it will be safe there, at least for now," she said.

"We may have no further use for it but leave it there for now. Time will tell," Samuel replied.

The girl looked at Colin warily. "You don't think he's . . ."

"I don't know what I think. I only know what was written." Samuel sighed as he stood and hobbled towards her. She guided him to a simple wooden table near the bed, and he sat again on a handcrafted wooden stool.

"My offer stands. He's a bilge rat if ever I saw one," Balaam snorted.

"You d-do talk!" Colin shouted, his voice finally escaping its captivity.

The donkey rolled his eyes. "Yes, and you stutter. Now that we've spoken the obvious, be silent."

"Both of you be silent!" Samuel pounded the table with his fist. "This infernal racket will bring the guards and I have enough worries."

"Wh-where am I? What is this p-place? Wh-who are you? How'd I g-get here?" *Give me some reason for my dementia, so the docs at the asylum will know what antipsychotic to inject me with.*

The girl handed Samuel an earthen cup, which he drank from deeply before answering. "I already told you who I am, as for these two . . ."

"Samuel, don't. He may be a spy," the girl warned.

"If he is, my dear, then it's already too late for us. Let no corrupt communication proceed from thy mouth but what is good, edifying, and grace unto the hearers, or so the Logos says." Samuel continued as he motioned towards the girl, "She is Alexandra, daughter to the high king and shield maiden defender of the kingdom of Gilead, and this one . . ."

Balaam trotted forward and lifted his head as he presented himself. "Balaam, royal prophet and Duke of the Seven Western Isles, Earl of Chestnut and—"

"He's a donkey." Samuel dismissed Balaam with a wave of his hand.

Balaam's muzzle sneered. "It wasn't always so! I was sent with a fleet to present a gift."

"And if the gift was chattering away like a fool and passing gas, then it's been given ten times over! Now be silent!" Samuel ordered.

"What brings you to our shores?" Alexandra asked. "You don't look like an Amorite. Your face is clean of their markings, unless they've started to brand their spies differently." Her eyes pierced Colin's.

Colin saw the likeness of Jennifer in Alexandra's face again and shook his head. "Y-you l-look just like h-her. You could be Jennifer's twin."

"Who is this Jennifer? Is she as strange as you?" Alexandra asked.

"Sh-sh-she's . . ." The words again stuck in Colin's throat. Whenever it was important, the words got in the way of one another. He could feel his cheeks flush. The frustration he'd felt his entire life was about to boil over.

"Shhhh." Samuel hushed Colin quietly and turned to Alexandra. "Help me to him."

Alexandra gently helped the old man to his feet and sat him beside Colin on the bed. Samuel ran his finger across Colin's face. Colin pulled back.

"Be still, boy. This affliction has caused you much pain. Let me do a kindness."

Colin relaxed and allowed Samuel to lay his hands across his face again. Then Samuel spoke a single word, as light as a whisper but in a deeper octave than any human could make.

"Libera," he whispered. The sound echoed through the room, and a breeze of fresh air flew across Colin's face, ruffling his hair.

Colin felt the tightness rise from his throat and disappear.

"Stutter no more," Samuel said and smiled.

CHAPTER 7

A Waking Dream

Thank you." The words slipped out with ease. Colin's eyes widened. "How did you do that?" His mind felt clear, as if some great blockage had lifted. He felt his throat. The usually tense muscles were lax.

"I spoke the Logos into you," Samuel said.

"Logos? You said that word before." Colin rubbed his throat and swallowed. "I don't understand."

"In the first light of creation there was the Logos," Samuel started. "The true word of the Maker. Through it, order was formed out of chaos, light from darkness, and our bodies from the clay. The Logos was passed down to us on scrolls to give us life and define our place in the world, but over the millennia we lost many of the scrolls, and those that remained"—Samuel faltered for a second, his eyes downcast—"we allowed others to change."

This is a great dream. I'll have to write it down when I wake up. Colin shook his head and smiled. Samuel's words had flown over him, his mind still reeling from the miracle. After a moment, his focus turned back to the old man. "Okay, so this Maker guy gave you the rules, and you blew it," Colin said as he nodded.

"More than that, I'm afraid. You see the Maker wrote in a language that no earthly eye could read, save for the chosen ones, the soothsayers. Kings and queens paid great sums to harbor these elite prophets, and in time, such comfort, such riches, corrupted them. New words were written over the old ones, and the teachings found inconvenient were blotted out. The people lost their way. The Maker must have sensed something amiss, for almost a millennium ago, he sent his own sayer to set a new accordance. The man performed mighty miracles, but when he spoke, his words were like burning coals on the people's heads. Those closest to him betrayed and murdered him." Samuel shook his head. "The Maker has been silent ever since."

"Sounds like you guys are in deep shit with this Maker guy." Colin smirked. He felt like he was back in Sunday school.

Samuel winced. "To put it mildly, yes," he said. "The Maker's hand left ours empty. Gilead has struggled with disease, famine, and war since the day our ancestors murdered his chosen one. Many believed us to be a nation cursed, but I never believed it until the light itself was taken from us."

Colin recognized Samuel's pained expression. He'd worn the same hollowed look over the last year. "I get that. You're stuck, helpless. Yeah, I get that."

"Do you?" Samuel replied. "I'll take that as you present it, then. When a man falls, it's a tragedy, but in time he stands again. When the world itself is broken, no amount of tears can bring solace."

"So this place is broken? You've lost everything?"

"Not quite. One true scroll was kept safe and handed down through the generations to me and still remains. It has been pieced together from pages of the Logos that haven't been burned or destroyed, but it was incomplete. Until today." Samuel held up Colin's folded parchment.

"My map?" Colin asked.

"Alexandra found it near you on the shore. Your map is of no concern to me, but when my fingers ran across the ancient letters on the other side, I knew the words were divine. Even if my eyes are blinded, I can still sense their power on the parchment."

"So, you can read those symbols? You know them?" Colin stared at the parchment. The faded letters seemed sharper now—clearer.

Are dreams always so vivid? Colin wondered.

"Would if I could," Samuel answered. "But more than a sense of the words is required. The sayer must be able to read them with his eyes. I hold a balm for this world in my hand but am unable to use it. But my friends here have helped me with the reading."

Balm. "The balm of Gilead? I read that on the other side. It sounds familiar. I've heard it before. Is it something physical? Like medicine, something I could use?"

"Our kingdom is so named, and legends say that the name itself and words like it were carried to our shores from some distant land. But the balm of Gilead?" Samuel mused. "Certainly, the kingdom has many potions and salves for ailments, but one that bears the kingdom's name?" Samuel thought for a moment more. "Long ago there was a terebinth tree whose sap could heal any sickness. Some say its sap could even bring the dead back to life."

Colin looked around the room and then down at his own hands. Was he really in a hospital bed somewhere, lying in a state like a vegetable? Perhaps his few remaining synapses were firing off the mother of all hallucinations before his brain finally died. He could only play it out. What choice did he have? He looked up at Samuel. "Where's the tree?"

"It's dead. Has been for over a thousand years. Somewhere deep in the Dead Wood, a barren weald to the east of Gilead and north of the Royal Road. Its story is a long one and suffice to say that that forest is not a place you should venture into."

Alexandra glared at Colin. "Where did you get that paper? Who did you steal it from?"

"No one. I guess it came in this box I bought—well, traded for—from Mr. Potter's shop. I'm guessing you don't have cell phones here, do you?" Colin already knew it was a dumb question. In a world where magic was a breath away, and donkeys talked, phones were most likely nonexistent. He slowly stood up, steadied himself from the dizziness, and went to a crude window. Past the high bluff the cottage had been built on, Colin could see the shoreline stretch away under the night. In the far distance, he saw a hundred points of light dotted across the water.

"Your words are strange," Alexandra said. "Sailfone?"

"Never mind." Colin sighed. "What are those pretty lights out there?"

"Those 'pretty lights' are the doom of the kingdom," Samuel replied, "the corsairs of the Amorites, laden with death, blockading Gilead's shores."

"Yeah, you said that. Gilead. This hut, these cliffs—this is your kingdom?" Colin asked.

Samuel turned to Alexandra. "Take him outside. Let him see the beauty that once was."

Alexandra opened the front door of the shack and nodded at Colin. He followed her out into the night.

Colin looked around and saw the cottage rested near the edge of a high cliff. A steep path led down to the shoreline and trees. Not more than a couple of miles to the south, past the olive grove and across rolling hills, a giant white stone wall stood easily a hundred feet high under the night sky. Great white spires rose into the sky and opened like lotus flowers behind it. Between the spires were countless small buildings, archways, temples, and, farther back, a grand castle built on a hill. The spires glistened in the moonlight, but as Colin let his eyes wander in amazement, he saw many of the city's towers were broken and in disrepair. The wall, too, had crumbled in portions, and extensive city sections looked dark and empty.

Wake up, buddy. You're not dead. This ain't no dream. Colin's eyes widened. *Holy shit.* "This is real? This is really real?"

"You *are* strange." Alexandra shook her head as she studied him. "Yes, Gilead is as real as you and I are."

She pointed to more walls perched atop the far cliffs. "The grand staircase climbs the cliffs to our western gate, what we call the Lion's Maw, and the Ambassador's Square near the western wall to the castle is nearly half a league, and that again to the eastern gate," Alexandra said and watched his reaction.

"It's huge. God, it's as big as two cities," Colin replied.

"Gilead was built thousands of years ago. It's survived storms, plagues, and sieges before. It will weather this evil as well . . . I hope. Ten thousand souls call it home."

Colin turned and nearly bumped into Samuel. The old man, led by Balaam, had quietly moved in behind them.

"Whether you're friend or foe is still a question to me, but I'd have you hear how we now stand on the brink," Samuel said and moved to sit on a nearby pile of stones. "Alexandra, you know this better than I, tell him your story—give him some understanding."

Alexandra reluctantly turned to face Colin, sighed, and began.

CHAPTER 8

Ill Winds and Omens

Egan stood alongside his men at the base of the Lion's Maw on the imperial docks. The torch fires were lit, and the merchants' vessels had been moored farther up the coast for their protection. He looked up at the gaping stone jaws of the lion's mouth high overhead. Its countenance had been chiseled into the face of the stone cliff by artisans working for nearly a hundred years, and it had withstood countless decades of weathering and war. Its muzzle protruded out high over the docks. The grand staircase set back a thousand feet from where Egan stood led into its maw and served as the only western entrance into the walled city far above him.

"The kingdom fails wherever I look, but still, old friend, you remain." He gazed at the craftsmanship of the stone masonry. "Perhaps even past the days of the last king you will be a testament of what was."

The white lion's head spanned the entire cliffside and crested the top of Gilead's high wall. Its massive paws were carved from the natural rocks of the harbor and spread out, like a sphinx, nearly fifteen hundred feet into the bay. Numerous wooden piers were bound on either side of them, allowing ships of all sizes to dock. In happier times, merchants had moored their vessels between its two great legs and made their way up the white stairway. The broad steps, now crumbling, still maintained their sheen when the sun set across their surfaces. The long journey up the staircase was eased by three lengthy terraces, fifty yards wide, the overhangs supported by great alabaster pillars. Each terrace was set higher than the last, cemented deep within the lion's jaws, and secured in the bedrock. Storefronts, carts, and kiosks used to line these landings, but since the darkness, the structures had all become empty shells of their former glory.

A grizzled man with a ruddy face wearing a burlap hat walked along the dock's edge. He carried a small ladder across his stout shoulders and an elongated copper wick staff with a flame dancing at its tip. A small child in an oversized coat held his free hand and waited quietly as the man paused, dropped the ladder, and lit the next lantern in his route. The child sneezed, and the lamplighter leaned down to better button him up.

"You're going to get me in trouble with your mother. Best get you home." The man paused and nodded. "Evenin', Chief."

"It's a foul night to have younglings out," Egan said. "You look familiar."

"Aye. His mum would agree but he loves to help as he can. It's Avery, Chief," Avery said and managed a smile. "I served under you, sir, for a short time, before the queen said different."

"Oh? I'm sorry," Egan offered. "I didn't know; can I ask why?"

Avery shuffled his feet in thought momentarily and finally spoke, "I guess I just said the wrong thing, or maybe didn't say the right one. But the Maker provides. Night, Chief."

Egan watched Avery lead his child up the grand staircase. His little light danced up the terraces and disappeared.

The shuffle of boots brought Egan's attention to his troop standing ready on the sand to take his orders.

Last in line stood his first officer, Salain. The old man had seen more battles than any other soldier in the army of Gilead, and his words were respected, though he seldom said what he thought. His most distinguishing mark was a scar across his left eye, something Egan knew the old officer used to intimidate recruits.

"See this, you sops!" Salain would say on their first day as he pointed to his face. "This is what happens to you when you step out of line, neglect your duties, or just piss me off." He'd then run his blade near the necks of those fresh faces, and every one of them would quiver in his boots.

Egan held back his smile. He knew his sergeant had gotten the wound from a triste with a scorned lover, but Salain's story kept the recruits in line. Egan stood before Salain and saluted. Salain returned the gesture.

"Every fighting man accounted for, Chief, awaiting your command," the old warrior said. "Your father would be proud."

"Good. Have the scouts spotted any approach farther down the coast?" Egan glanced towards the pinpricks of light far past the dark waves.

"None, other than their black envoy. It floats at a distance of roughly half a mile offshore. I'm concerned some of their agents may have snuck into the city by way of Northport. My privateer says otherwise, however."

Egan raised an eyebrow. "Since when do you hire privateers, Salain? I thought you hated their kind."

Salain followed his captain's gaze towards the far docks that rested between the outer edges of the lion's stone legs, where an unkempt sailor in muddied garb made his way to them from the shadows. "Nothing's changed."

The torchlight accentuated the young man's dark eyes and

slight scowl. Egan guessed he couldn't be much older than himself. He raised his hand to the sailor.

"Greetings, you must be Salain's man," Egan said and smiled.

The man glanced at Egan's outstretched hand but didn't take it. "I'm nobody's man. My name's Absalom." He turned to Salain. "Here's your report." He pulled a folded parchment from his pocket and offered it to Salain.

Salain grabbed it from his hands. "Fool! You address the chief warrant officer—the king's right hand. Show some respect!"

Absalom glanced back at Egan. "Of course, my apologies," he said, his brow lifted slightly.

Egan lowered his hand. There was no love lost between them.

Salain unfolded the parchment and scanned it. "The Northport authorities make no mention of the northern pass. Why?" he asked Absalom.

Absalom sighed. "You hired me to bring you reconnaissance of the sea, not inland. I never asked them. Now about the money . . ."

"I told you to get comprehensive scouting reports. This is incomplete," Salain growled at him.

Absalom folded his arms. "Well then, we're at an impasse. I anchored my ship in a soup of fog three nights ago in that province's dreary little harbor. The royal guard have seen little of the enemy, from what they can see at all. Some of their men have gone missing . . ." Absalom eyed Egan. "But I'm sure they're busy watching the pubs, as is the custom with the uniform." He looked back to Salain. "Now pay me."

Salain raised his hand to strike him. "Mouthy little cur!"

Egan grabbed Salain's hand. "Enough! Pay him. It's clear he's done his duty."

Salain grimaced but tore open a pouch at his side. He pulled five gold coins from it and slammed them into Absalom's open hand.

"Be off with you. Run to your floating derelict and let the leviathan have you," Salain snapped.

Absalom eyed Egan again, his sneer melting. "Well then, thank you." Absalom turned away and hurried up the grand stair.

"My apologies, Chief. It was a mistake to hire that impudent halfwit," Salain said.

Egan patted him on the back. "We must use the tools available to us."

"Aye." Salain nodded towards the ship lights in the distance. "How should we proceed?"

"I would that we'd ready our ships to meet them in battle, but the queen has ordered otherwise." Egan studied the distant lights on the water for a moment. "An embassy ship is being made ready. The Vizier is accompanying a gift of grain and foodstuffs to their vessels. He goes to negotiate with them. He's asked for a small detachment of guards to accompany him."

"Of course, Chief." Salain nodded curtly and bit his lip.

"Your eyes betray your thoughts," Egan said. "Speak your mind."

"Well, sir," Salain started but was interrupted by the bumbling call of the Vizier as he stumbled down the last few steps of the grand staircase behind them. Catching himself, he stopped to adjust his frayed curly locks behind his ear and then raised his chin to regain his self-important composure.

"He fears the Amorite response, yes?" The Vizier asked as he straightened his silk robe around his protruding belly. "And who could blame him? No, any common man would look at their mighty vessels and be concerned. But fear not. Sharper minds than yours know how to soothe angry men and turn them into friends."

Egan nodded toward the impish little man. He had never liked the corpulent bootlicker. The Vizier lacked a backbone, and his loyalties shifted with the wind. Egan wondered how much of Gilead had was sold off because of this great sage's counsel.

The Vizier clapped his hands, and nearby peasants began to pull two large carts of grain and fruit from the southern beachhead out to the farthest dock and load them onto a ship.

"How many of our own people would that feed, I wonder?" Egan asked as he watched them work, and Salain nodded.

The Vizier laughed. "My boy, this stock comes from the king's personal cupboards. We must all shoulder the burden of being a reputable host. I guarantee that in three hours' time our friends will depart from our shores, and I'll have renewed our accord with them."

"Friends don't mob your doorstep in the night," Salain murmured.

The Vizier smirked at Salain and then turned to Egan. "You should train your foot soldiers better, lad. They speak out of turn in front of their superiors."

Egan saw the retort was like a slap across Salain's face.

"Apologies, Vizier." Salain's lips barely twitched.

Egan leaned forward to within an inch of the Vizier's face. "As far as I'm concerned, Salain has no superior here. Now get on your ship."

The Vizier swallowed and backed up. "We shall have a discussion with His Majesty about rank and respect when I return. Select my retinue and let's delay no longer!" He brushed past them and boarded the vessel.

"Send me, Chief Warrant Officer," Salain said.

"Why in the Maker's name would you want to protect that snake?" Egan asked him.

"Few men have seen the Amorite legion up close and lived; fewer still have presided over negotiations with them. I can be your ears in their presence." Salain nodded at the advisor, who was busy making himself comfortable near the vessel's helm. "And in his."

"I would hate to see you lose your life protecting his," Egan replied.

"Who said anything about protecting him?" Salain smiled. "I'll use him as a shield if it comes to that."

They laughed, and Salain laid his hand on Egan's arm. "I've seen you grow into a fine man, Egan, one your father would be proud of. Give me the honor of serving your needs."

Egan nodded reluctantly. "Take care, friend, and be vigilant."

"Always." Salain nodded and saluted him before turning towards the ship to board. The vessel soon undocked, lowered its sail, and made for the open sea. Egan watched its outline diminish into the night and wondered if those lights on the water would bring back hope or Hell.

CHAPTER 9

The Ashes of Eden

Some of it I witnessed," Alexandra began, "and some I read later in my father's diary, but it all seems like a dream now . . ." Her voice trailed off as her eyes became lost in thought before she picked up the story again. "There was a time when I could play in the Western Square with the other children or ride into the city at my father's side on my white charger. I knew every street and alley. I knew the merchants in the bazaar by name. The kingdom was alive and wonderful. But things changed, and like many evil things, the seed of it was greed."

KING BRAEDEN WATCHED FROM HIS balcony as his young daughter sparred with Egan below in the castle courtyard. His warden Egan smiled as he helped Alexandra correctly hold the wooden sword. She half curtsied and laughed as she fumbled with the training tabard bound around her waist and flicked her blade to nudge him on the chin.

"She's enjoying herself, but I wonder if diplomacy wouldn't be a more appropriate skill to master, my lord," the Vizier said and nodded as Braeden turned to him.

"She'd need to learn patience first, I think." Braeden waved off the counselor. "I'll not begrudge her some sport. The weight of the bureaucracy will be on her back soon enough." Braeden turned from the balcony to his desk. Half buried under a pile of scrolls lay his sheathed sword, *Teacht Riocht*—the blade of kings. Braeden brushed the documents aside as he lifted the scabbard and weapon like it was made of glass. He partially pulled the hilt out and let his eyes scan the ancient letters chiseled into the base of the blade. "For now, let her imagine her problems can be vanquished so easily."

"True, Sire. Speaking of problems at hand, I have our latest storehouse report." The Vizier said as he touched the king's arm, and Braeden sheathed the sword again. "I'm sorry to say things have not improved." He held out his report.

Braeden took the advisor's scroll of figures and walked away without a word. The accounting needed no explanation. Nine years of famine had left his storehouses empty, his fishing boats rotting on the shore, and his reserves depleted. His people cried out for food, yet Braeden had nothing to give. When riding through Gilead, he'd see families begging for bread and children scrounging after rats.

The following morning, King Braeden sat alone in the Great Hall of Judah—the Hall of the Lion—and looked to the empty throne on his right. Sorcha, his wife, would've been succor; her soft voice would've brought some insight. But with the birth of Alexandra, she'd lost her strength and, within hours, died.

The sound of clumsy footsteps and heavy breathing echoed into the hall.

"Sire." The Vizier's voice brought Braeden's attention back. "The envoy to Cormorant has returned."

"What word? Will our neighbors offer us aid? Can we barter lumber for grain?" Braeden leaned forward. At best, the proposition was weak, but Gilead had no other allies.

The Vizier studied his expression before speaking. "They no longer wish to support us. Our timber has little value to them, and our treasury is empty. They say the Maker has cursed us, and they don't want to bring the same trouble to their households."

Braeden leaned back on his throne. *That damn prophecy. Must this old curse still besiege the kingdom?*

"Are we not past the days when we huddled round fires and feared every shadow?" Braeden asked. "One man was put to death, however unjustly, a century ago, and yet even now nobles whisper of a coming judgment."

"I share your sentiment, my lord, yet I have other tidings. We do have an offer—an offer I think you should listen to. A nobleman and his retinue wait at the outer gates. He's from beyond the western isles and seeks your audience."

The king's brow furrowed. Those living beyond Gilead's western sea were nomads, hunters, and pirates. They worshiped dark gods and, in years past, had raided his outposts and colonies.

"He has brought a caravan of gifts. Sire, surely you could at least acknowledge his generosity?" The Vizier asked, already knowing how the King would respond.

"Call the guards to escort him. I'll see this man, but he will not have free passage in the city," King Braeden replied.

The grand doors to the throne room opened within an hour, and a man wearing a gilded cloak was escorted in. His skin was pale, sickly, and dark bags hung below his small eyes. His sweeping bow was overdone, and when he smiled, Braeden saw that his teeth had been filed to those of a wolf's.

"Great and mighty King Braeden, I bring greetings from the thirteenth house of Talamar. I represent the Amorites. We have heard of your powerful reign and wise leadership, and we bring our . . . adulation." The man bowed again. He turned towards the doorway and clapped briskly. Thirteen gilded palanquins laden with silver trunks and carried by women in veiled hijabs entered the room. Braeden's mouth dropped as the servant girls lowered the litters and opened the chests. Each held piles of gold, diamonds, and precious jewels. "More will come, of course." The stranger smiled as he gazed at the king.

"What is this thirteenth house that they bring the riches of Solomon to my door?" Braeden asked.

"Your servants, of course. Our ruler would only ask a small boon in return," the man said. "A small measure to show that we are allies." His eyes gleamed as his hand ran across the lid of one of the chests. "We ask that your fleet no longer attack our mariners and traders, and you allow us to live peacefully among your people."

Braeden paused. He feared more was implied in the traveler's words. "Your mariners have been called cutthroats; your traders, spies."

"Ignorant terms thrown about by those who lack understanding of our ways. We're no different from you. We simply wish for the same liberty that your citizens enjoy." The traveler nodded toward the king with respect.

Braeden considered for a moment. He remembered hearing an excerpt from the Logos long ago, some warning of those who bring gifts uncalled for, but times had changed.

"We accept your gift and give you this promise. Our soldiers will not strike your people, as long as they follow our laws."

"Yes, wonderful," the stranger said. "I promise you, we will make your laws our own." He smiled wide, his fangs disquieting Braeden.

"You never mentioned your king. Who rules over this thirteenth house?" Braeden asked. "To whom do we send our thanks for these gifts?"

"Our ruler is but a humble man, of no consequence but of great means," the stranger said. "He also offers one more gift, a prize more valuable than all the treasures of Sheba . . . his daughter."

The stranger clapped again, and a litter carried by four male servants was brought into the hall from beyond the great doors. A woman sat atop it. A hijab concealed her face, but her burka reflected rows of inset emeralds, sapphires, and rubies. The servants lowered the litter before the king, and she stood, stepped away from her seat, and walked forward. She unveiled her hijab and let her covering to slip off her shoulders to puddle around her feet. Her amber eyes locked onto the king's, and her flawless sun-kissed skin gleamed in the torchlight of the hall. She wore a silk camisole and skirt, both laden with fine diamonds, and her flaxen hair shined as she moved her hips seductively.

"She is skilled in all the arts of nobility and medicine, and she will be an asset to your home," the stranger said.

"I'm honored to serve you," the woman said as she bowed low.

"What is your name, my lady?" King Braeden asked as he stood and lowered his hand to her, and for a moment, her gaze felt the same as his wife's had—warm, inviting, and enticing.

"Mariselle," she said as she took his hand. "You have kind eyes, Majesty."

"I leave you in peace," the stranger said and turned from the king. The man didn't bother to bow before he left. All in the room noticed, except the king himself.

"Five years passed," Alexandra said. "The gifts came in and our land thrived . . . for a while."

"There was food though, right?" Colin asked. "And peace—I mean, they kept their word. What was the problem?"

"Yes, with our new wealth we were able to import the sustenance our people needed until the famine ended, but we became entranced by their gold and seduced by their lies," Alexandra said. "The stranger never came again, but messengers brought more chests of treasure, and demands—always more demands."

KING BRAEDEN CAME UP BEHIND his daughter and hugged her. "Why does my daughter grieve?" he asked as Alexandra stared from the castle's balcony over the courtyard and toward Gilead's marketplace. He released her and turned her around to face him.

"Do you know they've disrupted Helen's wedding?" Alexandra said, her eyes red with tears. "They mobbed her and the priest as they entered the southern temple, tore her dress, and ripped his robe because he refuses to teach from their books. I don't care what promises you made them, how can they do that? How is that right?"

"Helen? Your handmaiden?" Braeden asked.

"Yes," she said. "These Amorites attack anyone who stands outside of their conviction. They're zealots acting like martyrs."

"They would no doubt say the same of our holy men," he replied. "What is important now is understanding, more than anything. Who can say what teachings are right or wrong these days? We must let go of archaic words that keep us bound to small-minded thinking."

"Did that, that woman convince you of that?" Alexandra replied, then turned and walked back into the king's chambers.

Braeden followed her. "Your mother was my happiness in life, Alexandra. Losing her left me empty for so many years. Mariselle can never replace her, but she is my heart's desire. She's given me such joy since your mother passed."

"I suppose she has. You've not been to Mother's grave for nearly a year."

"I mourned your mother for years now. She will always be a part of me. But it's time I move on. Mariselle has been patient and asked for so little."

"Do you think the mob will ambush your wedding tomorrow as well? Will they tear Mariselle's dress?"

"The people will rejoice tomorrow. I've made concessions to ensure it," Braeden said.

"Concessions?" Alexandra asked.

"Her dowry from her father was promised to be doubled if we married in the customs of her people."

Alexandra's mouth dropped. She looked around the room until her gaze fell on Braeden's sword, still sheathed and cast on the floor. She walked to it and lifted it to his desk. Her eyes ran across the broken leather strapping of the sheath.

"Alexandra." Braeden sighed. "You are royalty. You must control your emotions."

Alexandra wiped tears from her eyes as she studied the blade and sheath.

"*Teacht Riocht* will be yours one day. When I'm sent on my final voyage, my name will be etched above the hilt next to those who came before, and you'll carry it by your side."

"You don't carry it now. Why should I bother?"

Braeden shook his head. Her words stung. "Aye, it's been a marker of our family for generations. I meant to have it cleaned and mounted in the great hall. It's fitting I give it the respect due."

Alexandra raised her gaze to meet his. "And the Logos?"

"The Logos scrolls are to be stricken from our temples until their teachings better reflect the will of all our people." He cleared his throat. The words felt wrong in his mouth. "The treasures of our temple are to be stored until they can be reshaped into images that envision all gods."

"So, our teachings will be cast down? Our songs unsung?" Alexandra whispered, "Our heritage erased?"

"Alex, you must understand these Amorites are our lifeblood. Their gifts keep our nation alive." Braeden shook his head. "You're almost an adult now! Near the age where you'll be courted yourself. You know as well as I that the famine decimated our reserves; to this day, our crops continue to fail and barely sustain our people. We struggle to keep our borders free from raiders and the kingdoms to the east. Stop acting like a petulant child! They're just proverbs and names that can be changed. Words can be redefined, teachings can be altered. All that matters are the concepts behind them."

"And what of the gifts? I see them less and less with each passing season," Alexandra replied. "Their coffers bring only a little of what they once did. How many came last month, Father? How grand was the gift this time?"

King Braeden looked down. "One chest, with thirty shekels of silver."

"We've sold ourselves for a month's worth of bread?" she asked, disgusted. "What a poor wage for our souls."

"You don't understand . . . you're being stubborn . . ." Braeden could not look at her face.

"A lion once dwelt in the Great Hall of Judah." She shoved his sword towards him. "I wonder if he will ever return?" She turned from him and left the room.

The king looked out over the city and feared deep in his heart that she was right.

CHAPTER 10

A Thief in the Night

After receiving his pay, Absalom silently climbed the great white steps of the Lion's Maw. The privateer's wiry frame cast the slimmest of shadows on the marble stairs, and his footsteps were as silent as a feather fall. Pausing to pull back his dark locks of hair that hung to his shoulders, he tied them into a ponytail with a bit of string, ensuring his line of sight was unobstructed. Quick hands were only as good as a sharp eye. Absalom studied his reflection in a puddle of water near his feet. He was average in height, and unremarkable in every way; he was an every-man who could blend into the crowd and vanish—ideal for his line of work. As he made his way up and around the terraces lying within the mouth of the great stone beast, he saw that the merchant kiosks were empty, covered in dust and disrepair. Whatever commerce existed here had left long ago. He shook his head and continued up the steps until he came to the great western gate at the top of the cliff, which opened wide and was guarded by two sentinels.

"Evening, sir. Where is your business tonight?" A guard approached him.

"In the market district, where else?" Absalom noticed the guard gripping the hilt of his sword tightly. "Does the queen track our every movement now?"

"There's talk of invasion, spies within the walls, and the like."

"You'd hardly know one by questioning one, would you? Tell your chief he needs better tactics if that's his concern." Absalom tossed the guard a coin. "Let this speak for me."

The guard smiled as he caught the coin. "Have a pleasant evening."

Absalom smirked. It was always the same with that bunch. Their morality could always be counted on to grovel when it came to the clink of an extra coin.

Absalom moved forward into the Ambassador's Square. What could have easily been the center of any town in the land, this courtyard only made up the western edge of Gilead's sprawling boundaries. The plaza stretched nearly two hundred thousand feet around its perimeter and was lined with mansions and shops on all sides. Absalom remembered in days past, dignitaries were met by the King here. A sprawling purple carpet runner would be laid across the humble cobblestone so their feet might never touch the filthy walkways the commoners used.

He had been just a boy then, unaware of what the pomp and circumstance actually meant, a regal circus signifying a station he could never achieve, a reminder of his humble place in the world. Only a guard's swift kick to his stomach, when he drew too close to the runner, had impressed upon him the lesson. He was glad the King's jewel of a city was crumbling—seeing it slowly wither gave a certain satisfaction. But the people he knew here, the little ones who struggled to get by, kept him from walking away entirely.

Absalom made his way across the plaza to the eastern side and the winding Market Street that curved and wound into the city's heart. The houses here were less grand, tightly abutting each other, and felt more like home. Windows with their candlelight were welcoming eyes compared to the cold emptiness of the Square. His mother had promised them a home here one day, but he'd known her words were empty. Her gentlemen callers had rarely paid what they promised, and more often than not, she'd return to the hovel with a black eye or a bruised limb until one day she didn't return at all.

As Absalom entered the market district, he saw the same old bustling activity from vendors breaking down their carts and kiosks for the night, though the night was now a constant in the land. A call here for more rope, a laugh between two others, and promises of drinks to come. This portion of the city hadn't changed at all.

He had been only twelve when he found his mother's broken body in a back alley nearby, with no sign of the aggressor in sight. He wandered in a stupor for days until his growling stomach woke him from his daze. It was then that he learned his meager frame was an asset. It was here in the streets that he had learned to survive. He could move unnoticed and pilfer any vendor's stall with ease. Instead of a harsh and unforgiving corner, he found the district to be a banquet table open to any who braved to dine at it.

Alleyways broke out in all directions from the main bazaar here, and he'd explored each, save for the few that led southeast into the great cemetery. Every gutter snipe knew the field of tombs within the city walls was haunted, and most adults preferred to bypass it and brave the old sector of town instead. There, one could enjoy the fine delicacies of opium, liquor, and the company of whores before stumbling out of the crumbling eastern gate onto the moors.

Absalom wondered if his childhood hut in the old sector was still standing, but the impulse to visit it died quickly. Even if the landlord hadn't let it burn to the ground, there were no fond memories to see. The quiet desperation in his mother's soft sobbing at night would echo in his mind again if he saw those cracked walls and rotting doors.

Instead, he followed the market road as it ran northward out of the bazaar and into the temple district, a place he'd happily avoided as an urchin for fear of dying from boredom. The white marble columns and lavish finery on the Travertine walls and altars never spoke to him as they did to the religious types. His provider was the clink of an unguarded coin purse; his god was real.

As Absalom approached a brazier of burning coals, he saw his fence appear from the shadows. The grizzled face and hunched figure of the man in the dirty overcoat could have blended into any crowd, a fact Absalom knew this particular scoundrel took full advantage of.

"'Bout time, you sloth. Figured you was held up by that captain of the guard, or chief warrant officer or whatever it is they call him." The fence laughed.

"The day that boy-captain bests me is the day I retire." Absalom smiled. "So, what's the mark?"

"Not really a mark per se—but I thought you might be interested. What with the curfew and all the talk of invasion going about, many in the palace are eyeing their retirement funds early. One, in particular, might be a real catch. Seems the King has a chest he keeps well locked in his bedroom." The fence scratched at his chin. "Too heavy to run off with, of course, and too tough to break. A five-tumbler lock to boot. They say no one can crack it, but then I thought of you."

"I've never tried the castle before." Absalom eyed the road as it ran northward up a hill to the castle and its courtyard in the distance.

"Which is damn surprising, if you ask me." The fence continued, "You can hit any target and get out free as a bird, and there's the biggest mark in the land and you ignore it."

"I wouldn't say 'ignore'; I just have my reasons. There's a scab there I'm not sure I should pick."

"Scab, eh? I say rip it off. Royal wounds bleed gold." The fence slapped Absalom's back. "Either way, you're on your own. I'm leaving tonight for Northport. Too many things stirring here for my comfort. You ever figure a way and get out alive, let me know."

"Aye." Absalom nodded as he gazed at the castle walls. His brow furrowed. Perhaps it *was* time to reopen the wound.

CHAPTER II

The Best Laid Plans

And so those who spoke the truth were silenced, and the promise of more riches never materialized," Alexandra said as she gazed at the great city in the distance.

"But the queen brought peace at least; I mean your new mother—" Colin started.

"Never call her that!" Alexandra snapped. "She's a snake. Her lies are poison to my father's ears."

Samuel nodded as if he knew the story all too well. Colin followed Alexandra's gaze to the empty towers and darkened streets beyond the great wall.

"Do you know what it feels like to see everything you love being pulled apart, bit by bit? I had to sit there on a throne and watch it happen."

"I think so. Like a leaf in the stream, right? No direction, no control?" Colin offered. "You got pushed around, stepped on—a victim."

Alexandra glared at him. "I hate that word, but yes, we were all at the queen's mercy. They married when I was eleven, and every year after that I saw our traditions dismantled, one after the other. I saw our people grow callous and petty. I saw old friends driven away from the court." Alexandra glanced at Samuel. "Finally, a year ago, I knew I had to leave as well."

"Your father never came looking for you?" Colin asked.

"Less and less often, and then not at all. Samuel now seems to be a wanted felon. I've no doubt Mariselle had something to do with that," she replied as a gust of wind flew by, and she wrapped her arms around herself. "In any case, Samuel needed help while he studied his scroll. It's the only one left."

"Study?" Colin turned to Samuel. "You're blind. How could you?"

"The Maker has blessed me with assistants who have imaginative minds," Samuel said.

Alexandra smiled. "What little I can do, but you know as well as I that my skill with letters is limited."

Balaam gently pawed at the ground next to Samuel with his hoof, creating a character resembling the *A* from Colin's puzzle box. The donkey seemed to take the greatest of care as he finished. Balaam gently nuzzled Samuel's hand towards the letter written in the dirt.

"Leyo," Samuel pronounced as he traced the character with his finger. "Even a donkey serves the Maker's purpose."

"I was much more once," Balaam said, "but it seems this is my penance, to serve as requested." He glanced at Colin. "And babysit when needed."

Colin shook his head. "Look, I'm sorry, really. But this place, your problems—they've nothing to do with me." He turned back towards the path. "You know pain? So do I. My mom is sick. Christ, she's dying." Colin clutched the photo in his pocket. "I don't know how that horn got me here, I don't even know where here is, but if there's a chance that finding this balm can save her, I gotta try. I owe her that much. So point me to this dead forest and that tree and I'll leave you to it."

"Even if you made it to the weald's borders, you'd lose yourself in it within a day," Samuel replied. "For a year now, shadows have blotted out the sun, and the night has been ceaseless. Even under normal light, travelers who dare cross the shadow of those woods rarely return."

"Samuel, let him go. He's of no use to us." Alexandra sighed. "The horn failed us."

"Yeah, I think your magic conch screwed up." Colin shook his head.

"On the contrary, you have what we lack." Samuel dismissed Colin's statement with a wave. "A face that is unknown to the queen, and two good eyes. There are still a few loyalists to the crown within the city walls. One man in particular could reach the king quietly and hand him a message."

"Do I know him?" Alexandra asked.

"Doubtful. He was a jailor in the dungeons last I heard." Samuel replied, "His name is Rustag, and he owes allegiance to no one but King Braeden. While I might still have the king's ear, I'd never make it to his court, not now. I'll prepare a letter sealed with my mark, a letter that the boy could hand to Rustag and he, in turn, deliver to the king. There is a message the king needs to read, words long overdue. Accomplish this task, and you'll surely find his favor." Samuel glanced at Alexandra. "The boy might not be our savior, but he can help our cause while furthering his own."

"Whoa, who said anything about being your savior?" Colin asked. "I just need this sap. That's it. If I run this errand for you, can you guarantee I'll get it?"

"No, but I can guarantee you'll fail if you try to make your journey alone," Samuel replied. "The castle has a storehouse of provisions and medicine. Some of the Terebinth's sap may have found its way there."

Colin shook his head. The idea seemed far-fetched at best, but there were no other options save for wandering a land he knew nothing of.

"Fine. I'll do what I can," he said.

And the minute I find this crap, I'm gone.

"Samuel, is this wise?" Alexandra asked. "Mariselle's agents watch throughout the countryside and the city."

Samuel nodded as he took Colin's hand. "True, and that's why you shouldn't risk taking the Royal Road south. Instead, row my skiff past the Lion's Maw. There's still enough boat traffic to hide you from any prying eyes, if you keep your heads down. Once you're south of the harbor, go ashore and make for the eastern gate. You'll be nearly invisible, dressed in some of my robes." Samuel turned to Colin and continued. "Balaam will guide you. You'll look like a peasant, a nameless face in the crowd. A skill, I sense, you know something about."

"Do I have any say in this?" Balaam asked.

"No!" Samuel snapped. "Balaam, you know the streets better than anyone. Avoid the temple district. Take him by way of the cemetery and the abandoned quarter to the servant's entrance to the castle."

"The abandoned quarter? The cemetery? Those places are filthy, crawling with rats, thieves, and beggars," Balaam argued. "No sane human would wander there at night."

"Yes, yes, I know. That's what will keep you safe," Samuel replied. "Alex, you may go with them to the eastern gate, but no farther. Your face is too well known."

"Samuel, I've wandered those streets since I was small," she replied. "Let me take this message. I've years of experience eluding guards and going about unnoticed."

"Child, you are our hope should we succeed against this

growing darkness. Your father is old, and soon Gilead will need a ruler of your caliber. I can't risk you on an errand like this," Samuel replied. "Nor can you risk yourself. Your name carries power, and we'll need it erelong, I suspect."

Colin knew he was a pawn. Even in this bizarre world, he was awash between tidal wills that cared little for his well-being. He would play the part for now until the time was right.

"I've ridden the wildest horses through the southern fields, explored the typhoon swamps of Northport, and outwitted Mariselle herself," Alexandra said, her face flustered. "Don't treat me like an infant!"

"I've said my piece, Alexandra." Samuel replied quietly. "Sometimes wisdom comes with accepting your station and staying silent."

Alexandra folded her arms and turned away.

"Could I have some sort of weapon maybe?" Colin asked. "Some kind of protection?"

"Certainly." Samuel turned and placed his hand gently on Colin's head. "Factorem prohibeo periculum."

Colin waited for something more, but Samuel lowered his hand and smiled, satisfied.

"That's it?" Colin asked. "Aren't you going to at least give me a sword or a wizarding wand or something?"

"Power does not lie in objects but in the true words of the Maker," Samuel replied. "Words have brought armies to a halt, toppled empires, and moved mountains. More importantly, words can change minds and open hearts. Never discount that."

"Sure," Colin said with an unenthusiastic nod. He wondered if he could scrounge a stick from the nearby bushes. "Okay then, I guess I'm ready."

Samuel took his arm. "Excellent. Alex, help him saddle Balaam while I finish the note. Steel yourself, boy. Tonight, you sneak into a lion's den."

CHAPTER 12

The Broken Door

Queen Mariselle sat on her throne and stared at the dingy banners and standards that lined the high walls in the castle's great hall. Their once impeccable white silk tassels were now ashen and ragged. Like the decayed tapestries that languished over the fetid tables and dirtied dishes cast under them, Mariselle felt foul and sighed audibly as her counselor droned on from a scroll where he stood at her side. A long line of supplicants had formed past him, all hoping to curry favors or air grievances.

"That is, by large, the kingdom's current holdings, Your Highness," the counselor concluded. He paused and glanced back at the line of nobles eagerly waiting for a word with the queen. He turned back to Mariselle and lowered his voice. "If I may, before you begin today's audiences, I'd like to mention some concern I have with the Vizier."

"Oh?" Mariselle eyed him with interest.

"There's evidence he has not only pilfered from the treasury but also blatantly administered royal funds to a black market, used additional funds for gambling, and—"

"But that's not the real reason you want his head, is it?" Mariselle rolled her eyes at the counselor. Since she had taken the throne, the court had become a pit of petulant backstabbing and rumors. Where the king had had loyal allies, she'd found dogs bearing their teeth for a bone. "He's wounded you, hasn't he? And you wish to hurt him back."

"My queen"—the counselor shook his head and bowed—"I would never disgrace you with such a petty act."

"Petty?" Mariselle stared at him questioningly and stood. "Walk with me."

"Majesty." The counselor leaned in. "You've haven't held court in months, perhaps you should first attend to the people?"

"Let them wait." She strode into an adjoining corridor and up several flights of stairs. The timid footsteps of the counselor followed, and she smiled.

She flung the door to her parlor open and stepped forward into a room filled with standing mirrors, armoires, and wardrobes. By the light of a thousand candles, she gazed at herself. Her eyes followed the soft curves of her figure and the porcelain tone of her perfect face.

As the counselor entered the room, she turned to him and smiled before loosening her dress and letting it fall to her ankles.

"Tell me, advisor, do you like what you see?"

The counselor blushed and turned away. "Your Majesty, I . . ."

Mariselle laughed and moved to her wardrobe, pulling a fur-lined robe from it and wrapping herself again.

"You're a liar if you label your desires petty. If someone strikes you, you strike back. You take what is rightfully yours." She sat at a vanity and brushed her tresses. "And you never look back."

Those had been the words spoken to her a lifetime ago when she was neither beautiful nor strong. She had still been a child then; sixteen-year-old eyes saw the world full of promise before they became a victim to its grasp. But the magician had changed all that. He had taught her how to fight. And the price for his training?

Mariselle glanced at the thin scars that danced across the underside of her wrists. The robe hid the long, lean cuts that traveled up her arms, back, and thighs. Save her hands and face; her body had paid what had been asked. But the question always haunted her, if that price had been too high.

"THANK YOU, MY LOYAL SUBJECTS." A young Mariselle laughed, her matted brunette hair flailing in the wind as she flew past her older sister, Rena, and across the wildflowers surrounding them.

"There you are, girl, queen of the daisies." Rena wove the last flower of the crown in and laid it on Mariselle's head. "Though I'm afraid we can't hold court today, the scullery pots call."

"Let them scream, my hands will crack if I have to scrub another pan for that family." Mariselle stuck her tongue at Rena and folded her arms. "Lord Gervasis—how can you stand that man? He's a pig."

Rena smiled. "He puts a roof over our heads and bread in our bellies. I'll soon have enough coin from him for us to travel; maybe take a boat to Shinoa, or some camels to The White City?"

"He smells of onions and feet, and the way he looks at me . . ." Mariselle shivered. "Not to mention that little bastard Portney grabs at me when I walk by. I swear he put a dead rat under my pillow a fortnight ago. If he wasn't the lord's son, I'd wipe the floor with him."

"Listen to me, sis." Rena's smile dropped. "We need only finish out the year. Just mind your work and don't create a fuss."

Mariselle watched her sister's tired smile lessen. She'd heard her cry at night and knew the toll on Rena's shoulders was heavier than she let on.

"We're tough biscuits, you and me. Now c'mon, we're going to be late."

Their extended break hadn't gone unnoticed, and as they entered the servant's entrance to the manor's kitchen, a pasty noodle of a boy with buck teeth wearing an oversized stained doublet met them.

"You're late for prep. Father will have to dock you half a day's wage."

"Then, Master Portnoy," Rena said through a smile of gritted teeth, "it's best you leave us to make the night's meal."

"Not too spicy. You put too much spice in my soup last night. It tasted terrible."

"Aye, Portnoy." Mariselle nodded and moved past him to reach for a mixing bowl.

"'Master,' you little imp. I'm your master. Don't forget that."

Mariselle eyed him steadily before nodding. "Aye, master."

The boy backed away from her nervously before running down the hall.

Time flew past, and as the clock chimed the seventh hour, Mariselle strained and lifted the heavy silver platter of dumplings, hog meat, and fruits. Her back ached, and her feet were screaming. *A few more hours, then bed. Get through this damnable dinner, then rest.* As she placed the platter of food on the grand dining table, Portnoy reached beneath the tablecloth and pinched her upper thigh.

Mariselle slapped his hand away and glared at him. The boy smirked and grabbed a handful of meat for his plate. Mariselle glanced toward Lord Gervasis, who was enveloped in conversation with his house guest, oblivious to his son's antics.

"Truly fascinating, my good man. Your Lord of Talamar must be powerful indeed." Lord Gervasis nodded at the man in the gilded robe. The stranger smiled. His sharpened teeth disquieted her.

"Behold, my lord." The stranger let go of his goblet, and it floated an inch above the table for a moment before gently setting down on the wood.

"By some unseen hand!" Lord Gervasis marveled. Portnoy nearly choked on his meat as he watched.

"Wench, more wine!" Lord Gervasis shouted over his shoulder at Mariselle, who stood stunned at what she saw. The magician caught her eye. His gaze was almost admiring.

Mariselle grabbed the wine pitcher and poured the lord a cup before approaching the magician. As she drew close to him, her skin prickled with a chill. She sensed some electric force was about to strike, and when his eyes flashed jade in the candlelight, she spilled the wine over the lip of his cup, pooling it onto the table.

"Half-witted fool!" Lord Gervasis bellowed. "Get a towel!"

"S-so sorry." Mariselle bowed and rushed to the door before losing her footing and falling on her face. Wine doused the rugs around her. Portnoy's long leg retracted, and a coy smile spread across his face.

"Get out of my sight, you ass!" Gervasis stood and snatched her arm, wrenching her to her feet. "Send your sister to serve the rest of the meal. You're not worth the trouble."

The rest of the night, Mariselle scurried to clean every dish in the kitchen, terrified of what Lord Gervasis might inflict on her once the meal was over. But he never stepped through the kitchen doors, and as hours passed, she realized Rena was nowhere to be seen either. It was not until dawn, when Mariselle finally went in search of her, that she heard her sister's slight whimper outside Gervasis's door. Blood stained her backside.

"Just take me to bed, please," Rena mumbled as Mariselle approached her.

"What did he . . ." Mariselle started, but a look from her sister quieted the question.

As Mariselle laid her down on her cot, she saw a bruise forming on Rena's cheek.

"Anything, name anything I can do." Mariselle ran her fingers across her sister's hair.

"Just be silent, sis. He was especially cruel tonight, but his temper will pass."

"Especially?" Mariselle gazed at her sister.

"I do what I must. Soon we will be free of him; soon we'll have coin enough to leave and never look back."

As Rena slept, Mariselle took her sister's stained dress to the courtyard. A bucket of soap and lye water sat at her feet, and she scrubbed the blood from her sister's gown until the sun rose high in the early morning sky.

"That stain will always mark it, I fear," the magician's voice called from behind Mariselle as she doused the dress again. She turned to see the strange man approach her and sit on a bench at her side.

"I apologize, my lord, if I woke you." Mariselle looked down.

"Don't, my dear. It doesn't become you. Apologize for nothing; you're doing what you must to survive."

She gazed at him again, and immediately an electric chill washed across her skin. "I never heard your name."

"I go by many names, but you may call me Dagon."

"Lord Dagon, then." Mariselle nodded, his jade eyes holding hers.

"Lord Gervasis betrays his trust to you and your sister." Dagon nodded at the dress. "Where I come from even the servants demand respect."

"He . . . he takes his pleasure. There is little I can . . ."

"Oh no," Dagon's voice coaxed. "Don't finish the thought, girl. I can see it in your eyes: you're better than this, you deserve so much more. You're a rose surrounded by weeds. Don't you agree?"

Mariselle looked away and nodded. "Yes. Perhaps. But that's not my lot in life—one day, Rena and I will move on, and we can forget this all happened. They say the Maker has a plan for each of us in time."

"Now that, my child, is a dream. A fairytale. What kind of Maker would allow two lives to languish so? What Maker would inflict such heartache?" Dagon whispered in her ear, "The truth is you have no one but yourself in this life; you must take what is yours, or have it taken from you."

Dagon turned and spit into the dirt before using his finger to draw geometric shapes in the newly formed bit of mud.

"Let me show you what true power is." Dagon smiled at her and took her hand. "May I?"

Mariselle's eyes widened as she saw a pin, as thin as a sewing needle, appear in his hand.

"One drop of blood is all it takes."

Mariselle nodded, and in a flash, Dagon gouged her wrist.

"Gah!" Mariselle screamed and then bit her tongue as she saw the drop of blood fall onto the symbols drawn in the dirt. Suddenly the symbols waivered and rippled as if they were borne on water, and a green haze formed around the shapes on the ground. Through it, Mariselle saw Lord Gervasis counting his coin by candlelight. A knock at his door turned his gaze away, and Mariselle saw Portnoy enter his room.

"I heard crying, Father."

"The maid—I had to punish her earlier. Servants must be broken if they're to serve adequately. Remember that, boy."

"Aye, the young one is especially bothersome—cheeky and defiant. I can't stand her."

"That will change in time." Lord Gervasis chuckled. "Just remember, whatever you command of her, do so quietly and in temperance. She was brought in by promise of coin, and as long as you dangle that carrot, she'll stay."

The vision faded. Mariselle felt her hand tighten into a fist, and rage burned through her.

"So, you see the truth of it." Dagon pulled away and stood once again.

"I-I must take us away tonight." Mariselle held back the tears that welled. "Gather what we can and we'll leave."

"And by the rooster's call tomorrow, Lord Gervasis would have the town guard hunting you and a price on your head. You'd be forever running from his grasp for the prize you took from him."

"We'd take nothing of his, we'd—"

"Child, I speak of you." Dagon shook his head. "You're meat, bought and sold to the nobility."

"I-I-I . . ." Mariselle stuttered. His words were like a slap in the face, waking her from her dreams of a better life.

"You are better than this life, you deserve so much more. But to claim it, you must believe it. You must put your future in your hands." Dagon looked past the courtyard to the wood beyond. "There is a certain mushroom that grows under the pine and timberwold trees nearby. It lacks a smell or distinctive taste and holds a purple cap with black spears—do you know of it?"

Mariselle nodded.

"A small amount can paralyze; larger doses kill." Dagon eyed her.

"Why?" Mariselle shook her head. "Why do you care about my fate?"

"I see greatness in you. It's rare in this world, but when a wolf sees a wolf, it must howl. I see you sitting on a throne, and men like Gervasis kneeling to be your footstools."

Mariselle looked down at the bucket and soiled dress, and her thoughts drifted to Rena curled on her cot in a fetal position.

"I leave in a few hours' time, but if you choose to howl, you may find me in a month's time traveling through Tasal, a mile south of here. The door to your freedom is open; the question is, will you take that first step?"

True to his words, Dagon was gone by midday. As the weeks passed, Rena's demeanor fell, and soon she fostered a cough and fever that left her bedridden. Mariselle tried to tend to her sister's needs in the small moments between duties, but an infection had settled in her and spread from womb to chest. Lord Gervasis had no time to call a doctor for what he deemed was simply "a lack of will."

It was not until Mariselle found her sister lying motionless in bed, her dead eyes fixed onto the leaking rafters above them, that she knew her dreams for the future were dead. Gervasis offered little sympathy, and the gravediggers burrowed a hole barely deeper than three feet for the grave. No ceremony was given.

Dagon's words echoed in her mind until, one night, she made the journey to the woods and found the mushrooms he spoke of. She stared at her hands as she prepared the family their meal. The wound from the pinprick had healed, forming the smallest of scars. What was life but a fight? What were a few more scars?

Their bloated purple faces planted in their meals were worth the price.

Deeper graves were dug for Lord Gervasis and his bastard son, and while callouses formed for a time on her hands from the shovel work, no trace would be found of the bodies. As she pilfered Lord Gervasis's chests for wealth, Mariselle vowed that every liberty, every ounce of joy she squeezed from life's throat, would be for her sister as well. By the morning light, she had sacked the mansion for what it was worth and paid transport to meet Dagon.

A whirlwind of delights met her the day his ship carried them to Talamar. Over a barren wasteland, they traveled to his mansion, where Amorite slaves greeted them with gifts, fine robes, perfumes, and all the things she'd dreamed of. Days flew into weeks and weeks into months as she ate the finest cuisine and learned of art, music, dancing, and other noble pursuits under master tutors. While she struggled to learn the most complex waltzes, her aim at archery was unmatched, and even her instructors were astounded at her talent with a blade and bow. Sometimes present beyond them, watching her mature, was Dagon. His insatiable gaze still held her transfixed, and she craved to know him more with time.

A grand ball was announced at the estate. A great crystal chandelier was raised in the dining parlor, beckoning onlookers with blue, green, and purple light. Mariselle marveled as the servants struggled to secure it high above the hall with two knotted ropes tied to a single metal sconce in the wall.

She was given carte blanche to order the finest tailored garments, but her thoughts constantly shifted to the first dance with her benefactor. The vision of his soft touch drawing her to the court of hundreds filled her imagination. But on entering the ballroom, her dream shattered when she saw a line of young women standing ready and expectant of the same thing. She'd never thought to question Dagon's absences, always trusting they were for some official duty. Now, these strangers had intruded on her home, and she was a nameless face once again.

"The dance of choosing has begun!" Dagon called to his guests, and they applauded as the ten girls, including Mariselle, were led into the center of the parlor floor. The music began, and Dagon called the waltz.

Mariselle knew the moves as she swayed around rhythmically. She only needed to remember the tempo and timing. As the young women encircled Dagon, his gaze darted to each girl. If one misstep was taken, his voice shrilled, "Out! This one!" A guard then led the woman away. Another girl forgot to curtsy as the others did, and his voice called her off to the corners as well.

Soon only Mariselle and one other debutante were left. As the two spun and moved to the music, Mariselle saw the girl's movements matched and outdid her own. A cramp grew in her legs, and Mariselle knew the next misstep would be hers. She would again be cast aside, and her future would be stolen. As she spun with a perfect flourish, she saw a nearby set of sharpened flatware knives. With a flick of her wrist, she snatched a small blade and twirled to the chandelier ropes at the side of the room.

"The last mistake!" Dagon's voice boomed, but Mariselle ignored it. With a swift strike of the blade, she cut one of the long ropes and rushed her competitor. Shoving her to the floor, she encircled the girl's throat with the thick cord and turned back to fling her blade at the last straining rope supporting the crystals overhead.

With a wretched scream, the chandelier crashed as the girl was ripped upward by her neck. Her lifeless body slowly swayed high overhead as Mariselle turned and bowed to her master.

The music stopped as a collective gasp echoed across the room. Dagon's eyes twinkled, and he stepped forward.

"A true wolf howls tonight! My search is complete." He embraced her. All around, the horrified silence of the guests turned to tepid clapping, and Mariselle knew she had finally stepped through the door.

THE COUNSELOR'S VOICE BROUGHT MARISELLE'S mind back to the present.

"My queen, what do you propose then?"

"I've seen to your concerns." Mariselle said and smiled. "I've dispatched the Vizier to his final duty, and in turn, opened the door for you to take his place. All you must do is take the first step."

DAGON HEARD THE WHITE CITY'S envoy ship drop anchor next to his galleon as he stepped into the dark hold of his ship. The men would know to bring the sheep here. There would be no negotiation. The calves had been fattened and were ready for the knife.

He lit a nearby torch with a flick of his hand. Green and blue flames illuminated a gigantic hold of wood, steel, and bone that could house five hundred men.

From the shadows, he heard the rustle of his soldiers and the heavy grunt of a massive Akan giant, who growled as he approached.

"Soon, Molek, you shall feed," Dagon's voice called to the towering form before him. The hatch behind him opened, and a grizzled soldier was shoved down the steps, followed by a disheveled pudgy courtier who instantly withered to his knees. Dagon turned to face them and smiled as he saw their expressions drop into terror.

"No words need be wasted here, gentlemen. Know that you were pawns, and you have been played."

CHAPTER 13

SECRETS IN THE CELLAR

Colin studied Alexandra's confident hands as she managed the jib line of the tiny craft. Her story was not so different from his own. She was as abandoned as he was, navigating a world that cared little for her well-being, yet she still strode forward.

Samuel's skiff slid silently across the water. The breeze was barely enough to fill the boat's sail, but Colin was glad it wasn't stronger.

This thing's not safe for two people, let alone a donkey, Colin thought as he looked past Balaam, who was sitting hunched by the makeshift jib in the bow, to gaze nervously at the water line as it kissed the boat's edge.

Alexandra steered from the back, expertly guiding the tiller with one hand and holding the jib line with her other. "Don't worry. It will hold us. Our craftsmen still know how to keep a vessel seaworthy."

"This wall goes on forever," Colin said as he gazed up at the top of the cliffs. The great wall and its many towers were easily visible. "Samuel said there was a little harbor nearby. Why not just dock there and head in?"

"There's nothing little about the Lion's Maw," Alexandra whispered as they rounded a bluff and sailed into the bay.

Colin's mouth dropped. The mouth of the lion was easily a thousand feet high and filled most of the cliffside. Its fierce stone eyes and far-reaching paws looked life-like as if the beast were poised to spring on their little ship at a moment's notice.

"Holy shit." Colin gaped at its grandeur. "That's part of the city? It's huge!"

"Hush. It's the western entrance to the city. For over five hundred years Gilead has welcomed merchants, visitors, and dignitaries the world over by way of the grand staircase. Five thousand steps and three terraces lead up to the Ambassador's Square, the central bazaar, a temple district, and the castle. Guards often patrol the route, and there's long been a curfew. Even with Egan's help, we would look very suspicious. The eastern gate is farther inland and is less guarded. We'll sail south for a league, then set ashore and make for that gate as Samuel suggested."

"What made you finally walk away from all of that?" Colin asked. "Seems like a lot to give up for a horn and some parchment."

"Gilead is beautiful to see," Alexandra said as her gaze crossed the city's wall. "But she is dead inside now. An urn of ashes. The queen's reign has brought the city to its knees, and she intends to see its life drained entirely. I learned it my last night there."

"Looks like we have some time," Colin replied. "Tell me."

Alexandra nodded. "The night of my father's wedding to Mariselle was an omen of what was to come." She brushed away a tear and recounted all she saw.

THE PERFORMERS IN THE GRAND hall writhed and danced in undulations that seemed both erotic and grotesque, round and round in giant concentric circles. Shawled women stood in the middle, dressed in revealing gossamer and satin. They held up trained snakes that slithered from their hands to their breasts and then to their legs in circular motions. The women moaned and snorted like animals, letting the serpents caress their bodies. The dancers in the outer circles screamed a horrible cry and turned to the courtesans who were watching. In unison, the outer dancers pulled pouches from their sides, doused their mouths with it, and blew fire from their lips.

The crowd cheered and applauded. Mariselle and Braeden stood from their thrones and clapped. Alexandra remained seated.

"The little one's still holding a grudge, I see," Mariselle whispered to Braeden.

"She's adjusting," Braeden said as he gulped down the last of his wine from his goblet. He nodded to the nobility and the performers, then turned to his daughter and lowered his voice. "Stop pouting." He glanced at Mariselle and smiled before turning to Alexandra again. "We all must play a part, you know that. Now, stand and applaud."

Alexandra stood sullenly and gave the lightest of claps.

"Someone's been lax in their readings." Mariselle turned to Alexandra and whispered, "The Tome of Unity calls this spring equinox the night of love, when maidens are free to bestow their wiles on men of their choosing." She turned and called out to the court, "Drink friends; toast to your lovers, and to theirs!"

The dancers cleared the floor, and tables of food and wine were brought in. The crowd cheered and immediately rushed to the tables, grabbing meat, fruit, and liquor.

To Alexandra, they looked like pigs fighting over morsels in a trough.

"Best not to give my daughter ideas. She's enough of a hand-ful," Braeden said to Mariselle with a wary smile.

"No, perish the thought." Mariselle smiled at him and gave a quick wink to Alexandra.

Alexandra wanted to vomit.

"Now, my love, excuse me. I'm to meet with my maids and arrange housing for our many guests." Mariselle curtsied to him and moved down a passage from the hall.

"She always thinks of others," Braeden said to Alexandra. "I hope you learn from that."

"Of course, Father. Excuse me, I'm tired." Alexandra bowed her head slightly to him and left.

The castle hallways were always a maze, but Alexandra knew them better than any guard. She'd followed Mariselle many times, bit by bit, always stopping before her footsteps gave her away. In this fashion, she had discovered that the queen met with strange men in the lower store rooms away from prying eyes. She'd never gotten close enough to hear their conversations, but tonight she was determined.

She came down the last of the steps to the wine cellar. Several casks blocked a small alcove to the side, and dimly lit torches cast enough shadows to let Alexandra move closer and listen to Mariselle's hushed voice unnoticed.

"The ceremony goes as planned?" Mariselle asked.

Alexandra peeked around the barrel and saw two men, gaunt and covered with strange markings and piercings on their faces.

"Lord Dagon's hand will outstretch, and in a month's time, darkness will cover the land." His voice was as rough as sandpaper.

"Good. I've bided my time in this hole for over ten years, watching as others did Dagon's bidding and were rewarded. What of the waking? Has the deep one stirred?" Mariselle pressed.

"Our seers have felt movements far below, but more blood

must be spilled, and the horn must be found," a shriller voice hissed.

"Damn! How long must I spend in this infernal kingdom!" Mariselle spat.

"Dagon says in one year's time, he will come for you personally with all the power of the Black Throne behind him. Whether the beast awakens or not, this land will be your footstool," Gruff replied.

"This land will be my toilet," she snorted and took the men by the hands to a nearby table. "Now ravish me, as your blood payment." She dropped her gown in front of them, and they took her.

Amid their groans, Alexandra slipped away. She'd seen enough. She ran from the cellar to the Great Hall of Judah. Her father had passed out, slumped on his throne from the drink. None of the court had taken notice.

"Father! Father!" She shook him, and he moaned.

Alexandra sighed and gently helped her father, walking him to his bedroom. Alexandra nodded to the guards posted by his door, and they helped lay the king on his bed before leaving the room. Braeden half spoke and half-sung bits of verse, laughing at himself.

"I miss the old days," he said as she stood over his berth. "Miss your mother . . . miss your smile."

"Daddy . . ." Alexandra took his hand.

"I miss Samuel . . ." Braeden said before drifting to sleep.

Alexandra laid his hand down on the brocade coverlet. Her king—her father—looked old and fragile as he cradled himself around a pillow, grasping for a mate who wasn't there anymore, dreaming of days that no longer existed.

Alexandra saw the last light of his fireplace die. She stoked the coals, and a flame burst from the old, buried embers. She watched the fire, and that meek voice inside of her screamed.

I am here, and I'll intercede for him. I'll plant myself here and burn against this darkness until I'm spent. Alexandra rushed from Braeden's bed chamber. She went to the great hall, where the guests were still in the throes of debauchery. There, the captain of the guards snored, his gut to the floor. His key ring was exposed. Alexandra lifted the keys from his belt without a word and made her way to the treasury.

The guards said nothing as she unlocked the door.

The room was pillaged. Empty of any gold item. Where the scrolls of the Logos once lay, now an ash heap remained. She could see the remnants of their tassels. The holy candles, cups, and placards that had told the Maker's story were gone. Alexandra sifted through the debris until she came to a darkly stained flagstone barely higher than the rest of the floor. Mariselle's men had missed it, but she knew of its existence. With a grunt, she pulled it up and out. She reached down into the dark recess, fishing for a familiar shape until she pulled out an old conch, opened in the center to be used as a horn. Its green shell had been chipped and broken from years of mistreatment. This final relic was the last vestige of her faith. She gently wrapped it in an old oilcloth lying in a corner nearby, then reset the stone to its place before leaving the room. She turned to the guards.

"Who is your regent?"

"Your father, the king, as always," one replied.

"Remember your oath to him by forgetting this moment."

The guards nodded. "Aye, Princess. You were never here."

She turned and hurried down the hallway. Her mind was intent on the horn she now held in her hands. Perhaps the artifact could be of some use. Maybe it would awaken people who had slumbered for too long.

Alexandra made her preparations until dawn. She released her handmaidens from her service and inquired after Samuel's location. In the early morning light, she walked through the gates of Gilead dressed as a peasant, holding the wrapped shell, and headed towards the home of the last living soothsayer.

"So, I came to live with Samuel and Balaam." Alexandra smiled and looked away, wiping a tear from her cheek. "From princess to peasant."

In the distance, Colin could barely make out several figures on the docks at the maw's base and a vessel sailing towards their skiff. "Looks like they're sending a welcoming committee for us."

"Doubtful," Balaam snorted. "We're a speck in the shadows to them. If anything, they mean to parley with the enemy or fire on them."

"Either way, I don't wish to find out," Alexandra said and tightened her hold of the jib line. The sails filled with a gust of wind, and the boat moved south past the bay into the night.

CHAPTER 14

THE WATCHMAN'S SONG

The five-mile trek from where they moored the boat to the great eastern gate of the city was quiet. As they approached the last leg of their journey, Colin walked head down, deep in thought. Balaam kept pace, and on his other side, Alexandra walked, studying Colin with furtive glances.

"What troubles you?" she finally asked.

Colin glanced up at the sky. "I feel . . . out of it. Samuel wasn't kidding about the night being endless was he?"

"No. For well over a year now, we've seen no trace of the sun nor call of a morning bird." Alexandra stared at the pale moon. "Mariselle's seers dismiss it as a natural phenomenon, but Samuel thinks otherwise; he says the Logos foretold this time. In any case, this darkness hangs like a death shroud over the land."

"The scroll actually says that?"

Alexandra paused and recited, "'Awake sons of Gilead. When darkness lies around thy door, call upon the Horn of Joshua. My servant shall come as before.' There's more to it of course, but I never learned it. Samuel insisted I blow the horn, and for nearly every night, I have."

"So that was you I heard in the cave? Your horn call?"

"Aye, it may have been. This old conch is the last of Gilead's treasures, handed down from ancient times. It's said the Maker himself ventured to the edge of the world and used it to destroy the dark one's fortress, the Jagged Tooth, at the dawn of time and chained him within the ruins. Our royal line may only use the horn in times of great trouble to call for aid."

"Well, I hate to break it to you, but it doesn't work." Colin shook his head. "I'm no hero, and I can't save you or this place. I don't care what the old man says. I mean you're going to need an army, machine guns, tanks, maybe some F-16s. I think me getting washed here was just coincidence."

"I'm afraid you're right." Alexandra nodded reluctantly. "I'm not sure how to make the horn *work* at all. For the last few days, I've seen it glow, as if responding to some call, but neither Samuel nor I can make odds or ends of it. Perhaps it does more than call to others. In any case, it sits in Balaam's saddlebag for now."

"Yes." Balaam turned to them. "And I truly appreciate having to lug this beacon around for the world to see."

"As long as it remains hidden in your satchel, you should be fine, Balaam." Alexandra sighed. "The moon is dim and this darkness could extinguish a multitude of lights."

"The land of eternal night. Mr. Potter must be laughing his ass off," Colin mumbled and rolled his eyes.

"The Maker's ways are a mystery to us all," Alexandra said and nodded.

"Maker? No I meant the old man who sent me here. Mr. Potter."

"You're strange boy. But you mostly look the part," she replied. "I wish Samuel had found you some sandals though. Those things you wear on your feet are practically a beacon for trouble.

Your home must be opulent if they're considered common."

Colin looked down at his old Adidas sneakers, colored yellow, black, and blue. "Yeah, I guess they look weird to you. But this potato sack you've got me wearing seems to cover them well enough."

"This Danan's Point you're from, what's it like? Have the Amorites besieged your shores as well?"

"Danan's? Oh, oh right." Colin smirked.

"What did I say?" Alexandra glared at him.

"Nothing, forget it. No, no Amorites there, but I suppose we have our own problems. 'Things fall apart.'" Colin looked up at the walls, now much closer and higher than he had first realized.

"'The center cannot hold.' Yes, Samuel has read those same words from the Logos. Perhaps our homes aren't so different," Alexandra mused. "Maybe certain words drift between all worlds, waiting for someone to speak them."

"Are there many men up there, up on that . . . turret thing, on the wall?" Colin pointed to a solitary figure standing sentinel high on the wall, his figure illuminated by the bits of moonlight that peeked through the clouds.

Alexandra peered and smiled. "The watchmen—they stand along the wall at night. I thought they'd been disbanded."

"So, they guard the city? Are they archers?" Colin asked.

"No, they're volunteers that keep to the old ways. Their duty is simply to wake the people if danger draws near. They carry no weapons except their voices," Alexandra replied as they walked into the shadow of the towering city wall. "On quiet nights, they will sometimes sing to keep alert. To hear their voices in that fashion is a good omen and a great comfort."

Colin, Alexandra, and Balaam paused as they heard the solitary figure suddenly sing a verse, and in the distance, they could hear a reply with the second line. Then, a second later, another voice, farther away still, chimed in but still in tune with the others. In this fashion, they listened for a few moments to the song of the sentinels:

Beneath the sky, there is a wall, and I, its watchman, wary,
Listening for my true love's call, the maiden I will marry.
There she comes around again across the bristling heath.
There she is, my love, my life, and on her brow a wreath.
Her lips like wine, her hips so fine and buxom round her haunches,
Let me rest beneath her pine and climb upon her branches.
Let me taste your fruit, my love, until the night grows weary.
Leave me not alone again. A watchman's life is dreary.
Stand with me, my blushing bride. To you, I'll always harken.
Bury me right by your side, safe in the temple garden.
There we'll lie until the day the Potter calls us airy.
Till then, the ground will be kept sound by watchmen standing wary.

"They sound lonely," Colin said as he turned his eyes to Alexandra.

"They sing a song of Gilead; a song of longing for completeness." Alexandra gazed up at the walls.

Colin watched the moonlight glisten across Alexandra's neck. She was beautiful. *If all maidens look like you, I can see why they sing.*

She caught his stare, and he quickly turned away. She blushed. "Is there something you want to say?"

"Uh, n-no," Colin stammered.

"Funny, I thought Samuel's word had softened your stutter," she said and smiled.

Balaam rolled his eyes and coughed. "We're close to the eastern gate now, Princess. Let the boy and I continue alone."

"Yes, of course," Alexandra said.

"Be safe, Alex." Colin put his hand out to her. She smirked at the strange gesture.

"I could say the same to you." She unfastened her belt and let her gown fall to her feet. Dusky gray pantaloons covered her legs, and a black blouse with leather stitching on the sides hung loosely from her neck. A hood was attached, which she quickly pulled over her head to cover her hair.

"My lady!" Balaam snorted.

"Not tonight, Balaam. Tonight, I am a shadow that carries Gilead's hope with me." She leaned in and kissed Colin on the cheek. "You're a sweet boy, but you're out of your league." She gave him an affectionate squeeze and slipped away into the dense bushes that lining the wall's base.

"I, hey, wait!" Colin called out, but she was already gone.

"Don't waste your breath, boy. I fear she's right enough. Samuel should have sent her for such an important task," Balaam said.

"I can handle myself, and I can certainly handle delivering a note," Colin snapped as he slipped his hand into his pocket for it. It was empty.

"What the hell?" Colin frantically searched his other pockets. Nothing but the photo of his father and him remained. "I just had . . ." He looked up and realized Alexandra's affection was double-edged.

"Yes, clearly," Balaam said. "You're off to a wonderful start."

"She can't go in there! We have to catch her!" Colin exclaimed.

"Do we?" Balaam sighed. "Yes, I suppose if Samuel wishes it, we should. Get on my back. If anyone can outrun her legs, it's me, and keep your head down as we pass by the guards at the gate. I've enough of a burden watching you two."

Colin hoisted himself atop Balaam's back like a rocket and instantly fell off the other side. Balaam shook his head and kneeled on the ground, allowing Colin to secure himself better. Once Colin's legs wrapped around his sides, Balaam galloped forward through the brush and towards the great eastern gate of Gilead.

CHAPTER 15

Beyond the Eastern Gate

Colin gazed at the eastern gate of Gilead as they slowed their pace and approached.

The massive wooden doors towered fifteen feet high and opened to the residential streets beyond. He saw dulled and dirtied copper fittings fastened across their faces. Ornate gold-leafed carvings on inset panels of the door that could have once gleamed were sullied by the graffiti of vandals.

As they drew closer, Colin eyed the crumbling faces of two colossal stone lions on either side of the gate. Cracked and broken, their backs seemed to almost sag by the weight of the rotting barrels, crates, and waste piled on them.

Colin tightened his grip on Balaam's mane as they proceeded to the entrance.

"Easy, boy. You're about to see things you wish you hadn't. Don't be intimidated, and don't catch their eyes for too long," Balaam whispered.

As Balaam walked under the raised metal grill of the great

portcullis, two guards leaned on their spears and studied them with cold, cruel gazes.

Colin and Balaam moved forward into the shadowy street. Torchlight illuminated the hustle and bustle of drunks, some retching in the alleys, others laughing in a stupor. Colin and Balaam moved like whispers past a side street, where Colin spotted two men beating on a wailing woman in the middle of the road. The men paused as they spotted the pair.

"We have to do something," Colin whispered to Balaam.

"We're not here for that, boy! Be silent!" Balaam whispered back and quickly trotted past them.

The two made their way past leaning, storied homes with pink, blue, and orange lanterns hanging from their eaves. Colin could hear moaning, laughing, and crying from the dilapidated dwellings on either side of the street. Women and men, many covered in dark tattoos and rigid piercings, stood in the doorways.

"Ah, new flesh! Come taste our love!" a woman cried towards them.

"Nah, you're not that kind of man, are ya?" a man in a silk camisole called towards Colin as he passed. "Let me show you feelings you never knew you had," he offered, lips pursed towards Colin.

Colin looked down, disgusted.

"Keep off my coin, you whore's son!" the woman screamed at her competition.

"Filthy wench!" the camisole man screamed back and tackled her as Colin and Balaam quickly moved forward.

Balaam turned down a side alley past an abandoned temple. Colin glanced beyond the crumbling stone pillars at its entrance to a doorway barely lit by torchlight. Within, he spied long copper poles, all made in the shape of a naked woman with wings.

Colin pulled on Balaam's mane. "This is one of your holy places?"

"Hardly," Balaam said. "It's been littered with Asherah poles, the Amorites' tribute to the dark one. Nothing holy remains there."

"The dark one? The one your Maker defeated?"

"If you believe the stories, yes." Balaam snorted. "Most do not."

"Who is he? This dark one?" Colin asked as he watched the shadows run across the women's inhuman figures. A chill ran across his neck.

"He has no name, but he's timeless. The Logos says once he was a being of light but became the first falling star and has been compelling others to fall away since the beginning," the donkey said as he moved them past a ruined metal gate hanging open into the great cemetery. "Chained to the Black Throne, he sits at the edge of the void and casts a shadow over the Maker's creation."

"And this Dagon serves him?"

"All those who serve their own purpose do, whether they realize it or not," Balaam said as they climbed a small knoll surrounded by gravestones.

Balaam paused to catch his breath, and Colin felt the chill in the air as he watched the wisps of steam rise from the donkey's muzzle.

"This place feels off," he said.

"Aye, you're not the first to think so. The cemetery is the oldest part of the city, and one most people avoid. But this path will lead us past prying eyes in the market square to the castle courtyard, so I guess it has some use."

A six-foot-high cobblestone wall surrounded the area, and Colin wondered if it was in place to keep the living out or the dead in.

Balaam shook the chill from his mane. "It's best if we keep moving."

As they hurried past several graves, Colin saw firelight flicker next to one of the crypts. Men covered in strange markings danced about the fire. The crypt's doors opened, and one man came forward.

"Brothers, there's one here that's fresh and still a virgin!" he called to them and beckoned.

"They're not going to—" Colin started, horrified.

"I told you there are things here better left unseen." Balaam shook his head and quickly took them up a lane.

"How could Alex make her life in such filth?"

"Gilead was not always so. It was once a bastion of light. Now, the people are seduced by their basest natures and have forgotten themselves; forgotten their true names."

"Names? What is it with you people and names?" Colin asked.

"A name has power, boy. It speaks of who you are and what you're capable of. All living things have a true name, given to them at the beginning, but the world makes us forget." They walked forward in silence for several minutes. Even the grave robbers had left this area of the cemetery undisturbed.

A shadow passed ahead, jumping from a large tomb and darting around a corner.

"Did you see that?" Colin asked Balaam.

"Hush. There are worse things than Amorites in the night."

As they walked closer to the tombs, Colin felt the same cold presence he'd felt back in his mother's room. Somewhere close, something was watching them. Colin saw Balaam's ear prick up, and without a word, the donkey quickened his pace. They followed the path until they came to a locked gate leading to the temple district.

"This should be open," Balaam said. "Something isn't right."

Colin could feel the hairs on his neck stand as he slowly turned to see three sets of glowing yellow eyes move toward them from the shadows. The figures' presence darkened the sky, and black mist seemed to emanate from beneath their shrouded forms. The creatures were taller than men. Their cloaks covered their figures, their necks seemed long, and their eyes were the same yellow slits Colin had come to fear. Their clawed hands reached out, and their hoods dropped from their heads. With horror, Colin realized their torsos were scaled, and there were long slithering tails where their legs should have been- he saw demons: half men, half serpents.

They hissed in unison as they closed in.

"The shadows have become flesh!" Balaam snorted and backed up against the locked gate.

"No, no!" Colin shook his head. His heart raced, and at that moment, he saw every beating he had ever taken, every face that had ever caused him to cringe, and his fists clenched. A single word flashed in his mind, one he did not know but was compelled to speak. With a swift kick to Balaam's side, he screamed, "Animus!" His voice echoed throughout the graveyard.

Balaam's eyes narrowed, and he reared as if the word had branded electricity into his backside, then charged toward the creatures.

ALEXANDRA MOVED PAST THE CROWDS unobserved, noticing that once bright smiles were replaced with dull looks and paranoid glances. Like a mouse, she scurried from shadow to shadow, keeping her head down as she moved along the King's Way, the central road that led through the heart of Gilead, across the main bazaar, and eventually, to the castle. As she slid silently past the guards without their notice and entered into the main market area, she came to a small shack nestled between two boarded-up shops. She hopped a small worn fence and knocked on the front door, the sound no louder than a footstep.

A quiet voice responded from within, "Go away, we have no money."

"Helen, it's I, Alexandra," she whispered. "Please, I have need of you."

"Alexie child?" Helen slowly opened the door. Alexandra's face fell as she saw her closest handmaiden and the woman who'd raised her, gaunt and haggard, wearing simple rags barely stitched together.

"Helen! What's happened?" she said, embracing her friend.

"I would ask the same of you," Helen replied. "We were told you'd abandoned the kingdom; gone to live as a nomad. Which sounds just like you." Helen brushed aside a lock of hair that hung across Alexandra's face and smiled. "But where are my manners? Please sit, I can put a kettle on if nothing else."

Alexandra shook her head. "I could never leave this place for long. My heart lies here. How has a year's time brought you to this?"

"Avery and I make do." Helen beckoned her in and closed the door. "We scrimp and save, but Taran isn't well."

"Your little one?"

"Aye, he reminds me of you at that age. Always running wild, ready to take on the world. But his gait has slowed, and he coughs horribly at night," Helen said as she hung an ashen pot over the small fire in the hearth.

"I know someone who may be able to help him," Alexandra offered. "His name is Samuel, though the walk there can be long."

"With the curfew I doubt we'd make it back in time," Helen said. "You-know-who has instituted a city watch, and their taxes are high." Helen's smile faded as she turned to straighten a few meager blankets on a cot. "I hear they protect us from the rabble, but their manner is cruel."

"Your husband is a soldier in the king's army, Helen! How could such a ridiculous tariff be brought against you?"

Helen looked away. "Oh Alexie, I thought you knew."

Alexandra shook her head.

"Avery was demoted from his station. The queen saw him stripped of rank when he refused to enforce her ordinance to burn the old annals and histories." Helen moved to a humble table and set a few dishes aside, avoiding the princess's gaze.

"Burning the books?" Alexandra asked. "In the libraries?"

"Not all, just the ones that give mention to the Maker and his works." Helen sighed. "I suppose it was a stupid thing to fall low for."

Alexandra took Helen by the arms. "No. No, it wasn't. Stay true to his decision. You're his compass."

"I know," Helen said and nodded. "Now he's a lamplighter. He has friends still in the guard, and it's their quiet generosity that keeps bread on our table."

"This wrong will be righted. There is treachery in the Hall of the Lion, and I think Samuel, the man I spoke of, has words that will open the king's eyes to it." Alexandra held the sealed letter up.

"Didn't you hear? Your father's deathly ill; has been for some time now. Queen Mariselle tends him day and night."

Alexandra shivered. She knew her stepmother's hands were wrapped around her father's throat. "What illness?"

"Hard to say. Little word comes from the castle these days. But we haven't seen the king's face for several months. Rumor is he's not long for this world."

"Helen, can Avery get me inside the castle? I've heard word of a jailor who might sneak me to my father's bed chamber."

"Well I suppose yes, but why? You're the heir apparent, you could go straight there."

"No, there is no welcoming for me. Trust me on this, Helen. The queen would see me dead long before I reached the upper hallways of the castle."

"Then I'll take you to the market stands. Avery will be there with Taran and his wick about this time. He's always given access to the castle courtyard and could at least get you that far," Helen said grabbing her shawl.

CHAPTER 16

A Desperate Flight

Colin and Balaam burst past the dark creatures, knocking them over, and raced back down the lane. The serpents coiled and chased after them.

"They're following us!" Colin yelled as Balaam veered down a narrow alley of gravestones. The demons flung themselves around the tombs and closed in to pinch off their escape.

"They're cutting us off! We're dead!" Colin shrieked as he kicked at Balaam's sides frantically.

"Yes, wonderful! Keep saying such helpful things!" Balaam yelled back and veered again, running up the sagging side of a crumbling tomb to its roof and hopping to the next one and the next like they were stones on the water. The serpents hissed and raced forward at the bases of the tombs, slithering parallel to the donkey's course.

Colin clutched Balaam's mane as he stared, wide-eyed, ahead. They were charging towards the cemetery's wall, several inches higher than the tombs themselves.

"Wall! Wall! Wall!" Colin screamed and pulled back on Balaam's mane.

"Let's see them try this!" Balaam yelled back as he ran across the last roof and, with a mighty jump, hurled them into the air, barely missing the wall's ledge and crashing into a thatch cart on the other side. Colin held tight as they smashed through the cart and onto the street. Guards nearby ran forward, brandishing spears. "Halt!"

"New problem!" Colin yelled as he clung to Balaam, who darted past the guards, knocking them over in his wake.

"Always!" Balaam snorted as he careened down an alley and onto another street, then veered again onto the King's Way leading to the royal courtyard.

"Okay, slow down!" Colin called. "We lost them."

Balaam slowed his pace as they entered the great market. Stands, overhangs, and shops were littered with random goods. Crowds of people moved about, and merchants carried baskets of wares. "Let me have control here. Subtlety is key," Colin whispered to the donkey.

A group of guards on horseback turned onto the street before them. The captain's face went sour. "You! Boy! Halt!"

"Oh shit," Colin moaned.

"Wonderful leadership, very subtle," Balaam said and rushed to the right, knocking over a cart and sending pottery flying.

"After him!" yelled the captain, and his men gave chase.

Colin spun his head around as Balaam charged down another street. The guards rushed closer and closer. One soldier grimly eyed Colin, pushing his mount ahead to match Balaam's speed. He thrust his spear at Colin, and Colin grabbed it. The two struggled with it as they hurtled down the lane, their mounts neck and neck. The onlookers screamed and ran as the two riders knocked over merchant carts and crates between them.

Without warning, a merchant pushed a cart out from a side alley in front of Colin's opponent. Both man and horse collided with it and fell away. Two other guards replaced him within seconds.

"Go faster!" Colin yelled as he kicked Balaam's side.

"I'm a donkey! Not a race horse!" Balaam called back.

The lane split to the left and the right ahead. "Pick one, great leader!" Balaam demanded.

"Uh, right! No, left!" Colin screamed.

Balaam dashed ahead, down the left lane, and into a caravan of garments.

Reams of fabric went flying, covering both Colin and the donkey.

"I can't see!" Balaam screamed.

An unending ream of silk covered Colin's face. He could hear the guards' horses behind as he fumbled with it. "Just keep going!"

Balaam flew past scattering crowds, past screaming merchants, and right through a thatched wall.

"Yes, m'lady. Of course I can take you to the courtyard, but if what you say is true, then we must do so as the quietest of mice," Avery said and handed Alexandra his burning wick. Avery's blue eyes twinkled as he guided Taran to his mother.

"Mister Taran here nearly ran off again, but I think he's ready for supper."

The little boy jumped into Helen's arm, and she laughed. "Not minding, Daddy? Well, no pudding for you."

"Pudding?" Taran whispered and cocked his head.

"Well, at least that's what I call it." She winked at Avery.

"Aye, more like a dried biscuit with a bit of sugar"—Avery kissed Helen's cheek—"but made with love."

Alexandra smiled as she watched them. Life had stolen every comfort they had, yet they seemed richer than any noble family in the court.

"I can give you my hat; you'll appear as my assistant." Avery placed his oversized burlap hat on her head.

"Hardly a fit, Avery, but I thank you. Discretion is vital," Alexandra said.

Colin and Balaam, covered in fabrics, burst through the thatch wall behind them.

"You?" Alexandra's mouth dropped. The boy was barely recognizable in the tangles of linen.

Colin pushed the last of the ream from his face. "Alex, we don't have time!" He grabbed her arm, and Balaam stumbled a little.

"What are you doing?" Alexandra started and pushed back until the city guards bolted around a nearby corner behind them.

"Get on!" Colin screamed, and Alexandra hoisted herself on Balaam's back behind Colin.

"Yah!" Colin yelled and kicked Balaam forward.

"You've gained weight!" Balaam yelled back as he ran, the fabrics still covering most of his head. "Would it please someone to get this damn thing off me?" Balaam shook his mane furiously, but the fabrics still blocked his face and tangled about his neck.

One of the guardsmen rode alongside and swung his mace at them.

"Right, Balaam!" Alexandra screamed.

The donkey veered to the right. The mace missed Colin's head and collided with Alexandra's still-burning wick. Another horseman raced to their right. The rider drew a bow, notched with an arrow.

"Left!" Alexandra screamed.

Balaam veered to the left, and the arrow flew mere inches from Alexandra's face.

"This is insufferable!" Balaam yelled.

"Take the high road to the courtyard, we can lose them in the alleys!" Alexandra yelled.

The road again forked, the left route curving, the other climbing.

"Right!" Colin yelled and kicked.

"No, you fool, left!" Alexandra yelled louder.

"Which way?" Balaam cried out.

A spear flew overhead as more horsemen raced in behind them.

"Right!" Colin screamed. Balaam turned down the right path and into the courtyard of the great temple.

"Oh! Okay, maybe left," Colin called sheepishly.

Balaam raced forward up the white steps of the city's central shrine, a structure that Alexandra thought rivaled the size of any small village. Priests, dancers, and merchants screamed as the trio sprinted into the inner sanctum. Alexandra's wick caught itself on a tapestry, depicting serpents and pagan rituals. The flame leaped from the stick and danced up the banner, devouring the cloth like a starving wolf. Balaam sped them to a ramped altar and a twenty-foot-high statue of a many-armed god with a smug face.

"Dead end!" Colin yelled.

"I can jump it!" Balaam yelled back.

"No! No! You can't!" Alexandra screamed.

The donkey rushed them forward up the ramp as Colin pulled the last fabric from Balaam's eyes.

"No! No, I can't!" Balaam screamed in surprise, but his momentum could not be stopped, and the three flew into the marble deity, knocking it over. The trio collapsed to the ground. Fire arched overhead as the flames jumped to each Amorite banner in a feeding frenzy before spitting their ashes and rods to the ground.

Covered in soot and debris, Balaam shook himself and slowly stood. Alexandra felt the hands of the guards lift her and then push her to her knees. Colin was thrown down next to her. She saw Colin look up to see Mariselle in regal purple robes standing over him, but the queen's gaze was on the princess.

"The gods are kind indeed," the woman said as she leaned down and lifted Alexandra's face with her hand. "Two spies in one night."

Alexandra spat in her face. "Don't touch me, Mariselle!"

Mariselle wiped the saliva from her eye and smiled. "Charming. As always." She turned to the guards. "Send them to the dungeon. A public trial should be fine entertainment tomorrow. You can toss them into Korah's Maw afterward."

CHAPTER 17

A BLACK RESPONSE

&gan stared out across the dark waters. Something didn't feel right. The Vizier's ship had been gone for over an hour, and no flags had been flown. No signal had been sent either, as was the custom during negotiations.

"Chief!" A city watch captain bustled down the stairs and out onto the dock. He saluted Egan. "We've had a major disruption at the market. The city watch requests your aid."

"What is it, Captain?" Egan barely turned his gaze from the water.

"My men chased down some vandals, sir. They've caused quite a commotion; sparked a mob, it seems."

Egan sighed. A grand battle it was not. "Fine, take twelve of my men. Whatever the outcome from these negotiations, it will be a while yet I think."

The younger captain saluted and called twelve others with him. The platoon quickly made their way up the great stairs toward the city.

A recruit looked to Egan. "Chief, should we fortify the docks? They have a sizeable fleet out there. We could ready archers at the very least and—"

"No, we wait," Egan snapped and paced the jetty. "Sharper minds are at play." The words rang hollow in his mouth.

Hours passed, and fog filled the bay. Egan's men joked and chatted quietly among themselves. Egan leaned on one of the pier's pylons and skipped a stone across the water. It bounced perfectly several times before disappearing into the gloom. He sighed.

Then a call came forward from a watchman, high on the grand stairway: "Ship's approaching! Flying our flag!" His voice carried down to Egan and his men. Egan turned to see a ship, torches ablaze through the mist, sailing fast for the docks.

"It appears to be the Vizier, Chief," one of the recruits called.

"Yes, he has grand news I'm sure." Egan straightened his uniform. "Something I won't hear the end of for a fortnight."

"Sir, the ship's not slowing!" the recruit called again.

Egan peered through the fog. The torchlight was noticeably brighter, and it came ever closer. "Maybe recruit, maybe . . ." Egan started, but with a gust of wind, the ship broke through the gloom. Its sail was ablaze with fire, the banners of Gilead burning on the port and starboard sides, casting red light on the pig poles planted across the deck. The heads of Egan's men stacked four high were mounted on the poles. Off the main mast hung the bodies of the Vizier and Salain.

"No! No!" Egan screamed as the ship plowed forward, smashing through the small fishing boats tethered to the dock. Egan felt his stomach drop as he saw a great brazier strapped to the female figurehead of the ship. Barrels and crates were tied to it like some kind of sick gift.

Egan's eyes went wide as he spied a long-corded fuse burning its last at the bundle.

"Run! Run! Damn you all!" Egan called to his men, who were trying to throw tow lines on the ship's cleats as it sailed past.

The ship exploded, sending his men standing on the edge of the docks flying. Metal and wooden debris flew across the water and pinned five more of his men to the ground, instantly killing them. Egan was knocked back to the base of the stairs; the air sucked from his lungs.

Fire. Screaming. Chaos.

As Egan's eyes cleared, he saw his men running. Others, covered in flames, raced for the water. He could hear the watchmen's voices rise above the confusion.

"Attack! Awaken, sons of Gilead, we are under attack!" their voices cried overhead.

Egan stood, dazed, and saw black corsairs racing toward them through the fog. A war drum sounded a savage beat as the cries of the Amorites filled his ears. The ships slammed into the docks, and hundreds of warriors swarmed out like cockroaches.

He ran forward and tried to pull his standing men back, but they were leaped upon by countless attackers dressed in black, their faces covered by ashen masks, their hands wielding serpentine blades. Every beat of the drum brought another Corsair crashing onto the shore.

"Back! Form a line at the stair!" Egan yelled at his entourage to the right and left, but they ran in panic and were at once torn apart by the attackers. A small platoon formed a circle several feet away from him as he called again and drew his sword. He slashed his blade through three of the raiders before reaching his men and moving into the center of the formation.

"Move back, we can't hold the docks! Keep your shields up and move with my command!"

The guardsmen shored up their shields and held back the horde of spears, swords, and hands, their faces wincing with every spear thrust blocked.

"We push together now, then strike! Remember your training!" Egan yelled above the din. "Now!"

The soldiers moved in one fluid motion and knocked back the Amorite mob with their shields before shoving their swords and spears forward, impaling a line of the enemy's men.

"Yes! Again!" Egan yelled.

In unison, the soldiers shoved forward before slamming their weapons into another line of black-garbed warriors.

Egan's eyes gleamed. His moment of glory had finally come. He would end the invasion here and cement his deserved position and respect. In that brief second, he remembered his father standing over him at the shore. "Move forward!" he yelled.

A recruit turned to him desperately. "Sir? You just said we can't hold the docks. We're overwhelmed!"

"You heard me soldier! Forward!" Egan called again.

The soldiers pushed forward again, but their shields faltered.

The ground shook as if a great mass had fallen to earth. From the shadows, a giant of a warrior, nearly fifteen feet high with arms thicker than a masthead, strode forward through the water. His shoulders and chest, covered with bloodied plate mail, spanned a ship's width, and his large head, protected by an iron skull faceplate, was the size of a grown man. As he pushed past the Amorites, he slammed an evil spiked mace the size of a tree trunk to the side and sent five of the mob flying. His other hand held a wood and metal plate that Egan could only guess had once been the hull of a boat.

"What in the Maker's name is that?" Egan's mouth dropped.

"Molek! Molek! Molek!" the invaders chanted as the brute approached.

Molek howled and sent his mace flying into Egan's platoon. The weapon decapitated two recruits and sent another three to the ground.

Egan's hands trembled as he tripped over the body of one of his soldiers, and he dropped his weapon. Molek slammed his mace down on two more of Egan's men while the Amorites cheered.

Egan pulled himself back to the stairway as Molek strode to him and leered.

"Is this a great lion of Judah?" Molek scoffed. His guttural laughs echoed.

Egan turned and ran up the stairwell. He could hear the laughter and taunts of the black army calling at his back, but still, he ran. Only the cries of his dying men followed him.

CHAPTER 18

Unexpected Allies

Colin wriggled back against the dungeon wall from where he sat on the wet stone floor as a rat scurried in front of his feet. The hay in the dank cell smelled of urine and feces. How much time had passed? He looked up at the ceiling of the small stone room and the tiny barred window overhead. There was only darkness. He heard the hustle and bustle of people overhead on some distant street. Angry voices of a mob, muffled by stone and distance, still made their way to his ears. But the world here in the dungeon was as quiet as a tomb. Only shadows, cast from the torchlight, played across the stone walls. It could be midnight or morning; only the darkness knew for sure.

Alexandra paced in the cell next to him, chewing her lip. The dying embers of a nearby torch barely lit the end of the long hallway. Colin could make out the silhouette of a triple-locked door, no doubt leading to the upper hallways. Few of the other cells were occupied. He heard soft snoring across the way and a woman weeping quietly from the shadows farther down. Colin glanced at Alexandra, still pacing in the cell adjacent to him. "What time is it?"

She ignored his question for a moment before turning to him. "Does it matter?" She returned to her thoughts.

Colin watched the shadows of the bars flicker against the dungeon walls. "Eternal night, right. I guess it wouldn't."

Somewhere water dripped and echoed. Colin wondered if his mom had died in her hospital bed, alone, trapped in a vegetative state, too delirious even to realize he wasn't there.

Alexandra tried her cell door again. It rattled but remained solid. "You couldn't have gone back, could you? You couldn't have left well enough alone." She dropped her hands and glared at him.

Colin sighed and looked up. "Samuel told *me* to deliver the message, not you."

"You had no message to deliver!" Alexandra hissed back at him. "Not that it matters now. Mariselle reads it as we speak. Still, *I* should've been chosen for it. Be glad I took it. You said it yourself. This is not your fight! It's not your home."

"No, but I've been thrust into the middle of it—this whole train wreck you call a kingdom!" Colin shot back. "I made a choice. Deal with it."

"I blew into a shell hoping for a hero. Instead, I got a half-drowned helpless child,"Alexandra said and turned away. Her eyes avoided Colin's hurt expression.

"If I get out of this alive, I won't bother you or Samuel or Balaam anymore. I'll find this balm on my own."

The princess slumped down on her cell floor. She peered at Colin between the bars. He stared straight ahead, chin up, mouth taut. Alexandra's expression softened.

"What?" Colin said, glancing at her.

"Tell me of your parents. Is your father noble or in a trade?"

"He's dead."

She glanced away. "I'm sorry. What skill did he teach you? Surely your—"

"Look, I don't know how it is here, but in my world, fathers don't do squat. They don't show up to your games, they don't help you when you need it, they promise you the world one day . . ." Colin reached into his pocket, and his fingers grazed the old photo once more. The next day, they're gone."

"Yes, they are." Alexandra said quietly and smiled at him.

Colin glanced at her again. "I'm sorry about your dad. Your mom too. I can't imagine having to deal with the family drama you put up with."

"Helen was more a mother to me, and she was there when Father was gone. We all have burdens to carry." Alexandra nodded. "So, you mentioned your mother. What illness besets her?"

"Cancer. That salve Samuel talked about, I have to hope it can save her. I don't think there's much in my world that would."

Alexandra looked at him questioningly.

"It's a disease, except it's more than that . . . Something bit her." Colin's hand clenched. He could feel his eyes water. He cleared his throat. "Back in the cemetery, these . . . things were chasing us."

"Things?" she asked.

"I think they were the same things that attacked my mother, and I know I saw them outside of Mr. Potter's—on the beach." Colin clenched the cell bars and stood, facing the shadows in his mind. "They were like snakes but . . . well, they were like humans too. I was scared, you know? Really shitting my pants. But then, I don't know, I just got tired of being afraid. I got mad."

"Mad? That was your instinct?" Alexandra asked.

"Yeah," Colin said, shaking his head, "and I said something, I don't even know what it was—gibberish. And then I charged them." Colin shrugged as he ran his fingers across the stone wall.

"For a moment I thought that if I could do that, maybe I could somehow do the rest of it."

Alexandra had leaned in on the bars as she listened to Colin's story. "These things . . . they were snakes? Were they black, larger than a man, with yellow eyes?"

Colin glanced at her face. "Yeah. How did you know that?"

Alexandra's mouth dropped a little. "What you're describing are Hissith, black serpent beasts that serve the Dark Lord exclusively. It's said that to even lay your eyes on one means your death is imminent."

"Well, I've had some luck then," Colin replied. "I've seen them three times."

"You could've died, easily. You had no control over Balaam, over anything, and you faced them?"

"I had to or lay down and die, I suppose. Sometimes you have to just pretend you're stronger than you really are."

Alexandra nodded and glanced away, letting his words sink in. "You said you charged them with a word?" she asked.

"Yeah, it just sort of appeared in my head. I don't even remember what it was exactly."

"This word, it did something?"

"Well, Balaam certainly moved his ass when I spoke it." Colin smirked at his unwitting pun.

"You may have spoken the Logos," Alexandra said, "the language of the Maker."

"The words in Samuel's scroll? How could I?" Colin asked. "When I had that page, I couldn't make anything of it. How could I suddenly remember a word I don't even know?"

"I have no idea, but those that speak it have power over this world; visions of the future, the past; the power to bring your enemies low, or move past them unscathed. They say to speak with the power of the Logos, one can move a mountain with a whisper," she replied. "If we ever see Samuel again, we should ask him."

Colin leaned his head against the wall and closed his eyes. "Sure. I'll put that on my bucket list, right before they execute me in a few hours."

The large door at the end of the hallway unlatched and burst open. Two guards approached. The first was pudgy and short; his bald head was acne-scarred and covered with boils. He was dwarfed by his seven-foot-tall comrade whose enormous fists held a torch and whose shaggy unshaven face and broad shoulders made it look as if the first guard had trained a bear to follow him.

Pudgy swung a ring of keys as he approached and called out, "Well blimey, if we don't still get surprises these days. Ain't that so, Rustag?"

His comrade grunted. They paused at Colin's cell.

Colin immediately caught Alexandra's gaze, and she looked at the oversized jailor.

Pudgy nodded at Colin. "Me thinks you're new to this spot of the world. Sad, you won't be staying around long to get to know it. They call me Gunney." He mockingly bowed before Colin. "I'd say I'm pleased to have met you, but the truth is I couldn't give a shit."

Gunney stepped over to Alexandra's cell door and leaned in, smiling wickedly at her. "But you. No introductions needed." Gunney licked his lips and lowered his voice. "Old Gunney hears things he does, hears about princesses running off and returning, like a sweet young filly that comes back to the stable. Mayhap Gunney can help her, and she can help Gunney."

Alexandra backed away from her cell door.

"Ol' Gunney's got an itch, and sweet filly, you gots a fine set of hands!" Gunney turned the key in the lock. He let the door swing open and bang against the bars as he stared at the princess. "I've had a taste of most every young pilcher that's come 'ere—but never one quite so pretty as you, love." He glanced to Rustag. "Go watch the stair. M'lady and I need some alone time." Gunney turned back to Alexandra and unbuckled his belt.

She pushed back against the wall. "I swear I'll tear it off if you come near me!"

"Promises, love, such sweet promises—I like it rough!" He took a step forward.

Colin stood and grabbed the bars. "You want to tango, buddy? Come here! Don't touch her!"

Gunney smiled. "Oh I've had my share of your like as well—afterward I'll let you clean me off." He took another step towards Alexandra. "Now open that pretty mouth of yours and—"

Rustag slammed his torch on Gunney's head, and the pudgy jailor dropped to the floor like a rock. Alexandra glanced at Colin. His eyes darted back to hers.

Rustag took a breath as if the words were hard for him and then, in a deep rumbling voice, said, "Some here still serve the crown. Rustag at your service, m'lady."

"You!" Colin said. "You're the one Samuel mentioned. I was supposed to hand you his letter."

"Then hand it," Rustag grunted and held out his hand.

"Yeah, I don't have it anymore. I think your queen took it."

"Not surprising," Rustag quipped.

Alexandra stood and stepped over Gunney's unconscious form. "Do I know you? I think I would've remembered your face."

Rustag shook his head. "I'm Agronian. Your father paid a kindness to me when I was young and stationed me here. I rarely make appearances at court."

"You're a slaughterman? He let you live?" Alexandra's eyes widened.

"A slaughterman? That doesn't sound nice." Colin backed away from the bars of his cell.

She kept her eyes trained on the giant. "Nor should it. They're north men, savages that burn, rape, murder . . . and eat their victims. My father spent years on a crusade to wipe out their tribes."

Rustag stared at the princess, his cold expression unchanging. "Blood debt. What is owed, must be paid. An eye for an eye. A tooth for a tooth."

Alexandra nodded. "Can you get me to my father's chamber? Without being seen?"

Rustag nodded silently.

"Then come. We must hurry." She moved past the giant.

Rustag picked up the limp body of Gunney and tossed him into the now-empty cell before slamming the cage door closed and locking it.

Colin ran forward and shook his cell door. "Hey! Come on, Alex, don't leave me here!"

She turned. "I'm not leaving you to rot. I promise! But I need to get to my father, and there can't be any mistakes this time."

Rustag moved to the dungeon doorway and peered through. He turned back to Alexandra. "Princess, footsteps approach. We have no time."

Colin saw uncertainty wash across Alexandra's face.

"If you're caught again, they'll kill you on sight. I'll be back for you before morning." Her eyes pleaded with his. "I'll help you find the balm for your mother, I promise, but I just can't right now." She hurried down the hall, followed by her new companion.

Colin shook his door again. "Alex! Alex! I'm not helpless, I'm not!"

The two were gone. Colin slumped back down to the floor and put his head in his hands.

CHAPTER 19

THE GODS ARE QUIET

Mariselle paced the antechamber of the Hall of the Lion. She looked at the empty throne and the banners hanging high over it. They would need changing. The throne was barely adorned and looked to be little more than a peasant's stool—her seat of power would be more regal. It would inspire awe in her devout followers and terror in those who might question her authority. In time. Braeden, the old fool, was nearly dead, and this new correspondence they had intercepted could be the finishing blow-in time.

She looked down to the far end of the hall at her coven of witches and priests chanting over a bubbling cauldron. *Gods, how long will these simpletons take?* She strode to their gathering. Samuel's seal on the intercepted letter was unmistakable. The waxen *S* in concentric circles was the same she'd seen on hundreds of pieces of correspondence in the past, but this missive was different.

The letter was blank.

"Is this a joke?" she had uttered as she tossed it to her seer. And yet she knew the old man was more cunning than most of her spies. Perhaps some incantation could make the ink appear.

"Cast your incantations, force the words from the paper, or I'll have your head," she had hissed at her retinue, "and Dagon will have mine. Tonight we reap the harvest, and I'll have what I'm due."

Mariselle heard the echo of the mob's angry chanting outside. She paused and opened a nearby window, glancing out to see at least a hundred people gathered, screaming and shaking their fists in the castle courtyard. Her chief advisors dodged hurled rocks and ran towards the portcullis doors that led to the safety of the castle's interior. Their attempts at settling the masses had failed.

She turned her attention to the man and two women dressed in white robes standing over the pot of steaming mire. As they chanted, the letter floated on top of the mixture but remained unstained. Mariselle broke their circle and snatched the document.

"Where are you with it? How can I still see nothing?"

One of the women lifted an ankh from around her neck, waved it over the paper, and recited a charm. Nothing appeared.

"The goddess Athena requires patience for divination. The stars must align in Saturnia," she said and bowed.

"Eridwen must tie the energies of the forest into a configuration," the other woman offered.

"Ereshkigal remains silent on this, my queen. Perhaps the kingdom should prostrate themselves before his greatness, for a sign to come?" her sorcerer offered and bowed.

"Athena? Eridwen? Ereshkigal? We must prostrate ourselves, you say?" Mariselle smiled and nodded. She grabbed the wizard by the back of his neck and shoved his face into the boiling cauldron. The man frantically tried to pull up, but Mariselle kept his head submerged.

"They bow down to me! They serve my master, Dagon, and the Dark Lord before him, you stupid cows!" She finally released the wizard, and he pulled his face back. It was seared red and covered in blisters. He ran screaming from the room.

"Worthless! All of you!" Mariselle screamed and kicked over the cauldron. "Get out of my sight!"

The witches ran from the room, nearly colliding with one of her advisors who was just entering.

Mariselle saw the worm she had appointed some months back as weak, perverse, and easily controlled. The little fat man's only redeeming trait was his penchant for reading a room. He knew a lie when spoken, and even the subtlest gestures did not escape his expert analysis.

"Yes? What now?"

"My queen, your beauty remains unfettered, even in the—"

"Out with it!" she commanded. "Why does this mob broach my door?"

The advisor straightened himself and bowed again. "The recent commotion in the market has provoked them. Also, they feel the levies placed on them in the last year are unjust. They demand to see the king."

"Impossible. The king is indisposed, sick beyond aid." Mariselle brushed him off with a wave.

"As I have pointed out to them, yes, m'lady. But still they insist. Perhaps if you came out on the dais and spoke to their concerns. You are their queen, and your promises carry weight."

Mariselle mused over this. If Dagon were to give the kingdom to her in the coming hours, she would need to address her slaves. Perhaps kindling love in them now would ease their complaints later.

"Fine. I shall do what you and the rest of my court cannot." She tossed Samuel's note onto the smoldering coals exposed by the cauldron's absence and headed for the door.

"A wise choice, Your Highness," the advisor bowed. "Forget the old man's schemes. You have power over many; perhaps in time, over Dagon himself."

"Yes." Mariselle smiled. "Yes, you're right. I'm glad to see you take the initiative. Let that old bastard Samuel scribble his notes. I'll deal with the mob myself." She motioned him to follow her out the door.

As the pair left, flames continued to lick the edges of the paper but did not progress to the center as if some unseen cover was preventing it.

A strong breeze blew in from the open window, snuffing out the coals and lifting the paper in a whirl before pulling it out into the night.

CHAPTER 20

An Outside Hand

Samuel sat under a bushy olive tree high on the bluff and looked out toward the sea. A slight breeze played with his hair. His unseeing eyes no longer brought him the view, but he still favored the spot. The smell of the salt air and the breeze reminded him of happier times. *Even in these dark days, some beauty remains*, he thought as he heard the waves crash on the rocks far below.

Thunder rumbled overhead, and the breeze picked up. Samuel raised his head, waiting for the telltale drops to fall. "Rain, now? Well, old friend, you've been long absent."

Samuel pulled himself up by his staff and headed down the well-worn path toward his cottage. His feet knew the way. Every pebble and curve of the slope served as guideposts. As he opened the door to his hut, he immediately sensed a presence within.

"Who's there? Who troubles an old man before he sleeps?"

"You've done well, Samuel, but I have need of you again. Your work is not yet complete. I've sent a final message, and it must be read," a deep voice replied.

"Who are you?" Samuel reached out with his hands.

A hooded figure stood just out of reach and watched the old soothsayer momentarily as a father would gaze at his child. Samuel would not have been able to recognize him even if he could see, for the figure took many forms; no one in this world, save Colin, would have known his face.

A sudden flash of light encompassed the room, and Samuel fell to his knees. The darkness from his vision cleared, and Samuel saw his own weathered hands for the first time in a decade. He looked around desperately, but the room was empty.

"Who? Where are you? Who are you?" he cried, but the presence was gone. Samuel slowly stood and went to his bed. On the cot lay his scroll, and woven into its end seamlessly was the page of text Colin had brought with him.

"I see." Samuel kneeled before the scroll. "The Potter has given me back my sight and restored his word. His one true word."

Samuel traced his fingers across the lines of characters on the new page. And as the Logos became clear in his mind, he steadied himself with his staff. The prophecy read differently than he expected. It was at once more beautiful and terrible than he had imagined.

"Maker . . ." Samuel said as he studied the words with his renewed eyes. "What have I done?"

BALAAM STOOD SLEEPING IN HIS stall within the castle's stable. His locked knees kept his body from swaying, and the warm fire from the simple hearth near the back of the livery gave some comfort. His lips shuddered as he snored a little, and bits of hay fell from his teeth. His snort suddenly woke him, and his eyes opened wide as he realized he had dozed off.

After Mariselle had sent Colin and Alexandra to the dungeon, guards had shoved him from the temple to a squire who pulled with even more force as he led Balaam to the king's manger. "Ah, you reek!" The pimple-scarred youth spat. He held his nose and quickly kicked Balaam's flank, making the donkey jump forward with a start. The boy slapped Balaam's rear with a stick, spurning him on.

As he trudged into the castle courtyard, he wondered if the guards would spear him down if he kicked back at the brat.

"In you go! You've caused enough trouble for the night. I wouldn't be surprised if they send you to the knackers in the morning." The boy laughed as he whipped at Balaam's haunches again, forcing the donkey into the stall.

The sting of the stick had throbbed for some time, but Balaam had resigned himself to rest as best he could. The mission was a failure. No doubt the princess and the boy would be swinging by the gallows before long or fed to Korah's Maw as the queen had promised.

Click.

Balaam turned and saw the latch to his stall had unlocked, and the gate was slowly opening. He gingerly peered out to the walkway between the stalls. A wizened man in brown robes and a cowl stood near the doorway to the courtyard. The dark hood almost entirely obscured his face. The livery squire lay at his feet, unconscious, breathing deeply.

"Hello, again," the old man said.

Balaam's eyes widened. "It's you! I remember you! You're the wizard that cursed me!"

"Yes, and no." The robed figure smiled. "I am many things, Balaam. Tonight I am a messenger. And now you must be part of that message."

"I should kick you, and it'd be less than you deserved! This bloody punishment has gone on for long enough!" Balaam said as he glared at the stranger. "Of course, you'd probably turn me into a toad next."

"Be at peace, Balaam. You are not cursed. Your path will be straightened in time. I mean no harm." The old man adjusted his hood haphazardly.

"And yet here I stand on hooves instead of feet," Balaam huffed, "shunned by all, a feckless fool for others to burden."

"Your burden is greater than you know." The old man said solemnly. "For what you carry is at the very heart of the Dark Lord's plans. Yet you will usher it away, right under his nose."

"That old conch? In my saddlebags? He can have it."

"The conch and scroll are the axis of both what is and what is to come. You are the wheel, Balaam. In fact, your presence is vital this night. Go down to the eastern gate and wait for Samuel. Do not tarry," he said and vanished.

Balaam snorted and shook his head. "Potter preserve us, this day is strange."

He stepped over the squire and paused. Quickly glancing this way and that, he gave a swift kick to the boy's groin, instantly sending the squire into a fetal ball, moaning. Satisfied, Balaam moved from the doorway back out into the city.

CHAPTER 21

EVIL UNLEASHED

Egan's side ached as he raced up the final steps inside the Lion's Maw and through Gilead's western gate. His hands trembled as he tried to draw his sword and finally let it slide back into his sheath. The image of Salain's body, the slaughter of his men, and the massive thing screaming for his death were too much. Egan fell to his knees and gasped. In his moment of fending off the darkness, he had failed. Bitter tears rolled down his cheeks. And his father's voice echoed in his mind.

"Stand up, damnit," Egan whispered to himself. "Do your duty." But for a moment, his legs refused. He wanted only to die. He hadn't seen the attack coming soon enough, hadn't drawn back when he should have, and now nearly half his men were rotting in the sand. He felt like a boy again—timid, terrified, and utterly unworthy.

"There's still more to lose," he mumbled as he stood. He'd account for his failures after dealing with this crisis. He looked around the Ambassador's Square and knew the calmness here would be destroyed. Sleepy homes and shops lining the large green space of uncovered sod would wake to battle cries, thirsty blades, and flaming arrows. At the far end of the square, a patrol of guards made their way down the market road, which curved out of sight, leading to the city's center.

"They're too far. Has no one heard the watchmen?" Egan scanned the high walls. None of his sentinels were present. The initial call of alarm never resounded. Egan hurried to the nearest guard shack. A pool of blood lay within. Egan's stomach dropped. He drew his sword and crept around the side. Just beyond the torchlight were three bodies. The western watchmen's throats had been cut, terror sliced across their frozen faces.

A patrol of guards interrupted Egan's racing thoughts.

"Chief Warrant Officer? We heard your call . . ." a guardsman started and then looked down at the bodies. "Maker."

"Have you not heard the explosions? Close the gates! We're under attack! Their agents are already within our walls!"

"Yes, sir!" his man called, and with a yell to the other guards, the men ran to the archway and worked the winch, slowly closing the massive wooden doors and drawing down the iron lattice in front of it.

Egan looked around the square.

"Where's the rest of the city guard? Why is no one at his post?" Egan yelled at the guard.

"Apologies, Chief, a great commotion occurred not two hours past in the market, and now protesters rally in the castle's courtyard. All hands have been called to quell the people."

"I sent men to handle the market problem, not break up a rally."

"Chief, it's much more than a drunken row. Half the city is racing to crack open the castle doors. Those you sent would be hard-pressed to pacify such a mob." The soldier looked down.

"The watch corrals the people when barbarians are at the gate? Who made the order?"

"Well," the guard said, shifting in his boots nervously, "the queen herself, Chief."

Egan threw out his arms. "What mire have we sunk into? What madness? Go, send messengers to the eastern gate and the castle barracks. Spread the word. The watchmen on the stair have been calling the alarm for nigh twenty minutes. Echo their warning! And reinforce this door, the demons below will not find it much of an obstacle," Egan yelled and ran to a nearby horse, pulling himself onto its saddle.

"What about you, Chief?" the guard called out.

"I'm going to have a discussion with the queen!" Egan kicked at the horse and sped down the market road towards the castle.

THE INNER HALLWAYS OF THE castle were empty, much to Alexandra's relief. Rustag seemed loyal, but he was also dangerous, and any unwitting servant who happened to slow their progress might become a victim to his fists. The giant was surprisingly agile and quiet for a man his size, and she almost lost sight of him as he moved ahead. Finally, after several twists and turns, they came to the king's bed-chamber.

"Please stay near the door, I might need your protection if we're found," Alexandra said and rested her hand lightly on his arm.

Rustag grunted. "With my life, m'lady."

She entered the room. Within, she saw a wisp of a man lying in bed, his face as white as the sheets that covered him.

"Father!" Alexandra ran to his side.

Braeden's breath rattled, and he seemed barely conscious of anything, his hollow eyes staring at the ceiling.

"Father, it's Alex! What has that witch done to you?" She slowly pulled up his head, now light as a feather.

Braeden coughed, and his eyes brightened a little. His focus shifted to Alexandra's face.

"Daughter?" his weak voice whispered.

"Papa, I never should have left you," she said, tears filling her eyes.

"No tears now . . . so happy to see you . . ." Braeden whimpered, his voice breaking. "Don't mourn me. I'm nearly well. Mariselle attends me nightly with her cures. She says the pain is normal, and I'll soon be right."

Alexandra sighed and wiped her tears away. Her hands trembled. It was as if every nightmare she had ever dreamed had come true at this moment, and there was no one to shield her from them. Panic shot through her like a thousand icy needles until she caught her breath. And in that instant, Colin's words came back to her mind.

"Sometimes you have to just pretend you're stronger than you really are."

Alexandra bit her lip. She was her father's caretaker now. "Her cures?" She looked around the room.

"We'll soon be together again, Daughter, in the great hall— you, your mother, and I." Braeden's voice wavered and drifted as if he was on the verge of sleep.

"Papa, where are these cures? Where does she keep them?" She gently shook her father back to consciousness.

"By the fireplace, there," he mumbled, making a slight motion to the alcove opposite the chamber near the fireplace.

Alexandra moved around to see a table had been set there, and an alembic boiled a viscous green fluid on it. Across the table, she saw a burlap bag, the bottom of which was wet. She carefully opened it, and the pungent odor of rotten fruit and bitter almonds wafted up her nose.

"What alchemy is this?" she mumbled, tossing the bag off the table. A twisted root lay nearby. She picked it up and sniffed.

"Mandrake root, we were always told to stay away from it—it'd explain why you're so thin. Still, to be so weak and delirious, no plant could do that without something more . . ."

Alexandra's mind raced as she searched the chest under the table and found a long glass vial. A cloth membrane had been tied to the top, and a trace of yellow fluid stained its bottom. It smelled of rot. Then, in the corner, she noticed a tall basket vibrating slightly. A heavy stone was placed on the top. A chill ran down her neck. Only one living thing could fit in that container. She straightened herself and gingerly approached the container. Every inch of her knew what was within and wanted to run from it, but she needed proof of Mariselle's scheme if a tribunal was called.

"Presumption can be questioned," Alexandra said as she drew closer, "but the truth is under that lid." Carefully lifting the stone and setting it aside, she removed the basket lid and stepped back.

Nothing.

She stepped forward again and slowly peered over the lip of the basket.

A black cobra sprang up from within. She screamed and fell back, knocking over the basket. The serpent slid out and coiled itself at her feet, its hood opened wide and its fangs extended.

Alexandra looked down at her unprotected feet. She could move them, but the snake's size meant it would reach her before she could roll away. It hissed again, taunting her to try.

She shimmied back, and the snake shot forward.

Rustag's massive hand caught it by the throat. The serpent turned and bit his arm over and over again. Rustag snarled and pulled the viper from his arm before grabbing its head and snapping its neck. He threw the carcass into the burning coals in the fireplace.

"Rustag! Are you alright?"

The big man slumped to the floor and rubbed his arm. "With my life, m'lady. It will mend."

Alexandra looked over the wounds; the venom oozing from the bites was the same pale yellowish color as the fluid in the vial.

"I'd see you to a healer, if one were left," she said. "We have what we need now, Rustag. Mariselle used that thing to poison the king. We can bring her before a magistrate and take back the kingdom!" Alexandra hugged the giant. Rustag gently put his hand on her shoulder before wincing.

"Can you walk?" she asked him.

"Serpent's bite was minor. I have strength yet," he said, lumbering to his feet.

She turned to her father. He slept fitfully.

She turned back to Rustag. "Thank the Maker. I need you to find an old soothsayer. His name is Samuel. He's old in years, blind, and carries a staff."

Rustag nodded. "I remember him. He served in the Hall of the Lion. He smelled of lye and dirty sheets."

Alexandra bit her lip. "If any man can heal your wounds and bring Father back from the brink, it's him. Leave by way of the eastern gate. His cottage is a little over a league northwest of the King's Way, near the northern shore." Alexandra returned to the table and drained some of the alembic's contents into a flask before stowing it in her pocket.

"You will be defenseless." Rustag looked down at her, his bushy brow wrinkled.

She looked around. He was right. No room off the main hall would be safe from Mariselle's grasp. She glanced out the window to the city. A large crowd had formed in the courtyard, and in the distance, past the Ambassador's Square and the western gate, she heard a resounding boom. She looked out to one of the crumbling spires. The nearest one loomed over the castle courtyard;

its doorway was only two hundred feet from the castle's entrance. The nearby guards had left their posts to hold back the mob.

She turned to Rustag. "I know where I can stay with him. Please help me carry our king."

Rustag nodded and walked to Braeden's bed. He lifted and cradled the old man in his arms like a child, and together the three crept from the room toward their freedom.

CHAPTER 22

A MEETING OF MINDS

Samuel dropped off the back of the wagon and waved to its driver as it pulled up to the eastern gate. He had been lucky to find a caravan of farmers fleeing down the King's Way toward the city. Word had spread like wildfire about the Amorite attack, and people were clamoring for protection.

The soothsayer rushed through the gateway just as it started to close. Overhead he heard the watchmen's alarm and pressed forward. Farmers and peasants from the surrounding countryside pushed past him to get behind the city's walls. Samuel held his scroll tightly under his cloak as families jostled him to move faster.

"Leave your carts!" a guard yelled over the frantic crowd. "Move in an orderly fashion!"

Refugees lifted their small children above their heads and passed them on to strangers closer to the gates. The great wooden doors continued to close, and the mob became even more hysterical. Samuel pushed his way to just within the walls before falling to his knees. Looking up, he saw Balaam standing before him, waiting patiently.

"Balaam! You are a friendly face!"

The donkey leaned in and whispered, "You can see plain as day. I should've expected as much."

Samuel propped himself up with Balaam's help; then, the two walked several steps away from the chaos of the crowd.

"Not until tonight, I assure you. But it's a story best told elsewhere. I need to find Alex and the boy right away. Their lives are in jeopardy," Samuel whispered to the donkey.

"I thought you knew that already," Balaam replied. "You sent them into this madhouse, after all."

"Them? Alexandra is already inside the city? Fool girl was supposed to have waited!"

"Yes, I've found she's quite selective in following your advice. The boy, however, dutifully ignores it completely and ran us right into the city guard. Was that your plan all along?" Balaam tilted his head at Samuel.

"I thought he was an expendable agent. I gave him a blank note with my seal on it—something that, at the very least, would remind the king of the silence between us. It may have been too subtle a message." Samuel ran his hand across his forehead. "Now it seems I've laid our last card too early on the table. That boy means more to us than I first thought." Samuel turned his gaze back to Balaam. "Quickly, where were they taken?"

"Last I saw they were being taken to the dungeon. We'd normally have little chance at them, but this evening is off. Half the city is running about in a panic. Terrors are haunting the graveyard. The guards have their hands full. We might be able to slip in."

Samuel looked at the watchmen and turned his head toward the distant western gate. A faint cry of battle echoed in the wind.

"A great many calamities are unfolding tonight, I fear. Let's move swiftly," Samuel said, hoisting himself onto Balaam's back.

CHAPTER 23

CHAOS IN THE CITY

Egan rode his horse down the alleyways parallel to the market district. He pulled in the reins as he reached a high slope in the cobblestone street. All around him, he saw the people locking their shutters and barricading their doors. A lamplighter and his wife and child scurried past. Egan recognized Avery from the docks.

"Avery? Hold a moment."

Avery turned as he pulled his child to his side. "Chief!"

"And you"—Egan gazed at Helen—"you're the princess's handmaiden, yes? Has the word of the invasion reached the castle?"

The couple bowed, and she replied, "Helen, sir. Yes, I was once. The only invading forces I've heard of is the rioting mob at the castle court. Even the people here in the market now pillage their neighbors' stalls for food."

"Aye, Chief," Avery continued, "I've got the family to think of. We're done with this place. Let Gilead destroy itself."

Egan looked past them and saw she was right. Peasants ransacked the stalls as merchants struggled to fight them off. Others were rushing past the bazaar up the northern road to the castle. Chants of "Injustice!" and "Down with the king!" echoed down the cobblestone streets. Torches were lit and thrown onto stalls, and to Egan, it seemed as if a great pot was boiling over, scalding anyone who drew close.

"I understand, but there are greater threats than these," Egan said as he surveyed the chaos. "As we speak, a legion of Amorites claw their way up the great western stair, and I fear the eastern gate will soon be sieged as well. You'd be safer in our walls than outside them."

"Then evil must come in threes, Chief," Avery said. "We ran into the princess Alexandra herself not long ago. Word is she was captured along with her servant boy—" He paused, caution spreading across his face.

Egan motioned to the man. "Go on, please, speak your mind."

Avery sighed, then slowly continued. "Well, sir, it's just that . . ."

"That woman." Helen shook her head, disgusted. "The king's illness and all this chaos is born of the queen. Alexie was looking for safe passage to see her father alone. I fear she's in danger."

"Love—careful with your words." Avery put his hand on her shoulder.

"Well someone has to say it!" Helen shook her head. "That woman has only been the biggest blight on our nation since she arrived."

"I'm always loyal to the kingdom and Alexandra's people," Egan said as he eyed passersby. "But Avery's right—to speak ill of the queen in these times can bring a stiff penalty." The image of the Vizier crept into his mind. The worm's station had grown ever since the new queen was crowned. Others far more deserving, like Salain, had been left to diminish. Occasional incompetence in the ruling class was one thing, but Egan couldn't remember one policy in recent years that had provided for more than Mariselle's gain. Perhaps some truth lay in Helen's words.

"Apologies, Chief." Avery bowed low. "We misspoke."

Egan saw a familiar look of defeat wash across Avery's face. "I understand your concern," Egan replied softly. "Gilead has been cast under a shadow for many years. Now is a time when we must draw together, no matter our station."

"Aye, and you'd have one more good man at your side, if it weren't for that twit on the throne." Helen huffed. "But don't mind me. What do I know?"

"You're right." Egan laughed. "Avery, your wife's a jewel and her words are true, if not subtle."

"Don't I know it." Avery smiled. "She's as subtle as a brick."

Helen elbowed him, and he laughed.

"Perhaps I should have you both in arms," Egan quipped. "But Avery, I know I need you more than any lamp does. As chief warrant officer, I reinstate your commission—if you'll take it."

"Are you sure, Chief? My old hands can barely—"

"Yes!" Helen smiled and glared at her husband.

"Well, yes then." Avery smiled and saluted.

"You two have backbone to speak your mind to me. Go to the Ambassador's Square, Avery. Call on others on your way. We must reinforce the western gate. The Amorites have no doubt secured the beachhead by now and must be ready to march up the steps."

Helen took their son from her husband as worry spread across her face. Egan turned to her. "Hold your fear, lady; your husband was a great soldier once, and I believe him to be that still. Many will be wounded this night. Call upon those you know who can dress wounds and set up a tent near your husband's station. All of Gilead must stand against the evil on our doorstep."

Helen bowed. "Yes, my lord."

Avery took her by the hand, and they headed westward down the alleyway.

Egan moved on through the grand bazaar, and soon the rampaging crowds surrounded him. As he rode past an overhang, three rough men grabbed his legs and pulled him from his horse.

"Get off me, you fools! I have official business!" Egan cursed as two thugs held him to the ground while another tried to snatch his mare's saddle.

"He's a uniform!" a fat one yelled.

"All the better! He'll have gold!" another said, laughing.

Egan struggled against their weight and looked around frantically for help, but the guards were nowhere to be seen.

The third thug cut the saddle from his horse and kicked the mare. "No more high-and-mighty for you, Governor!" He laughed at Egan as the mare ran off into the mob.

"I'll have your heads!" Egan screamed as he struggled with the other two. Their hands reeked of sewage and kept his head to the pavement as they leered over him.

THUNK.

The saddle thief's smile fell from his face as he dropped his prize and collapsed to the ground dead, a dagger protruding from his back.

"What in the nine hells?" The larger thug let go of Egan and spun around. Standing before him was the mouthy privateer from the docks, Absalom, holding a dagger in each hand.

"Drop your trifle, squirt. We have business." Absalom sneered as he spoke.

The oaf ran at him, grasping for his throat. In the flash of an eye, Absalom ducked under his arm and slammed a dagger into his side. The thug fell to his knees, screaming in pain. Absalom grabbed him by the back of his head and slit his throat. The oaf's gaze went wide, and he fell on his face, dead.

The third leaped clear of Egan and backed away.

"Run away, little mouse, before you get stepped on," Absalom said, staring at him coldly.

The thief turned and ran down an alley. Egan steadied himself and stood.

"I owe you thanks. Absalom, yes?" Egan asked as he caught his breath.

Absalom kneeled and searched the oaf's pockets until he found his pouch. He peered inside, counting the coins. "They owed me money," Absalom said. "I was collecting a debt, nothing more."

"You're handy with a blade. We could use your skill near the western gate. The Amorites have begun their siege of Gilead."

"Gilead can fend for herself. I've no interest in dying for her," Absalom said.

"Yet you say 'her.' She's a mother to you as she is to all of us, and she needs your help this night."

"My mother was a whore," Absalom said and raised an eyebrow. "Of the finest stock, fit for a king. Nothing became her so well as the rags she was left to wear before she died here, in the gutters."

Egan's eyes lowered. "I see. Perhaps when this conflict is over the king will revisit some of his policies."

"Oh, yes." Absalom said and sneered as he motioned towards the mob fighting in the streets. "He is ever so prudent when it comes to us all."

Egan shook his head. He had no time to reason with the man. "Change comes from within, Absalom. I wish you well, whatever path you choose." He stepped over the thief's body and moved back into the crowd.

Absalom watched him go before slipping away.

Egan trudged his way up the King's Way toward the castle. Dodging the protesters that swarmed around him, he called out the alarm, but the raging din of the mob drowned out his words.

CHAPTER 24

FATE'S PRISONERS

The king! The king!" the mob chanted in unison, their fists flying. Mariselle stood several feet above them on the royal dais. She smiled and nodded, gazing across the unshorn and gaunt faces below. It was in their nature to be violent. She would tame them soon.

"Take note of the loudest ones," she whispered to one of her advisors nearby. "I want them in chains by week's end." She raised her hand as if accepting applause.

"Great people of Gilead, hear the words of your humble queen." Her melodic voice echoed across the courtyard, and the crowd quieted. "We live in troubling times, it's true. But I will not balk nor shift blame to another. My heart's been broken by the king's illness, and I've not attended to your concerns as I should have." She wiped a forced tear from her eye.

Some in the crowd nodded.

"Name anything I can do to appease your concerns and I will make it so," she said and smiled.

"Your Majesty!" one commoner called out. "How is it that thieves and vandals can rampage through our markets, and yet the guards lift barely a hand! The taxes they impose are ridiculous. The city lies in ruin—constant darkness day and night— and now these Amorite slavers hinder our ships and fishermen! How can the king still be indisposed, for a year now? Where is the law?" His words echoed in the courtyard, and like a wave building and breaking on the shore, the mob again cried out and cursed her.

Mariselle leaned close to her advisor. "That one goes to the gallows."

She turned back to the crowd and waved down their voices with her hand.

"Ever direct you are, good man. I agree it's been a dark time, but don't let hate fill your speech. For those same ships that illuminate our shores have come to our aid. Our walls have been filled with fear-mongering spread by a fanatical few for decades. Over these last few years, finally, we've opened our minds and hearts to new teachings, new ways of understanding, and complete acceptance and unity with those that only seek our goodwill. The king, as beloved as he is, has left us with failed policies, debt, and a burden we cannot shoulder alone. So, for a short time, we ask that all classes give extra in efforts to stem the tide of crime in the city. Our neighbors, the Amorites have brought peace-keeping forces to help us in this just cause." The last words rolled off her tongue.

Her advisors nodded and clapped. "Well spoken, my queen."

"Let the cattle chew on that," she mumbled through the facade of her smile and wondered how the same fools would sound when they were being burned alive on an altar.

"And what of tonight?" a merchant yelled out. "What of our ruined stalls and shops?"

"Our tireless watch caught the miscreants not four hours past," she replied. "We were to fine and release them in the morning, but I feel as if the people should have a say in this. Yes?" She turned and posited to her counselors. They nodded in unison. The crowd cheered.

Calls to "string them up!" and "flay them!" resounded across the courtyard.

"Grab the wretches and let them face their victims," she called to the guards. The soldiers saluted and left.

"I am ever your servant," she said as she bowed to the mob, and they cheered.

COLIN HELD THE BLACK STONE from the puzzle box in his hand. Once more, he tried to scratch his name onto the dungeon wall, but always on the second letter, his hand would shake, refusing to form the shape of the vowels in his mind. Whatever power blocked his ability to say his name had also woven into his muscle memory. He slid the stone back into his pocket and sighed. He had long since stopped trying to break open his cell door. The rusted iron bars seemed like they would give way at first, but he soon realized that not even the hardest obsidian could slice through them without months of effort. *They never show you all the downtime those cons have in the movies.*

In the cell beside him, Rustag's former comrade, Gunney, slowly sat up and rubbed his head.

"Morning, twinkle eyes," Colin said without a glance.

"What rot is this?" Gunney looked about before standing and rattling his cell door.

"You, my friend, have been hoodwinked. Up shit creek without a paddle. Welcome to the club."

"Eh? What creek is that?" Gunney turned to him.

A shadow eclipsed the torchlight in the dungeon corridor momentarily, and Colin straightened, clutching the stone in hand, ready for whoever might approach. A cloaked figure emerged from the shadows and studied Colin before turning away.

"What's that, a silent warning?" Colin spat. "Checking up on me for your queen?"

The figure paused. "Hardly. I'd heard the princess was here. My mistake."

"You're no guard. I've seen those guys move," Colin called. "And I doubt you're from her retinue—not fat enough. So my guess is you're just as much of an impostor as I am."

The figure lowered his hood. Dark locks fell across his face. "You're very observant for a peasant."

"I'm no peasant," Colin replied. "I don't live here, just visiting and ready to get the hell home. Help me out of here, and I can help you find the princess."

"You're not in the position to help anyone." The man smirked.

"She owes me; Alex owes me. I can put in a good word for you." Colin leaned close to his bars. "I know where she went and the lug she went with. Get me out of here."

"If you're lying, you're dead." The man sighed and pulled a lockpick from his pocket.

"I'm dead already," Colin said as he watched the man shift the tool into his cell keyhole. "Good luck unlatching this rusted piece of..."

The latch clicked, and the door swung open.

"Who are you?" Colin asked and eyed him incredulously.

"Absalom." The man nodded at him.

"Take me to the storehouse; wherever they keep meds," Colin said as he stepped forward.

"That's not part of the deal." Absalom frowned. "You've got no bargaining chip here."

"And the princess has no ordinary bodyguard. I think he's

what you call a slaughterman." Colin kept Absalom's gaze; he would not be badgered this time.

Absalom's face went white for a moment. Colin continued, "You obviously know this place well enough. Get me to wherever they keep the herbs or medicines, then I'll take you straight to her."

"You are either very brave or very stupid." Absalom eyed Colin. "Yes, I know the storeroom; I've pinched an item or two from there in my formative years. It's nearby. But keep up, I'm not a nursemaid."

"What of poor Gunney?" Gunney pawed at Absalom through his bars. "If you're looking for the filly, Gunney can help." He licked his lips and revealed a salty smile. "I'll even hold her down for ya."

"Even I have standards," Absalom said, slapping his hand away.

Colin followed Absalom down the dungeon corridor to a stairwell beyond. At the entryway, he gingerly stepped over an unconscious guard.

Absalom nodded. "Blackjacks are wonderful tools."

They went up the stairs to a narrow passageway barely illuminated by a brazier at the far end. Absalom held up his fist as they approached a four-way intersection. He pushed Colin against the wall, covering them in shadows. Two guards walked past them, the stench of soured mead in their voices.

"What the 'ell does she want them for?" One guard grumbled to the other.

"Who knows? Run 'em through on stage, I suppose." The other shook his head. "Better them than us. Them folks want blood, and you can bet she'd serve us up if it suited her."

They turned within inches of Colin's body and headed for the dungeon. He held his breath. Without pausing, they moved into the stairwell and downward toward the cells.

Colin breathed again.

"We have no time." Absalom pulled Colin by the arm and turned down another passage.

A moment later, they reached another door. Absalom tried the handle, and it opened.

Colin pushed past him into a small alcove with shelving and a few unmarked bottles.

"Where the hell do they keep this balm?" He snatched up a few bottles and studied them in the low light.

"Most phylacteries of any worth are labeled and, my guess is, have been snatched and sold off by now." Absalom shook his head.

"Nothing? You guys have nothing?" Colin scanned the room. "What kind of kingdom is this?"

"One that's rotting to the core," Absalom said as he watched the hallway. "Find your cure and let's away."

"Why are you in such a hurry to meet Alex? Who's she to you?"

"You could say I'm curious. She may have a key I need. Beyond that, it's none of your business."

Colin sniffed at another small bottle and set it aside. "Samuel was right. There's no balm here, or if it was here, it's gone now." Colin turned to Absalom. "I need to get to this Dead Wood. There's a tree, a terebinth tree I have to find there."

"First, he commands me to break him free; now he demands I lead him to the nastiest spot in all of Atlantea?" Absalom pulled a knife to Colin's face. "You forget yourself, my boy. I've humored you till now, but my patience has a limit."

"Alarm!" The call of the guards echoed down the hallway.

Absalom instantly stowed the knife and slipped out the door.

"Wait!" Colin gasped and followed him down the hallway. As Absalom ran past a brazier, he tossed a small pouch onto it, extinguishing the flame with a hiss.

Three guards ran down an adjoining corridor, torches in hand and swords drawn.

"We have escapees! Find them!" one yelled.

Absalom tailed the last guard briefly before turning down a side passage. Colin took a breath and tried to follow his movements. The guard spun around and slammed his sword hilt into Colin's face.

"You little wanker!" the guard spat as Colin fell to the ground. Another two guards stepped up, dragging Gunney behind them by a chain.

"Where's the girl?" the guard demanded, kicking Colin's side.

"They had an inside man," Gunney called out. "He overpowered Gunney, he did. Left me to rot in the cell, while they ran amok."

Colin glanced to the darkened hallway Absalom had fled down, but it was empty. He was on his own again.

"And they left one of their own to roam the halls? Is this true?" The captain turned to Colin.

Colin knew no lie that would save him or Alex.

God, give me something here.

"There were two of us, yes. Only your man Gunney remains." Colin chose his words carefully. "Last I heard he wanted a piece of the princess for himself."

"She bought you, you little lecher? Traitorous sack of dung!" the guard growled at Gunney. "Both of you will answer to the mob."

"No! Please! I'm only a loyal servant!" shrieked Gunney as he fell to his knees. The guards grabbed him and pushed him forward. The other snatched Colin by his shirt and pulled him to his feet before shoving him ahead. Colin took a breath to steady himself. Whatever his fate, he would face it standing.

CHAPTER 25

TRUTH BE TOLD

Alexandra sat beside her father; he moaned slightly as his withered frame curled into a fetal position. She pulled her cloak over his shivering body and gathered more hay under his head. The moonlight broke through the clouds and touched down through the gaping hole in the spire's roof to illuminate the king's face.

"It's little comfort, I know. But Rustag will be back soon with Samuel," she whispered.

"Where's my wife?" Braeden struggled to sit. "She tends me."

"No, Father. She doesn't." Alexandra gently pushed him back down. "We're not in the castle—look around. Mariselle has all but overthrown you, and now she has the kingdom in an uproar."

Braeden stilled as he listened to the echo of the mob outside and Mariselle's screeching voice above it. He shook his head. "No, this damnable illness has weighed on her. I've been a burden to her . . ."

"Father, she's trying to kill you. See for yourself." Alexandra pulled the flask of poison she took from his chamber and uncorked it. She pointed to a nearby patch of weed growing through the cobblestone floor and gently tilted the bottle. A solitary drop landed on its green leaves, curling them to gray. "Behold, your medicine."

Braeden closed his eyes for a long moment before finally responding, his breath rasping in his throat. "You're right. Of course, you're right."

Alexandra watched her father stare at the ashen plant as if he were watching the death of an old friend.

"Leave me. I'm not fit to rule if what you say about Mariselle is true."

"You bore the weight of the kingdom alone for years." Alexandra corked the bottle again and set it aside. "I can hardly blame you for wanting companionship," she continued and took his hand, letting her warmth soak into his chilled fingers.

"No, but I am to blame for not listening to the ones I love," Braeden replied, his voice cracking.

Alexandra nodded, holding back tears. "I don't know how you managed to rule so well for so long—the famine, this siege, Mariselle. I need you to be strong, Father, because I'm not. I can't do what you do. I don't have the answers the people need. I'm not equal to the task."

A slight smile spread across the king's face. "No one is. Not a day went by when I didn't second guess a choice I'd made. But therein lies the weight of our station, Daughter. The choices we make in this life will impact others for years to come; we only fail if we make no choice at all." Braeden hit a coughing fit for a few seconds before settling again. "Make no mistake, the choices are never easy, but they'll always be yours."

Outside the tower, Alexandra could hear the crowd suddenly cheering. Braeden turned his head towards the noise. "Has some fortune finally come our way?" he asked her.

Alexandra stood and opened the door slightly to peer out.

Through the shadows and above the heads of the mob, she saw Mariselle standing atop the castle porch and dais, addressing the crowd, her retinue standing to the side. Guards approached from behind her and shoved two prisoners forward to face the jeering crowd. The wretched jailor Gunney cowered, and Colin stood next to him.

"No, Father," Alexandra replied. "Things have just gotten much worse."

CHAPTER 26

The Triage

Rustag waited in a shadow-filled alley off the bazaar. The looting had come to a head, and now open brawling filled the marketplace. His arm throbbed and constricted. The venom was working its way up to his shoulder. He sighed, knowing what needed to be done. The giant squatted in the alley and tore a swath of fabric from his shirt, tying it tightly above the bite marks. His arm screamed in pain. He gritted his teeth and squeezed the wound. Pus squirted out, and he moaned in agony, knowing his strength was waning.

His hand shook as he sucked in a breath to pinch again, terrified of the white-hot burning. Yelling and gruff voices nearby pulled his attention and stayed his hand.

Peering into the mob, he saw a familiar face: the soothsayer Samuel, riding atop a donkey. The old man was struggling to pass a group of thugs beating on each other when one of them turned and grabbed Samuel's robe, trying to yank him from his mount.

Rustag grimaced. This, at least, was something he could

weather. He stood and forced himself into the crowd. With a sweep of his fist, he knocked Samuel's attacker to the ground. Rustag grabbed the donkey's bit, pulling the beast and the old man back into the alley.

"Unhand us, cur! I am the royal soothsayer." Samuel tried to pull away Rustag's hand. "I have urgent business at the castle!"

Rustag groaned as the pain shot through his arm again. "As does all of Gilead . . . hrumph."

Samuel's eyes narrowed. "Do I know you?"

"Perhaps, my name is Rustag. Your face is known to me."

Samuel's eyes widened. "And your name to me."

"I've been sent to lead you to our king."

"Yes! Good!" Samuel nodded. "Is there a boy with him? A stranger with a strange tongue?"

"No. We left that one in his cell. He'll keep . . . I think." Rustag replied, closing his eyes as the venom seared through his veins. "The king lies dying, and the princess attends him."

Samuel's face went pale. "Then the rumors were true. What ails him?"

"Much of it is the same venom"—Rustag's chest tightened as he gasped—"that courses through my wound."

Samuel slid off Balaam's back and gently laid his hands on Rustag's massive arm. The wound pulsed at the prophet's touch. Rustag moaned as Samuel studied it.

"The venom is strong but not fast. I have little succor to give you here. My balms are over a league away; no doubt it would reach your heart by then and well . . ." Samuel shook his head. "Still, I can slow its movements. Hold still." Samuel breathed in and brought his mouth close to the bite before breathing out a single word.

"Spissus."

The word echoed down the alleyway, and Rustag instantly felt the hairs across his body stand on end. The pain dulled, and his breath flowed more easily. A slight chill moved across his arm and into his chest.

"What did you do to me?" Rustag breathed easier.

"I spoke a word of the Maker," Samuel replied. "A word of healing."

"The Maker?" Rustag chuckled. "The Maker abandoned us to our folly. Condemned us to . . . ourselves."

Samuel smiled and shook his head. "Until this night I might have agreed with you, but I've heard his voice with my own ears now. I've seen his final words with my eyes!" Samuel pulled his scroll from his robe and unrolled the newest portion for the giant to see.

The words glimmered across the parchment, and Rustag's mouth dropped.

"I believe a new speaker has come," Samuel continued as he stowed the scroll in his robe again. "The Logos has been restored, and I must see that Gilead follows in kind."

"I'm no scribe," Rustag replied, deep in thought, "but I believe you."

Samuel looked out to the ongoing riot in the streets. "I fear this route will get me no farther."

Rustag nodded at the opposite end of the alleyway. "We can take the temple road, through the cemetery . . . It runs closer to the castle's perimeter and opens to its courtyard. The princess hides the king in the broken spire there."

The donkey suddenly shook his head and snorted. "I'll not venture there a second time, thank you kindly. My last jaunt had me almost killed by things I'd rather not see again."

"Talking donkey?" Rustag's eyes widened. "Perhaps the poison runs through my head now."

"Ah, yes, I'm so accustomed to Balaam, I forget he's a bit of a shock when people first meet him," Samuel said, distracted, as he stared down the dark alley, studying the graveyard in the distance.

Rustag followed his gaze to the towering alabaster crypts and gravestones, which were silent amid the chaos everywhere else. Not even birds seemed to intrude into that quarter. The gate to the cemetery creaked open with a passing breeze.

"I think whatever you saw, Balaam, has left." Samuel turned to face them again. "At least I hope so. That path is the most direct, and time is of the essence now. The words I spoke over you slowed the poison, Rustag, but it didn't stop it completely. Can you make it to the Ambassador's Square, near the western gate? In the clamor, I heard some say a healing tent is being erected there."

Rustag nodded. "I could . . . yes. But my duty is to the princess . . . I cannot leave her."

"Your duty is also to the cause she serves. You've a strong hand and a good heart. I'd hate to see you succumb to your wounds. We'll have need of you soon, I'd wager."

"Perhaps, then . . ." Rustag looked down and clenched his fist, testing his grip. "I see the truth in what you say. Tell the princess I will return."

"I will." Samuel turned to Balaam and patted him on the neck. "Now forward, friend. We still have quite a walk in front of us."

"It'll be a run if I have anything to say about it," Balaam replied.

The giant watched as the old man and his donkey strode into the shadows, and for the first time in years, he smiled.

SAMUEL SPOTTED THE PRINCESS'S FACE peering from the slightly opened doorway of the broken tower. They had traversed the cemetery without incident. Much to Balaam's apprehension, the once locked gate leading to the castle district lay on the ground, ripped from its hinges—as if some powerful force had rammed through it and escaped into the night. Samuel saw that the mob ahead filled the archway to the castle's courtyard, but no eyes were on the broken spire that rose within its perimeter several yards back. The crowd's anger was palpable as they screamed for blood. Mariselle's voice echoed outward from within the courtyard; her soothing tone seemed only to feed their hatred.

Samuel wondered how soon that hatred would be redirected toward them. The witch had a way with words. The venom on her lips could confuse as well as kill.

Alexandra motioned for Samuel and Balaam to enter as she opened the door. Without a word, the two made their way through the crowd and to the tower doorway. She ushered them in and promptly shut the door again.

"Thank the Maker, I was wondering if Rustag had found you. Is he far behind?" she asked.

Samuel smiled. "Yes, our paths crossed, though I never imagined a jailor could be so overwhelming. He's somewhat the worse for wear. I sent him to the Ambassador's Square by the western gate. He can be treated there, and I think the men stationed round will have more of a need for him than us. Gilead is under attack."

Alexandra's mouth dropped. "No. The Amorite blockade? I knew they had surrounded Gilead, but the negotiations . . ."

"Were a ruse, meant to keep us pacified until they were ready to strike. This war was a long time coming, and we're not nearly prepared for it." Samuel looked past Alexandra to the king lying on a pile of hay, shivering slightly under her cloak.

"Samuel? You can see my father?"

Samuel smiled at her. "The Maker is good, his ways unknowable, his hand delivers." He moved to the king's side.

"Then there is some good in this horrid night," Alexandra said and nodded, taking it in stride. She moved closer to her father. "Mariselle has been poisoning him—a mixture of devil roots and serpent's venom. He's delirious now, fitful and hardly breathing." Her eyes filled with tears as she handed Samuel the bottle of poison.

"Hello, my lord. I'm happy to see your countenance again," Samuel said to the king while he uncorked the phylactery, eyeing its contents. "Yes, Mariselle's work. Crude but potent."

Braeden's gaze slowly focused on Samuel's face. "Samuel? Is it really you?"

"Yes, my liege." Samuel took the king's hand and kissed the royal signet ring on his finger.

"I thought you were dead." Braeden smiled.

"Not yet, my lord. The Maker has entrusted me with a final task," Samuel said. "I must ready Gilead for battle and anoint my successor."

"Successor?" The king feebly shook his head. "I know I stand at death's door. I have one charge more for you as well. Come closer . . ." The king motioned for Samuel, who bowed close to Braeden's whispering mouth.

CHAPTER 27

A Painful Price

Her father's voice was so soft that Alexandra couldn't make out what he was saying, but Samuel's smile fell as he stood again, still looking down at the king.

"I will try, my lord. If I can find him, I will try," Samuel said. "But I've been given the final page of the Logos, and the Maker has made its words clear to me. I believe the lion of Judah will roar again before the dawn. You will stand with your people once more, and you may be able to deliver the message yourself."

She watched Samuel take a small knife from his cloak and winced as he sliced his palm. He laid his bleeding hand on the king's forehead and spoke softly over him.

"Infirmatate sua, sanguinem meum."

Braeden coughed violently. Alexandra gazed on as she saw the veins in her father's arms and neck pulse black, and flow into Samuel's arm. Samuel choked for a moment as the king's coughing subsided. She saw the color instantly return to her father's face and his eyes clear.

"What did you do, Samuel?" Braeden asked as he shakily pulled himself to sit upright.

"Father!" Alexandra wrapped her arms around him, and Braeden kissed her cheek.

"There, child, I'm fine. I'm fine. Samuel?" Braeden looked to the old soothsayer, who had kneeled momentarily to steady himself.

Samuel slowly rose to his feet. His face had become as white as a sheet. A festering sore now covered the wound on his hand. "You're healed, my king. I now carry your burden."

"No, Samuel. There must be some other way," the king cried. "Speak those words over yourself!"

Samuel ripped a swatch of linen from his robe. He gingerly wrapped it around his wounded palm. "Those words were meant for you and you alone, Your Majesty. Alex, I'll need you to take this." Samuel pulled the scroll from within his cloak and gave it to her. "Along with the horn in Balaam's pouch, these are the greatest treasures in Gilead. This scroll is the complete and untarnished word of the Maker, the only one in existence. I daresay these are the reasons the black fleet has come to our shores."

"My people, I come before you to right a litany of wrongs!" Mariselle's voice echoed from the courtyard over the din of the mob.

"She's the reason they've come to our shores." Alexandra nodded past the doorway. "Father, you should call a tribunal, have her brought before the court for treason!"

"I fear it would do little good. She would be found innocent immediately. She replaced our magisters with Amorites years ago," Braeden replied.

"Justice will be served!" Mariselle's voice echoed again. "Tonight I bring you the wretches responsible for the violence in the market."

"And now those Amorites are about to put the boy to death," Alexandra said as her mind flashed back to the dungeon. Leaving him in the cell had seemed prudent enough at the time, but even her father was helpless now to stop the execution. Before the mob could cry for his blood, she had already sentenced him to death. She would be responsible. The fact hit her hard. "Is there nothing we can do?"

"The Amorites are mere puppets for the Dark Lord," Samuel said. "I was able to read the final chapter of the Logos, and our world is entering black times. That document you hold is a beacon. It will shine a light on the lies that darken this realm."

"And the Horn of Joshua? That old conch?" Braeden asked.

"That conch is far more dangerous than we ever knew. I thought the old prophecies said it was a horn of calling. I misinterpreted it. It's a horn of waking."

"Waking? How is that dangerous? What does it wake?" Alexandra asked.

"Death! Death!" The crowd outside cheered.

Samuel shook his head and stood. "There's no time to explain right now. You must see that those treasures stay in the right hands."

"Certainly." Braeden nodded. "As soon as I can stand, I'll have it sent to my treasure room, guarded by my most loyal men."

Samuel took the king's hand. "My king, you are great, but you are not the one chosen for this. By hiding it away, you would help destroy the very kingdom you struggle now to protect. These belong to the boy."

"I still don't understand. Why did you send him?" Alexandra shook her head. "Samuel, he didn't have a chance. It was a fool's errand. And now because of your message"—she looked back to the door—"and my arrogance, he'll die."

"I sent him with a blank note," Samuel quietly replied. "There was no message for the king. Only a chance for him to make a judgment and to know I was watching; to see my mark and remember the silence between us. I now see the folly of it."

Alexandra's eyes flashed. "You mean to say you sent us as expendable agents to make a point?"

"We want their bloody heads!" voices echoed through the doorway.

"I didn't send you," Samuel said as he paced the room. "Balaam recounted to me your exploits. You stole the note of your own volition. I wasn't sure what would happen to the boy, but I couldn't risk our exposure or endangering you."

"Well, you failed on both accounts!" Alexandra yelled.

"And while we bicker, he stands alone," Balaam said and snorted. The donkey turned, nudged, and opened the door with his muzzle, so they could all spy the scene in the courtyard. As Mariselle flourished on stage, two figures were pushed to the forefront. Colin was one of them.

"Wonder upon wonder," Braeden whispered, gazing at the donkey. The king pulled himself up from the hay and moved to the doorway, his breathing still heavy. He paused at Balaam's flank. "Uh . . . pardon me."

"Of course, sire." Balaam immediately bowed and moved away.

Braeden peered out at Mariselle, standing high above the mob, across the courtyard. "That woman has made a mockery of this kingdom. I've been a fool to let her tongue lull me so."

Mariselle's echo called as she gestured at Colin, "This scoundrel has destroyed your bazaar, stolen your property, and I fear, sown the seeds of discord, violence, and hate on our most venerable citizens."

Samuel turned to Braeden and placed his hand on the king's back. "You were as blind as I was, but now we both see clearly. Stay here a while longer with your daughter. Your strength is not fully returned. I will go to the boy's defense."

"You're in no shape to challenge her. Let me at least call to some of my guards to escort you."

"You have cried out for bread! For relief from your suffering," Mariselle's voice continued, "but what relief can I provide when my hands are bound by deplorables such as these?"

"You'd be hard-pressed to find them, my king," Samuel replied. "Gilead is being eaten away both from the outside and from within. Even now, Dagon's fleet attacks our western gate while Mariselle pulls all attention and resources to her charade." He stepped through the doorway.

Mariselle pulled a dagger from her sleeve. "Tonight we will cut this disease from our kingdom!" The crowd cheered.

"Wait!" Alexandra called to him. "Is that boy . . . Could he really be our hope in all of this?"

Samuel paused and turned to face her. "If there is still hope at all, it rests in his words."

She wondered at this as the old man disappeared through the doorway, like a whisper carried on the wind.

CHAPTER 28

THE COURT OF FOOLS

Colin flinched as he was shoved again on the high-standing dais to face the screaming mob nearly twelve feet below. Gunney cringed beside him as the crowd's calls echoed into the night. Mariselle's smile faltered when she saw the princess was not among them. She turned to the captain. "Where's the girl?"

"She's escaped, my queen." He frowned at Gunney. "I'm sorry to say one of my own had something to do with it."

Gunney shook his head. "No, m'lady, never! Gunney's loyal, he is!" The captain slammed his fist onto the back of Gunney's head, silencing him. The little man whimpered and bowed low.

Mariselle leaned closer to the soldier. "Find her. Use every last man if you have to, but she mustn't escape, and do it quietly."

The captain nodded and signaled for all but two of his men to leave with him into the castle's interior.

"M'lady," one of her advisors whispered, "now may be an opportune time to finally claim what you're owed by making an example . . ." He nodded at Colin.

"Yes, I know. Two birds with one stone." Mariselle's face changed to a wide smile as she turned toward the crowd. "Citizens of Gilead, it is up to you to judge the miscreants who befouled our market and brought chaos into the streets." She made a sweeping gesture with her arm. The crowd cheered. "These two represent all that is wrong with our fair kingdom! They take what they want, with no regard for the people or property they destroy." The crowd booed as Mariselle continued her accusations. "Even now, evidence is coming to light that these two are responsible for the princess's disappearance, a kidnapping the king and I have grieved over for a year."

Colin shook his head, unbelieving, as the mob pumped their fists and screamed louder.

"Reports are coming in that these two even orchestrated raids on incoming shipments of grain and supplies for the city!" Mariselle continued.

Colin glanced around. His mouth dropped as he saw the mob's frenzy intensify, devouring every word she spoke.

You've got to be kidding. "That's complete crap!" Colin said. "You're throwing me under the bus. You're not even giving me a chance to explain!"

"Silence!" A guard slapped Colin, and he bit his tongue.

The queen's advisor leaned in and whispered in her ear. She nodded. "I've just learned that before they were apprehended in the great temple, they disrupted a unity ceremony and assaulted several priests. But I am fair—let it never be said I wouldn't offer grace. So, in accordance with our just laws, let them answer for their crimes. Let them admit to their deeds—and they may receive some mercy."

Gunney, wide-eyed, shook his head again. "No, please, Gunney ain't got no complaint with nobody!" The crowd jeered at him, sending a few stones flying over his head.

A guard nudged Colin forward to address the crowd. He

looked across the angry gaunt faces of the mob. How many of them were screaming at the world and at their pain as much as they were at him? They were starving children screaming at their mother for a crust of bread. They wanted answers to questions they didn't know how to ask. They wanted completeness for a hole inside them that they didn't know how to fill.

What can I say? How could I even start to explain how I got here or why? These people want blood. Colin looked down. There, just below the dais, was Samuel. The old man was again facing Colin with the same uncanny stare. Lightning crackled in the distance, and thunder bellowed overhead. The crowd screamed louder.

Mariselle frowned and stepped forward, raising her hand to calm the mob's voices. She turned to Colin. "Speak, worm! You and your ilk have conspired against our kingdom, against our freedoms, against our unity. What do you have to say for yourself?"

Lightning flashed across the sky. Colin saw a slip of parchment carried in the wind floating high above the castle.

Drops of rain began to fall, and the paper dropped and dipped in the breeze before landing at Colin's feet on the dais. Colin slowly leaned forward and picked up the parchment. The broken seal across its edges was clearly Samuel's; it was the same message Colin had carried the night before.

How the hell? Colin's mind wondered for a second, before a word appeared on the blank page. "Venia," Colin mouthed.

In an instant, the mob disappeared.

COLIN WAS FLOATING IN SPACE, somehow alive and conscious, a speck adrift in the infinite. The harsh screams of the crowd had been replaced with a silent emptiness that was both vast and suffocating.

Before him, the magnitude of a star field pulsed, and with a resounding boom, the sun burst into existence. Colin covered his eyes; glaring light surrounded him, broke through his hands, pierced his clenched eyelids, and filled his mind. He expected to be engulfed in flames, but he felt no heat. The glare lessened. He slowly moved his hands away and drew his gaze to the void below him, where he saw a planet form from nothingness within seconds. A brown orb grew in size until it filled his view. Water swept across its surface, and mountains formed. Atmospheric clouds lifted from the waters, making the planet lush and green.

In a flash, he was standing on a grassy hill, surrounded by evergreens, overlooking the city of Gilead far to the west.

What is this? How can I be here? How? Colin's mind raced as he watched the city's walls grow like plants out of the ground, gleaming white and new. The city's spires rose like flowers, and the castle, a white jewel in the center, built itself up.

Colin realized he was watching something he wasn't a part of, like a time-lapse scene in a documentary. He was witnessing the birth of Gilead. Days and nights flew by.

My God, this is like virtual reality on steroids. His mouth dropped as he watched the city take shape over what must have been hundreds of years. Clouds formed overhead, casting the kingdom in shadow. Time slowed to its normal course. Then a beam of sunlight broke through and touched the field before the city's gates. A child in simple robes appeared before the city, and then in the blink of an eye, Colin was standing before him. The boy's brown locks shined, and his face glowed with light. Colin stumbled and knelt as the child touched his forehead. For a moment, Colin felt entirely at peace. The city's gates opened, and people flooded out to surround the boy.

What's going on? Colin wondered as he was pushed to the side. The child reached his hands out towards the crowd. People grasped for his touch, and their faces became joyful as they did.

Colin stood amid the crowd as they bowed to pay the child homage one by one. A mighty wind swept across the valley, and the trees, in turn, bowed low. Colin looked up and saw the sun and stars appear together in the sky, seeming to bow in unison. The boy called to each star by name and then turned his gaze to Colin, breaking through the vision as if to say, "I know you too."

In an instant, the child was now a man. He was taller than Colin, bearded, and his locks hung low at his shoulders, but his eyes held the same light. The crowd now screamed at the man. They were striking his sides and back. Rioting around, kicking and hitting him until he fell to the ground, bleeding. The sky turned black as lightning and thunder rolled overhead. The land had become a lake of sewage. Colin looked around to see the castle had melted away, replaced by barren woods and a mob who tied the man to a gnarled, leafless willow tree nearby.

Colin's eyes opened wide. He screamed for them to stop, but his voice was silent. The man continued to stare at Colin, his gaze never wavering, and amid the crowd's screams, his voice whispered to Colin's mind: "You are a beast tamer, a mountain mover, and a speaker of the words."

The mob jeered at the stranger as they stuck him repeatedly with spears. Blood gushed from his wounds and soaked down to the tree's roots like a crimson waterfall.

Colin saw he was now standing in the blood, holding a spear that pierced the stranger's side. He gasped and let the weapon drop from his hand.

The ground began to shake, and he fell to his knees, watching as the mob surrounding the tree scattered in all directions. Thunder roared across the sky, and a bolt of lightning shot down from the clouds, striking the man and setting the tree ablaze in a fiery explosion. Colin was hurled back into the muck as the tree split down the middle. His eyes were blinded, and a dull ringing hung in his ears until his vision returned.

He slowly opened his eyes and saw he was kneeling before the same tree, long since burned and dead. Time had passed again. Centuries had flown by. He looked up to see the body was gone. Singed into the tree trunk was a single word: "Venia." Colin's eyes filled with tears as he realized his hand had dealt the killing blow.

"I . . . I'm so sorry, I didn't mean to do this to you. I'm so sorry."

MARISELLE SNATCHED THE PARCHMENT FROM Colin's hands. "Where'd you get this?"

Colin's eyes refocused. He was standing on the dais again. The rain was pouring down. The mob was screaming for his blood. The vision had passed.

Mariselle screamed at him again as she grabbed the back of his neck. "Gaping at them won't save you! Now, beg the mob for your life before I cut you down right here!"

Colin looked up towards the crowd, the hairs on his neck still standing on end. His mind reeled in shock from what he had just witnessed.

"Venia," he whispered.

A slight breeze washed across the mob's faces, and for a moment, they became silent. The word was with and in him, and somehow he felt changed.

Colin looked down to find Samuel's gaze again. The old man stood directly below the dais. His eyes widened at the sound of Colin's voice. Samuel turned to the crowd and held out his hands.

"If you wish to kill a fugitive, kill me!" Samuel cried, but Mariselle drowned out his voice.

"It's him!" Mariselle glared at the prophet and then yelled toward her guards, "Samuel, traitor, kidnapper—arrest him!"

"I will have a word on the boy's behalf," Samuel called back, "then you may do what you will, Mariselle!"

The guards pushed forward to the old soothsayer and grabbed him.

CHAPTER 29

The Bulwark Falls

As Avery hurried to meet the guards at the western gate with Helen and Taran in hand, he wondered at his change in station. In seconds, Egan had cleaned away the tarnish of his demotion, and now he was called to carry much more than a wick. He wondered if his hands would remember how to hold a blade. As he approached the western wall, he heard the Amorite drums of war echo up the stairs. Snarling voices could be heard rallying down the massive steps as they set fire to the terraced sections below. Avery ran past the gate to the balcony and steps leading downward. He peered over the high wall and saw the white steps of the grand staircase stained black with the shuffling bodies of hundreds of dark-armored attackers making their way up the terraces.

Thum! Boom! Thum!

He looked to the soldiers behind the wall at his side and saw the glances of dread that spread across them as the deadly rhythm of the Amorite drums drew closer.

"Helen," Avery said, turning to his wife, "how do I do this?"

"You accept it, love." Helen searched his eyes. "You be the man I know you are, the one I fell in love with all those years ago. You do it for me, for him . . ." She nodded to their son and placed her hand on Avery's chest. "But most of all—you do it for you."

Avery nodded and watched Helen take their son to the far edge of the plaza where a medical tent was being fashioned. A few wagons, barrels, and poles had been brought together to face the onslaught, but Avery knew it would not be enough to hold the Amorites back. During his long run from the bazaar, he'd garnered five or six more soldiers, who had all but given up trying to secure the mob that made its way toward the castle. Word had continued to spread, and now he saw another handful of city watchmen and soldiers approach. He beckoned to them.

Thum! Boom! Thum! The drums pounded louder, and the Amorite chant echoed upward: "Death! Death! Death!"

Guards pushed more carts and wagons to the barricade and quickly released the door chain, allowing the doors to slam shut. A beam was placed across it and steadied with iron poles.

"Archers? Any of you?" Avery asked the group of men approaching him. A few nodded. "Take the ladder yonder and move to the top of the walls 'round the western gate. The rest of you help build up the barricade. Those doors won't hold forever."

He turned to see Helen direct several women to the triage tent. Her eyes held his momentarily, and she brought her hand to her bosom.

"Love you," he mouthed, and she followed suit before leading Taran inside. A large brute of a man lumbered in after her, gasping and clutching his arm.

"Maker, we already have wounded," Avery said and turned to inspect the stacked barricade growing near the gate's base. Old wood beams had been hastily sharpened and placed amid sandbags, barrels, and crates. Workers rigged the pieces together with rope.

Avery saw the riggings tremble slightly as the percussion of drums and feet made their way up the stair. The gravel at the foot of the barricaded gate bounced across the cobblestone as the Amorites drew closer.

"Make the knots fast, boys. There'll be no other shield for our people after this one," Avery yelled. The men nodded and checked their work. The barricade formed a giant horseshoe facing the gate. Several spearmen stood across the space within, readying their weapons, while a score more stood on either side of the makeshift blockade. Archers now lined the high wall, standing next to the few watchmen who had left their eastern positions on the bulwarks.

Nearby, shop owners and townspeople held their homemade weapons with shaking hands. A few wore spare hauberks of Gilead or carried shields and swords. Both the old and the young, men and women, stood ready, fidgeting in armor they had never worn before, holding weapons they could barely use.

"Death! Death! Death!"

The guards' weapons shook as the attackers' voices echoed up the stair.

Avery could see the fear and uncertainty in the people's eyes. He moved to them and called them into formation. "Steady up! Rows of seven all of you!" The people quickly moved into formation.

"Those of you wearing chest plates or pauldrons, keep your bindings tight! The last thing you want is to be tripped up during the battle."

The soldiers nearby smirked as they watched the civilians struggle with their gear.

Avery shot them a sharp look, then continued, "I know many of you haven't held a weapon; you may feel unqualified for it. But tonight is not a skirmish of mercenaries. It's not a military exercise. We are fighting for our lives."

Thum! Boom! Thum!

Avery continued speaking as he inspected the civilians. "I would gladly die defending any one of you. You're the reason the rest of us go into service. You're the heart of Gilead. Any professional soldier here would do well to remember that." He glanced back to the guards, and they nodded as others turned to listen.

"Tonight, there is no difference between soldier and civilian, no rank between professional and novice. We are all brothers- and sisters-in-arms. These agents of destruction now on our shore would see your bones smashed into the ground; would see your children's blood run in the streets! Our leaders have urged us to relinquish all that we hold dear to these savages in hopes of unification. They have stripped us of every asset and called us deplorable if we questioned them. They have sold us a false bill of sale for peace, at the cost of our souls. Is your life so dear, your peace so sweet, that you would trade it for chains?"

The people around him chanted "No!" as thunder rolled overhead.

Avery cried above the din, "They come now with their drums and spears, with their cries of death. The wail they will hear will be their own! We are battered and bruised, but we are not broken! Tonight, make THEM feel terror!"

Lightning arced across the sky, and Avery saw the people's faces had turned from fear into anger. "Make the lightning of our glory sear their eyes! Make the thunder of our voices shatter their ears! Archers find your targets!"

The plaza echoed in unison as Avery led them in chant, "Gil-e-ad! Gil-e-ad! Gil-e-ad!"

Avery's soldiers slammed their weapons on their shields. The people turned their formation to the gate as they answered the Amorite call with their chanting.

Thum! Boom!

But the drums faltered.

"They are at the gate!" the guards called down. "They stand uneasy!"

Silence fell upon the square for a moment. With his men, sword, and shield in hand, Avery took a position as the rain began to fall.

Boom! Boom! Boom! The savage drumbeat began again, echoing faster.

A fiery cauldron flew over the wall and exploded behind the barricade, sending soldiers running and screaming. The gates lurched forward as the Amorites pushed against them.

"Shields up!" Avery screamed. "Hold the line!" A shower of fiery arrows flew down into the plaza. The people screamed and ran for cover.

The battle for Gilead had begun.

CHAPTER 30

The Second Gift

Colin felt the rain sluice down and soak his shoulders as he watched the burgeoning mob in the courtyard clamor to cover themselves in the downpour. Only Samuel, standing next to him on the dais, seemed unfazed by the storm.

Colin searched the soothsayer's eyes.

He can see. My God, the old man is looking at me.

Had Samuel seen the vision as well? Could he really calm the crowd? What words would be heard through their cries? Colin's gaze swept across the screaming mob. How could people so easily forget what had happened? How could they fall so far? But he knew it wasn't forgetting. It was not wanting to face it. They would rather smash their mirrors than look at themselves—and Samuel looked as fragile as glass as he faced them.

His voice could barely be heard over the crowd's chants and screams. Before them, finally, was a face to put to the misery of the last few years—someone to be held accountable. The guards on the outskirts of the mob scoffed as they watched the old man trying to face the same rabble they could barely repress night after night.

Colin watched Mariselle laugh as the scene played out before her.

Samuel raised his hands to try to quiet the screams of vengeance before him. He looked down as they jeered at him.

Then with a quiet breath, he spoke: "Pacem."

A gentle breeze went out from his lips and across the faces of the mob. Instantly they quieted. Colin wondered at it. The old man uttered the same voice that had breathed through Colin moments before. These words must be the Logos that Samuel had mentioned, but how and where this power manifested was still a mystery.

Mariselle glanced at her advisors, and they shook their heads, dumbfounded.

"People of Gilead!" Samuel began again. "I'm not your enemy. I've been given words, words you need to hear from the Maker himself. You've broken his laws and you suffer because of it," his voice carried beyond the edge of the mob.

"We don't care what you have to say scum!" a man called back from the crowd. "Don't waste your breath on us with that Maker rubbish! We don't give a rat's ass for your opinion, much less a set of contrived commandments!"

"Yet you scream out for my blood?" Samuel asked. "You demand justice, a right to cancel out all the wrongs done to you?"

"You're damn right!" the man screamed back.

"The same commandments that you mock are the foundation of the laws you demand to be enforced! Even if you tossed aside the laws, wouldn't you still know the difference between what's right and wrong? Wouldn't you still want retribution if your neighbor stole from you?"

"Don't try to spin our words! You three are responsible for all of this!" the man yelled. "You're on trial, not us!"

Colin gazed at the agitator for a second. In the flash of an eye, he saw the man pickpocketing people in the mob during the commotion. Colin shook himself. The vision was over just as quickly as it had started. Something was happening to him.

Am I having an aneurysm? Did that happen?

Samuel glanced at Colin knowingly, then addressed his accuser. "Your name is Fergus. You're desperate for gold to pay off those lenders; desperate to do it without your wife's knowledge. So desperate, you stole from the pockets of those around you just moments ago."

Colin's mouth dropped. *Is Samuel reading my mind? Or perhaps I'm reading his. How could we both share this knowledge?*

Fergus's eyes widened, and he began to back up. "What sorcerer are you? How do you know my name?" The people around him felt for their missing coin purses and grabbed him.

Samuel raised his hands. "Peace, please. The only power I have comes from the Maker. Enough blood has been spilled tonight."

The mob pushed Fergus to the perimeter and left him while Samuel grasped Colin's arm to steady himself. A silence settled over the people, and even the guards looked at Samuel in awe. The old soothsayer's hands shook slightly as he leaned on his staff, ready to address them again.

Mariselle pushed past him. "I think we all know what is real. Real joy has come from the freedoms given to us by the Amorite teachings, not simple parlor tricks. Our inner truth gives us meaning. No matter the name it's given in, no matter the god you worship, it makes no difference. We're no longer enslaved by the old faith."

Some in the crowd cheered. Others were quiet, less sure.

Samuel snorted. "So, you seek your own inner happiness without the Maker? With every prize you've attained, with every base action you've committed on yourselves and on each other, have you felt fulfilled? Have you felt contentment? Or like a thirsty man drinking from the sea, do you constantly crave more?"

The audience listened intently as Samuel continued. "The truth is that nothing in this world can satisfy you completely. You were not made for this world! You were made by the Maker as vessels of life. Without him, you are an urn of ashes." He turned to face Mariselle. "Outwardly beautiful, but on the inside full of decay."

Mariselle backed away.

"How dare you!" a woman yelled out. "Who are you to speak? If I love a man or a woman, what is it to you? My needs are my own! I was born the way I am, I shan't be ashamed of it! If there is a Maker, he made me this way!"

The sight of the woman flashed another vision in Colin's mind; she lay with man after man and woman after woman, drunk and delirious each night, alone and despondent each morning. The name *Aiela* appeared in his mind.

"Your name is Aiela," Samuel replied. "You've had six lovers in the last two years, and you've left all of them. They promise you their hearts, but they trample on yours. You pour your life into each of them, and they take it, until you've nothing left to give. They've left you as an empty chalice, chipped and broken."

The woman's eyes welled with tears, and she turned away. Samuel rested his gaze on the rest of the mob. "You claim to be victims, but the truth is, you've all made choices in your lives that have changed you little by little. One mistake led to another, and the truth that you hold dear today was not the same truth as the day before. You've lost sight of the only beacon that can guide you in the storm. You've lost sight of the Logos. With each choice, you slowly spin the wheel of your life towards restoration or ruin, but make no mistake. You are always at the helm."

Colin watched the crowd's reaction. Something in the old man's words had touched them. Their fists lowered, and their eyes searched inward.

Samuel continued, "I'm not a great man. I'm old, powerless, poor, and by all accounts, a lost cause, but still I see what you cannot. Twenty leagues from here is the ashen tree, where your ancestors murdered the man the Maker had sent. In that carnage, the Maker allowed your people to see how far they'd fallen from his laws and, at once, left you a message that was never relayed—until now."

Samuel paused. Only the echo of the rain spoke out.

"Venia," Colin said, and the word's meaning finally became clear in his mind, two hands coming together, two frayed cords joining to become one.

Samuel nodded at him and called out, "You are pardoned."

Mariselle grabbed Colin by the back of his neck and shoved him off the dais, sending him toppling twelve feet below.

"Enough! Is this a circus that we let the fools admonish us? You wanted justice for tonight, I give you your criminals!"

Some of the crowd began chanting again, but their voices were few and far between.

Colin picked himself up. His side had taken the impact, yet he felt like he had landed on feathers. He looked up at Samuel.

The prophet smiled at him. Mariselle motioned to her guards. The brutes grabbed Samuel's arms, but the old man focused on Colin.

"You're here for a reason, lad," Samuel said. "I was wrong about you."

"Your words. I saw them in my mind before you spoke. I saw something," Colin replied. "What did you do to me?"

"Nothing, boy. The Maker's power is sufficient, made perfect through suffering; so the Logos says."

"Shut it!" a guard yelled and slapped Samuel. Blood ran from the old man's nose, but he held Colin's gaze. Two more guards pushed their way through the crowd toward Colin.

"No!" Colin shook his head at their approach. "Samuel, we can fight. Use your words to protect yourself. You're the only guide these people have!"

"Not anymore. I pass that title to you. You are the last soothsayer."

The guards pushed past the last of the crowd surrounding Colin and grabbed him from behind.

"The gods have indeed blessed us!" Mariselle laughed as she called to the masses. "Standing before you is the master orchestrator of your turmoil! A wretch whose dogged belief in a dead god has crippled the king and the kingdom! His words are empty; his lies to be pitied. Truly a wasted life."

Samuel faced her, his eyes steel. "The words of the Maker are flawless, like silver purified in a crucible. They protect the needy that call out. They are a shield from the viper's tongue."

Mariselle glared and yelled over his voice to the crowd, "Even now you pause? You have been wronged! Take your justice! Claim them! Kill them both!"

Half the crowd pushed toward Samuel and Colin, swayed by Mariselle's words, screaming for death. The other half held them back and pushed them away. To Colin's eyes, it was as if two great waves had crashed against each other, struggling to turn the tide. Those in support of Colin and Samuel grabbed at the guards, while the angry grasped for Colin's neck.

"Back off, the lot of you!" the guards holding Colin screamed at those lunging for him. Wherever their true loyalties lay, he could tell the guards were just striving to maintain some order in the chaos. They formed a tight circle around him, their eyes wide as the mob pushed them into a corner.

Mariselle spat at Samuel. "Where is your Maker? Call him this night, so my master may slay him! We will leave his body on the heap with your own! Let him behold the might of—"

Samuel raised his voice even louder: "His might breaks their teeth and rips out their fangs! Silentium!"

Thunder boomed overhead, and with another flash of lightning, Mariselle's jaw shattered.

Blood poured from her mouth as her teeth fell to the ground at her feet. Her retinue screamed and ran from the dais as she fell to her knees, moaning. Her tongue went limp as bits of bone splayed across her hands. Her guards pulled her to her feet. One of her advisors grabbed a spear from a nearby soldier.

"Samuel!" Colin yelled. But it was too late. Mariselle's counselor ran at the old soothsayer, piercing the spear into his back.

Colin screamed as Samuel fell off the dais and onto the ground at Colin's feet.

"Samuel!" Colin collapsed beside the old man and held Samuel's head as he felt the soothsayer's blood run across his lap. "Samuel? Please . . ."

Samuel's blank stare told him enough. The crowd around him was speechless.

Egan burst through the mob at the far edge of the courtyard as the crowd moved away from Samuel's body and Colin's kneeling figure. He glared at Mariselle.

"What evil is this! What have you done?" his voice echoed across the courtyard.

Mariselle motioned toward the chief warrant officer.

Two armed men rushed Egan. He unsheathed his sword. He ripped through their torsos with a flash of steel and moved forward. "People of Gilead, there is a traitor among us, and she stands before you! She has sold us to an army that now murders our men and women at the western gate. The Amorites now siege our walls! To arms! To arms!"

Mariselle held the remnants of her jaw, her gown stained by her blood. She stumbled as pain racked her body. Her eyes widened. She shrieked and pointed to Colin.

The mob was still for a moment. Then, in unison, attacked Mariselle's men at the bottom of the dais. The soldiers nearest Colin cut down any who came within striking distance and pushed Colin back to the castle's entrance way.

Colin turned to run, but two of the queen's men tackled him to the ground and slammed their gauntleted fists into his face until he knew no more.

CHAPTER 31

Korah's Maw

Colin sat with his mother at their coffee table in their kitchen. As he munched on toast, she slowly sipped coffee from her mug and sighed.

"You gotta be strong now, hon," she said as she gazed at him. "They'll eat you alive if you let them."

A DROP OF WATER SLIDING down Colin's cheek brought him back from the darkness and the dream. The clang of metal on metal was the first sound he heard in his daze. His body was still; his knees were pushed against his chest. His back was hunched against cold iron bars, bruised and spasming with pain. He felt the ground swaying back and forth like a ship on the sea. Blood running from his nose to his lips tasted of copper.

Slowly—it'll hurt.

He opened his swollen eyes. Rusted metal bars filled his vision. Colin turned his head slightly and felt searing fire shoot across his neck and into his chest.

Where the hell did they put me?

He saw his prison was small enough to keep him from standing. The top of the cell was rounded, and the metal floor was flat; yet still, the sway told him terra firma wasn't close. The drops of water landing on his face and the cool chill of the dark breeze whispered he was somewhere outdoors, not in the castle's dungeon. The soft, steady rhythm of rain became clearer in his mind. *It's almost peaceful,* Colin thought as he strained to look below him. *If I could just be home enjoying it.*

Lightning flashed, and Colin saw the high gallows holding his cage up. A mechanism at the top of the wooden arm was connected to his cell by a long rope leading downward. His mind flashed an image from a history book he'd scanned in class. A prisoner was held in a human-sized bird cage, left to rot. *A pillory is what they called it. How high up am I?*

Lightning and thunder cracked again, and Colin saw another pillory cage across the dark expanse. Inside was the runt who had been in the dungeon with him—Gunney. The little man pulled and clawed at his bars like a frantic caged rat. He reached his hand out through the bars and tried to grasp for the rope running from the arm of his gallows, but the line was just out of his reach.

Below and to his right, Colin heard movement and hushed voices. They were busy, working on something. The lightning flashed again; through the rain, Colin saw a troop of men erecting a command tent, putting together huge wooden ballistae mounted on wheels, and readying several oversized iron-tipped bolts. *The Amorites,* he thought. *Great.*

To his left, Colin saw that the line of men ended abruptly as if some natural barrier in the darkness stopped all ingress. Lightning arced across the sky, and Colin's eyes spotted the reason. He was hanging out over a sheer and vertical chasm that split the earth and held a large gorge of water running far inland from the sea. Colin spied jagged rocks sticking up like teeth in the depths of the channel beneath him, surrounded by a miasma of seawater swirling around them. The water rolled in long waves from the distant breakwaters, then funneled down the canyon gorge to this endpoint. Colin saw the influx of surf smash around and through a crudely made latticed gate connected to either side of the gorge, running across its width.

Are they trying to catch fish? Colin wondered. But the spaces throughout the lattice seemed much too large.

"Watch your foot!" one of the workers growled at another below. The tent was now up, and in another flash of the night sky, Colin recognized Mariselle's ruined face. Coarse stitches ran from her neck up to her mouth. She was staring up at him. She turned toward the command tent and motioned to a nearby guard. Colin watched as she leaned in and whispered in the guard's ear. Colin couldn't make out the words. The guard nodded and moved to the foot of Colin's cage. Mariselle's disfigured smile spread across her face as she gazed at him; still-bleeding gums and a few scattered teeth were all that remained. She went into her tent.

Colin's guard called up to him, "Don't think about using your voice powers on me, boy. I'll spear you before you get two words out. Or maybe I'll just drop you early."

Colin leaned back and sighed. "Go ahead. I can swim."

The jailor laughed. "You can? Can you swim faster than the beastie? That I'd like to see!"

"What?" Colin asked.

The guard signaled to another man standing below Gunney's pillory. The jailor yanked the rope attached to the gallows arm, and Gunney's cell split in the middle. He shrieked as he fell into the chasm. Colin winced as he watched the little man fall, sure he would be impaled on the jagged rocks between the waves. Suddenly gigantic jaws flew up from the water and bit him in half. A flash of light revealed the flat gray belly of the beast as it splashed back into the water, smooth like an eel but a thousand times larger.

The black silhouette of the creature filled the bottom of the watery chasm. Another lightning flash revealed a double set of jagged teeth sinking below the waves as its four black eyes stared up at Colin in anticipation.

The remains of Gunney's body were pulled below the water. The rolling wash turned crimson as lightning flashed again. Colin's hands locked around the bars of his cell, and he shut his eyes, not wanting to see more.

Colin's jailor laughed again. "I'd welcome you to Korah's Maw, but you won't be staying long."

AN HOUR HAD PASSED. KING Braeden stepped out from the ruined spire and approached his chief warrant officer, Egan, in the castle courtyard as the guards moved around him, working to pacify the crowd.

He paused as a soldier finished his report to Egan.

"Chief, she's nowhere to be found. In the chaos she must've escaped the city."

"Aye, and taken half our servicemen with her," Egan said and nodded. "We've no time to root her out further. Take our remnants to defend the western gate."

"Aye, Chief," the solider said and saluted, turned to bow to the king, and left.

Egan took a knee. "My lord. Thank the Maker you're with us. I'd feared you were nearly dead."

"And I was, I nearly was, if not for my daughter and her friends. Thank you for your service and your warning."

Egan stood. "We need all available hands at the Ambassador's Square. The Amorites have attacked the bay and, right now, march up through the grand staircase of the Lion's Maw. I've had the western gate barricaded, but I fear it won't hold for long."

"Unfortunate, but not surprising. There is little coincidence that Mariselle's betrayal coincides with the attack. I had no idea how divided my forces had become. I've sent a personal detachment of my guard to route her from the castle, but if what your man says is correct, she's long gone. She's brazen, but she's not stupid," Braeden said, his eyes calculating. "How many men do you have at the square now?"

"No more than a company or so." Egan's eyes roamed across the courtyard, counting every able body capable of holding a weapon. "There are more willing fighters within the city walls that I can round up. Some civilians are capable of holding their own as well."

King Braeden's brow raised as Egan chuckled to himself. "Something amusing?"

"Sorry, my lord. A privateer I came across by the name of Absalom was exceptional with a knife. Showed more spine than half of Mariselle's mercenaries. I suppose—"

Braeden's face went white. "Did you say 'Absalom'?"

Egan paused. "Sire? You know of him?"

"I'll send the rest of my guard to your aid as soon as we've seen to these people," Braeden said, avoiding Egan's gaze. "Have your officers set up a command post at the central bazaar, near Market Street. It will be our fallback point, should we need it. Take everyone you can now to the western gate; I'll follow once I've said my goodbyes to him." Braeden nodded at the body of Samuel, which was covered by a tattered sheet.

"Yes, m'lord." Egan nodded and turned away.

Braeden approached the body and kneeled beside it. "Well, old friend, it seems all my sins have come back to haunt me tonight. I envy your peace."

CHAPTER 32

UNSTAINED HANDS

Mariselle gazed around her tent. A simple cot, a table, a chair, a chest, and a crudely made vanity were now the only luxuries she enjoyed.

Their retreat from the city had forced her men to scavenge the bare essentials. The mob would be rioting in the castle now, pawing at her furs, soiling her sheets. Her soldiers needed a little time to regroup; then, the masters of the house would return.

"An inquisition will be needed," she mused. "Every piece of filth who's trespassed will be found and made to watch as we draw and quarter their families." Her fists clenched. "Every mark on me will be revisited tenfold."

She moved to her chair and stared at a hag in the chipped vanity mirror. The scarred and emaciated face reflected was one she no longer recognized. The dark stitches running from her lower lip across her mouth and cheek were hackneyed work at best. The surgeon's handiwork had even left a permanent sneer.

Mariselle wrapped her fingers around a dagger on the stand and stood facing the physicker who returned to her tent.

He smiled as he bowed low. Rubbing his bloody hands on his apron, he said, "It was an honor, my lady."

"How could I thank you . . . for such *fine* work?"

The surgeon glanced up. "With what constraints I had, I hope you'll find it agreeable, in time. I'm but a humble sculptor, of sorts."

She smiled at him as he bowed. "Is this your opus?" She pointed to her face.

The physicker stood. "M'lady?"

"I hope so. It will be your last," Mariselle spat and arced her dagger across his face. He screamed and fell backward to the ground, clutching his eyes. Mariselle pounced onto his chest and plunged the blade deep into his heart, holding down his grasping hands until they fell lifeless to his sides. His face was a river of blood.

"Fool," she said and stood, pulling her blade free from his chest. Her last remaining advisor coughed behind her. Mariselle spun around, dagger ready to strike again.

"My lady." He immediately cast his gaze away from her face. "The seers have read their bones. Lord Dagon wants an audience with you."

Mariselle eased her grip on the blade and swallowed the lump in her throat. Her master only dictated these tête-á-têtes when he was angry. "Bring in the altar then. We have enough blood to summon the vision," she said.

The advisor bowed low and pushed back out through the tent flap. Moments later, two soldiers carried in a wrought iron stand, waist high and adorned with animal bones and leather. Hieroglyphs were roughly hammered across its side. Her seers hastily made this one, sacrificing a horse to finish the job. The smell of rotten meat purveyed the tent as flies landed on some still-sinewy cartilage decorating the front of it. Mariselle stared at it in disgust. The Amorites had mastered many skills, but craftsmanship was not one of them.

"Leave me," she ordered without turning to her men. They hurried out, eager to be away from the stench. Mariselle approached the altar and held out her hand. In her other hand, she grasped her dagger and placed it across her palm, ready to draw blood. She paused as she stared at the lines in her palm. How often had she wondered about her future when she was a girl? Gazing across her hand's lifelines, she'd imagined living at court, married to a nobleman or even a prince. Her lily-white fingers would pick dandelions in the field, and she'd form herself a crown. How many of those dreams had fallen by the wayside?

Dagon had promised her riches, a kingdom of her own, and a true love to sit by her side. She only had to make his mark, a prick of blood; merely a gesture, he'd told her, of loyalty. But as the years went on, more marks were needed. More was always asked, and the worst scars he left were the ones in her mind as he forced her to see and do things she'd never believed she could. Now even her face was gone. All that remained were her hands, still unblemished.

The vision altar always demanded one willing subject to spill their blood. She'd been spared the deed until now. She held the dagger at her palm, ready to make the necessary cut, then she looked down at the dead physician at her feet. Years of serving under Dagon's foot had taught her there was always an easier way.

"I've paid enough this night." She leaned down and ran her hand across his brutalized face, cupping his blood between her fingers as best she could. "Your blood will suffice."

She hesitated before standing and letting the slow trickle of crimson drip onto the altar. Unsure if the dark magic would work.

The bone and metal framework of the shrine shook of its own accord. Mariselle knelt before the altar. The lamps in the tent dimmed, and an intense heat washed over her. Mariselle glanced up at the large shimmering face that appeared before her.

"Master Dagon, I'm here as called. What is your bidding?"

Dagon stared at her, his serpentine eyes seared into her own. His face, what she had once thought of as fair, was now as pale as a corpse. His long dark locks partially obscured his grimace. Mariselle had learned to withstand his gaze, unlike his many other minions, but his pupils would elongate, giving her the distinct feeling she was staring at a reptile.

"My ship still waits offshore. Why is there resistance at the gates? You were told to have the city open and waiting for my occupation. Now my men throw themselves on Gilead's spears."

"Master, forgive me, the city was wrapped around my finger, but over the last few days some . . . unforeseen issues arose." Mariselle bowed her head.

"Unforeseen? Should I tell our Lord that you have uncovered some fault with his designs?" Dagon growled.

"No! I misspoke. You see . . ." Mariselle's mind raced. How much could she safely say? "There's been an uprising, but I was able to quell it and kill Samuel, the last soothsayer. He'll no longer be a problem."

"How many troops bear arms behind the walls?"

"Well, Master, I'm . . . I'm not entirely sure. I was forced to leave the city from the eastern gate. I'm only a half league away at Korah's Maw, and I'll soon regroup with—"

"A half league away? You quell an uprising a half league away? Liar!" Dagon screamed, his eyes blazing.

Mariselle covered her face and looked away. "No, I all but crushed them. Their defenses are pitiful. Your men will have no issue pushing past their last gate!"

Dagon's visage wavered over the altar.

"What of the king and the Horn of Joshua?" Dagon asked.

"He's on death's door. We looked for the horn. It was … missing." Mariselle said.

"He was to be dead by now, and the horn in your possession! Have I placed my trust in a witless dog that you bring me these scraps?"

Dagon's face again wavered and faded. His eyes searched around the room.

Mariselle clenched her fist as she caught his gaze again. "I will do whatever you ask of me. Name it, and it will be yours."

"Your vision fades. Did you draw fresh blood for the altar?"

Mariselle's eyes turned away. "Of course, Master."

"My seers say our victory is no longer absolute. What are you hiding from me?" Dagon glared at her.

"Nothing of any import. Before we fled the city, I captured a stranger—a boy."

"He accompanied the soothsayer?" Dagon frowned.

"He was caught separately, but they knew each other, it seems. The boy's speech sounds off; he's not from Gilead nor any country I've heard of. Though I did hear him whisper the Logos. He's a zealot, nothing more. I'll have him killed soon."

Dagon's eyes opened wide. "Listen to me, wench, our master knows the old prophecies. If you value your life you must not—"

Dagon's face wavered and faded into nothingness. Mariselle looked around the altar. "I'm not a fool. He can save the reprimand. Killing a boy is hardly a challenge."

She stood, dusting soil from her knees. The altar could not be used for another day, but no further instructions were needed. The Dark Lord would see her worth soon enough, and she may be raised above even Dagon's station in time. She turned and walked to the tent opening. The zealots were playing their end game. They would be crushed. There would be no more mistakes. Gilead was almost within her grasp. Perhaps after the boy's death, she would be rewarded. Perhaps this time, Dagon's promises would be kept.

CHAPTER 33

The Dead and the Living

Rain drizzled on King Braeden as he stood at the entrance to the royal crypt in the cemetery. The seal had been unlocked, and the doors opened. He stared at the darkness within. Alexandra stood solemnly by his side, holding a handful of lilacs. Braeden shifted in his chest plate as he glanced at Alexandra's flowers wilting under the downpour. So little beauty was left in the world now. The remnants of light were being smothered by darkness, and the world held its breath waiting for the final ember to die. Balaam was reverent as he gazed at Samuel's body. Around them, five guards stood vigil with torches. The mob was quelled once Mariselle fled the city and Braeden appeared. The remaining guards were cheered at the sight of their king, once again healthy and stalwart in his command. Four men carried Samuel's body, covered by a sheet, on a simple litter to the tomb's doorway.

"This was meant for me. I should be the one, not him," Braeden whispered.

"Samuel knew his path at the end," Alexandra said taking his hand. "He knew you could change things."

"Can I? Even now our forces are dying. I led Gilead to this ruin. How many lives have been lost because of my arrogance? How many lies did I tell myself and others?"

Alexandra turned to face the shrouded corpse and placed the lilacs on Samuel's body. "I know custom says lilies, but you always liked these more. Thank you for your kindness," she said. Her eyes welled with tears, and she quickly brushed them aside. "Sorry," she said as she turned back to Braeden.

"No, Alex. Weep. I've been wrong. Your heart's a hearth fire in a world where so many others have gone cold."

He looked at her. It was impossible to tell where the raindrops ended, and her tears began.

"He will rest with our ancestors," Braeden said and motioned to the guards. They carried Samuel's body into the crypt. A soldier approached the king. He paused for a moment before removing his helmet.

"My lord, we searched the dungeon and the castle. There is no sign of the boy or his body anywhere."

Braeden glanced at Alexandra. "Would he have run? Fought his way free?"

She shook her head. "I don't know. I don't think he could have freed himself. Mariselle's guards grabbed him and . . . I don't know."

Braeden saw the dread in her eyes and nodded to the guard. "Thank you. Ready my horse."

"I'll be riding to aid Egan at the Ambassador's Square," he said, taking Alexandra's hand. "If I fall, you will rule Gilead. You'll wear the crown and have to make your own choices." He paused as the guards exited the tomb and sealed it with a marble flagstone etched with the sigil of Gilead. "Make wiser ones than

I did. I wish I had more to give you, but at the very least, I must tell you the truth."

"You won't die . . ." Alexandra started.

"Alex, I'm no warrior. I'm old. If this night ends with my death, you must guide Gilead back to the light. I begged Samuel to carry my last burden, and now it seems I leave it to you." But he paused and shook his head, holding back his words.

"Father, what?"

"I asked Samuel to do something I should've done a long time ago. Before your mother died, before Mariselle cursed our shores, I took a lover," Braeden breathed. "She bore a child."

Alexandra's mouth dropped. Braeden continued, "You will rule Gilead, but you must make provision for your older brother. I dismissed his mother because of her station and left little to provide for either of them."

"Why?" Alexandra shook her head. "How could you?"

"There is no excuse. Egan mentioned that he met your brother, and I fear his life is now in danger. I've shirked my duty too long, allowed too many others to tend to the damage I've caused. At the very least, I can help defend the city. At the very least, I owe him that. I owe all of you that."

"Who is he? What's his name?" She peered into his face, but Braeden turned away. A guard brought him his horse, and he hoisted himself onto it.

He nodded towards his men, then glanced at her one last time. "She named him Absalom. I hope one day you'll meet him."

"And you're only telling me this now?" She stared coldly at him. "All these years."

Braeden searched her eyes. "Daughter, I've found two things to be true in this life: that no choice is ever easy, and that no path is as clear cut as you might imagine. I have done some evil to achieve what I thought was right, but the weight of those choices is heavier than I could have ever imagined. You were right about Mariselle." He turned and mounted his steed. "You were right about me as well." Braeden nodded to his guards. "Farewell, Daughter. Know that I love you."

With a flick of the wrist, he charged forward with his men, his eyes on the battle ahead but his mind on the children he would be leaving behind.

EGAN MARVELED AT THE COMMONERS as they bellowed their war cries, grim determination in their eyes. Women, farmers, and old men pressed hard against the gate as it bulged from the ramming attackers. Others stacked quivers filled with arrows for the archers on the high wall—as efficient as any platoon he'd trained. As more guards arrived to reinforce their efforts, he stopped one boy busily dousing out flames created by the occasional volley of fiery arrows that landed in the courtyard.

"You've held them this long without soldiers?"

"We're all soldiers tonight, sir. Your sergeant, Avery, was right. I'd rather die standing than live on my knees." The boy nodded and hurried away.

Egan spied Avery supporting his troops and repositioning reinforcements to hit their targets better. The lamplighter was a natural in battle.

With a loud crack, the western gate splintered open. Egan watched in horror as its great bronze hinges snapped loose. Hundreds of obsidian-mailed Amorite warriors surged through the small opening into the Ambassador's Square like black spiders flooding out of an egg sac. They shredded through the men nearby. The defenses were failing again. Egan screamed the order to charge, and three platoons of soldiers ran to defend the barricade. His men pushed back against the black tide of warriors, cutting down row after row.

"Hold them, men—hold them for as long as you can!" Egan yelled. He signaled to Avery and his archers, stationed high on the surrounding wall. "Send your arrows inward!"

"The walls, Chief!" Avery shook his head and pointed to the stairwell below. "They're scaling the walls!"

Grappling hooks flew over the upper battlements. Some latched onto the stone surfaces while others careened into the archers, sending them flying off the ledge. Like locusts swarming a field, Amorites crawled over the embrasures. Avery pushed back those he could reach before slicing through the connected ropes with his sword, letting those still ascending fall to their death.

"I need your aim!" Egan called to Avery again. "Call your men back or we are routed!"

"The barricade!" Avery commanded his archers. "Send the arrows to our inner barricade!"

The archers on the high wall turned and fired upon the attackers flooding the plaza through the broken gate, laying fifteen down in a pull. A rain of fiery arrows arced up from the Amorite ships in the harbor and impaled five bowmen.

In the chaos, Egan spied a solitary dark warrior scale an embrasure and tackle Avery from behind. The two fell from the high wall onto the cobblestone street of the plaza. Another wave of fire toppled more archers like dominoes as the second wave of Amorite climbers reached them.

Amid the flames, Avery stood and steadied himself, blood running down his leg, the crushed body of his attacker beneath him.

"Reporting for duty," a low voice rumbled behind Egan. He turned. The large brute from the medical tent stood before him, his arm bandaged, his giant hand clasping a battle-ax. "Rustag, at your service."

"You service all of Gilead." Egan nodded. "Can you fight?"

Rustag smiled. "I can kill."

"Good, you'll want a shield for . . ." Egan started, but Rustag rushed past him before he could finish. The large man dove into the wall of Amorites swarming at the barricade, swinging his ax in full circles. Five warriors were knocked back, while three others instantly lost their heads.

Egan ran to Avery's side and saw a wicked-looking dagger lodged in Avery's thigh.

"I can't walk—leave me!" Avery yelled as he held back the blood running from his wound.

"You will walk!" Egan commanded. "I've enough blood on my hands." Egan forced his arm around the lamplighter, supporting him. "Now move."

The pair pressed forward a few steps simultaneously, pausing only when attackers came at them. Egan drew each to the ground with a flash of his blade.

"You formed this defense?" he asked as he moved them back past a line of soldiers.

"Aye, Chief, from the ragtags." Avery chuckled. "Even the smallest will fight if their spark is fed. Certain death has a way of feeding us all."

"No, it's you, I think," Egan replied. "You're a beacon to us all. I'll not see you extinguished."

As they hurried forward, he could hear Rustag laughing wildly as he mowed down warrior after warrior. Gilead's soldiers rallied behind him as they pushed the Amorites back to the gateway and beyond the broken door to the head of the steps.

Egan pulled Avery past the rear barricades and waved to Helen, where she was triaging soldiers near the tent across the square. She froze as she saw them approach. Her assistants pushed past her, rushing the dying into the shelter. She screamed Avery's name as she ran to them.

"He'll live, but you must move those wounded back to the market district. We can't hold the bastards back all night," Egan said as he helped Avery into her arms.

"Aye, my lord. I can carry Taran, and help Avery." She glanced at the soldiers hobbling to cots within the tent. "But there are many here to move. I'll ask the other women to see these men are helped to the bazaar, but you may still keep the gate." Her face lightened as she nodded at Rustag toppling more warriors across the square.

The Amorite drums sounded again behind the gate, and Egan's soldiers paused throughout the plaza at the invaders' rising chant.

"Molek! Molek! Molek!"

The dark warriors at the gate retreated down the steps, and Rustag paused to catch his breath as he peered into the shadows beyond.

"Come back, whelps!" Rustag laughed.

The gravel on the cobblestones bounced as if some great mass were climbing up the last stairs.

Egan knew that sound, and his stomach dropped. The insane fear and hopelessness returned as he stared at the gateway in horror. "Get back! Rustag, get back!"

Rustag's smile dropped as a shadow rose above him.

In an instant, the remains of the great western gate were ripped from their hinges and thrown into Rustag, tossing the slaughterman aside like a ragdoll.

Molek ducked under the archway and roared. The men at the barricade ran as the giant hurled his war hammer across the plaza into the medical tent.

Egan turned to see his wounded men's bodies buried beneath its weight.

The giant lifted his head and howled again. The Amorite mass flooded past him back into the plaza, devouring the remnants of Egan's soldiers.

"Retreat!" Egan screamed, knowing it was already too late.

CHAPTER 34

THE BEAST

Lightning cracked overhead as Colin watched Mariselle emerge from her tent and move to the gallows, suspending his cage. He pressed his face to the bars to catch her gaze.

"Mariselle, look you don't need to do this . . ." he started.

"No more talk," she said, yanking on the pillory's drop rope. The bottom of the cage flew open. Colin screamed and locked his fingers into the latticed side. The metal cut into his skin as he dangled over the dark chasm.

"Damn you!" Mariselle screeched and pulled out her dagger, slicing the support rope in half. Time slowed as Colin felt himself falling with the cage into the dark foam far below.

He hit the water hard, slammed under the wash by the weight of the framework surrounding him. He struggled against his cell as it pushed him farther down under the water line into the abyss. His sleeve caught a jagged edge of bars and tangled his arm. Water filled his mouth. Colin shut it, desperate to save what air he could. The cage folded around him like a hand as he landed on the soft murky bottom.

Door, opening, something, look for it.

No opening in the bars seemed wide enough to fit more than his arm.

Where's the side of this thing?

Colin reached out with his free hand and tried to burrow his fingers under the edge of the cage. It was too deep to dig under and too heavy to lift. The darkness was all-encompassing. His hand raced across another edge of the cell and found it had also buried itself below the agitated muck. Colin settled his frantic mind. The last of the air was leaving his lungs.

Dark. Cold. This is where I die.

A thousand dreams flashed in his mind: climbing El Capitan in Yosemite, buying a boat, and spending time with his mom. But finally, his thoughts rested on Alex's face.

Yeah, that's the one. The thought surprised him.

From above, Colin saw the lightning flash through the liquid glass, illuminating the pit surrounding him. The beast was there, staring at Colin in the darkness, beating its massive tail back and forth, its four eyes gazing through him. Colin pushed away from the side of the cage, tearing his sleeve free.

The creature rushed forward. Its massive jaws opened wide.

It ripped the cage and Colin from the soil and shot upwards, breaking through the water like a missile with the metal mass wedged between its wide serrated fangs. Colin gasped as they broke the surface and felt fresh air fill his lungs again.

Within seconds he was shoved underwater as the beast drove the cage into the chasm wall. The cell squealed in agony as it collided with the rocks. Lightning flashed again. Colin stared at an infinite row of bloodstained teeth inches from his face. He hung on to the bars even harder. As massive as the creature was, it couldn't swallow the metal barrier surrounding him.

The beast gnawed its razor jaws into the metal, struggling to reach the boy in the center—one by one, the bars folded under pressure. Colin shrank back, afloat in the center of his collapsing cell. The great beast tore the cage from the rocks and carried it upwards. The monster broke the ragged pillory through the foam again, and Colin gasped for life.

Far above, Mariselle's men jeered and laughed. Above it all, Colin could hear her voice: "Tell me when he's dead," she ordered and walked away.

The beast rammed the remnant of the cage against the exposed rocks. The jagged reef held the framework in place as the creature's tongue slapped against Colin's leg, savoring his taste. Colin screamed and tried to pull himself up from its touch. With a moan, the metal hinge collapsed into the monster's mouth, and Colin's cocoon opened like a cracked egg, leaving him completely unprotected.

The creature dropped hold of the cell and swerved to the far side of the dark pool. Colin saw the beast bash against the latticed barrier blocking the way to the sea.

It wants out. It's as much a prisoner here as I am.

The creature turned and rushed forward again. Colin desperately felt for something, anything to defend himself with.

Pacem.

The word flashed in his mind. Colin dismissed it as he pulled a loose long bar from the broken cell and held it out, a miniscule defense against the reaper rushing nearer. The creature's gaping jaws filled his sight, and he screamed as he held the bar aloft.

It struck something solid, and he grasped it harder. Again, they were under the water. Lightning flashed overhead once more, illuminating the pit. Colin saw the bar he clung to was caught between two huge incisors, holding him like bait on a line. The beast chewed ferociously at it like a horse working its way through a broken bit.

Again, the word *pacem* appeared in his thoughts. They broke the surface.

"Pacem!" Colin yelled before water once again blinded him and filled his mouth. The creature slowed, and its jaws paused. Its head broke the water line. Rows of teeth surrounded Colin. "Pacem!" Colin gasped again. The creature closed its mouth shut, and darkness filled Colin's vision.

"God, no, please! Please! Pacem!" Colin cried. But the beast's tongue was still. Colin lost his grip and fell into the cavernous mouth, waiting for the pain and loss of consciousness. He landed against a back row of teeth, but they remained static.

The beast remained almost motionless as if Colin's words had lulled it to sudden sleep.

Colin felt around in the dark. Saliva, serrated edges, and muscle. All was still.

Libertas.

Another word appeared in Colin's mind. It formed a padlock and then shattered into darkness. Without a second thought, he spoke.

"Vincere libertas, amice." The voice was not his own.

The creature shot forward and smashed against the barrier. Colin rolled into the beast's front teeth, but its jaws remained shut. The creature bashed against the barrier again and again. The thick stench of rotten fish and decayed flesh filled Colin's nostrils. He wanted to gag, but there was air here, and he forced himself to breathe. He had to.

Another burst forward, and Colin heard a crack outside his fleshy prison. The beast surged forward again as if some unseen hand was leading it.

The barrier—my God, the thing has broken through.

In the darkness, he waited for the teeth to open again, for the tongue to wrap around him and pull him down into the creature's gullet, but the rows of razor teeth remained motionless.

Colin could feel a slight trickle of water leaking from the corner of the creature's mouth and draining down its throat. The rancid air was warm enough to be comfortable. In the blackness, Colin reached out and felt the bar still lodged among the rows of teeth above him. He dropped his hand. The metal rod wouldn't save him now. Better to be swallowed and die quickly than let the struggle drag on.

The beast moved ahead with purpose, and there in the mouth of death, Colin felt something different, a feeling that came across him slowly like the sun breaking through the clouds.

Pacem. The word became evident in his mind. *Peace.*

"WHAT?" MARISELLE SIGHED AS HER advisor entered her tent and bowed.

"The boy is dead."

She nodded. Not the cleanest win, but a victory nonetheless. Her advisor paused, his eyes darting to and from her face.

"What else? Speak!" she demanded.

"The beast seems to have broken through the sea barricade."

"Just as well. It served its purpose. We have more pressing matters to deal with."

Her advisor looked down and shuffled his feet like a guilty child.

"Anything else?" Mariselle asked.

"Your Highness, there are . . . messengers . . . on the outskirts of the camp. They wish to speak with you."

"I'm not holding court. Retrieve the message yourself." She moved past him and sat at her vanity. Picking up a hairbrush, she began straightening out her long brunette tresses.

"I'd rather not. They are quite adamant that it be you and you alone they see. They won't leave the shadows nor come close to our campfires," her advisor replied. "They claim to speak for Lord Dagon."

Mariselle lowered her brush and stared at him in the mirror's reflection. "Are they human?"

"No, Highness." He shook his head. "I didn't get that impression."

She stood and cleared her throat. "Hissith. I should've known."

"Should I rouse the guards?"

Mariselle shook her head. "What good would it do? They'd be slaughtered before they could draw their blades." She turned and walked out of the tent.

CHAPTER 35

A COVEN OF DEATH

Where?" Mariselle asked her guards standing around a campfire a few meters from her tent. They stood on edge, sharpening their blades. One of them nodded down the path, past the glow of the flames. She moved forward into the shadows. A chill filled the air as she followed the path into a hollow overlooked by a row of indigo bushes. She paused as the bushes rustled.

Two serpentine figures on the crest of the hill reared an entire foot higher than her. Mariselle glimpsed their tails. Their dark woven hoods covered their upper torsos and faces, but their tails were unmistakable. Their voices hissed in perfect unison.

"Ssss . . . boy. Where is he?"

Her skin prickled as she faced them. "He's gone. Dead. Fed to the beast there in the maw."

"Mussst have boy." The demons writhed. "Massster wants the boy!"

"You'll have to swim after him then. I wouldn't be surprised to see him shat out farther up the shore in a day's time."

"No!" They hissed louder. "No time! Take your camp back to cccity, reinforce the lord's warriorsss, then move to hisss ship. He isss waiting! We will finisssh what you could not." They moved back into the shadows and were gone.

Mariselle backed away several paces before turning. As trained in the dark arts as she was, she couldn't imagine what those things would want the boy's body for. Perhaps it was part of Dagon's design, or maybe it was tied to some punishment in store for her. As she hurried back to the safety of the camp, she wondered if Dagon had both in mind.

THE AMBASSADOR'S SQUARE WAS LOST and burning. Egan looked away from the rampaging flames that filled the district. The invaders had paused their pursuit to regroup, allowing Avery, Helen, and Rustag time to move the trickle of survivors down the market road to the great bazaar and the king's command post in the city's center. Egan had thought Rustag was dead when Molek threw him, but amid the chaos, the barbarian had stood again and cleared a path out of the square for those who could run to make it out.

Helen had been only inches from the tent when it had collapsed. She clutched Taran to her side in their escape with Avery, but the women she had brought to help were dead. Egan wondered how many friends she'd lost in that moment and at the calm resolution in her eyes as she strove forward without complaint.

Egan paused as he made his way up the market road, spotting his reflection in a puddle of water. His face looked haggard and desperate. His mind flashed to Molek, the giant now leading the marauders. At the first sign of battle below the grand stair, he had left wounded men as he ran for his life. How could he ever be what he claimed? How could he ever hold their gaze again?

"Your face betrays your feelings, Warrant Officer," King Braeden said as he approached. Egan immediately knelt.

"My lord, forgive me. My defense of the city has failed."

"Still, you held back the Amorites far longer than any other man here could claim and, I'll wager, far longer than they expected." The king smiled at him. "Stand, please."

Egan stood. "Speak your will and I'll do it, Your Highness. I could form a squad, a vanguard, and rush them at . . ."

"And get yourself killed in a few moment's time? No," Braeden replied. "We'll hold here at the market as long as we can and then, if need be, fall back to the castle. What's important is to ensure that the eastern gate is free and clear. I know many have sought refuge within our walls, but now I want you to lead the people out onto the moors *away* from Gilead. I'll stay back with a host of guards as a distraction. They want my head, not yours."

Egan's mouth dropped. "My lord, how could I leave you alone? Let me fight them! Let my final death cry be championed in Gilead's memory!"

"There will be no one left to remember you if you don't lead my people away," Braeden replied softly. "Egan, a great man is different than a prominent one. Being a leader means serving others first."

Egan nodded. The king beckoned to five of his soldiers. "Follow your chief by way of the cemetery to the eastern gate and lead our people to Northport. My stewards there will house you, and together you may make your plans." Braeden turned back to him. "My daughter, Alexandra, should be waiting for you by the royal tombs. Please keep her safe. She is in your charge."

Egan signaled to the soldiers to round up the people throughout the district. "Move quickly, we have little time!"

The war drums of the Amorites began to resound again in the distance.

As the guards moved ahead, herding a long line of families, he turned to look at his king one last time. The distant fires illuminated Braeden's solemn face, and Egan knew he would not see its likeness again.

CHAPTER 36

MOVING BEYOND THE PAGE

Alexandra fastened the overly large helmet to her chin. The eye slots were barely within her range of vision. The chain shirt and thick gauntlets were going to make intricate movements difficult. Slipping away from her guards at the cemetery had been easy enough. Making her way with Balaam to the nearly empty armory had also presented no problem. But standing five feet, four inches in armor that was meant for a six-foot man was almost impossible.

"You look ridiculous," Balaam huffed.

"I don't give a rat's ass what Father thinks. I'm not leaving him to die on the battlefield," her muffled voice replied from under the oversized helm.

Through her obscured view, she found the weapons. None were as ornate as her father's blade, but they might serve. Heavy maces, bastard swords with edges the length of a small child, and massive shields were everywhere, but after tugging at their handles, she didn't bother trying to pick them up. Then, from the corner of her eye, she spotted a dagger stuck into a closet door. She tossed off her gauntlets and closed her hand around the blade's hilt. It fit perfectly. She yanked it from the door and stumbled back. Her helmet fell to the ground and rolled up next to the Logos scroll she had left near the doorway. Alexandra bit her lip as she glanced at the manuscript.

"Samuel left it in my keeping, but it's more of an anchor than anything." She turned to Balaam. "I can't fit it on me, and well, this place is no good at all."

The donkey's eyes went wide. "Don't you dare. I'm already stuck with that conch gouging my side."

"Balaam! I need you to take this." Alexandra picked up the scroll and moved toward him.

"I'm not a courier, m'lady. I'll stay by your side, as is my duty."

"Well, I'm going to the front lines," she replied.

"I'll be happy to carry your message elsewhere," Balaam chuffed. "But this scroll is much more than a parcel."

She pushed it into the saddlebag lying across his flanks.

"I know. That's why I need you to take it somewhere safe—or to someone who can keep it so . . . The boy, I think. Maybe he should be the one, if he's still alive."

"Are you sure there's no other treasure you'd like me to ferry about?"

"A ferry can move, at least. I have no other options. If Samuel was right, the boy must have these. He's our one hope—though I don't really see how he could be."

"You fancy him, don't you?" Balaam asked.

Alexandra took a step back. "Why would you ever think that?"

"I've noticed the way you look at him. A bit of fancy, I suppose, is no bad thing."

"He's hardly at my station, Balaam."

"Aye, and when has that ever stopped you from doing what

you liked?" Balaam scoffed. "Of course the chief warrant officer has eyes for you too, so you have your pick of the litter."

"Egan and I are friends. He's loyal to my father."

"Yet he seems preoccupied with your safety."

"I'm the princess; it's his job. Besides, he's at least ten years older than me," she said and smiled. The thought had crossed her mind, but she had never presumed their playful banter while training years ago had been more than that.

"Eight, by my counting, but I'm only a donkey." Balaam snorted.

"Excuse me, but the last thing I need right now is to be courted. Especially not from some strange lad who can barely speak or from a would-be warrior, playing patrol through the city." Alexandra immediately bit her tongue. Her harsh words already stung false.

"Egan has risked his life for us, my lady," Balaam replied quietly.

"I'm sorry. You're right." She nodded. "I suppose my duty as future queen would be to find an acceptable suitor."

"Not your duty, Princess. Just your heart—it makes no difference to me who you favor. Chief or boy."

"Can you find the boy? Can you help him?" Alexandra put her hand on Balaam's mane.

"Doubtful. I'm a donkey, not a tracking hound. But I can try. I know the witch spoke of Korah's Maw. If he still lives, perhaps I'll find him there." The donkey nodded and moved to the doorway. "And me rescuing him with the kingdom's treasures dangling from my rear is absurd, but desperate times . . ."

"Thank you, and Balaam?"

The donkey paused. "Yes, Majesty?"

"Take care of yourself as well," she said, wondering if she would see her companion again.

Balaam bowed his neck low. "It's been an honor . . . my queen." He turned and walked out into the night.

Alexandra gathered her helmet and followed a few minutes later, deciding to leave the gauntlets off. Barehanded, she could at least hold a horse's reins and her weapon. As she moved across the empty, rain-swept courtyard toward the stables, she paused to look around the open grounds. The mob had dispersed at the sight of the king, and some order had returned, yet she felt like everyone was saying goodbye. As if some great chapter of her life was coming to a close, and she had been left behind to close the book.

CHAPTER 37

STRANGE BEDFELLOWS

Balaam's heels echoed on the cobblestones as he trotted towards the eastern gate again. In the distance, he could hear the fighting and see the flames engulfing the city's western half. He wondered if perhaps he should've followed the Princess instead.

"Completely reckless," he muttered to himself. "At this point, I should know better. I just hope the old stranger is watching. I hope he sees how much prudence I've learned."

The donkey skirted the cemetery, still wary of its shadows, and found his way to the portcullis of the eastern gate that opened to the moors beyond. There he saw Gilead's chief warrant officer speaking with one of his soldiers as a steady line of people hurried by them into the city.

"Chief, we've just reopened the gates to let more in. I can't send them away."

"We won't be. We'll be leading them to Northport, as the king ordered. Gather the guards; pull them from the barriers at the bazaar, if needed. The people are our priority, now. The people and the Princess."

A soldier ran up and saluted. "Sorry, Chief, she slipped away. I looked everywhere in the vicinity."

Egan shook his head. "How could she not be there? She was your charge!"

"Yes, sir. She, well, I turned my back for a moment, sir. We were leaving the cemetery you see, and, well, she was gone."

"She's the heir to the throne! If she dies, Gilead will perish with her! Are you sure she's not among the tombs?"

"No, sir, we checked. Even the rabble have cleared this area since yesterday. A few men are still searching the castle. Perhaps they'll find Her Majesty."

"Very well." Egan sighed. "Organize the people and ready them to leave. I'll do a final search around the tombs myself." Egan took a deep breath and strode away down an alley that led to the cemetery gateway. Balaam followed in the shadows, at a distance.

"The girl needs a defender. He's as good as any," Balaam mumbled as he trailed Egan past the open gateway, stone monuments, and crypts. Emblems of trees and faces adorned many of the crypt doors. Half-broken statues of cherubs watched the pair creep by.

"Damnable night," Egan muttered, pausing to look across the white-marbled monuments. He approached the royal mausoleum and ran his hand across the freshly sealed door of Samuel's entombment.

Balaam stumbled on a cobblestone, then quickly scurried behind a crypt.

Egan turned toward the noise, but Balaam stayed hidden.

"Princess?" Egan paused to listen. He slowly wrapped his hand around the hilt of his sword.

Balaam sighed. There was no easy way to do this. He stepped up behind the chief. "He was a rotten old codger, but he was my friend."

Egan spun around to face the voice, and his sword flew from its sheath.

"What? Who?" Egan looked past the riderless donkey. "Come out! I'll not play games with you!"

"Good. I hate wasting time," Balaam replied.

Egan dropped his sword, and his mouth followed.

"You . . . you speak? You speak!" Egan's eyes widened.

Balaam sighed. "Yes, I hear that a lot. Look, the Princess is who you're looking for? Yes? She's on her way to her father's side. I should think she'd need some help. She won't listen to me. Never has."

"What black magic has Mariselle spun here? How can you speak?" Egan picked up his sword and held it outright as he slowly approached the donkey.

"Mariselle had nothing to do with it. It's a long story, but I doubt we have time to get into it. Suffice to say Samuel gave me shelter when no one else would." Balaam stared at the crypt door for a moment in silence. "Safe travels, old man." He turned back to Egan. "Best if you hurry along. I'd try the castle."

Before Egan could respond, a guard emerged from the shadows.

"Chief!" the soldier called.

"The donkey. He can . . . well, he's a donkey that . . ." Egan stared at Balaam as the donkey scooped up a patch of grass into his mouth and smiled at him wryly.

"Sir?" The soldier looked at him quizzically. "Chief, you must hurry to the fields outside the eastern gate. Mariselle and her men were spotted approaching from beyond the King's Way. We did as you said—we have a line of families outside the walls, nearly a half mile long. I doubt we can herd them all back inside in time. They have nowhere to run."

"How many men are with her?" He asked.

"Easily twenty, sir. Though I'd wager more are following. We have only six armed men, including you. I can close the gates but we have no defense beyond that."

"More lambs for the slaughter." His brow furrowed. "No. Not again. Those within the walls have some protection at least. Go then, ensure our men have the weapons they need. I'll meet you outside the gate in a moment. This time we'll bring the fight to them."

The soldier saluted and slipped away into the night. Egan eyed Balaam without a word before turning away. After a few strides forward, he paused. "Whether you be a mad dream or not, I hope she is as determined as you claim."

Balaam watched as the young chief straightened and moved forward, ready to face whatever fate had in store outside the gates.

ABSALOM WAITED IN THE SHADOWS for over an hour, watching as Mariselle's men ransacked the halls for valuables before they fled, and then continued to listen for any sign of footfalls for some time after. Patience was an old friend, one he had learned to trust. It had served him the finest valuables over the years, and tonight it would lead him to a prize he might retire on. Finding the king's chest by way of the Princess had been fruitless, his bargain with the strange boy a waste, but perhaps these detours had their place. All eyes were outward to the siege; for a short window, no one minded the castle itself.

He moved silently down a stone hallway. The tapestries lining it had been partially torn from their rods or left cluttered on the floor. His shadow crept in and out of doorways like a mouse, furtively darting, pausing to listen, then moving again.

"Not a bloody soul," he whispered to himself.

He came to the Great Hall of the Lion. The feasting tables had been knocked on end, and platters and broken chalices lay strewn about. Mariselle's retreat from the palace with her entourage had been a hasty one.

He approached an upended chair and lifted a goblet from the floor.

"You probably took all the wine as well." Absalom shook his head as he tossed it aside. If the sounds of battle were to be believed, he knew his ship was in ruins. The harbormaster was most likely dead. He would find no compensation for his losses there. But here, here—

The sound of armored boots on stone echoed into the chamber. Absalom slid into the shadows behind a large stone pillar.

"Any luck?" a guard's voice called.

"None, and I doubt we will with further search. Princess Alexandra wouldn't have a reason to return here. I've already checked the royal quarters; what little is left of them. Mariselle stole everything, save for the king's chest. She probably didn't have the key and the damn thing weighs a ton."

"Aye, I wouldn't be surprised if that witch ran off with half the treasury. Come on then. The chief won't like it, but there's no sign of the Princess here."

"I'm more worried about the king. Now that he's up and about again ..."

Their voices trailed off as they left the great hall.

Absalom walked back into the light and glanced up at the empty throne.

"Up and about, are you? Needed one last conquest before you finally drop?"

Still, the king's chest sounded promising. The bastard owed him something before the city imploded, and the old man was going to pay.

After a few twists and turns, Absalom found his way to the royal quarters, and what he guessed by the size of the chamber was the king's bedroom.

The room smelled foul, like death and decay. He saw a charred serpent's body smoldering in the fireplace.

"What in the nine hells were you up to?"

He spotted a large dark walnut trunk at the foot of the bed. Three inset locks adorned its front. He kneeled beside it. Scratches and gouges decorated the face of the chest as if several hands had tried to break the locks or pry open the lid.

"You couldn't quite manage it, could you, Mariselle?" Absalom said as he pulled a leather pouch from his belt and unrolled it. A set of lockpicks gleamed before him in the torchlight. Within seconds he had selected the correct sizes and went to work on the locks, massaging the tumblers with the minutest of movements. After a few moments, all three locks unfastened, and he opened the lid.

The chest's interior was empty save for a leatherbound journal.

"You've got to be joking." Absalom slumped onto his rear and palmed his face. His father hadn't left one cent for his daughter. At least he was consistent. Absalom reached in and grabbed the journal. He thumbed through a few pages. It was a ledger of sorts. Many of the pages were facts and figures, lists and invoices, but as he continued to scan them, he saw more and more of them contained personal entries. Then his eyes froze. Absalom saw his name. His eyes reread the passage over and over again.

It makes my heart glad to see Alexandra happy. Still, I wonder of the other—Absalom. I've spotted him from time to time in the marketplace . . .

"You knew," Absalom whispered. He closed the journal and clenched it in his hand. "And you did nothing."

"Nothing is all you'll have once we've locked you away. Put your hands up!" a guard in full armor yelled, standing in the doorway, holding a dagger.

Absalom dropped the journal and jumped to his feet. He drew his blade.

"Who are you? What business do you have in this chamber?"

Absalom studied the guard and took a step forward. This soldier wore his armor wrong, the bindings were loosely tied, the man's stance was off, and his voice sounded like . . .

The guard lunged forward with the dagger. Absalom spun to the side and grabbed the guard from behind, ripping his helmet off. Absalom held the blade to his attacker's neck and saw that it wasn't a man. The head of long hair was in tangles, and the skin was too fair. Only one female remained in Gilead's palace . . .

"Princess Alexandra?" Absalom's grip on her loosened.

"I'd say you have me at a disadvantage, but . . ." She twitched her dagger, and Absalom glanced down. She had her blade angled up into his crotch. "Bring your weapon closer, and you'll be a eunuch."

"I'll back away if you do the same," Absalom replied. He fingered the grip of his dagger.

"Fine," Alexandra replied.

"Fine." He nodded.

The two simultaneously separated to opposite sides of the room and faced each other.

"Who are you? What business do you have rifling through my father's things?" she asked.

"No one of any import, I assure you," Absalom replied. "Your father owed me a debt. I was fool enough to believe there might be something of worth for me to collect here."

"My father pays all his debts. I doubt he'd ever take up with someone like you," Alexandra said.

"Then you'd be right. He hasn't acknowledged me once in my lifetime." Absalom stowed his dagger and looked around the room. There was nothing else worth taking.

She paused. A light of recognition spread across her face. "You're him, aren't you? The bastard?"

"I've been called worse." Absalom kneeled and stowed his lockpick set.

"Sorry. You're Absalom, yes?" Alexandra asked and gazed at him.

Absalom stood again and mockingly bowed. "At your service, m'lady."

She folded her arms. "You picked an opportune time to claim your inheritance. With all that's going on, what did you plan on doing?"

"I could ask you the same." Absalom smirked. "I doubt that armor is your normal attire, and you look a fool the way you hold a blade."

"I know which end does the stabbing," she retorted.

"And do you know where our father is now? I'd like to have words with him. If the Amorites haven't chopped him to pieces yet."

"Bite your tongue! You may be blood, but he's still your king."

Absalom ignored her chide as he approached her. "But the question remains—why are you wandering the castle dressed as a guard? Unless . . ." Absalom stifled a laugh. "Are you planning on secretly joining him on the front lines? You are, aren't you? How precious."

"It's the least I can do, and it's better than skirting about in the shadows, pillaging whatever you can get your hands on," she said, raising her dagger again.

"Tell you what, Princess. You take me to your father, and I'll pretend you're the real deal. I'll even help you fasten that helmet on tighter so it doesn't blow off in a strong breeze," Absalom said, taking a few steps closer to her.

"Why should I? I won't let you harm him," she replied.

"There are more than enough people within the walls of the city that want him dead. I just want . . . answers. Otherwise—" He rushed forward and tried to grab the knife.

Alexandra instantly sliced his finger.

"Gah!" he backed away, nursing his hand. "We'll both find ourselves in quite a mess. I'll be locked in my cell"—he glanced about the room—"and you'll be locked in yours."

CHAPTER 38

In the Belly of the Beast

The beast had been swimming for nearly an hour as Colin stared at the row of jagged teeth keeping him interred. How many miles had they gone? How far out to sea were they? If the monster ever let him go, there'd be little chance of him swimming back. Even worse, if the creature happened to open its mouth while deeply submerged, tons of water pressure would instantly collapse on him. Colin saw his head popping like a balloon.

"Well, kid," he mumbled, "how the hell do you get out of this one?"

You don't. The reply seemed to crop up quite naturally in his head.

"I don't? I don't. Great. Thanks for that." Colin shook his head.

Nothing you've done has been of your own accord. Why do you insist on relying on it now? The thought blinked into his mind again as if someone were speaking in his ear.

"Ok, so maybe I can think up another one of those words? Expelus Meus!" He shouted at the teeth barring his way, but nothing happened. It had been worth a shot.

The words are a gift, the voice echoed in his mind, *given at precisely the right time.*

"God, or whoever," Colin called, "I need to live. I can't do this on my own."

He sighed and shimmied back from the teeth. He closed his eyes. Suddenly he felt a surge upwards. The smell he had come to tolerate was now even more rotten. Colin covered his nose and peered down into the dark throat of the creature. He heard a flood of saliva rushing towards him from the monster's stomach.

Oh no. Not that, he thought just before warm green bile flooded around him, clinging to his skin and plunging up his nose. He gagged and instantly tasted the putrid essence in his mouth.

The beast crested the water line and vomited Colin up with the rank bile.

Colin coughed and retched as he swam free from the acidic mucus. He felt the powerful thrust of the creature's tail as it moved below his feet and back to the depths. The sound of rain dancing on the water filled his ears and rinsed the slime from his hair. The cold salt wash was a welcome taste. Then, barely visible in the night and closer than he'd dared to hope, he saw cresting waves breaking on a shore. He swam for it and grasped at the packed sand as the tide carried him to the beach. Colin gagged as partially digested fish and phlegm clung to his skin, and he threw up. After several seconds he collapsed and let the waves wash over him, carrying away the mess.

Time passed, the cold of the night air crept up Colin's arms, and he shivered as he stood on unsteady feet. The rain had not let up. He looked around and saw that the waves had thrown him into a small cove that cut into a forest. Nothing looked familiar. If what Samuel had said was true, he couldn't expect the morning sun anytime soon. Moonlight peeked through the clouds.

Colin staggered up the sandy shore and collapsed again to get his bearings. The trees towered over him like redwoods, but all of them seemed to be dead and leafless.

Cold. So cold.

He forced himself to his feet, eager to escape the breeze blowing across the water, and stumbled farther into the woods, following a hillside up. He tripped over a root hiding in the shadows and tumbled down an embankment in a single motion.

Colin rested for a moment amid the crushed leaves and bracken. "Nothing's ever easy, is it?" he griped as he stared into the starless sky.

No, baby, but who said it was supposed to be? his mother's voice echoed in his mind.

A canned response she'd given him on bad days when he felt like the world was closing in to smother him. It all seemed like a lifetime ago.

Now get back on your feet.

Picking himself back up, he clenched his fists.

Must get warm. But warmth was a ghost in this place, hiding in the shadows, always just out of reach.

CHAPTER 39

A Call beyond Reason

Chief, I can help you," Avery said, clutching his bandaged leg.

"If you did, I fear your wife would attack me from the rear." Egan smiled and patted his shoulder. "Rest for now. The night is long, and I know I'll have need of you again soon."

Avery nodded as he hobbled back to Helen's side and took Taran's hand when the child tried to squirm away.

"I'll settle these two, my lord," Helen called, "and tend to those that need it. Just send them my way."

Egan turned and assessed the people rushing by him. Most of them were women, children, or the elderly. None could hold a weapon—even if there had been extra to give.

"The castle armory is too far," Egan said, shaking his head. "There must be something they can use." He grasped the old leather sling at his side and wished it was enough. Turning his focus to the incoming crowds, he moved toward the eastern archway and portcullis. Two ladders went up from the ground to the turrets on the high wall, but no weapons were stored there either. Perhaps some people could slip by in the darkness and scatter across the rolling hills, but not enough. Mariselle's men would be on them in moments.

Standard tactics would not work here. How could an unarmed man fight a multitude? There were going to be far too many refugees fleeing to go unnoticed.

"Fog's rolling in, Chief. They might slip away." One of his guards pointed to the haze creeping in across the moors.

"Peasants with their families, carts, and belongings in tow?" Egan shook his head. "Not for long. They'll be slaughtered like cattle, and I will be the one who funneled them to their deaths." He felt like a fraud, a child making at war with nothing but a stick in his hand.

What did you ever see in me? His thoughts dwelled on his father's face. *This night will go down as the blackest in Gilead's history.*

Then it struck him—the image of his father standing in the doorway of their home all those years ago, beating his club, screaming himself hoarse to keep the sabers away.

"How far is Mariselle's vanguard from us?" Egan asked the soldier.

"Well, the watchmen say maybe half a league. We can see their torches in the distance."

"That's ten minutes as the horse rides. Call all the people back!"

"Chief, I'm sure our armory in the castle has weapons enough for the people to use."

"And how fast could you run with an armload of them?" Egan replied. "By the time you got to the castle, her men would be on us. I need you here, helping the civilians find cover."

"But sir, we have nowhere to hide them! Even if they were to run into the cemetery."

"They're not going to hide *behind* the walls, man. They're going to hide *in front* of them. Douse all the torches in the archway and the turrets. Have every elder and infirm line the great wall. Tell them to put their damn backs to it! Be sure they spread out, shoulder to shoulder!"

Egan ran ahead to the gateway. "Back all of you! Line the walls! If you can climb a ladder, come to me!" Several women and boys came to his side, and he motioned them up. "Stand an arm's length apart up there, and be ready to make some noise!"

The soldier ran to Egan's side. "Forgive me, Chief, but they'll be sitting ducks!"

Egan smiled. "Do you think so? Come with me!" He led his man through the gateway and to the outer wall, diverting people from the gate to line up against the great stone barrier. With hesitant nods and wary eyes, they followed his commands and shuffled shoulder to shoulder down its length, nearly disappearing into the shadows and the mist.

"That's it! Keep going the entire length! No doubling up!" Egan cried and motioned to two of his soldiers to help those who needed it. He nodded to his assistant to follow him as he walked several feet away from the city's wall. He turned around to face his man. "Now, how many 'ducks' do you count from where you stand?"

The soldier bit his lip and peered through the haze. "Hard to say, sir. They're hard to see in this light. Not that there is any."

"Exactly! And if you're only a few feet away how much less visible will they be from several hundred yards?"

"Perhaps, but they're still just . . ." the soldier began.

Egan turned to the people lining the wall. "People let me hear your war cry! Whoop!"

A few meager yelps reached Egan's ears. He could sense the fear and confusion the people felt. Egan cleared his throat.

"Listen to me, and listen well. You know this eternal darkness is unnatural. We've all suffered and bumbled our way through it for the last year. But we can turn the witch's weapon against her! She doesn't know the number of our fighting men, and in that alone we can make her pause. So, whoop like your life depends on it! Cry 'Gilead' with all your might! Those above, high on the walls, beat your chest and howl! Let their ears hear the mighty roar of your voices!"

The people's voices raised in a low chant.

"Louder! Louder!" Egan waved at the people on the walls. "Louder, all of you! Put the fear of the Maker into them!"

The howl of three hundred voices came together, and as if orchestrated by an unseen hand, the chant of their kingdom filled the night.

"Gil-e-ad! Gil-e-ad! Gil-e-ad!" they cried in unison.

Egan turned to the soldier. "Now how many fighting men do we have?"

"It sounds like . . . like we have an army!" The soldier's voice was barely audible over the chanting. "This is unheard of, where'd you learn this?" he asked Egan.

"From my father. Come, have our soldiers mount their horses and brace for combat. We'll drive forward to meet them and take them down, one by one if needed, with a sounding army at our backs."

CHAPTER 40

Moving Targets

Balaam crossed the moors and over a rolling hill into a hollow. The eastern gate and the refugees swarming to it shrank behind him. The boy was probably dead, but Balaam had sworn he'd try. The conch horn and scroll inside his saddle bags shifted, and he paused to shake and adjust his flanks.

"The two greatest treasures of Gilead are secured with a bit of cinch." He sighed. "Why don't they just paint a target on my back and be done with it?"

The donkey paused to look around. The heath and high grass would offer even less protection.

"Why in the Maker's name did I agree to this?" He snorted. "How exactly am I supposed to find anyone out here, let alone rescue them?" But he knew the answer before he finished uttering the words. He'd been forced to learn one insidious fact in all his travels. Life moved you forward, no matter your plans, even if the path ahead was unclear. Korah's Maw was still some distance, and he knew the trail was hard to follow even in daylight. Perhaps another refugee would know.

Balaam looked about him and realized no one was near. "This won't do," he mumbled to himself. The distant chanting echo of people's voices rolled across the hilltops before their cries were quieted by thunder overhead. For a time, he wondered at it until the wind spurned him to move on, occasionally pausing to shake raindrops from his ears.

"Hooves?" He turned his head, listening. "Someone ahead, just over the ridge. Probably lost too." He galloped up the hill and right into Mariselle on her steed. She reared her mare back.

"Enemies! Draw your weapons!" the queen's advisor called from behind. Ten soldiers raced past Balaam down into the hollow behind him but found nothing. They quickly returned and encircled the donkey.

Mariselle steadied her horse. She glared at Balaam, but she didn't recognize him to his great relief.

"The rider must have heard us approach and left the ass. He'll be warning them. We must hurry and strike the gate before they can rally! Grab the donkey. We can use it to haul the supplies!" She rushed past Balaam, and her soldiers followed.

The last Amorites in the vanguard threw a noose around Balaam's throat and dragged him along in the rear. The rope dug into his neck, but he kept his head down. One of Samuel's proverbs echoed in his mind.

Even a fool is thought wise when he is silent.

CHAPTER 41

In the Grasp of Giants

Molek gazed on as the dark horde of Amorites broke through the doors of homes and shops throughout the square, setting fires with their torches. Curtains, beds, tables—everything burned. The few people still hiding within their homes were pulled out by their necks and slaughtered in the street. The warriors became more violent, furious, and crazed with every new victim cut open.

Molek surveyed the carnage and laughed as he watched his little men have their fun. Why Master Dagon was so anxious about the resistance was beyond him. These sheep were no threat. He would soon start collecting his usual trophies. Every city they had toppled along the way had added to his collection. From every empire he crushed, he took a necklace of heads. Tonight's strand would be the greatest yet, and he knew whose head would adorn its center—the cowering officer who had run from him at the docks.

Yes, his would do nicely.

THE FOREST FLOOR WAS SPRINKLED with pine needles, bark fragments, ferns, and stones. In the sparse moonlight, Colin collected what kindling he could find. Once he had an armload, he carried it to a clear spot near a large stone outcropping. The massive jagged rock formed the likeness of an arrowhead angled towards the sky, and he welcomed its meager shelter from the persistent rain. His hands shook as he tried to build a fire. The chill and damp had worked their way from his fingers to his arms and legs. He stopped every few seconds to wrap his arms around himself for warmth.

Sticks should be angled like a teepee. Have to get air to the bottom. But his hands ached with the chill, forcing him to stop and breathe into his cupped palms. He finally steadied the kindling onto each other and paused to study his handiwork. *It's unsteady, but it should hold . . .*

A strong wind blew in above the upper branches, sending his kindling flying across the forest floor.

"Damnit!" Colin exploded and kicked the stone outcropping with his foot. "Ouch!" He knelt and fingered his stubbed toe within his sneaker. The cold crept to his core.

Heat. Need heat. Screw the pyre. Just a stick. Just one little spark.

He got up and searched for any piece of wood that might hold a flame longer than a second or two. Colin's neck tingled as if some presence was nearby, watching him. He turned to see the shadows behind him, but no trace of a living thing stirred.

He finally found a large chunk of bark and returned to the outcropping. He backed up against the massive rock and knelt beside it.

"Okay, I rub some sticks together and I'm good." He knew

it wasn't that easy. But he grabbed a nearby twig and rubbed it furiously against the bark.

The twig snapped. Colin clenched his fists again and shook the sting from his fingers.

"Okay, something harder, something . . ."

Again, Colin felt eyes studying his moves. He spun around. "Hello?"

Only silence answered. He clenched his fists and slowly turned back. He remembered the stone. The stone he'd found inside Mr. Potter's box that he still carried in his jeans. Since his time in the dungeon, he'd forgotten all about it. He searched his pant legs and felt it still in his pocket. He pulled it out with the crumpled photo of him and his father camping. His body shivered as he peered at the picture.

"Slow and steady wins the race, son," his father had said and smiled as Colin had worked to start their cooking fire that day. "It doesn't always come easy, but if you keeping trying it will eventually come."

His mother had been there and had nodded as she looked on.

"Why's it gotta be so hard? Can't we just get a burger or something?" Colin had whined as he struggled to get a spark. "I suck at this. I'm just gonna fail."

He remembered how his father had knelt and tousled his hair.

"I guess that's why persistence is failing nineteen times and getting it to work the twentieth, buddy. So, if you're going through hell . . ." He paused as he looked at Colin's mom.

"Keep going," she said and winked at him.

Another shiver rippled across Colin's body, bringing him back to the present. The thought of his mother returned to him. Was she still comatose in a hospital bed, alone? What hell was she facing? What dark corner between life and death was she trapped in? *I don't have time to freeze to death.*

He took a breath and steadied his hand as he gripped the stone. He ran it up, and down the bark, and for a second, he saw a trace of smoke.

The rock broke through the rotten piece of timber. Colin balled the photo in his fist. He wanted to scream. It was just another lie, just another way to fail.

"You're doing it wrong," a deep gravelly voice said from behind him.

Colin spun around, but no one was there. He looked to the shadows but saw nothing. He pulled himself up to the top of the outcropping and peered into the forest's darkness.

"Come out! Whoever you are!" he yelled.

"Would you mind not standing on my head?" the voice grunted. Colin felt the stone shift underneath his feet, and he fell backward off the rock and onto the ground. There before him was the most enormous face he'd ever seen.

CHAPTER 42

An Unhappy Reunion

King Braeden stood on the rooftop of a shop near the bazaar gate to see. The fires from the Ambassador's Square still raged. The light rain did nothing to quench the flames. Below the shop, Braeden watched as his meager retinue of guards and volunteers piled barrels, carts, and timber into the archway. The barricade would do little against the horde slowly making its way to them. Braeden looked to the sky. "Maker, help us," he whispered.

A low grunt caught the king's attention. He turned to see Rustag standing behind him. The towering man was not unknown to him. Braeden had wanted the Agronian to serve in the guard years ago, but Mariselle hadn't liked his demeanor and insisted he be kept as a jailor for the lower dungeons.

"Thank you for your service, Rustag. Without you, I fear more people would have perished tonight. I wish I could give you a proper reward, but I doubt I will have anything to offer come morning, if this night ever ends."

"Morning will come, my king. I'll fight to the death to ensure you see it," Rustag replied.

Braeden shook his head as he looked past the archway and down the curving cobblestone street leading to the square. The Amorite battalions would be forming. He could hear their rallying cries.

"They'll be here soon. If only I could stop up this archway . . ." Braeden said.

"Perhaps this man can help then. He seems intent on talking to you," Rustag grunted and motioned at the stairway behind him.

Absalom stepped forward.

Braeden gazed into his son's eyes for a moment. The boy had become a man.

"Rustag, you can leave us. I'll be quite alright," Braeden said.

Rustag glanced at Absalom and nodded to the king before trudging back down the steps.

"You're trusting . . . Father," Absalom said.

"If you wanted to kill me, I imagine you would've done so by now." Braeden folded his arms.

"I found this," Absalom said, tossing the patriarch his journal. "So you knew?"

Braeden looked down at his journal and thumbed a few pages. "Of course I knew, Absalom. I've watched you since you were a baby."

Absalom nodded and bit his lip. He moved to the wall and stared at the flames burning the western quarter.

"And . . . nothing? You wouldn't acknowledge me? Send some succor for my mother? I wasn't worth it?"

Braeden turned and stood beside him, following his gaze across the city. "No, son . . . I never felt that way. It's true I never loved your mother. It was a single night's tryst. But you . . ." He reached out to Absalom, but the privateer instantly backed away.

Braeden continued, "Months later I caught her eye in the marketplace. She was selling fruit and heavy with child. I knew. I had my men leave food for her while she carried you. The night you were born, I was there. Your mother gave birth to you in the castle. My own personal surgeon delivered you. As a young man, I sailed to the western isles, conquered the northern lands, and saw countless battles, and I was stalwart throughout. But when I first saw you, I was afraid. And ashamed."

Absalom turned to his father. "Ashamed? Then I'm glad I ransacked your palace. Consider it payment past due."

"No, Absalom, I was ashamed of myself. I was afraid of what others might have said. And as you grew and Alex was born, the truth became harder to tell. I wish I'd had the courage then. Leaving you was a mistake." Braeden finally faced his son. "There are no words to express how sorry I am."

"You are sorry. But the deed is done." Absalom replied and turned away for a moment, lost in thought. "Perhaps in time we'll speak on it again, but for now I'd ask you to keep your spies tethered and stay out of my life. I was planning to leave the city until your friends came knocking." He looked back to the narrow market road leading to the distant fiery blazes.

Braeden nodded. There were more pressing matters. "My worst fears are realized tonight. Gilead is doomed."

Absalom's eyes flashed angrily before he cleared his throat and finally spoke. "In my time scurrying the streets, I learned how to pick many a lock. I wonder if you're aware of the lamplighter stations."

Braeden glanced at Absalom. "Of course. We keep wicks, oil, and sundries in them; hardly a defense."

"Those sundries include a peculiar black powder, and when mixed with the whale oil you import, it makes a rather nice bang."

Braeden's eyebrow raised. "What are you saying?"

Absalom smiled cruelly. "I'm saying if Gilead is going to die, let her go out with such a blast that we take them with us." He pointed up and down the market street and the homes and shops lining it. "They'd make wonderful tinderboxes, don't you think? Ready to burst on the Amorite's ranks as they pass."

Braeden shook his head. "People's homes . . . some of them may still be in hiding."

"And they will be burned alive regardless!" Absalom laughed bitterly. "I'm sorry I have no grand scheme that clears you from all guilt, but if you truly care for your people, you'll do what's required, no matter the cost."

Absalom's words stung like a slap in the face.

"I see." The king mused for a moment. Egan and his men had hopefully evacuated any remaining people from their homes, but there was no way to be sure and no time to check. Any that remained would die in the flames in an instant or die at the hand of the Amorites, slowly. There were no good options left. "And what men would you have me send to risk their lives in this venture?"

Absalom looked out across the city. "She's more a mother to me than the woman you bedded. I know every street, every back alley, every crack in her cobblestone."

"Fine. Take Rustag with you. Gather the supplies as quickly as possible. Set the charges."

Absalom turned and hurried down the steps past a soldier standing sentinel—a soldier who stood uneasily in a chest plate and helmet much too large, who'd heard every word of their conversation and wondered if her father's son was as forgiving as he seemed.

CHAPTER 43

THE WAKING OF THE MOUNTAIN

Colin stared into the giant stone face. What had first appeared to be simple crevices in the huge rock now gazed at him; slight outcroppings above the holes moved up slightly like eyebrows, and a long curved crack below it opened to a dark cavernous mouth that echoed when it spoke.

"If you insist on building a fire, you'll need the right rock for the task."

The ground shook slightly beneath Colin, and a chunk of black obsidian-like rock tumbled down the stone face and rolled next to Colin's foot. Shock set itself into Colin's face like rust on metal.

"Please . . . please don't kill me." Colin gulped and crawled back up against a tree.

The face furrowed its stone brow and peered at him. "Should I kill you? I had not thought of that . . . but perhaps . . ."

Colin shook his head frantically. "Please no, no."

The face softened. "No, crushing you serves no purpose. You're already such a tiny pebble."

"What are you?" Colin asked and wondered if he could get to his feet quick enough to run.

"I am . . ." the face said. "I am as old as the mountains. Indeed, in the first dawn, I was a great mountain, but time has worn me down . . . time and wind and water."

"What magic controls you? Do you serve Mariselle? The Amorites? Dagon? What do they call you?" Colin asked as he pulled himself up.

"Many questions for such a small pebble. I serve no one, save the Maker. What am I called?" The face looked down as if deep in thought. "I had a name, but I've forgotten it. It was a good name, I think . . . but I've been asleep for so long."

"Are you real?" Colin shook his head as he stepped closer to the face.

"As real as rock. Yes. But you've posed a good question . . . my name . . . hmmm."

Colin looked around the woods. "Do you know where we are? You see, I'm lost and . . ." Colin's hands started to shake again with cold.

The face looked up at him. "Yes, I do see. You're here."

"No, I mean where is here?" Colin asked as he rubbed his hands together, his teeth chattering.

The stone face raised an eyebrow as if trying to comprehend. "Here is here, and there, and there." His eyes gazed out across the expanse of the wood. "It's all the same to me. I'm everywhere, you know. Every rock is part of me. Every stone forms my being." The face stared at Colin and frowned as he shivered. "I can stand the rain and water, but you, little pebble, are made of flesh. Make your fire."

Colin knelt beside the wood he'd dropped and picked up the

flint the great rock had given him, careful not to turn his back to the behemoth.

"Use the stone you have with the one I gave you. Two stones can make a spark when they're the right ones."

Colin knocked his stone against the dark flint. A spark caught hold of the timber. He quickly blew on it and added nearby pine needles until the smoke became a slightly warming blaze. He sighed as he sat beside it and gazed at the face across from him. "Thank you. So, you're . . . you're everywhere? You're in the mountains in the distance and here?" Colin asked.

"My mind wanders when I'm not sleeping. Sometimes I am the bedrock of a mountain peak, sometimes I am in the watery deep, but most times I am here. This place holds my memory . . . This is where I began."

Colin looked around. The dark, leafless wood seemed an unlikely nursery. "You began here? How?"

"How else? I was formed from the dust—like you, like everything. This was the Maker's garden once. All life was chipped from this place. But the green left long ago, and all that's left are dead trees and silent stones."

"Dead trees? The Dead Wood? Is that what this place is called?" Colin asked.

"It's a new name for this place, but yes. Long ago it was called Erewhon."

Colin's mind raced as he thought out loud. "Samuel told me about this . . . The vision showed me this place . . . Tell me, is there a tree nearby, a great burnt tree, a tree that a man once . . . died on?"

The face became sullen. "Who are you again? I was so caught up trying to remember my name, I never asked for yours."

Clearly, the creature knew of the tree if Colin could only convince it to tell him. He tried to speak his name, but the words were silent again. Finally, he sighed. "I . . . I can't speak it for some reason. Maybe there's a curse on me, but I can't seem to say it. It's almost like I've forgotten it too."

"A name is a powerful thing, little pebble, and to call one's true name can render even a stone heart to dust. The Maker named us all, and by our names, we are defined. To forget your name is either very good . . . or very bad. I'm not sure which. But at least I am not alone in forgetting mine."

"I guess . . . well, in my vision a man called me a 'beast tamer.' I survived in the mouth of . . . well, whatever that thing was before it dropped me here," Colin said.

"Then Beast Tamer you shall be called, but I doubt that's the sum of it. I've not spoken to a human in eons, so I will call you . . . Beast Tamer, Stone Speaker . . . until it gets longer, as most names do over time."

"Your name must be huge then, whatever it is."

"My name was longer than the great Sanhedrin mountain range, more mixed than the shifting sands of Arabah, and deeper than the abyss at the edge of the world. I think . . . it held great power." The stone face frowned.

"What can I call you then?" Colin asked. "Like a nickname? Or do you like 'Big Rock Face'?"

"A nickname?" The face frowned. "This word is new to me."

Colin sighed. "Like a temporary name, a short name, you know?"

"Hmmmmm," the great stone rumbled in thought for a moment. "'Crag' . . . I think that was part of my name. Yes, 'Crag' will do . . . though it's woefully inadequate."

"Right, okay, Crag. Look, do you know about that tree? If this is the Dead Wood, then it's here and I have to find it. Samuel called it the Gilead tree. Ring any bells?"

"I have no bells to ring, little pebble. But I do understand. It's not a place you should visit. The ground there has long been cursed. Nothing will grow near it. Not since those people killed the Maker's man on the tree. However, a nice quarry is not far from here. Sometimes it fills with water. I find it quite peaceful. You should go there."

Colin shook his head. "Crag . . . I need to find the balm of Gilead. The only reason I came into this world was to find it. The tree is the only hope I have of saving my mother."

Crag's rocky brows raised. "You came from another world to save one you love?"

Colin nodded.

"You were called then? By the Horn of Joshua?"

Colin shrugged. "Yeah, I guess so."

"Mmmm . . . little pebble, you should have said this earlier."

"Why would it matter?" Colin asked him.

"The horn is one of The Ten. It only calls those who will have a serious impact on our world, but to what end is a mystery . . . even to one as old as I. The Maker told me of these things long ago. I never thought it concerned me until today. I will shift the wood for you. The path will lead you to the tree."

"Okay, thanks, I guess." Colin stood and watched as the ground slowly shifted before him, parting the wall of trees to his right and closing the gap of trees to his left. Colin turned to Crag. The face seemed almost entirely rock-like again.

"Crag . . . what do you mean, 'The Ten'? Are there more of those weird conches out there? Are they dangerous?"

"Little pebble, that is a story for another time, and I grow tired. Take the flint and your own stone . . . roll down the slope I've given you. It's clear you're not meant to gather moss here."

"But Crag . . . I need to know, am I in danger?" Colin asked again.

"You've always been in danger, but how you choose to roll through it will either shape you or break you. Farewell."

Crag closed his eyes, and his countenance disappeared into the rock.

"Crag?" Colin called, but there was no response. He turned to the small campfire and rummaged through the pine needles on the forest floor until he found a large stick. He took off his shirt, ripped the arm sleeve off, and wrapped it tightly about the stick until he formed a makeshift torch.

"This will have to work," he mumbled as he put the remnants of his shirt back on and knelt to set the torch ablaze from the cindering campfire. He moved down the dark forested pathway, holding his torch high, hoping its flames would be enough to ward off the darkness pressing in on him.

CHAPTER 44

THE SACRIFICE

Mariselle spurred her horse forward as it raced across the moors. The eastern walls of Gilead were less than a mile away. The flight from the castle had been swift, but her grasp on the kingdom was weakening with every moment the king breathed. Now that she had recovered and regrouped, the time to retake Gilead had come. The long ride back from Korah's Maw would end with Braeden's head on a stick. No more illusions, no more deceit. As Lord Dagon attacked the Lion's Maw from the bay, she and her men would retake the city's eastern half. Through the fog, she spied the silhouette of Gilead's great walls looming in the distance. The executions would go on for days.

"Faster!" she screamed to her men. "We will enact a justice so complete the streets will run crimson with their blood, and the first will be that little wench—Alexandra."

Behind her, her guards kept pace on their black steeds, swords drawn and ready to cleave. As the high wall of Gilead loomed ahead, Mariselle glanced back and saw that her entourage numbered at least twenty capable Amorite warriors. The sheep at the gate would be no match.

Then the battle cry of "Gil-e-ad" reached her ears. Mariselle pulled up her horse to a trot, and her men followed suit.

"Damn them! They've rallied," she said, turning to her advisor, who followed closely behind. "Take my cargo and spoils round to the shoreline and meet me at the docks. I'll not have my things damaged in this skirmish, short as it might be."

"M'lady, are you sure you won't come with us? Storming Gilead's walls, even with your guard, seems rash at best," he replied.

"Does a lion kowtow to a lamb? I'm ruler over this kingdom, and it's time it pays me the respect I deserve, whether by will or by force. Begone!" Mariselle commanded and motioned to the armed warriors behind her.

The advisor bowed and turned his mount to the back of the line. Four servants, bearing a wagon of chests and towing the captured donkey behind, followed him.

A guard brought Mariselle a black obsidian bow and a quiver full of arrows. She fitted them around her. "It's been an age since I've used these, but one never forgets," she said to her man and notched an arrow into the line. She turned to her warriors. "Form a wedge. We'll cut through their resistance at the gate and ride straight for the king's throat!"

The Amorite guards formed behind her as she spurred her steed forward. The battle cries rolled across the moors as they darted through the mist. Mariselle dug her knees against the saddle and let the reins loose as she readied her aim, confident her warhorse knew to keep its course. She hoped the princess was among the defenders. The brat's death would settle all questions of sovereignty.

EGAN WATCHED THE FOG ROLL across the foothills of the eastern moors and waited in the darkness alone, crouching low to the ground in a hollow. His horse stood quietly in some thorn bushes nearby. It was a meager camouflage but one he hoped would hold up. Two of his five men were closer to the wall, ready to race forward on their horses from the southwest, and two more men were poised to attack from the north side. This was not how he'd learned to play at war. When he was younger, he had imagined leading a squadron of troops in glorious battle, marching in even rows under the sun. Yet now he stood in the shadows, on a razor's edge between desperation and annihilation, scared to death. He remembered his eagerness for battle when he was a squire and wished he could cuff that young fool's head. Perhaps courage came from necessity alone, not from will, and to lean on others was no great weakness.

His thoughts drifted to the shore of his childhood as he toyed with the sling he carried. In simpler times, the answers were clear.

The sound of racing hooves brought his attention back as the Amorites raced across the high moor above him. He knew it was time. Mariselle flew past, making her charge on the eastern gate. Egan mounted his horse and darted up from the bushes to follow her war party. In the dim moonlight, he drew his sword and spied her leading the vanguard. Egan pushed his horse harder and came up behind the back line of her warriors. In a flash, he sliced his blade through the backs of two men. They fell from their steeds like rocks in the water. Two more of their number turned their horses to give chase, and Egan led them around a hill away from the others. From the corner of his eye, he saw two of his men swoop in from the shadows and pierce Mariselle's formation from the side, cutting through three of her soldiers before vanishing into the darkness again.

"Shore up!" Mariselle screamed. "They're upon us!"

Mariselle pulled her horse to a halt. She looked around desperately for the attackers, but Egan and his men were nowhere to be seen. The Amorites readied their weapons as another two of Egan's soldiers raced past and cut down the guards on either side of Mariselle. She shot her arrow, but it missed the mark and landed in the chest of one of her warriors. He fell from his horse and crumpled to the ground.

"Damnit! I said shore up! Protect me!" she screamed again, and her remaining men formed a circle around her on their horses. Mariselle notched another arrow. Egan had whittled her fighting force in half in a few moments.

Egan could hear the echo of "Gil-e-ad" from the walls and spied his prey, checking her flanks, but only shadows greeted her. He saw his chance and encircled Mariselle's troop from the right while two of his men came at them from the left. Her circle of protection crumbled as Egan smashed through it. She screamed in the chaos, and her horse flew forward, terrified. She clutched at its mane, trying to balance herself as it rushed towards the high wall.

The moon peered out from the clouds, laying bare the wall and the ruse at play. In that instant, Egan knew his plan was about to fail.

———

"Open the gate!" Helen yelled at the eastern wall. "He's out there!"

The large doors opened a sliver, and Helen rushed out from the eastern wall peering at shadows at its base.

"Taran!" she hissed. "Please, any of you? My little one got loose!"

"Here, lady." A woman called and beckoned her to the wall's edge. At her feet squirmed the toddler. He rushed to Helen's side.

"You should be within the walls with your baby!" she whispered to Helen.

"There were so many wounded." Helen sighed. "I looked away for a moment and he was gone. I fear there's little shelter within."

"Aye, I saw you." The woman nodded. "How fares your husband?"

"He's recovering. I think he's raring to fight, actually." She tussled Taran's head. "As is this one."

The woman nodded. "A little lion of Gilead."

The boy broke free from Helen's grasp and ran out from the wall onto the field. "Taran!" Helen screamed and chased after him.

"Forward, men!" Mariselle's voice howled like a banshee through the mist. "They've played us for fools!"

She burst from the shadows like a wolf, notching an arrow in her bow and flying towards the child on her horse.

"No!" Helen screamed.

———

AVERY'S LEG WAS still ablaze from his wound, but he needed to know Helen was safe. He moved around the gate, keeping to the waning shadow, and to his horror, saw his wife running into the broad moonlight toward their toddling child. He watched Helen push Taran aside as Mariselle shot an arrow. It perfectly pierced his wife's chest. Helen fell to the ground and was trampled as the steed sped past them.

"Helen!" Avery screamed. But he knew it was too late.

CHAPTER 45

THE STEADY BLADE

ing Braeden watched Rustag and Absalom move down the street below and disappear into the shadows. His son's words weighed on him. Once again, he had sent another in his stead, forcing someone else to clean his mess.

"Soldier." He motioned to the armored figure standing behind him. "Ready my horse and the men. Whether Absalom's trap fails or succeeds, I'll not be unready to face the enemy."

A shadow emerged at the king's side, and a guttural laugh echoed in his ear.

Braeden spun around and caught the assassin's blade hand. A serpentine dagger stopped inches from his face. His arm shook as he held back the dagger's embrace.

"Father!" Alexandra's voice screamed, and the armored soldier behind him jumped onto the Amorite, knocking him off balance.

The assassin fell back, and Braeden kicked him away. His eyes widened as he saw his guard's helmet fly off and his daughter struggling to pin the killer down.

"Alex? Guards! Guards!" Braeden yelled.

The assassin smashed his fist into Alexandra's face and threw her off. Another royal guard ran up the stairs and plunged his sword into the Amorite's side. The assassin screamed and dropped his dagger before grabbing the man by the neck and throwing him from the roof. The Amorite reached for his dagger but found nothing. Turning around, he met his blade as Alexandra pushed it into his chest.

The Amorite fell, lifeless. Braeden looked at his daughter standing above the killer, bruised and bleeding from her nose.

He embraced her. "How in the Maker did you . . . No, never mind. You're alive, that's all that matters."

Tears rolled down Alexandra's face. "How could you expect me to stay away? How could you think I'd leave you to face this alone?"

Braeden nodded. "I shouldn't have. But you're all I have left. How long have you been here?"

Alexandra wiped a tear from her cheek. "Long enough. I saw all of it."

"Absalom despises me, as he should. I'd hoped to reconcile with him privately if possible, but these dark days led to brash action and reckless words—from us both." He paused for a moment, deep in thought. "Still, he risks his life to free us from Mariselle's grasp. His heart beats for Gilead."

"And if your bastard son will fight for you, why wouldn't I?" Alexandra pushed away from him.

"The night is long, Alex. Don't take my ill planning as a slight," Braeden replied. "I know you are capable. You're as strong as your mother. I won't ask you to sit idle again."

Braeden pulled *Teacht Riocht* from his side scabbard and studied it for a moment before turning to his daughter. "Kneel then."

She kneeled, and he placed the blade at her shoulder.

"Though some would say the kingdom is your birthright, I believe succession should be clear. Or else claims to my throne will bring another war to our doorstep. The weight of the crown will bring you enough worries on its own. I name you knight protector and heir to my kingdom. You fight for our future as much as any man here. Just don't fight it alone."

"I-I won't father. Thank you. Thank you for trusting me."

"Rise, my lady." He offered his hand, and she took it. "Find Egan. Help him if you can." Braeden looked over the armor fastened about her. "I know you can."

"And you? Will you promise to be with me come the morning?" she asked.

"No matter what happens to me, daughter, I will always be with you," Braeden said and hugged her.

Alexandra nodded as she pulled away and turned toward the steps leading down to the street below.

Mariselle brought her horse around. The woman had not been her intended target, but it mattered little. The rest of the commoners would fall as soon as her remaining men could be rallied. She raced back toward the fighting on the moor. If the king's soldiers were bolstering the walls with defenseless peons, they were desperate, and any fighting men on the field were no doubt their last. She ignored the peasant who had run out into the field to grab the child and darted toward a grouping of her guards fighting off three guerilla attacks. She notched another arrow, but a shadow at her side lunged, throwing her from her horse. Gilead's chief warrant officer landed on top of her and slammed his gauntlet into her side, making her drop her bow.

Mariselle delivered a swift knee to his crotch and pushed him off. She leaped to her feet, brandishing a twisted dagger in each hand. Like a cobra, she stabbed her left-hand blade into Egan's shoulder as he struggled to stand. Egan screamed and slapped the other blade from her right hand. He stood, wrenched her blade from his shoulder, gasping from pain. Mariselle took a step back.

"Come, boy! Make your last misstep here and be done with it!" She spat as she pulled another dagger from her belt and smiled. "I've outmaneuvered you and your pathetic people for years and—"

Egan slashed his sword forward in a perfect arc and severed off three of Mariselle's fingers. She wailed as she dropped her weapon and fell to her knees—blood gushing down her hand. The last vestige of her beauty, the last reminder of herself, was gone.

"Enough!" Egan screamed and pressed the blade to her chest. "Tell them to drop their weapons, or you die here and now!"

"Stop!" Mariselle croaked. The pain from the wound coursed throughout her body and clouded her senses. Her men dropped their weapons.

"You've killed enough innocents tonight, witch, and you'll answer for it," Egan barked at her. "Call off your men at the harbor and perhaps the king will spare your life."

"My men?" Tears rolled down her cheeks as she clenched her hand. "You give me too much credit. No. What you see rampaging through the city is not my doing alone. The full might of the Black Throne has crushed your kingdom. The Dark Lord has sent Dagon, Lord of Death, to your shores! Kill me if you wish, but you and your friends will be hanging from the archways within a day!"

Egan pulled Mariselle to her feet. His other men had Mariselle's warriors kneel while they restrained them.

He faced Mariselle with cold, steel eyes and grabbed her bleeding hand. She flinched. He pulled a loose swath of fabric from his tunic and wrapped her wound, never breaking his stare.

"You're under arrest, for crimes against the kingdom. You'll face a tribunal and see justice done. May the Maker have mercy on you."

"Pathetic pup!" Mariselle spat into Egan's face. "Do you seriously fancy yourself in command? You're a joke. A fraud. A mouse to be stomped."

"If there's no hope for me . . ." Egan set the tip of his blade to her neck. "Then there will be no mercy for you."

Mariselle's eyes went wide as she saw the quiet rage in Egan's face and felt the sting of his blade biting into her neck. Then, as if the universe were responding to her outrage, she felt a strange force pulling at her. The ground became as pliable as water, and she felt herself sinking into it. Egan's shocked face melted into the darkness.

Suddenly, she was falling into an empty abyss, and then, in an instant, she landed hard on rough gopher wood. The impact was painful. She looked up and saw she was on the deck of a ship under the same darkened sky. She had somehow been ripped away to another place. A familiar face came into view. Standing over her, staring with those nightmarish reptilian eyes, was Dagon.

"I should have you killed," his voice echoed in her ears, "but you'll serve a purpose yet."

Mariselle felt the saliva leave her mouth and wondered if Egan's blade would have been better.

CHAPTER 46

The Trap is Set

Absalom backed into Rustag and dropped the barrel of black powder onto the hard cobblestone. He winced, but the barrel rolled an inch and stopped.

"Damnit, fool," he yelled at Rustag. "We'll die if we're not more careful."

"Then watch where you're going," Rustag grunted and returned to the lamplighter shack for more of the explosive material. He returned, hugging four of the barrels in his massive arms.

Absalom wondered if the slaughterman's lumbering strength would become a burden when stealth, speed, and agility would be required for rigging their trap. However, four hands were better than two in a pinch, and the pinch was ever-tightening.

Absalom helped Rustag move the remaining barrels to a small wooden cart and paused to count the stock. His eyes danced over the leather skins of lamp oil, leaking grease that dripped down the wheels, and the thin corded rope was hastily thrown on top of it all. "I'm not sure it's enough, but we don't have time to scavenge for more," he said.

"I can hear their war drums. Let's finish this," Rustag replied and peered down the alleyway. The sound of the Amorites' laughter and slaughter was louder now.

Absalom nodded and beckoned Rustag to follow him down the road.

Rustag took hold of the cart's tongue like it was a feather and quickly pulled the wagon after him. The two men turned onto the main thoroughfare—the market road curved for several hundred yards ahead here. The glow from the fires reflected on the windows of the homes lining the street. Absalom turned back and saw the archway leading to the bazaar in the distance.

"This is as good a choke point as any," he whispered. "The bastards won't bother scaling the inner walls when they can come right up to the front door. Help me." He hurried over to the nearby doorway of a house. Rustag followed behind, carrying a barrel of powder, a skin of oil, and the hemp line. Absalom pulled out a lockpick and coaxed it into the lock. He placed his ear to the door as he began working it.

"Now just one little click and . . ."

Rustag kicked open the door and pushed past him. "It's open," he grunted.

Absalom picked up his lockpick and went inside. He surveyed the living area and grabbed the line from Rustag. "I'll leave you to opening the other doors on this street," Absalom said. "But before you do, give me the rope there and the oil and powder. I'm going to make a fuse."

"Will that bit of string burn like you want it to?" Rustag fingered the line in his hand. "Seems like it might smolder."

"Normally I'd say you're right, but if we coat it in the oil and powder itself, it should burn much more quickly. Grab those tables and chairs and anything else that you see. When this barrel goes off, we need as much debris flying out as possible."

Within a minute, Rustag had piled furniture up against the windows facing the street. Absalom finished coating the line and, with a quick thrust of his dagger, punctured the barrel and placed the end of the fuse into it.

Rustag nodded and hurried out the door to the next house, grabbing more barrels from the cart. Within several minutes they had set charges up and down the street throughout the homes that lined the road. Absalom covertly placed and tied together the long fuses leading from each house to one single knotted line in the middle of the cobblestone street. As they worked, they softly called out to see if survivors hid in the empty homes. No answers came.

The shadows of the Amorite troops reflected on the path ahead as their torch fires came closer.

Absalom and Rustag crouched next to the knotted fuse in the middle of the street.

"It's not the subtlest ignition point, but it'll have to do," Absalom whispered. "All we have to do is light it and run."

"It will be good to see their bodies flying in burning masses," Rustag replied.

Absalom glanced at the giant man kneeling next to him. "You're demented. Do you know that?"

Rustag nodded and smiled.

The black armored warriors flooded into view; many carried torches, setting the buildings ablaze as they approached the choke point trap. Absalom watched nervously as smoke billowed from the windows and fiery tendrils coursed up nearby rooftops. One meandering spark could easily set off the fuses, but a slight breeze kept the embers from traveling near them.

Thank the Maker for small miracles, he thought as he spied a runt of a warrior pounding on a cruel-looking war drum made of bone. Others in the front of the horde ran forward on all fours like wolves chasing prey.

"They're barely men." Rustag grimaced. "They need to be put down." He pulled out a piece of flint and a stone, ready to start the spark.

"Wait! Just a little closer . . ." Absalom hissed. "We can only do this once."

The horde marched forward, their torchlight eating away the shadows in the street. Absalom knew he and Rustag would be spotted within a minute or less.

As the mass drew closer, one scout tripped on the fuse and paused. The Amorite slowly pulled the rope up from the street and saw its line arc up to other houses on either side. The warrior crept into the doorway of a home to investigate.

Absalom's face went white. The trap would be discovered.

"Light it!" Absalom hissed to Rustag. "And pray to the Maker that we can outrun the charge!" He turned and raced at the Amorite, blade drawn, as Rustag lit the fuse.

Absalom could hear the spark chasing his heels.

CHAPTER 47

SIGNS OF BETRAYAL

Balaam locked his knees to counter the ship's sway, but stumbled on the deck as a large breaker hit the vessel's side. The journey to the Amorite ship had been uneventful. The barge had met Mariselle's advisor and the rest of her servants on the coast only a mile from where they parted ways. With a good deal of grunting and cursing, her counselor had managed to climb aboard, nearly falling into the wash in the process. Now, the vessel's captain cursed in his Median dialect as he navigated to Gilead's harbor.

"Sit yer arse down, fool!" the captain yelled at the advisor. "Likely as not, we'll take cannon fire off the port and starboard, and I'm not getting paid to deliver corpses."

The advisor quickly sat on a coil of rope.

"Not there, ya fool!" the captain barked again, and Mariselle's man jumped up again. Balaam watched in horror as blazing fireballs, catapulted from the decks of the Amorite ships in view, blasted the docks and high walls of the city. In the dim firelight, he could see figures on each vessel working with expert speed as they prepared the next barrage of heavy stones, covering them in pitch and setting them ablaze before sending them flying. As the barge weaved between the anchored ships, Balaam counted their number—at least twenty—but it was not until they had reached the back of the blockade that he saw the actual threat. A massive vessel, easily the size of three of the others combined, with four masts and three rows of cannons protruding from the ship's side gun ports came into view. Upon the masthead was a horrific face that Balaam could only glance at before turning away. A crane line dropped from the colossal galleon, and a platform was lowered to the barge. Balaam was pushed onto it along with several barrels and the advisor, who clung to the ropes for dear life.

The crew of the black galleon wore the same frightful masks as the soldiers attacking Gilead. Balaam wondered if it had some other purpose besides putting fear into their enemy's hearts. Perhaps the men were scarred, or the faceplates kept them from feeling shame as they ravaged their victims. As he peered around at the deckhands, his attention was instantly drawn to midship. Between the masts was an altar of bone, easily five feet high and adorned with gaudy finery and fabrics. A green iridescent haze floated above it, and Balaam sensed something very evil was watching him, the deckhands, everything, through the haze.

He watched as the crew moved barrels from below the ship's deck to the lift. The barge that had ferried Balaam had quickly moved away, and small landing boats had come up alongside the ship in its wake, waiting for the powder kegs to be lowered to them. The ship's captain opened one of the barrels and studied it. Black powder ran through his fingers. He sealed it and moved it into position to be lifted out. Within a minute, the Amorites had lowered the barrels into the first skiff, and another small boat pulled up.

"They're supplying the whole fleet," Balaam muttered as Mariselle's advisor moved past him.

"Well, I have the report. Where is Master Dagon?" the advisor questioned one of the deckhands. The sailor nodded behind the counselor, and the little man turned, abruptly pulling back. A gaunt figure with reptilian eyes loomed over him.

"Ah. Lord D-Dagon," the advisor bowed.

"Is this all she sent?" Dagon asked as he peered at Balaam and the other cargo. Balaam looked down, for no reason but to give the illusion that he was as absentminded as any beast.

"Yes, well, for now, but you'll be happy to know she's storming the city from the east and—" the advisor started.

"Where's the boy?" Dagon interrupted.

"The boy?"

Dagon's eyes widened.

"Oh yes, of course, well, Her Highness fed him to the beast in Korah's Maw. Your, uh, messengers didn't seem to think that was sure enough, despite Her Majesty's assurances."

Dagon clutched the advisor by his arms and pulled him to within an inch of his face. "Her assurances are worthless," he whispered. "I wanted him alive and brought to me. You have no idea what she's let loose. Your services are no longer needed."

Dagon grabbed the advisor by his throat. The man's eyes went wide as he gagged for breath. Dagon opened his mouth wide, and black bile gushed, forcing its way down the man's throat. The counselor shook violently as the putrid essence streamed from his ears and eyes. Finally, Dagon released him. He collapsed like a wet rag onto the deck, lifeless and pale.

Wiping the sludge from his lips, Dagon turned to the altar and began muttering strange words over it. Balaam watched as the green haze grew and then, as if the air itself was being warped by heat, shimmered as a dark fog appeared. The ship's mast appeared to twist as the haze floated up next to it. Even the deckhands momentarily stopped their duties and took a step back. A hollow crack echoed across the sky, and Mariselle fell from the haze onto the ship's deck in a flash of light. She lay at Dagon's feet for a moment before looking up.

"I should have you killed," Dagon said, "but you'll serve a purpose yet."

Mariselle cringed at his words as she lay at his feet.

"This was meant to be a brief engagement." Dagon walked past her to the altar. "Now I find my warriors are whittled away by half-measures of a ragtag army."

Mariselle slowly stood with uneasy steps. She cradled her hand, which had been wounded recently judging from the bloodstained cloth it was wrapped in, as she moved next to the sorcerer. "Sire, I can tell you they're not nearly as well-armed or cunning as you might believe. Their gates are garrisoned by harmless civilians and . . ."

"You let their greatest asset escape."

"The princess is a child, my lord," Mariselle continued. "She's no threat."

"The boy!" Dagon screamed. "Since the horn's call, I've sensed him hovering, like a fly in my ear. There is something to him, something I can't put my finger on."

"The boy?" Mariselle shook her head. "The boy is dead."

"And the horn? The old man's scroll? Do you have them?"

Mariselle swallowed. "My lord, the scroll was lost some time ago, and the horn . . . Well, it's only a shell. A poorly made trifle. I could have a grander one made for you . . ."

"You have no idea what it is." Dagon's eyes flared. "Nor the wrath unleashed on both our heads if we fail to obtain it." He moved past her to the ship's railings and pulled a long silver chain from around his neck; a black bone whistle was attached to the bottom. He pursed it to his lips and played a single note.

Balaam's eyes widened as he caught sight of a faint green glow emanating briefly from the saddlebags across his back and heard a muffled sound echo back.

Dagon spun around and scanned the deck. "No, could it be?" He moved past Balaam and ripped open one of the crates on the deck. "I heard it!"

Balaam backed away and peered around. Soon there would be no hiding it and nowhere to run. The whistle glistened in the moonlight as it dangled around the sorcerer's neck. Dagon turned to face the donkey. A questioning glance spread across his face.

"Could it be?" He grasped the whistle once more.

"I told you I found nothing in the castle!" Mariselle motioned to Dagon. "I suspect Samuel kept them in his shack."

Dagon dropped the whistle to his neck again and glanced back at her, scowling.

"When we march into the castle and slaughter the last of the resistance, I'll have a dispatch find them," Mariselle continued. "It should be easy enough. The civilians are harmless, at best."

Balaam saw his chance. He leaned forward and wrenched the whistle and its line from Dagon's throat. Quickly he bit down on the piece and felt it shatter in his mouth before he tried to swallow it. The shards caught in his gullet, and he threw them up instantly.

Dagon spun around. "Damnable beast!" He kicked the mule aside and stared at the broken instrument in the bile.

Disgusted, he turned back to Mariselle. "Pray you're right, woman. The Dark Lord requires them, and he gives far less grace than I do." Dagon moved past her to the bone table. Mariselle glanced back at her advisor's lifeless body and breathed to steady herself.

"See now." Dagon motioned toward the haze still hovering above the altar. Mariselle turned to study it. The green miasma formed a smoky circle in midair. Figures came into view through the mist as if seen through a cloudy glass. Balaam moved from his corner of the deck unnoticed. He slowly made his way behind the sorcerer and saw in the green vapor the silhouettes of Absalom and Rustag as they positioned powder kegs among houses within the city.

"Your harmless civilians are about to spring a death on my warriors," Dagon breathed as he watched the figures intently through the haze. "They will fail, of course."

"How?" Mariselle asked.

Dagon turned to face her and smiled. "Because you will keep my men alive." He pulled a curved bone-handled blade from his belt.

Mariselle backed away. "I'm your chosen, your w-wolf."

"Every dog has its day," Dagon replied, "and now yours draws to an end."

CHAPTER 48

THE FINAL GIFT

Colin made his way under the dark dead limbs of the ancient forest. His meager torchlight barely lit the path around him. The rain had stopped, but the cold was chilling. As he followed the trail, he felt it begin to slope downward. His feet left small pools in the wet ground, and the snapping of branches echoed as he shuffled forward. His breath steamed in the frigid air. He was thankful for the torch fire, holding it close to feel its warmth. After a good hour, the path widened again until Colin came to a clearing. A small hill rose in the middle of the clearing, and atop it was a lone gnarled tree, blackened and lifeless. A cruel split ran from the top branches to its lower trunk.

Colin's eyes widened as he stared at it. It was as if time had stopped since that ancient day of bloodshed and seared the scar of that act permanently into the land. Colin shivered. The foul smell of rot wafted from the soil. How could something so ugly offer hope?

The clearing was silent—no bird calls, no owl cries. Even the wind was mute. As Colin moved up the hill to the tree, the ground became harder and as lifeless as the woods around him. No blade of grass grew here, and the puddles were filled with brackish water the color of blood.

Samuel must've been wrong. People came for healing here? It's practically a cesspool.

Colin reached out to the blackened husk of one of the tree's roots. A chill ran up his fingers as if he had pressed on a meat locker door. He brought his torch closer, and there, in the deepest part of the tree's split core, he saw a tiny bit of amber resin. His eyes searched around the limbs for any other indications of the balm, but the tree was barren.

This must be it. Whatever other magic this thing had is gone. Maybe . . .

A stabbing pain ripped through Colin's shoulder.

He felt the bite and jerked around to see a hooded Hissith towering over him, his blood dripping from its fangs. Colin fell back as the demon slashed at him with its claws. He threw his torch at the beast, singeing its side. The Hissith howled and slithered back into the shadows. Colin glanced at his wound and saw the bite was already infected. Venom bubbled from the puncture and, like acid, was eating away at his shirt. Colin's arm felt numb. He reached for the still-burning torch, but fiery needles shot through his arm and into the base of his skull. His hand fell lifelessly to his side. He grabbed the light with his other hand and waved it frantically around in case the beast tried to attack again.

Hissssss.

The sound was behind him now.

Colin strained his neck to see two sets of serpentine eyes watching him from the gloom just outside the torch's light.

They inched closer.

Two voices broke through to Colin's mind, coherent but wholly inhuman.

He will sssleep soon. Already he weakensss.

Yes, sssleep, little morsel. Drop the nasty flame and dream.

Hisssss. Perhapsss we take a bite? Before we deliver him?

Yesss, a little bite. He is fresh and sssweet.

"You take a bite and I'll burn your ass to the ground!" Colin screamed at them.

The Hissith paused.

He hears usss? How can he hear usss?

"I hear you very well!" Colin yelled and lurched forward with the torch. The creatures retreated a few feet.

What can he do? Only a boy. Alone. Sssleep, little morsel.

The serpents' voices enticed him, and his eyelids weigh down. All he wanted was to do as they said. His breathing became labored, and resting sounded divine. Surrounded by darkness and death, how could he hope to stop their attacks? Already his torchlight was burning low. Colin's gaze blurred as he watched the embers dying. He searched for words, some magical phrase that might turn them away, but his mind was empty. Samuel may have marked him as the next soothsayer, but without the Logos, he was nothing. The desire for sleep built like a flood bursting through the dam of his conscious mind.

Colin clenched the torch again and shook his head clear.

No. I didn't come this far for . . .

Fog filled his brain again. The serpents' voices seemed almost melodic as they spoke to him.

Releassse and rest.

Give in and die.

The cruel words sounded so sweet. Colin leaned back against the tree. He couldn't hold back the flood anymore.

"Maker, I can't do it," Colin whispered.

One of the Hissith rushed forward and coiled atop Colin's feet, pinning him against the tree. Behind it, the other drew closer, ready to strike. Colin felt the bark rub against his skin. Its woody splinters pressed up against his bite wound. The demon's crushing tail pulsed on Colin's legs, cutting off the blood flow, and its yellow eyes filled his gaze. Colin's vision darkened as the monster pushed back its hood to reveal its whole countenance. Too exhausted to resist, Colin felt consciousness fleeing from his mind as the bark scratched deeper into his flesh.

Something sticky pushed into his shoulder. Colin turned slightly and saw some of the tree's sap had dropped into his wound.

Warmth surged across his body.

The hairs on his neck stood on end as if a trumpet had called them to attention, and his vision cleared.

The serpent faltered, its trance broken. A name appeared in Colin's mind.

"Your name," Colin gasped, "was Simiel."

The Hissith drew back as if it had been slapped.

A new vision filled Colin's mind, and he spoke again.

"You were made a cupbearer to the Maker, and the others called you out. You had to choose in that great battle before the first morning. You were unsure. You wished to be more."

It doesssn't know me, the Hissith spat. *How could it know me? What magic is thisss?* The great serpent backed away.

The heat from the sap spread across Colin's body, and his strength returned to him. The fear melted into rage.

"You wished to be more, so you followed the Maker in quelling the uprising, but still you did not fight; you were too afraid to stand against the darkness. And when the fallen were cast out, you were as well. You are craven, Simiel," Colin said as he steadied himself and stood. "You are a coward."

The Hissith screeched as if it had been struck and fell back. The other serpent rushed at Colin from the side.

Colin turned his head and spoke: "Sile!"

The serpent fell to the ground as if it was pinned there.

"You are Azrael, once anointed by the Maker; and yet you were cast out too. All you know now is anger." Colin knew the voice he spoke with was not his own. He had become a vessel of the Logos. He had fallen in his weakness and had been brought back as something new.

Sssilence! Shut itsss mouth!

"Run back to the Black Throne! On your bellies crawl. May your limbs be broken and useless!" Colin's voice thundered.

The great serpents screamed in pain as their arms ripped backward. They fell into the mud squirming and flailing.

"Back!" Colin commanded. "Tell your master you've failed. Tell your master a soothsayer remains."

The beasts scrambled across the bracken pools, using their great tails to propel them forward through the muck, down the hill, and into the darkness of the woods, crying in agony until their voices faded into the distance.

Colin stood at the tree and waited. After several moments passed, he no longer felt their presence. His muscles relaxed. The power within him dissipated.

He turned toward the tree and peered closely at the bark he had pressed against. Emerging from the timbers was more of the resin. Colin gingerly raised his wounded arm as he ripped another swatch of fabric from his shirt and pulled the resin globules off the tree's bark. His eyes glanced over the dead tree again, and wondered if it had anything left to give.

Good enough for now, if it doesn't dry up by the time I need it.

He folded the fabric around the sap and pushed it into his pocket, his finger brushing against the smooth stone he still carried. The image of his mother lying unconscious crept into his mind again. The old feelings of powerlessness returned to him.

How the hell am I ever getting home?

"With a choice," Mr. Potter's voice echoed behind him.

Colin spun around to see a cloaked figure standing at the edge of the clearing.

"You! You're here!" Colin slowly approached him. "You can fix all of this, can't you?"

"I can only offer you a choice, my boy." Mr. Potter lowered his hood to reveal his worn face. "You may leave now, or you may stay. How you choose will affect the lives of many."

"That's . . . not fair." Colin shook his head. "That's not fair! You know she needs this." He held up the balm in his hand. "She needs me!"

"Yes, *she* does." Mr. Potter nodded and knelt. He quietly etched a crown into the mud. "Her very life may hang in the balance, and with her, the kingdom."

"Alex?" Colin asked. "Is something going to happen to her?"

"Her life hangs in the balance as much as your mother's," Mr. Potter said. "It's for you to tip the scale one way or the other."

"I don't know how to save these people." Colin's voice cracked.

"With the same words you saved yourself—if you choose to speak them. You have the Logos in you, and through you, it will name all that is in the light and the darkness."

"Can you guarantee my mom will live?" Colin searched Mr. Potter's eyes. "Promise me?"

"I can only promise that you can make a difference here and now," Mr. Potter said, offering his hand. "Take my hand to go back to the world you know, or take the path to save this one."

The way before him was dark, surrounded by dead wood, each tree mirroring the next. Colin paused. There was no easy answer, no sure choice. Finally, he took a breath, closed his eyes, and stepped forward.

CHAPTER 49

By Fire and Blood

Absalom sprinted to the open doorway ahead of the burning fuse and tackled the nearby Amorite scout from behind, slamming the warrior to his belly. Shrieking, the man spun to his back with surprising speed and clawed at Absalom's throat. The warrior's nails dug deep into his neck, locking into a vise grip on his Adam's apple. Absalom struggled to rip the man's hands away.

"Drakkath ak guluz!" the scout screamed at him and smiled a vile grin. The fuse's spark burned past them as they wrestled, and Absalom knew they would both be blown apart in a few seconds. He loosened his grip on the scout's hands, allowing the pressure on his throat to increase. The attacker broadened his grip to get a better hold, and Absalom saw his opening. Instantly he shoved his palmed hand up into the killer's nose, snapping the bridge and driving the bone straight into the scout's brain. The warrior fell back and collapsed on the wooden floor.

Absalom staggered to his feet, jumped over the body, and raced back through the doorway, straight into the Amorite army rampaging past. Savage faces filled his vision, and he felt daggers slicing across his body.

Rustag grabbed his arm and pulled him free. Absalom looked up to see his comrade had four enemy soldiers on his back, yet he had still managed to make it to Absalom in the midst of the mob.

"Run, you fool!" Absalom gasped.

There was a split second of silence before he saw fiery explosions burst from every doorway and window on the street. The invaders were thrown like rag dolls in all directions. Others were engulfed in flames and impaled by flying debris. Then the closest house behind them exploded.

Absalom felt himself being lifted off the ground and thrown ahead. The fast-approaching cobblestone filled his sight before it went black.

A fog of screams and explosions echoed in his mind when Rustag's hand swatted his cheek, waking him from the stupor. His vision cleared to the burning devastation around him. A full two-thirds of the attackers were dead or dying. Farther down the street, others fled back to the Ambassador's Square. Absalom gazed at the burned bodies around him. No one would bar the pair's way now. The giant looked down at him.

"Still alive?"

Absalom barely nodded.

"Good enough. We just sent the bastards a little love note. Let's return to the king."

Rustag helped Absalom to his feet, but he immediately collapsed again. The slaughterman grunted and lifted Absalom over his shoulder.

"Thank you, I . . ." he gasped.

"Shut up," the slaughterman mumbled, "you talk too much."

Absalom smiled as they made their way back to the last barricade.

KING BRAEDEN LOOKED OVER THE burning maelstrom and smiled at his guard. "Our city burns, yet she gives us a chance at life."

"What now, my lord?" a guard asked.

"There is no other defense. We must not lose this advantage. We'll chase them back from the streets to the square and out to the docks. Ready my horse. Bring the last of the guard, and send a messenger to Egan at the eastern gate. He can rally what forces he has and bring them to the shore at the base of the Lion's Maw. We'll cut the Amorites off from their ships, cast them from the great stairwell, and finish this."

The guard nodded and moved down to spread the word. The king took a deep breath and clenched his fists. The fires of his youth burned again in his chest. *Teacht Riocht* reflected the glow of the flames in the distance. The names of his ancestors etched onto the blade gleamed in the firelight.

"Tonight, you and I will have our final dance together."

CHAPTER 50

A Light in the Darkness

&gan helped the townspeople off the battlements. The eastern gate was secured. He turned to Avery, who stood over his wife's body, covered by a blanket. The lamplighter held his son in his arms.

"I'm so sorry, Avery. I don't have the words to tell you . . ."

"There are no words, Chief," Avery said as he gazed at her. "She did what needed doing."

"I knew my plan was a long shot at best," Egan said. "But if I'd stopped to think of the cost . . ."

"There's always a cost, my lord." Avery looked up at him grimly. "Everything we do in this life has one. You did what you knew was best, and for the sake of the others, at least, it was."

"I'll give you time to bury her."

"No," Avery said, "not yet. Taran needs a home, and we have nowhere else to go."

"I can take him." The woman from the wall approached them. "I'll see that he's safe. Your wife would want you to protect him; to protect all of us."

Avery laid his hand on Helen's side and said, "Tend yourself for a time, love, and I'll tend to those who have a reckoning due them. I know you'll be with me when that happens." Avery removed his coat and laid it over her before nodding at his captain—and friend.

Egan turned as a messenger ran to his side. "News?"

"Chief, the Amorite forces have been pushed back to the Ambassador's Square!"

"And what of the explosions we heard?"

"The king's operatives laid a trap; though half the city now burns, it has taken the lives of many invaders. The king wishes you to take what forces you can muster round to the docks at the Lion's Maw."

"Cut them off—yes, it would work. A few private docks lay off the beaches south of the bay. We could launch from there, if any boats remain," Egan said as he gazed past the eastern gate to the moors and beaches beyond. "Still, entering the bay would make us targets of their fleet. Thank you, soldier. See to your duties." Egan saluted the man, and the soldier turned away.

Avery's voice broke his thoughts. "Chief, if I may, I'd wager most of the Amorite ships' crews will have mostly sailors. Their deadliest warriors have already disembarked. A small fighting force could infiltrate and board one ship with little resistance. With one of their vessels, we could slip through their blockade easily and make our way right to the docks, surprising their land forces from behind. Likely as not, most of their soldiers have already climbed the great steps to the Ambassador's Square."

"Would it be enough?" Egan asked. "Even a schooner with two score men to fight with us would not be much of a barricade to stop the foot soldiers' retreat, and we have fewer men than that here." Egan looked around and quickly counted roughly ten men able to hold a blade.

Alexandra stepped out from the shadows to Egan's side. "Then we attack their warships instead." she said.

Egan's mouth dropped. "Princess! Where did you—"

"There's no time to explain. I'll not sit idly by in this fight, and I swear, if you command me to leave, I'll race ahead of you into battle."

"My charge was to protect you."

"You'll need protecting as much as I will. If Avery's plan is to work, you'll need all the help you can get."

Egan looked over the sullied armor Alexandra wore. She looked older, more mature, and almost elegant in the dim light. "You wear those well. I won't argue it further then."

"That's wise," Alexandra responded and smiled. "I left a skiff on the southern shores when I first entered the city a night ago. Others are often docked there as well. With all the carnage at play, I wouldn't be surprised if some were abandoned by their owners running for their lives. The boats could easily ferry us to one of the Amorite ships."

Egan glanced back to Avery. "Assuming we do take control of one of their vessels, do you really think we can wipe out their whole fleet? Even with enough shot, we'd be outnumbered on every side."

Avery shook his head. "Wipe out? No. I'm suggesting we cause as much chaos as possible"—his fist tightened around his sword hilt, and his brow furrowed—"and by doing so, we muddy their logistics and cut off their one chance at escape. We've been given a window. Their army is in disarray, and if we distract their fleet, their barrage will stop and their men will be stranded on the shore."

Alexandra nodded. "At the very least we can buy my father time to oust them from the city. When they run for their ships, they'll find only splinters."

"Aye." Avery spat. "We'll make them bleed some and let their cries fall silent on the sand."

Egan looked on at his men: each readied their weapon and nodded back—ready for whatever fate might bring.

"You've shed blood with me here to protect your families," he said to them, "I won't demand more of you or think less of you if you choose to stay by their side."

"We're waiting Chief", one of the soldiers replied. "Give the order."

Egan nodded. "To arms! All fighting men! Gather your weapons and say your goodbyes. The Amorites shall see what true wrath can do!"

THE TREES HAD NOT THINNED as Colin had shuffled onward, but the ground had become increasingly bog-like, making each step a chore. He paused to catch his breath and felt a great rumbling beneath his feet. Panic would have set in had not a huge but familiar stone face burst from the ground to tower over him.

"Crag?"

"Hello, little pebble. Or I should say Beast Tamer, Stone Speaker? Ah, now that name no longer fits . . . You've outgrown it. You are something more now. I can sense it."

"I thought you were gone—sleeping, or whatever it is rocks do."

"I laid deep in the earth for a time, but sleep could not find me. Then I stretched to the roots of the scorched tree, and it spoke. It hasn't spoken in a very, very long time."

"The dead tree spoke?" Colin wondered why this surprised him after all he'd seen.

"Ah, but it's not dead . . . Nothing ever really is. It gave you its last gift."

Colin patted his pocket. "Yeah, the resin. It's the balm of Gilead, isn't it?"

"Humans gave it that name, but it does heal."

Colin nodded. "I have it, or at least some of it. But I'm not heading home just yet. I have to help Alex, I just don't know how exactly. Or how I'll even reach her for that matter."

The stone face shifted its gaze to the west and closed its eyes, listening intently. After several moments, Crag turned back to Colin.

"A rock cannot roll uphill. If one way is shut . . . another way always opens. I think the tree, the earth even, has wakened me for a reason, little pebble. I think you are right. There are grave matters to the west . . . The old stone walls of Gilead are groaning in pain."

"They might keep groaning. I'm not even sure what I could offer. Words of encouragement?" The memory of Alexandra's disdain as she walked away from him in the dungeon still stung. "I don't understand this power I have. I've got no clue what I'm going to do."

"Pebble, you are rolling and gathering mass as you move. You are . . . growing. You are much more than you realize. I cannot say what you will become, but I feel, in time, you may move mountains. But if you only see yourself as small, how can you expect others . . . to see you differently?"

"But what if I fail?"

"You only fail . . . if you do nothing."

Colin took a deep breath and then nodded. "Okay. But who knows how long it will take me to get there? It has to be at least a day's journey. Hell, it could take a week. By then, will my arrival even make a difference? Maybe if I were on a boat or something I could get there faster."

"But you are not on water. You are on soil. And for one such as I, soil spreads as easily as water. Come, Beast Tamer, Stone

Speaker, Serpent Crusher. Step onto my hand . . ."

The ground shook violently again as Crag's huge rocky fist erupted from the ground and opened. Though granite, the stone hand was as smooth as polished marble. His fingers were seven feet taller than Colin himself. Colin climbed into Crag's massive palm.

"I will protect you, but it will be . . . bumpy," Crag said.

Colin nodded and sat, holding his legs tightly to his chest. "I've had worse rides."

Crag's other stone hand broke from the ground and covered Colin completely. Then his fists shot downwards into the soil, and in an instant, they were gone.

CHAPTER 51

The Might of the Dark Throne

Balaam stepped back as he watched Dagon pull Mariselle next to the bone altar.

The green haze of energy above the ship's altar spurted and flashed. Mariselle's mouth dropped as she gazed into the mist. Looking past her, Balaam saw a vision of the Amorites burning and screaming as explosions tore them apart.

"What would you have me do?" She turned to Dagon. "I don't have the power to protect them from this!"

"You won't protect them. You'll bring them back! Blood for blood!" Dagon hissed.

"You promised me your forces would conquer—you promised me the throne!"

"I lied." Dagon slammed a bone dagger into her side.

Mariselle gasped, staring down as Dagon cupped her blood and sprinkled it on his altar.

"Bareth dak! Mogz sakath!" he uttered over it, then turned to her. "Do not be alarmed, my sweet. The dagger both drinks your blood and keeps you from dying. Every drop of your life will bring back a soul."

Mariselle's knees crumpled as Dagon hoisted her onto the altar and set her body so the blood slid slowly down upon the bone surface.

Balaam looked on in horror as Dagon moved away, leaving Mariselle whimpering in a fetal position on the altar. The queen of lies, who had mocked and destroyed his friends, was now reduced to a weeping child, gasping for breath. It would be a fitting end to her, but every sacrifice his friends made this night would be for nothing if what Dagon said came true. Alex, Egan, King Braeden, and perhaps even the boy would be walking into a trap. Everything good in Gilead was about to be destroyed. And at that moment, Balaam's fear turned to anger.

KING BRAEDEN AND HIS LAST guard raced forward on their horses past Absalom and Rustag toward the Ambassador's Square. The pair's efforts would be rewarded, but he could not ask them to brave another encounter on his behalf. As his vanguard flew down the burning street, he saw the corpses of his enemies scattered on every curb and doorstep. This would be nothing compared to his blade singing death down on those who remained. He guided his men through the flaming rubble littering the cobblestone road, but he stopped in his tracks as they came within sight of the square.

Burning husks stirred. Charred hands once again grasped their weapons. The flaming dead slowly stood and strode toward them. Only their black eyes had any sign of humanity. The burning mob screamed as they surrounded the king and his men.

"Draw your blades! And fear no wound, for we are already in hell!" the king commanded, unleashing his sword on the clawing masses.

CHAPTER 52

UNDER COVER OF NIGHT

olin pulled his legs in closer as the stone walls of Crag's hands shuddered. The pitch blackness intensified as he heard the earth give way before them like water. Colin could only guess at the speed at which they traveled under the soil.

A loud crack shook Crag's fists as the living stone pushed through something more solid than dirt.

Was that a boulder? Granite? How deep are we?

There was no telling. When the great sea monster had swallowed him, Colin found himself feeling helpless. Still, the air was breathable and somehow still fresh. Like a leaf in a river, he had no control; yet somehow, he was surviving. Perhaps believing in the Maker meant giving him the burden of what's to come along with what has already happened. Colin wondered at this until his head hurt. The rhythmic wash of the earth around him and the knowledge that Crag would protect him was enough for Colin to release his grip on his legs. He laid down in the darkness and slept for the first time in over a day.

THREE SMALL DINGHIES FLOATED SILENTLY through the fog bank, rounding the shoals. Egan sat at the bow of the lead boat and nodded past his two guardsmen to Alexandra seated in the stern. She waved a small lantern, and Egan saw that two more lanterns several yards back followed suit.

"Keep the signal going. The fog's been a boon for keeping us hidden from their fleet, but we could just as easily become lost in it," Egan whispered to her.

"Are you sure we're even moving in the right direction? It's soup, for all I can see," she whispered back.

Egan nodded as he heard the waves crash against the rocky cliffs off their starboard side. "I'd recognize this shore anywhere. Now keep low—we should be rounding the point to the harbor soon."

As soon as the words left his mouth, the boat rounded the bluff, and they came face to face with the full force of Dagon's fleet. All the ships' bows pointed to the northeast, and the Lion's Maw.

Alexandra's face went white. "So many . . ." she uttered.

"The Amorites have brought their entire navy to bear on us," Egan whispered, realizing how naïve he'd been to hope they could hold the docks. "Bring us closer to that one," he directed the oarsmen and nodded at the nearest schooner. "Do it quietly."

The dinghy pulled alongside the great ship and waited as its two siblings came to bear and rested beside them. Above, Egan could hear a few vitriolic voices mumbling on deck, several snores, and the opening of a hatch or two. Several closed cannon hatches along the schooner's side were almost within reach.

Too small to climb through, but they might make a decent foothold, Egan thought and signaled to Avery in the second boat. The old soldier nodded and leaned over his bow to hand Alexandra several yards of rope with a grappling hook attached.

Alexandra mouthed, "Are you serious?" to Egan as he measured the length of rope on his arm and raised it back to throw.

Egan paused and shrugged.

Lightning and thunder cracked overhead. The lull in the storm had ended. He saw his chance and let the hook fly. It caught perfectly onto the deck railing and was muffled again by another deep roll of a thunderclap. Rain poured down, and he strained to see if any faces appeared over the side to scream the alarm.

Nothing.

He nodded to Avery and Alexandra and began to pull himself up the side of the ship. Halfway up the side, he wriggled the cannon hatch open with surprising ease and used its small portico as a foothold to hoist himself up to the deck railings.

When Egan's eyes became level with the deck, he saw it was nearly deserted except for a few sailors scurrying back to the stern of the ship. A stack of large crates and barrels near the railings blocked much of his view, but he heard no footsteps behind them. Only one watchman stood near the mast, his back to Egan, grumbling as he tried to shelter a spark in his pipe. Egan pulled himself over the rail and signaled Avery to throw another line. Within several minutes the squad of men had pulled themselves up. They followed Egan's lead and crept behind the stack of crates, readying their weapons.

He eyed their cover. There were too many of his men to fit behind all the crates. "This won't last," he whispered to the men. "We'd best move soon, or we'll be caught dead to rights."

Carefully peeking back over the railing, he saw Alexandra tie the other two boats to the first, then climb up the ropes.

"Still have your dagger, Princess?" Egan whispered in her ear as she pulled herself over the railing.

"Still have your courage, Chief?" she replied and smiled.

Egan nodded to Avery and the others, and the group broke apart. Avery led several men to the ship's stern while Egan crept up on the man near the mast.

With another flash of lightning, Egan's knife laid the man dead, and he beckoned Alexandra on. The crew at the stern scrambled for their weapons as Avery and his troop tore into them. With each flash of lightning, Egan stood behind a new man, cupping mouths before slicing his blade across their throats.

As Avery approached the ship's captain, the man turned and spat, instantly drawing his blade.

"Biteless cur! I'll sling your guts across the mast and—"

Egan's sword silenced the man from behind, and the captain toppled over, dead.

"Apt timing," Avery said as he leaned on one of the ship's dinghies lashed to the deck. Quickly scanning the deck's perimeter for any more resistance, he finally nodded to Egan and motioned the men to the hatch leading down into the hold. Between rolls of thunder, Egan could hear the faint snoring echoes from below.

"This will be bloody, friends. Do your work, and do it quickly," he whispered to his men, then turned to Alexandra. "I know you can protect yourself, but don't follow us down there."

"You must not think much of me if you expect to stop me from—" Alexandra started.

"It's not what I think of you, it's what you'll think of me when you see what I am about to do. There is no honor in it."

She kept his gaze for a moment before finally nodding.

Egan turned toward the open hatch and descended into the darkness with his men. A torrent of screams and blades tearing into flesh and bones filled his senses. Only Alexandra's last look kept his hand steady.

CHAPTER 53

TIDES OF RUIN

Hushed voices mixed with the soft patter of rain falling on the medical tent in the castle courtyard. Rustag awoke to a candle burning low by his cot. Two women and a man were bringing poultices to the wounded men lying beside him. The nurses had pushed two cots together to hold Rustag's girth. As he rolled his weight onto one, he heard it creak. He pulled himself up from its weathered canvas and looked at Absalom lying next to him. His comrade looked battered and broken but alive.

"Still breathing, friend?" Rustag grunted.

Absalom's slight snore told him enough. That man needed rest. The townspeople around them had given what aid they could behind the fortifications, and though a small part of Rustag wanted to stay, he knew his duty was to stand by the king's side. Rustag stood slowly, clenching his fists as the muscles in his side cried out in pain. Finding an old blanket, he laid it on Absalom.

"Rest then. I'm needed elsewhere." He turned to leave, then paused. "It was a good plan . . . I liked the explosions."

As he moved past the fortifications, he saw the king's vanguard farther down the stone street, fighting desperately against a fiery horde. Rustag grabbed a nearby polearm and made for the battle.

EGAN EMERGED FROM THE SHIP'S hatch and climbed onto the deck. The fresh sea air was a comfort after the stifling stench of death below deck. His face and shirt were covered in blood.

Alexandra's face turned white.

"It's not mine, Princess," he told her, wiping the blood from his blade. "Though we lost many."

Avery came up after him. He, too, was covered in gore, and a large gash ran across his brow.

"My salves—I should have brought them," Alexandra said as she ripped a strip of cloth from her shirt and bound it around Avery's head.

"My lady, I'll see more than this by morning's light, I'm sure," Avery said and smiled. He turned to look up at the sky. "If morning ever comes, that is. This foul darkness has been with us too long."

"Maker, look at that." Egan groaned as they saw the Amorite fleet launch another volley of brimstone over the city's walls. "Still they pummel us. Any resistance the king can muster will be blown apart once they near the western gate."

Avery gripped Egan's arm. "The men have counted the guns on deck and below. We have balls and powder enough to take out five of their vessels, if not more. It will make a dent."

Egan nodded. "Then have the men below deck put all the cannons on the starboard side. Powder them as well. We'll have one chance at a surprise, and I won't waste it." He turned to his men nearby. "Lads, go and bring the deck guns to bear on that." He pointed to a brig several hundred yards to their starboard side. "When I give the word, we fire. I'll take the helm and Alex . . ."

She nodded.

Egan's tone softened. "I'll have another man come up to help, but we'll need you to lift the sails. There's a bit of breeze coming off the port. It should be enough to move us into position. This won't be easy. I won't be able to protect you."

"I'm not asking you to," Alexandra said and held his gaze.

"You realize once we hit one of their fleet, they'll loose all their guns on us? We'll have

little time to shift our aim," Avery said.

"We'll do as best we can," Egan replied, shaking his head. There were no other options.

Egan's men moved the underdeck cannons and brought them to bear on the brig to their

side while Alexandra, Avery, and a few others positioned the top deck guns and pulled the

sails high. As the wind filled them, Egan took the helm and brought the schooner around.

"Fire all guns!" he yelled, and with a thunderous boom, the ship's cannons shot their payload.

DAGON LOOKED PAST the haze. The visions the black magic gave were often murky at best, leaving his eyes tired. He pulled his gaze away. A thunderous explosion echoed across the sky as he moved past the altar. He looked up. No lightning flashed.

"What trickery is this?" he mumbled, running to the ship's side. Before his eyes, he saw one of his vessels explode into a ball of fire.

"Drop the sails! Bring us about!" he screamed to the helmsman. The great black galleon shuddered and then, as the sails filled, turned to face the fiery din. From behind the flames,

Dagon saw the rogue schooner sail fleetly past, making its way toward the docks.

"Full speed, Captain! Ram them!" he yelled. The black galleon picked up speed and pressed forward, dead on target.

EGAN STEERED THE ship forward, and as it slid by its target, he saw the brig's deck was aflame. Its men were scrambling and screaming amidst the fires. Others were jumping ship. Another Corsair came into view.

"Ready your aim!" Egan called. "Fire!"

Another Amorite ship blew apart in a cloud of debris and flame. Egan turned his head toward the rest of the fleet. Corsairs stopped their siege, shifting their sails and angling at them. A volley of shots flew across the deck and destroyed the railing.

"Get down!" he screamed, instantly searching for Alexandra's form on the deck. She peered around from the mast, then returned to help with the sails.

Another Corsair drew alongside them. Its deck guns echoed as cannon balls blew apart the schooner's sails and sent the main mast crashing down. Two of his men were crushed under its weight.

Alexandra dodged the debris and reached the helm next to Egan.

"We're dead in the water!" she yelled above the noise.

Egan looked to the docks and grand staircase. Though the Lion's Maw loomed over them, they were still too far from the shore to disembark. He ran to the hatch. Below he saw Avery and his men loading their cannons. "Fire when ready!" he called to them. Their guns roared as the Corsair moved past them and pulled hard to port, making a loop for a return attack.

"We barely scratched them. Load your guns! Hurry!" Egan called. "They're turning for another round!"

His gaze shifted off the bow. The entire fleet was racing toward them. "Well, Princess, you wanted their attention. We've got it."

"Egan, look!" Alexandra pointed behind him, her face white.

Egan spun around to see a war galleon bearing down. Its screaming figurehead was only a few yards away.

"Egan! The starboard side! Turn the ship!" she screamed.

The galleon slammed into their hull.

CHAPTER 54

A Crack in the Armor

Balaam stumbled as the black galleon lurched forward, smashing into its mark. Dagon held tightly to the railings, facing the impaled schooner as he commanded his warriors to ready their weapons. Balaam steadied himself, crouching low on the deck. Amid the chaos, the donkey saw the altar had been left unguarded. Mariselle lay across it, and the green energy floated just above her.

"To hell with this," he spoke softly to himself. "If I die, I'll die more a man than a donkey."

He sprinted toward the bone table. He dislodged the bones from the altar's base with several swift kicks, and the rest collapsed under Mariselle's weight. Thunder rolled across the sky, and he felt a rush of wind rip across the deck as if a great chain had snapped. Balaam saw the walking dead collapse through the misty haze that floated over Mariselle's body. She rolled off the remains of the altar, barely breathing, and the green ball of energy above her instantly disappeared.

"Thank you," Mariselle whimpered and pulled the knife from her side. She dropped the blade on the deck as her eyes went blank, and her body shuddered one last time.

Dagon spun around and caught Balaam's eyes.

"What have you done?" he screamed. The ship lurched and shuddered again, and the sorcerer stumbled to his knees as his warriors jumped the railings down to Egan's schooner. When Dagon looked up, Balaam's back hooves connected with his face.

His nose shattered, and he collapsed to the ground, unconscious.

"Excuse me," Balaam mumbled as he stepped over Dagon's body.

BURNING HANDS RIPPED AT BRAEDEN'S men, sending them into a panic.

"Cut them down!" the king screamed above the dead's moans. "They're still flesh and bone!" But terror had crept into the small platoon's ranks, and he saw his guards pulled into the flames by the demons everywhere he looked. One fiery husk grabbed at Braeden's leg. His horse reared and screeched, and Braeden fell from his saddle. Hitting the ground, he quickly rolled to his feet, ignoring the pain, and arced his blade at his attacker. The undead jumped and throttled his horse like a pack of hungry lions on their prey. In seconds, the mare was consumed.

"Damn you back to hell!" Braeden screamed and brought down his sword on the nearest fiery husk.

The horde paused to stare at the king like he was a child brandishing a toy. They turned and encircled him.

Rustag burst through the circle and impaled the nearest attacker against a wall with a polearm.

Braeden desperately lashed out with his sword, just missing his marks.

A crack rent the sky as if it had been cleaved by a mighty ax, and a boom of thunder echoed down the street. The flaming legion fell to the ground, lifeless shells once again.

King Braeden stumbled as he backed away and turned to see Rustag at his side. The street was quiet save for the sound of the blazing fires.

"Maker—you've downed them all! How?"

Rustag stared in disbelief at all his fallen foes lining the street. "It was not my doing, my lord," he said. "Some greater powers are at play."

"No doubt, but the Maker's providence has fallen on us." Braeden smiled. "We live."

"Do you hear that, my lord?" Rustag said, looking around as another sound emerged above the noise of the flaming wreckage. Braeden could hear the echo of the Amorite drums and the enemy's maniacal chant in the distance again.

"The Ambassador's Square. They still hold it," Braeden replied. "Help me find any of our survivors. Then we'll move forward."

Rustag nodded as he pushed aside some wreckage and helped those few men he could find. After several minutes the two had gathered only a handful of soldiers who could still stand and fight.

"It must do then," the king said as he led the party past the burning remains of their enemies. "Let us be done with this, once and for all."

CHAPTER 55

OMENS AND WONDERS

His mother's voice called to him across a sandy shoreline, and Colin watched as the water pulled back farther and farther. Half buried in the exposed silt, he saw countless faces crying in agony. As the water continued to retreat, Colin moved forward, careful not to step on any trapped people. Then a solitary figure stood ahead of him, his back to Colin. The man wore Samuel's burlap robe.

"Samuel? I know now. You were right," he offered as he touched the old man's arm.

Samuel's voice echoed in his ears: "The horn. It's so much more than I thought. You must . . ."

The man turned to face him. His green reptilian eyes peered into Colin's. This wasn't Samuel.

"Give it to me!" the man yelled.

Colin knew he was facing Dagon. The distant water line came crashing forward and surrounded them.

Colin screamed as he was sucked under the massive wave. He was tossed and thrown in the chaos. Water filled his lungs as he was pulled into the depths until he came to rest, floating in front of some gigantic form.

One great eye opened and filled Colin's vision.

A leviathan had awakened.

Colin stirred and sat up. He was still safe in Crag's fists, still deep beneath the earth, moving toward Gilead. The darkness was a comfort; the blackness kept his mind from wandering.

CHAPTER 56

BURNING THE PAST

Alexandra winced as she watched Egan dodge a blade aimed at his neck. With a quick turn, he outmaneuvered his attacker and planted his sword into the man's back. A hand grabbed Alexandra's shoulder from behind, and without thinking, she elbowed her attacker in the face, knocking the sailor over the side railing. Avery guarded her flank, holding off two more men.

"This is insufferable, they'll just keep coming!" Alexandra yelled to Egan.

Egan looked past the broken mast to the jib sail in the bow. It rustled loosely in the wind. He called to a sailor nearby, "Send a man to the jib line and make it taut, then go to the stern. Work the wheel as best you can. We must dislodge from the galleon if we're to target more ships."

Egan turned to her. "The forward sail won't bring us much closer but it may be enough to help dislodge us."

"This must be their command vessel." Alexandra peered over

the fighting men and across the railing to the high deck of the galleon. "I don't see Dagon, but I have no doubt he's here."

"You'd be right!" a voice called out from the black ship's bow. She turned to see a donkey leap from the railings and crumple on the schooner's deck before her.

"What in the nine hells?" Avery yelled, his mouth wide as he held his sword toward the beast.

Balaam shakily stood up on all four hooves, his balance uneasy from the saddle and the pouch still hanging from his side.

"Balaam!" Alexandra ran to him.

"Would you mind sticking that at the actual threat?" Balaam nodded at Avery's sword.

"How are you even here?" she said, pulling his attention back. "I sent you to find the boy!"

"A fool's errand to be sure, since I got little more than a league outside of the city before I was captured," Balaam replied. "I have no idea where our friend is, but you should know old green eyes may soon wake from my little kick, and he won't be happy."

"Dagon? So, he's aboard?" Egan pressed the donkey.

"He is, but your greatest threat still lies in the city. Dagon is using some sort of black magic to raise those that have already fallen to attack the king anew. I may have knocked a notch in that spell for the time being—"

"Does the king live?" Alexandra asked.

"I can't say, the glance I had of it all was cursory. But I'd wager if he does, he needs our help."

Alexandra turned to Egan and pointed toward the boats lashed to the ship's side. "We should take these boats to shore. We can't take down any more of their fleet. Let your men handle their crew!"

"I won't leave soldiers behind," Egan replied. "Not again."

She paused and surveyed the loyal men on the deck. Leaving them here would mean their death. The old feeling of panic washed over her again. She had to choose, and there were no easy answers.

"I hear you . . ." She hesitated. "I-I . . ."

The men turned their gaze to her and nodded, awaiting her command.

"I'm sorry," she whispered, but five of them stepped forward before she could continue.

"My lady, we will serve however you see fit," one of the men said.

"No!" Egan took the man's arm. "I can find another way. I'll not have your blood on my conscience."

Alexandra shook her head. "And what of your king? My father—your lord—is facing their entire legion in the streets. This isn't a play at honor, and I'm not asking you! Chief, set down the dinghies!"

Egan studied her face for a second and nodded. "Yes, Your Highness." He turned to Avery. "You and the men will have to make do."

"Go then, Chief," Avery saluted. "We'll do our best to dislodge or at least scuttle the ship long enough to give you a window."

Alexandra grimaced as she saw what remained. More of Dagon's warriors had latched onto their vessel's sides to climb the railings. Soon her men would be outnumbered. Other ships in the fleet had changed their trajectory since the galleon had hit them. Still, more vessels were landing on the shores and unloading reinforcements. They would soon lose whatever foothold Gilead had gained in the last hour.

Avery turned to Alexandra. "I will stay and fight, my lady, but I fear it will make little difference."

She knew he was right. Dagon's forces on land and sea were unending. She felt like she was standing on a crumbling sand castle, defying the rising tide. She looked to the Lion's Maw high above them. The last symbol of her home that had not been destroyed. Would it weather the destruction of their land? Would its mouth be silenced?

Mouth silenced. Shut the mouth. An idea formed in her mind.

Alexandra turned to Balaam. "Do you still carry the conch?"

"And the scroll, yes." Balaam snorted. "Dagon was within mere inches of finding them, but I improvised. You should know he was able to call to the horn—until I ate his whistle. Samuel was right. I think there's more to that old shell than we understand."

"No doubt, but now is not the time to unlock its mysteries." Alexandra looked back to Avery. "My father would give his life to protect Gilead, and I must follow suit. We'll move ahead, but when you hear the horn's call . . ." She nodded at the deck guns and then looked to the grand staircase. "Do your duty as well. Fire all remaining cannons on the Lion's Maw until it comes down on them."

"My lady? What if you—"

"Do it!" she said without hesitation.

Egan and Avery quickly lowered the deck dinghy off the starboard side to the water below. Alexandra climbed down into it. Balaam was another matter, and it took a few missteps before he finally jumped into the little boat with a scream. Egan quickly followed, and the three steered their boat away from the wrecked schooner. They watched from a growing distance as Avery rejoined his men to fight the attackers on the ship's port side.

"He'll be lucky if he can get to the cannons at all," Balaam said as they neared the shore.

"Avery's a survivor," Egan replied as he paddled. "He won't fail us."

Amid the battling ships' confusion, the three made their way to the sand without incident. Egan helped Balaam disembark after Alexandra jumped onto the shore. Then he pulled his blade from its sheath. The trio looked farther up the shoreline to the grand staircase at the base of the stairwell. Two platoons of warriors were forming at the water's edge, helping to unload barrels and supplies from one of the corsairs.

"I ran from this spot only hours ago; now I scuttle by again." Egan sighed and turned to the others. "Stick to the cliff walls and shadows as much you can."

They slipped by the warriors unnoticed within a few moments and began the climb up the staircase. As they ran up the steps, Alexandra wondered if the terraces would become her tomb.

CHAPTER 57

THE MONSTER AND THE KING

Colin felt the vibration of rock sliding on rock. Crag's voice echoed into the small dark chamber. "We are coming to the stone of the city now. I will take you a little farther . . . I think."

Colin looked up and responded, "Yes, then help us! With you, we could easily smash the Amorites."

"Hmmm, there is a great power above the surface. It will be difficult to split the soil . . . I don't know how helpful I can be, little pebble. The Maker may only wish me to ferry you."

The rumbling stopped. After some time passed, Crag's voice once again echoed. "Deep magic here. Not to be toyed with . . . It weighs heavy on the soil. Even I may not be able to break through."

"Try, Crag. I need to be up there. I need to speak the words."

"Yes . . . I believe you do," Crag said and strained again.

As King Braeden entered the Ambassador's Square with his men, his mouth dropped. The beauty of Gilead's most prestigious landmark was now in ruins. Regal architecture burned in the continuously raging fires and the once green plaza was littered with bodies. Amid the chaos, he saw a monster towering over hundreds of rabid warriors, barking orders.

"They call it 'Molek,'" one of the soldiers whispered in his ear, "an Akan from the north."

Molek snatched a dying man from the ground and tore him in half with a grunt.

"I don't care where he's from," Braeden replied, beckoning his men forward. "He's going to hell."

Molek turned and saw the vanguard's approach. "Fresh meat, boys! Attack!"

The mob rushed to meet them. Molek's footfalls shook the earth as the horde drew closer.

Molek slammed his giant club into the king's guards, sending them flying back. Braeden dodged the giant's swing. "Back, you fiend. Go back to the hole you came from!" the king screamed.

Rustag rushed the giant's leg and pierced his polearm into the monster's foot, piercing through the boot. Black blood gurgled up, and Molek howled in pain. The giant reached for Rustag, but the slaughterman raced behind him and skewered the hulk's Achilles tendon. Molek fell backward, screaming in agony. The black soldiers that had crowded around took a step back. Molek fell to his knees and caught Rustag in a vice-like grip.

"Now you—you're worth a killing," Rustag grunted, "though your grip is soft."

Molek's eyes flared, and he squeezed Rustag. The slaughterman gasped and dropped his weapon. Molek flung Rustag into a burning shack several yards away, then limped to his feet, pulling the lance from his heel. King Braeden now faced the giant alone.

"Little man with a little crown," Molek's guttural voice echoed. "I've brought your kingdom down. Bow to me. Bow to the might of the Black Throne, and perhaps I will spare your life."

The king stood, trembling. Every choice he'd made had brought him to this moment. For every mistake he had committed in his life, for every weakness, he would not fail this time. Though everything in his being begged him to take a knee, he remained on his feet. He lifted his sword at the giant. His eyes glanced to the names of his grandfathers that adorned the blade, and he knew they stood with him.

Molek's grin faltered, and Braeden saw a glimpse of uncertainty flash in the monster's eyes for the briefest of seconds.

The giant snarled, and with one deft stroke of his club, the king was dead.

Molek turned from the decimated body and howled in victory. The black legion around him cheered.

CHAPTER 58

The Last Pawn Falls

Dagon pulled himself up. His skull rang. Blood sluiced from his shattered nose. He sat back on the deck and moaned as he clenched his broken nose in his fist. With a sharp jerk, he straightened the cartilage, screaming in pain, and then released his grip. A stream of crimson trickled across his face. "Damnable beast," he muttered as he stood. His men were fighting around him, boarding another of his corsairs on the port side. His altar lay in ruins. Mariselle's body was crumpled in the corner of the deck.

Dagon's mind reached out to the minions he had ripped from death and set on the last vestiges of the king's men. They had been beaten down again, and their souls were too far gone into the nether to retrieve. The Dark Lord would know by now of the resistance and Dagon's failure to crush it. Their next meeting would not be cordial, and Dagon knew he would be in chains for it. Those who went to the Black Throne in the Jagged Tooth rarely returned. The king had been subjugated. His kingdom was all but gone now. How had this sortie floundered so severely?

The boy is still alive, the whispers in his mind told him. *Some other will is at work.*

Dagon raised his hand, channeling his mind's eye across the fleet and to the city high above, searching. The foolish old man was dead. He sensed his champion had already bested the king and ravaged his body. Yet the people's will was not broken. Then a vision unfolded in his mind, and he saw the danger more clearly than ever before. The outsider was rising—the boy who could read the words. Dagon turned to his helmsman. "Stop the attack, Captain. Bring us round to the docks and have the fleet unload all remaining soldiers on the shore! We must reach the Ambassador's Square."

"Lord? We'll expose our flank to their ship," the captain said.

"I won't repeat myself," Dagon replied. The captain saluted and called the others as he moved to the helm.

The great black galleon turned, wrenching the smashed schooner to her side. Dagon's ship plodded forward into the crowded bay, pulling to the shore. The fleet followed in unison until the invader's fleet covered every inch of the beach. Dagon disembarked and led the rabid masses to the stairway. Gilead would be his, even if he had to take it himself.

ANOTHER OF AVERY'S MEN FELL at his side. Dagon's deckhands fought like savage animals, and with the Amorite fleet all around him, Avery wondered when their cannons would ring in the death blow. No men could leave the sortie to fire the guns on the Lion's Maw as the princess had commanded. The fight was going on longer than he had hoped. At this point, he was merely buying them time.

With a sudden crack, the black galleon wrenched forward and veered to the side. Avery heard an Amorite voice call from the shadows of their deck and felt his ship shudder as Dagon's massive vessel shrugged theirs aside and veered toward the shore. The Amorites on deck immediately stopped their attack and jumped over the railings as if a queen ant had commanded her workers to a new target. Avery's men looked around in confusion.

"Sir, should we fire on them?" one soldier asked. "Their stern is to us."

"No." Avery held his hand up. "The beast has been distracted, and we haven't the men to stave off another attack. Watch them, but get the deck guns ready and pointed to the high terraces."

Avery watched as each ship landed on shore and countless soldiers disembarked. "They're reinforcing. They're going to make a play for the square. They're going to march right up the lion's throat," Avery mumbled. He turned to his men. "Bring all guns on and below deck to bear on the stairwell and the terraces above. When the horn sounds, empty every last round on them."

CHAPTER 59

THE STONES CRY OUT

Alexandra turned to Egan and Balaam as they topped the third terrace. The ruins of market kiosks and wagons lay around them. "They'll bring more troops, I have no doubt of that." She scanned the narrow passage and nodded at the nearby crates and barrels. "We can slow their progress with this debris, perhaps long enough to bottleneck them before they reach the square above; long enough for Avery to do what he needs to do. Help me build a barrier to the stairs here, as fast as you can."

The three quickly moved to push the rubble and wreckage into a huge pile that blocked a large portion of the stairs below them. She looked at Balaam as the donkey struggled to push a cart into place with his head. "Your hooves are spry but pushing wreckage is not your forte. I'll need the horn now."

The donkey moved closer to her, and Alexandra opened his side pouch. Next to the scroll was the green conch shell. She grabbed it.

"Take the scroll upwards. If any of them live to see the day .

. . If the boy lives, give it to him. Samuel would've wanted that."

The donkey gazed at her momentarily and then quietly moved up the stairwell. Egan cleared his throat. "On any other day, I would've said that was an odd send-off."

"On any other day, we wouldn't be here," Alexandra said, smiled, and turned to the makeshift barricade at the stairs' edge. Three wooden carts were overloaded with hay, barrels, and timber. They swayed precariously at the lip of the stairs. "Will they burn?"

Egan studied the carts for a moment. "They might. Enough to scatter anyone who gets in their way, or yours." Egan walked to a lone torch fixed to the far wall of the terrace. He pulled it from its sconce, then peered over the outer edge to the harbor far below. Troops were already making their way up the steps.

"They'll be here soon. You'll want to sound your horn. We can make a go of it until Avery brings it all down on us."

Alexandra shook her head. "He'll bring it down on me, Egan. My father still needs help, and Balaam is no fighter." She took the torch from Egan's hands.

"Alex, I can't let you do this alone." Egan shook his head. "I need you. I mean . . ." Egan stammered, "the kingdom . . . needs you, we all do."

"Egan—" Alexandra smiled and said, realizing she'd decided without panic or thought. Success or failure no longer mattered. The mask of strength she had cowered behind had become part of her spine, holding her up to face the darkness. "If my life buys Gilead a moment longer or saves even one soul, it will be worth the price."

Egan nodded. "I wish we'd had more time, truly."

They held each other's gaze.

The echo of the Amorites' feet drawing closer broke the moment.

"As do I," she replied and turned to face her fate.

EGAN CREPT INTO the cobblestone plaza, blade drawn. His mouth dropped. The majestic square he had tried to save only hours before was now in ruins. A fire burned across the archway leading to the market street, and the homes that had once lined the square were shattered and strewn like the bones of some great animal. Black smoke hung low in the sky. Pillaging and fighting had transformed the once elegant plaza into a burning pit. Far to one side, he spied Balaam, crouching among the wreckage of the burned shops and a broken fountain. He shifted his gaze to the commotion rising in the center of the square. There stood Molek, dangling the king's lifeless body over his cheering comrades.

The hairs on Egan's neck stood on end.

"Molek!" he cried.

The giant paused and turned. A wicked smile spread across his lips. He tossed the king's body aside as he strode forward. The Amorites around him watched on, eager to witness another death.

"My trophy has arrived," Molek growled, clenching his fist around his club.

Egan ran forward, his sword aimed at Molek's legs. The giant quickly moved and kicked him to the side. Egan crumpled to the ground and turned to see Molek's face over him, laughing. Egan stood again and swung his weapon at the monster. Again, Molek dodged the attack and laughed. Egan knew the beast was toying with him. He swung his sword a third time, and Molek caught the blade in his hand. The sword cut deep into the giant's palm, drenching it with his blood. He took the hit without a cry, wrapped his huge fingers around the blade, and wrenched it from Egan's grasp, squeezing it until it cracked and shattered. He shook the pieces from his bleeding fist like a splinter, then raised his club above Egan's head.

Instantly, the ground shook, and Molek staggered to the side. A rocky spire erupted from the cobblestone directly below the giant's feet and threw him back. His eyes widened as the granite spire opened, and a boy walked out from its recesses.

Colin looked around at the devastation and the encircling enemies. He turned to Egan, who was struggling to stand.

"You?" Egan started. "How—where did you . . . ?"

"I'm here to help," Colin said simply as he offered his hand to the chief.

"Get out, man! Can't you see we've lost? I can't protect you!" Egan cried as he saw Molek move behind the boy. Colin glanced back at the giant briefly before turning again to Egan. "Egan, if a boulder marks a man's path, he only needs to ask for stronger hands to move it."

Molek howled and raced toward the pair. The ground rumbled again, and a second massive stone spire erupted from the earth. The granite formed into a hand and grabbed hold of Molek, tossing the giant into the burning archway.

Bloodied and battered, Molek steadied himself as he looked up at the great stone form looming over him, and for the first time, Egan saw fear in the abomination's eyes.

CHAPTER 60

The Tomb

Dagon pushed past his guards as they climbed the steps of the Lion's Maw. He surveyed the destruction as they crossed the first terrace. His army had done an adequate job of destroying every building and shop on the platform. As they climbed the stairs to the second terrace, he felt that strange outside presence again. It seemed closer. "Some older magic," he said as he crossed his arms, focusing his mind. "This boy is using something stronger than even I know of."

His men followed him to the stairway leading up to the third terrace. The stone supports around them shook, reverberating from high above. Dagon reached out with his mind to his champion and sensed the giant's fear.

"Do not fail me, Molek," he uttered. "Our boon is within reach." He turned to the mass of warriors and screamed, "Ahead you fools! Support Molek! Throw your lives at them if you must!"

The black soldiers raced ahead as a tremor shook beneath their pounding feet. Dagon peered over the ledge of the terrace and down into the harbor. Even more of his ships were unloading his army. It would be done, if every last warrior had to die to take Gilead and retrieve the horn.

HEAVY MARCHING BOOTS echoed up the steps to Alexandra's position at the top of the staircase. It was time. She set her torch to the carts piled together and breathed a sigh of relief when she saw the flames consume them. She looked out toward the harbor, put the shell to her lips, and blew. Once again, the Horn of Joshua sounded into the night.

Time seemed to slow as she spied Avery, far below, signal his men to fire.

The cannons roared, and the Lion's Maw began to crack from the assault. Cannonballs flew across the base of the great maw, smashing into the stairwell and the Amorites climbing it. Another volley pummeled into the first and second terraces.

Alexandra heard the screams of soldiers below her. A third volley flew high over her head and exploded into the steps leading up. She was thrown to the ground as rubble dropped all around her. She inched her way to the carts as the ground shook violently and shoved one down the steps.

"GO FASTER!" DAGON spurred his men. "Damn you all!"

The warriors ahead of him raced to the bottom of the next flight of stairs. A flaming cart smashed into them and exploded, sending fiery debris everywhere.

Dagon watched the chaos unfold as another flaming cart cascaded down the steps and followed ten more of his men over the ledge.

"What in the nine hells are you doing?" he screamed at his remaining warriors, who scrambled to regain their footing.

Another volley of cannonballs collided with the stairwell, killing the bottleneck of warriors scrambling to make their way up the steps from below. Burning rubble rained down on them from every direction. The air was thick with dust.

Dagon peered through the destruction, and his senses reached out to the third balcony above. He instantly saw his prey.

He pushed past his guards. "You cowards! You're being cast back by a child!" The sorcerer held out his hand, and an unseen force ripped between the ranks of his warriors, shoving them aside. He raced up the steps.

———

ALEXANDRA FELT THE walls quake around her as another explosion rocked the terrace. A small piece of rock fell from high above and struck her back. She crumpled to the ground, stunned for a moment. She tried to regain her footing, but her legs wouldn't move. There was no pain. She pulled at her leg to no avail. She was helpless.

With her final ounce of strength, she pulled herself to the ledge again. She wanted to see Gilead's waters one last time if she was to die.

She looked down at the chaos she had created and smiled. Perhaps death was no horrible thing. It felt almost peaceful. Even the violent shaking of the terrace seemed to steady as her vision dimmed.

A cold hand ripped her from her stupor. Enraged green reptilian eyes filled her sight.

"No, little one, you'll not leave this mortal coil until I let you. You are nothing more than a pawn, and you will be played." Dagon ripped the horn from her grasp. "This was meant for greater things."

Alexandra watched as the sorcerer fumbled with the horn. His cloak was torn, and his hands were burned. Finally, he stowed the shell under his arm and pulled her to his chest. His stink made her gasp.

The stairwell shook once more, and debris fell like rain around them. Amidst the chaos, Dagon dragged Alexandra up the final flight of steps.

CHAPTER 61

The Fall of Judah

Colin spotted Balaam braving the destruction erupting throughout the plaza. The donkey raced toward them. The Amorite onlookers ran for cover as their champion's body collided with a nearby wall. Crag's behemoth stone hands ripped through the ground and tossed Molek again. Balaam dodged Molek's feet as the giant stumbled into his path and nearly careened into Colin and Egan.

"Balaam? Where did you come from?" Colin called out. "Are you okay? The princess?"

"She holds the last terrace, boy." The donkey flinched as the earth shook around him. "I would've stayed with her but she thought you should have this—in my satchel."

Crag threw Molek to the far corner of the plaza. The giant collided with the buildings, and they collapsed like a house of cards. Colin reached into the satchel as Egan searched desperately for a weapon amidst the nearby wreckage. Another tremor rocked the masonry at their feet, and they stumbled. Colin finally managed to pull out the scroll and opened it. He caught his breath.

"This is . . ." he began, his eyes darted across the script. The foreign letters and symbols wavered and melded into fiery words he could understand.

Egan glanced at him. "Samuel's scroll. I thought it lost. Not sure how that can help us any more than your large friend over there can."

The trio watched as Crag burrowed under the streets, splitting the cobblestone before erupting again to tower over Molek.

"Hmmm, old root. Once a sapling of the Maker . . . now twisted into a weed," Crag spoke down to the giant, like a father speaking to a petulant child. Molek cowered as Crag raised his great fist over his head.

"All weeds must . . ." Crag paused as the Lion's Maw archway and the stairway leading down collapsed in a cloud of debris that flooded into the plaza like a wave.

<hr>

As the great Lion's Maw broke apart high above, Dagon lurched up the last steps, pulling Alexandra past the ruined gates and into the plaza. The archway exploded overhead and filled his vision with dust and rubble.

The sorcerer shot his free hand upward and felt the weight of the falling stone archway hold above him. His mind could keep it afloat for no longer than a moment, but it would be enough time. He was clear with a few more steps, and the burning debris smashed to the ground behind him. He looked up and marveled at the great stone man towering over his broken champion.

"An elemental," Dagon said as he clutched the princess tighter to his side. "How quaint." Dagon raised his arm toward the stone behemoth. "You are stone. Stone rends before the Black Throne. You are life. Life shatters before the Dark One's fist!"

THROUGH THE DUST and haze, Colin heard Crag speak out.

"You . . . you are not of the Maker. Stop!"

A thunderous crack echoed in the courtyard, and Colin looked up to see Crag's towering form split asunder from head to base and shatter. Massive boulders flew into the air and crashed into the homes surrounding the Ambassador's Square. The great stone behemoth was no more.

"Crag?" Colin stumbled back.

Dagon emerged from the dust cloud. His arm wrenched tightly around Alexandra's neck, the horn slung at his side.

"Molek! Rise!" Dagon called out. "Let the power of the fallen one fill you! Let his wrath surge life into your veins!"

After a moment, Molek lumbered from the rubble to stand behind Dagon. His face plate was shattered. He ripped it from his head. Blood and tissue protruded from the giant's skull.

"Destroy them!" Dagon commanded.

Molek roared with fury as he raced toward the trio.

"We always meet under bad circumstances, it seems," Egan said looking at Colin with shock. "I have no weapon left to use, no ploy left to play. I misjudged you, boy. You stand with us at the end; for that, you have my gratitude."

Molek raced closer, and the ground beneath their feet shook.

Egan stepped forward, bracing himself for the giant's blow. "I've failed Gilead. I pray she forgives me."

Colin reached into his pocket and grasped the familiar stone he'd carried since Dana Point. A vision of Egan skipping rocks with his father flashed in Colin's mind.

"Everything you need, you've already learned," Colin said, handing the rock to Egan. "I think this is meant for you."

Egan gazed at it for a second and then felt for the old sling draped over his belt.

He turned to face the thundering giant and took a breath to steady himself. Rolling the smooth stone into the pouch of tired leather, his fingers remembered the perfect grip and angle as if he were once again a boy at the seashore.

The pounding earth screamed, yet Egan's aim was sure and perfect. With one final cry, the chief officer let the stone fly. It sailed through the air perfectly and planted itself between Molek's eyes. The giant stopped in his tracks. A long groan echoed from Molek's mouth, and his stare went blank. Then, like a long-dead evergreen, he toppled to the ground. His lifeless body hit the cobblestone, and the impact echoed throughout the city, making Gilead shudder one last time.

Dagon's eyes widened as he stepped back and wrenched his arm tighter around Alexandra's neck. "So now we come to the end game!" Dagon's voice echoed across the courtyard. "For a century, we've planned your fall." The sorcerer yanked Alex forward as he drew closer to them. "Your city burns, your people have sold themselves to us, and your king lies dead in the streets!"

"Let her go," Colin called out, "or I swear to God we'll end you!"

"Such brave words—I'd expect them coming from the boy-captain, but you? You're not even that, are you?" Dagon spat. "You're nothing. You'll always be nothing."

The sorcerer's words cut Colin sharper than any knife. It was the same voice that had echoed in his head every day of his life.

"I'll let your little battle mean something, though, for all of you." Dagon eyed the scroll in Colin's hand. "I'll let the bitch live. I'll give you your kingdom back and set you up as high rulers of it. I'll have my forces retreat, and you'll be heroes, for a small price."

Alexandra bit Dagon's arm, and his grip loosened enough for

her to scream, "I swear if either of you do any such thing, I'll tear your hearts out myself!"

"Why should we trust you, demon?" Egan asked. "What would stop you from destroying us at your whim?"

"What's to stop me now?" Dagon yelled back, and Alexandra could only cry as his hold on her tightened again. "Even now a hundred soldiers surround your harbor, and more are coming, I guarantee it."

"Lies," Egan replied as he stepped closer to the sorcerer and Alexandra, his eyes desperately searching for a way to free her.

"My master and I came for two boons, one of which your princess so eagerly gave me earlier . . ." Dagon patted the horn at his side. "Now hand me that rag in your hand, boy, and finally, bow—all of you. Proclaim your fealty this one time, and all that you see is yours."

Colin and Egan glanced at each other for a second.

"How many more lives will you sacrifice for your petty honor, Chief?" Dagon stared at Egan. "How much blood will it take to wash away your incompetence? It's a small thing the Black Throne asks of you. You'd be wise to accept it."

Egan looked at his empty crimson-stained hand and shuddered.

Colin wondered how many lives they could save if they gave in. Wasn't peace worth kneeling for? Wouldn't it be a better path?

No. It'd only be an easier one, a voice echoed in his mind.

Egan's mouth dropped as Colin walked forward to face the sorcerer alone.

"Do you really expect to stop the inevitable?" Dagon snarled. "The Dark Lord's will is unstoppable. Your small victories are nothing."

Dagon pulled a knife from a sheath at his side and held it to Alexandra's neck.

"Stop!" Colin called.

"Your lives are forfeit," Dagon hissed and ran the blade across Alexandra's throat. Blood drenched her skirt, and she fell to the ground.

"No!" Colin screamed.

Egan fell to his knees, stunned.

Colin stared on as Alexandra whimpered for a second and then quieted. Her lifeless body was an island in her blood.

CHAPTER 62

The Soothsayer Speaks

Tears filled Colin's eyes, and the words came to his mind.

"You're right, demon. We are nothing now. We have no army or city left, no power . . . I am weak—nothing compared to you and your master," Colin said, his voice cracking as he suddenly felt the Maker's presence wrap around him. Electric chills ran across his skin. "But what you've taken was not ours to begin with, and what you offer is not yours to give."

Dagon took a step back, and Colin moved closer to him.

"There is a Maker of all things, who is older than you or the Dark One you serve, who has called each thing into existence, and has given each thing a name . . . even you."

Colin opened the scroll, and Dagon stumbled back. The Logos spread into Colin's thoughts.

Colin peered into Dagon's eyes and saw an ailing old man, near the turn of the century, take a voyage west under a different name than the one he was known for now.

As Colin searched the sorcerer's gaze, he saw ancient hands barely grasping a ship's railings as it returned to the California coastline. Once ashore, Spanish missionaries were paid to lead the enfeebled man back to the tiny cove he had discovered nearly fifty years earlier. When he was much younger, he had fallen into this world once before and found himself floating in an unknown sea. He'd become lost and lured into the service of the Dark Lord, who promised him his freedom, great wealth, and eternal life in this new world if he returned when called. The Hissith bite was enough to compel him back. The old man knew his life was ending on Earth and left nothing for his kin save a little wooden box and a map with his initials, R.H.D., on it.

Colin's mind focused back on the present. "I'm not the only stranger here. You were the first, Dagon. Except it isn't Dagon, is it? You've been here so long, been so twisted, that you've forgotten your own name."

Dagon's mind cleared, and at that moment, he remembered.

"How many lives have you squelched to lengthen your own?" Colin continued. "How much of your soul did you sell, Dana?"

"No!" Dagon shook his head. "Stop! You can't know that!"

"Richard Henry Dana is your true name. Remember it. Remember every moment and every betrayal," Colin's voice echoed out, and Dagon screamed, grasping his ears like they were on fire.

"You filthy little swine!" Dagon threw out his hand at Colin, but his power was gone.

"Nolite et videte!" Colin commanded, and the image of binding ropes filled his mind.

Like a freight train, a powerful force hit the sorcerer, and he buckled to the ground.

Colin watched terror spread across Dagon's face, and for the briefest of moments, Colin thought he saw hundreds of spirits appear around them. Their cold silent stares focused on the man that had betrayed them. Every base act Dagon had committed engulfed him, and his hands shook as he lowered them. His green eyes faded to brown. They were human again, weary and red with tears.

Two spirits stepped closer to tower over him.

"Mariselle . . ." Dagon's face went white. He turned to face the other. "Aukai?" His mouth dropped with odd recognition.

Colin watched on as Dagon's skin aged within seconds. His hair turned gray, and his forehead filled with wrinkles. Now, only an ancient and feeble man kneeled there. The great sorcerer Dagon was no more. Only Richard Dana remained.

Without a second thought, Colin spoke again, and the Logos flowed through his lips.

"Veni, veni Emmanuel, captivum solve Israel," Colin called. "Save us, Maker, free your people from this blight."

Dana screeched as Colin's voice grew stronger. "Liberum corde suo. Free his heart, and rejoice Gilead—for the sun breaks!"

Dana shook violently as seizures racked his body, and the horn dropped to the ground.

Colin continued speaking the Logos. From the distant corners of the city atop the high wall, the remaining voices of the watchmen joined his until a choir of resonating speech filled the plaza. Dana looked up in terror as a dark mist formed around him.

"No! It's not my time yet. I can still . . . No, master!" He cried out as his arms bent backward, his shoulders shifted inwards, and his neck twisted around.

Egan stood and ran to Alexandra's side. Only Colin kept the sorcerer's gaze as the abomination shifted, inverted, imploded in on himself, and then was gone.

CHAPTER 63

HOUSES OF HEALING

Colin heard the thunder roll one last time before the darkness parted and sunlight broke through the clouds. Beyond the Ambassador's Square, the morning light glided across Gilead's harbor, and every Amorite ship, save Avery's, was set ablaze as if they were matchbooks set too close to a flame. The remaining warriors in the square screamed in horror and fled from the sun's rays into the shadows of adjoining alleyways.

Colin turned to Alexandra's body and saw Egan holding her head; tears rolled down his cheeks. Balaam sat next to him, staring bleakly at her.

"She's gone," Egan started, "I couldn't save her. I . . ."

Colin ran his hand across her face and let it fall to his side.

Putting his hand in his pocket, he felt something soft—the fabric fold of resin he had taken from the dead tree. He pulled it from his pocket and opened it to reveal that the small amount of balm was still intact. He looked up. It was meant for his mother, but that was another time, another world. He looked around and saw the ruin of Gilead. Now, more than ever, the people needed her.

"Every world needs some light," Colin said, sliding the resin across the deep cut on Alexandra's neck. "Even if it casts shadows elsewhere." He knew his mom would agree. He pressed the last of it to Alexandra's lips.

The bleeding slowed and stopped, and before their eyes, the wound mended. Her face filled with color again, and her chest rose with breath.

Egan gasped, smiling through tears, and Balaam's ears perked up.

"I'll stay with her," Colin said, placing his hand on Egan's arm. "You have a job to do, Chief."

Egan nodded, rubbed the tears from his eyes, then turned and called, "Awaken Gilead! Call forth the watchmen!"

His voice resounded across the square, and within moments, the news spread across the city. The retaking of Gilead was at hand.

ALEXANDRA GAZED AT THE FIRST sunrise in over a year. Like a long-absent lover finally returning, its warm rays kissed her face and, for a moment, made her forget her cares. She turned back to her bed to reluctantly wait for more news. Egan had insisted she mend for a time before she took on any duties, and she knew he was right. Her wounds had healed entirely save for a small scar on her neck and a few bouts of exhaustion. From the reports, it had taken Egan and his men nearly two days to rout and kill the remaining Amorites within the city walls. During that time, the wounded were tended to and search parties were formed to scour the wreckage for survivors. Several of the citizens came forward to give aid to each district. Her father's body was soon found. Despite the stroke of Molek's club, he was unscathed and intact, hugging his sword to his chest as if sleeping in the Maker's hands. Days later, she found Absalom recovering in the healing tents. There at his side lay Rustag, battered and broken but alive. The privateer watched over his sleeping friend.

"I owe him more than I can repay," Absalom said to Alexandra as she approached.

"Then that makes you friends," she replied and sat beside him.

"It's not a bond I'm eager to carry," Absalom quipped. "Though I'm glad I could help him, and you. If only to bring some order to this place again."

Alexandra paused. She had been there, listening, when Absalom had spoken with her father. There were wounds here she had no idea how to mend. "If things are to be set right, it should start with us."

The rogue folded his arms as he met her gaze.

"You're family," she continued. "It's long past due that you be treated as such."

Absalom's expression softened a little, and the brother and sister watched their injured friend in silence for a time.

A day later, Avery buried his wife on the bluffs near Samuel's old hut. Alexandra stood next to Colin and others, unsure of what to say.

"She always loved the ocean," Avery said as he stood over her grave. "I'd hoped one day we would build a home of our own here, but I could never scrape together the money for it. I didn't deserve her."

"You were all she wanted, Avery." Alexandra put her hand on his shoulder, watching Taran play nearby. "You were there, and that's all that mattered."

The following morning at dawn, the people of Gilead walked down to the shore. There, on a floating pyre, they placed King Braeden's body. Skiffs tethered to the raft pulled it past the breakers before it was set free for the tides to pull out into the ocean. Three women stood to the side of the crowd and sang a dirge and then a song of redemption. Their melodic voices carried across the shore. A line of soldiers held their oil-dipped arrows nocked and at the ready.

Alexandra turned to Colin and Egan standing nearby, struggling to hold her emotions in as she pulled the king's sword, *Teacht Riocht*, from the sheath at her side. Her father's name was now etched onto its surface.

"I'm sorry, Alex . . . if it means anything," Colin whispered.

"It does," she said, raising the blade overhead before lowering it to signal the archers. A torch was passed among them, and within moments a hundred flaming arrows hit the pyre and set it aflame. "He was imperfect, but he loved this place. He loved me."

"The king is dead!" Egan called toward the crowd. "Long live the queen!"

The trumpets of Gilead blew as Alexandra watched her father's cradle be enveloped by flame and water. She looked down into her hands and wondered at the great conch that she held. Dagon had risked everything for it.

"Such a strange prize to covet," she mused. "We must take the time to find the answers in the Logos. Samuel saw something there."

But prophecies were seldom deciphered easily. It was a mystery they might never understand. Such was the motive of all evil things: to shatter without reason, corrupt what is beautiful, and destroy without regard. And so much had been lost. She turned to her friends. Egan looked past her to the pyre. Colin caught her gaze and smiled.

She wondered why he would risk so much for so little in return. He was so much more than what she had first thought. Perhaps even the smallest voice could shake foundations. Maybe even in this dark world, there were beacons of light.

CHAPTER 64

THE PARTING

As true night settled in, Colin stood near the breakers curling off the shore where he had first come into this world. He paused to gaze at the stars. The constellations radiated as if they were rejoicing. "They're brighter here but not so different." His gaze fell to his companions who had come to see him off. He had rested, and Egan and Alexandra wanted him to stay, but Gilead was not his home. His life, his problems, and his mother were waiting.

"I know what you sacrificed for me." Alexandra said. "I wish I could give you something for her."

"This place was worth it. You were worth it," Colin replied. "And I'm not entirely certain I didn't gain something I can use."

"Well, at least now you can speak without stuttering like an infernal monkey," Balaam chimed in, and Colin smiled. The donkey continued, "I daresay you saved all of us, boy. Thank you."

Colin laughed. He had never been able to give them his name. He cleared his throat. "Uh . . . Colin. Colin's my name."

The word finally fell from his lips. His eyes widened. He could say it.

"It's a strong name—Colin," Egan replied and stepped forward. He handed Colin a gold signet. "It's not much, and I'm not sure it will survive your trip home. If I could give you all the riches of Gilead, it would not be enough."

"Thank you. Take care, Egan," Colin said. "Keep the Logos safe. Keep Alex safe."

Colin caught Alexandra's gaze once more. *Perhaps if there'd been more time.*

And for a second, he thought her eyes agreed.

"With my life," Egan replied, smiling at the new queen.

Absalom shook Colin's hand. "Avoid tearing up any more cities, if you please."

"You should talk," Colin laughed.

Rustag nodded at Colin but said nothing; the acknowledgment was enough.

Colin turned toward the water and moved forward into the breakers. As the icy waves encircled his waist, he turned to face his friends one last time.

"I hope this works," Alexandra laughed. "Or you'll be soaked for no reason."

Colin winked at her as she pressed the Horn of Joshua to her lips and blew, and with a resounding call, a giant wave washed over Colin, blurring his vision. Within seconds, he was swirling in the waters and then deposited back into the sea cave a universe away.

CHAPTER 65

WHAT WE CARRY

Colin gasped as he pulled himself onto the sandy floor of the sea cave. The water here had not warmed. As he stood, he saw sunlight crest the rocks and roll across the water to him. The tide was out, and the fog had lifted.

What day is it? How long was I gone? he wondered as he carefully made his way out the side passage and onto the trail that led back to the beach. *Four days maybe? Five? A week? A month? Is she still alive?*

He paused as he rounded the last outcropping of the cliff and came to the sandy beach. Mr. Potter sat tending a campfire. He waved Colin over.

Colin peered at him as he came closer. "It's you. I guess you've been waiting for me?"

Mr. Potter smiled as he handed over a metal skewer with roasted chicken and peppers. Colin instantly felt his stomach grumble and sat by the fire's edge.

"I was with you every step of the way, my boy. You never left my sight."

Colin pulled at the hot food, nearly dropping it in the sand.

"Oh, now careful there," Mr. Potter laughed as Colin devoured the morsels. "Wouldn't want you choking after all you've been through. I had to take a personal hand in things to see it along from time to time, but it all turned out. It always does."

Colin swallowed the last bit of chicken. "You're more than . . . well, more than you appear to be, aren't you?"

Mr. Potter leaned in, a gleam in his eye. "You are too, Colin. Remember that."

"You gave me back my name, didn't you?"

"I simply held onto it until you could appreciate it," Mr. Potter said and stood. Colin dusted off his jeans and got up. The old man looked down at the campfire and nodded. The glowing embers cooled instantly. Colin gazed at Mr. Potter and wondered why that seemed so natural. The two walked farther down the shore.

"Mr. Potter, I have to get to my mom, but I didn't save any of the balm. I want to believe she can make it, but I'm not sure if I have the words for that. I'm not sure if I have the . . ."

"Faith?" Mr. Potter offered.

"Yeah, I guess," Colin replied and looked down. After all he had done, he still felt like a failure.

"Faith's a funny thing," Mr. Potter started. "Not something you get once, and then break. It's something you have to pick up every day. Something you choose to carry, every day."

Colin looked up and saw they had somehow traveled to the San Clemente Memorial Hospital parking lot.

"H-how?" Colin stammered.

"Go see your mom, Colin. You've got everything you need." Mr. Potter's voice echoed in Colin's ear.

Colin paused and looked around; Mr. Potter was gone. "Of course." He sighed and pushed through the hospital's main doors and went to his mother's room.

He lingered at the doorway and saw her frail figure breathing. Shaking in relief, he moved forward and put his arms around her neck. The bite mark was gone. Colin leaned back and studied the lines across her face.

"Mom?"

She didn't respond. Only the steady beeping of the medical monitors could be heard.

"I'm so sorry," he whispered. "You know, I had it, I had what you needed, but I had to make a choice and . . ." His vision clouded with tears. "I don't know what to say."

Colin sat for a time next to her, holding her frail hand. The glow of the harsh lights overhead made her skin look pale and paper thin. Colin studied the deep creases in her palm. Years of worry and sacrifice had left their scars. How often had she wanted to kneel before the onslaught of life? How many times did she stand for his sake? Colin wondered how many great battles were fought silently every day, behind every face. He concentrated. He was a soothsayer now. He had to know the words. Whatever ideas came to mind seemed to dim from his memory within seconds. Finally, he bowed his head. Plain English would have to do.

"God, I don't know if you can hear me," he started. "But I could really use your help right now."

"She needs her rest." A nurse broke Colin's concentration. "We'll let you know if there's any change."

He looked up, nodded, and stood. He turned toward the door, defeated.

The long walk home exhausted him, and as he approached the front door of his apartment, he yawned. Reaching under a nearby rock, he found the spare key and let himself inside. He paused and instinctively waited for some corporeal nightmare to make itself known, but there was nothing. No dark presence or Hissith lurked—only soft furniture, plush carpeting, and a hot shower that he spent half an hour enjoying.

The rest of the day, he slept fitfully. The horrors he'd faced haunted his dreams, but none more than the image of himself standing alone over his mother's grave.

He awoke the following day, and a sense of peace filled him. He had planned to return to his mother's bedside, but he knew staring and waiting would do nothing. Life still needed to be lived, and it was a Monday. He wondered how far behind he was in his assignments. He'd check on her after school.

Colin parked his bike at San Clemente High School just as the first bell rang. He turned down the empty corridor toward his locker and saw Jennifer waiting for him. She smiled as he approached.

"Colin, I was wondering if I'd see you today. Were you sick? I heard something about your mom."

"She's recovering, at least I hope so."

Jennifer's eyes widened. "Oh my God, you didn't stutter. Colin, that's great!"

"Yeah, I guess it is," he said and smiled as best he could.

Suddenly he was pushed forward into his locker. He turned to see Red sneering at him.

"Well holy shit, the little bitch doesn't stutter. I bet you still piss your pants and cry though."

Colin faced the skinhead as Jennifer backed away. Gazing at the bully, he realized he felt absolutely no fear. After facing sea monsters, demons, and an army of savage warriors, Red Arnold didn't seem so bad.

"Oh, what, you eyeballing me now?" Red snapped as he stepped closer. "You finally grow a spine?"

"It must have hurt," Colin said quietly, peering into Red's eyes.

"What the hell are you talking about?" Red laughed.

"It must've hurt, when your dad used his belt on you all those times."

Red was stunned as if he'd been slapped.

Colin continued, "And when you wet yourself just last week because you were so scared, running to your mom's room, screaming for help, but she didn't open the door. It must have hurt."

Red's eyes widened, and he clenched his fists.

Colin took another step forward. "She closed the door because she knows she'll be next if she says anything. And you hate him for that, don't you?"

"What is this? A joke?"

Colin stared at him quietly, knowing.

"Shut the hell up, man. You don't know me!" Red screamed.

"But more than that, you hate yourself, because as much as you hate your dad, you'd do anything to get his approval. To get him to say he's proud of you."

"Asshole! I'll kill you!" Red's cheeks flared.

"They named you Reginald, but you call yourself Red, because that's all you see when you look in the mirror after he's done with you."

Red threw himself at Colin, but Colin stepped aside. Red fell to his hands and knees, paralyzed by the truth in Colin's words.

Colin took Jennifer's hand. "Come on, let's go."

Jennifer stared at Colin in awe as they walked away. He knew who he was and why he was alive at that moment. And like the stone he'd carried with him, he carried the faith that his mother had finally opened her eyes and awakened.

EPILOGUE

Colin rolled his eyes and blushed as he sat at the dinner table and listened to his mother fussing over the pumpkin pie she had just pulled from the oven. Jennifer stood next to her and laughed as his mom prattled on.

"And then, of course, there was the time he tumbled down the stairs in front of us, naked as a jaybird, and said, 'Momma I'm clean!'" His mother laughed as she pulled the oven mitt from her hand.

"Too much! Colin you were so wretched, your poor mum deserves a medal," Jennifer said and winked at him.

"Yeah, she deserves something," Colin mumbled and glanced about the room. Their little apartment was already dressed with holly and pumpkin-scented candles. A box of Christmas decorations had been pushed to the side, awaiting its grand reopening. Things had almost become normal with the advent of the Thanksgiving holiday.

"Now, when do you expect your parents to arrive, dear?" his mother continued.

"Well, Dad's a bit of a tortoise so—"

"Don't even get me started on that. Colin has cement feet in the mornings, why—" Lane paused, mid-thought. "Now, what was I about to do? I swear I dropped ten I.Q. points when I was sick."

"Mom, the toothpicks are in the third drawer on the left," Colin called out.

"Ha! Well, wouldn't you know it? I swear you've got a sixth sense about you." Lane shook her head and pulled the toothpick box from the drawer before taking one and placing it in the center of the pie. "Oh, good. It cooked right this time."

Jennifer giggled and discreetly turned her head to him to silently mouth, "You're a weirdo."

Colin smiled knowingly. In time, she would come to understand. He had accomplished more than he had ever thought possible in that world, so why not here?

Neither success nor failure is final, my boy. Be wary of what you foster with your words.

The voice echoed in his mind, and he straightened in his seat.

"Mr. Potter?" Colin whispered.

But no response came. The following day, Colin found the old man's shop at the marina was gone, but a part of him knew it would be. He had hoped to touch base with the sage one last time, but like the mist surrounding the harbor on that fateful night, he was nowhere to be found. Mr. Potter's final words haunted him; were they meant to encourage, or were they a warning? The question lingered in Colin's mind.

THE MAGISTER OF SLAUGHTER RAN his elongated pale fingers across the blackened wall until they came to chains that would lift the metal gate into its reaches. His empty eye sockets had long been sewn shut, but he knew the room well enough. Behind him, he heard the shuffle of many feet that could only mark the entrance of the sload—half-men, half-beasts—that served the Black Throne through mindless labor. He remembered they resembled mole-like creatures, nearly as blind as he but strong and resilient. They were a select few servants of the Dark One that could withstand his presence.

The sload carried a man's twisted and battered form into the room and tied him to a large wooden wheel that sat upright on its side, facing the cavernous darkness that lay just beyond the gate.

The corpse smelled of rot, and the sload cursed and spat as they fastened the body at the wrists and ankles to the device.

The Magister smiled. Though the smell was horrid, he took some solace in the fact that his once great and mighty contemporary was now nothing more than a sack of rotting flesh.

"Leave us," the Magister croaked, and the sload quickly shuffled from the room. He moved forward to the corpse and ran his fingers across the man's face, pausing to rest them on his sagging eyelids. "You shall miss these, brother. I do not envy what is in store for you."

The Magister turned around to face the gateway and pulled the chain, opening the iron portal, before he secured the chain to a wall hook. His feet stepped forward to a ledge he knew dropped into an eternal abyss. He took a breath and moaned loudly to signal across the great expanse. After all the air had left his lungs, he stopped and waited.

A resounding chorus of inhuman screams responded. The room shook violently. The Magister steadied himself as he felt the structure around him move. The stones of the walls and floor quivered as they were ripped from their foundations within the great tower, but somehow the room remained intact.

The Magister could feel the chill of wind rushing against his face as the room moved forward into the darkness, floating across the eternal chasm.

The tower of the Jagged Tooth defied natural law. Space and time served only the Dark Lord here, just as *his* very presence defied the Maker. The room finally slowed and stopped, hovering in the darkness.

A great mouth pressed against the gateway, and the Magister immediately stepped back. He remembered the one time he had seen the master and knew the rows of teeth lining his mouth were sharp and wickedly long. A giant forked tongue salivated and slid across those teeth.

"His body was reclaimed from the wastes as you commanded, my lord." The Magister bowed low and stepped to the side of the gateway.

The giant lips moved, and within the guttural echo of his voice, the Magister could hear the cries of millions of souls that had been swallowed.

"Live again!" the Dark Lord's voice bellowed.

The body twisted and writhed on the table as if it were possessed, and then with a gasp, Dagon awoke.

ABOUT THE AUTHOR

Glen Gabel worked as an educator for years before dedicating himself to writing novels, short stories, and screenplays. Glen's short story, "Where Light Has No Purchase", was shortlisted as a finalist in Reedsy's Writing Contest in April 2022 and published in the 2022 Bardsy Character Anthology. He lives in Idaho with his wife and wonder-pup, Duke. You can read his latest work by visiting:

WWW.GLENGABEL.COM